Alabama's Redemption

A Novel by Hale Meserow

ISBN-10: 0615488005
ISBN-13: 978-0615488004
(Published by Marathon Publications)

ACKNOWLEDGEMENT

For Sue: my editor, accountant, willing sounding board, and life partner. Plus she puts up with me.

PROLOGUE

It was good to be white then.

American soldiers, sailors, and airmen stationed in Europe had recently come home from crushing the German regime that had threatened to end free civilization and usher in a thousand-year oligarchy. Two American atomic bombs had landed on populous Japanese cities, erupting in a fury that shocked even their designers.

White faces came home with a swaggering triumph that belied the utter relief of simply surviving mankind's most savage and destructive conflict ever. Bands played for them, parades honored them, and a grateful nation could not stop grinning and laughing with them. White faces found mates, jobs, God, and money. Life was good.

Black faces, which had faced the same dangers, had fought the same battles, had cheered, screamed, bled, died, and sacrificed just as much as their fellow American fighters with white faces, came back to a very different welcome. Black faces came back to a devil just as evil as Hitler, just as inscrutable as Hirohito, and just as arrogant as Mussolini. His name was Segregation, and he ruled with an iron hand.

Such was the state of the world in Louisiana when Alabama Denton arrived in New Orleans.

"The steps of a man are established by the Lord,

when He delights in his way;

though he fall, he shall not be cast headlong,

for the Lord upholds his hand."

Psalm 37:23 (ESV)

CHAPTER 1

Alabama peered through a swatch of leaves in the gathering twilight toward the meadow. From his relatively comfortable perch on a thick branch of an ancient oak with his back against the trunk, he was satisfied that he was quite hidden from the view of even the most ardent Nazi who might be scanning the woods with binoculars. He had been in that tree, having scaled it with the help of spiked attachments which fit onto and off his boots with a simple lever mechanism, for most of the afternoon. He longed for a cigarette but knew it to be foolhardy to light one. Patiently he waited, scanning the meadow for movement.

The very day Alabama had heard about the war, he told his mother and father that he was going to enlist. His mother wailed. "You mah only chil,'! she cried. "What Ah goan' do if'n you get yosef killed?"

"Mama, Ah kin get strung up heah jes' as quick as get killed in dis war," Alabama replied. "Least in the Army Ah kin make some money. Learn me somethin'."

While his mother bawled, rocking back and forth on the rickety wooden chair on the porch, Alabama's father took him aside and placed his hand on the young man's shoulder. "Prendergast, you go on and get yo'sef inta that Army if'n they take you," he said solemnly. "But be a man, you hear? Don' be disrespectful, but don't be kissin no white ass. You unnerstan'?"

Alabama nodded. He wasn't particularly fond of his father, having endured beatings and long, long hours digging in the earth for him in an effort to grow corn and vegetables to sell in the local farmers' market. But he knew this was a very special moment. "Ah make you proud, pappy," he replied. The old man pursed his lips and nodded. His eyes filled with tears, and a stream of them ran doggedly down his weather-beaten face, navigating their way through his week-old white stubble and onto his bib overalls. He dropped his hand from his son's shoulder and shuffled back to console his weeping wife.

It was well into the spring of 1942 when the news of the conflict had actually reached the black farmers scattered around Selmon, Alabama, because news tended to keep itself private from blacks. It was only when Alabama, then called by his name Prendergast, was purchasing seed corn at the local black general store that a fellow farmer mentioned that he was thinking of going off to the war.

"You *crazy*, Henry?" the proprietor exclaimed. "Why you be wantin' to fight crackuh's war for him?"

The farmer, a tall and strong young-30's dirt scratcher with a family of five children, chewed on a stalk of grass and mused. All heads in the store turned toward him and all ears flexed, intent on his answer, for this was a question that had been posed before with no satisfactory answer. The farmer replied in a rumbling voice "Gettin' hard to feed dem chirren. Hear tell the Army gives a man three squares and some money 'sides."

There was general murmuring at this answer. Several heads nodded, some almost reluctantly.

"You figure you can feed yer family from dat Europe?" the storeowner asked.

The farmer shrugged. "Ah don' *need* no money if'n they's gonna put food in mah belly," he replied nonchalantly. "Figure if they's payin' me besides, Ah kin send it back to Mazzie. She kin come down heah and buy food from you. Long's she keeps the chickens goin', they's eggs and stewin' meat. Long's she gets some corn in the ground, they's some pone an' brayud. She do all right."

2

The storeowner regarded him. "If she goan' do all right, Henry, how come you got to go off and fight?"

The farmer pulled the stalk out of his mouth and looked around the store. His thick lips brooded, and he frowned as he formed an answer. At length he said "Samuel, you gots you a nice store heah. Gots you supplies, gots you shelves to put 'em on, gots you folks comin' in and out an' givin' you dey money. Me, I got two acre, and das' low ground on de edge of de river. Floods now 'n den, sometimes when they's a crop in the groun', and den Ah lose dat crop. Sides, Ah don' think da land is really mine, tell ya the truth, 'cause Mr. Mercer, he be comin' down now and agin in his Ford auto*mo*bile and makin' like Ah jes' squattin' on his two acre. Ah got me a piece 'a papuh sayin' it belonged to mah pappy, but you know what *dat* worth." He made a gesture as if he was wiping his rear. "Reckon any day now my family be tossed off dat two acre, papuh or no papuh. Den what? Den what we got?" He stared hard at the storeowner, a deep scowl on his face.

The proprietor stared at the young man, sighed, and shook his head.

"We got flat feet, das' what we got," the farmer replied to his own question. "We got feet dat best be movin' on. To what? Who *know* what? Jes' off Mr. Mercer land, das' what. Jes' gone, wif nuthin'."

The murmurs increased in volume. It seemed every black face had an opinion, and there were no white faces within a mile to counter them.

"So you be thinkin' mayhaps you kin make some money," the proprietor asked rhetorically.

The farmer nodded. "Yep. Mazzie smaht. She find a hidey hole, save up some. Mayhaps nuf' to buy me somethin' like you got heah. Den Ah kin quit scratchin' in the dirt like a chicken and put my feet up at night. Den my chirren get a full belly, ever' single day."

The proprietor sighed. The truth was that he had inherited this store from his father, and it had originally been built and given to his great-grandfather as a gift for a lifetime of loyal service from the plantation owner who had owned him and lost him to the Emancipation. Such an event was very rare indeed, and the proprietor knew how much it would cost for the dirt farmer to actually set himself up in business from scratch. Still, he nodded. "Mayhaps," he replied with only a hint of encouragement.

The farmer looked down at his cracked, ancient boots, footwear that had belonged to his father before him. "Anyhow, das' what Ah be thinkin'," he mumbled. He scratched at an invisible mark in the worn floorboards with one foot.

Alabama, his eyes wide and his ears burning, left the store and waited outside. When the young farmer came out with his goods, Alabama sidled up and said "Howdy!" He offered a grin of peace.

"'Day," the farmer replied, loading his supplies into a rusty wheelbarrow for the long push back to his two acres.

"Ah done heah you talkin' 'bout de Army," Alabama offered.

The farmer glanced at him, nodded, and returned his attention to the barrow.

Alabama kicked softly at the packed red dirt. "So, Ah was wonderin'," he stated. He stared at the farmer.

The farmer straightened up, a full head taller than Alabama's mature height of five feet eight inches. At nineteen years of age, it was unlikely that Alabama would grow much taller. He had resigned himself to that fate. "Wonderin'?" the farmer replied.

Alabama nodded. "Yassah. How's a fella get himself into dis heah Army?"

The farmer explained to him that there was a recruiting office in Montgomery, a full two day's walk south of Selmon. "Dey be lookin' at ya, seein' if you's fit enuf to fight," he said. "If'n dey like ya, ya go in dat day. Dey feed ya, putcha in a uniform, and teach ya fightin'. Das' the way Ah done heah it tell."

Alabama stared into the dark brown eyes of the farmer and licked his lips. "Ya think Ah be fightin' size?" he asked eagerly.

The farmer looked him up and down. After a moment, he shrugged. "Don' know," he replied. "Mayhaps. Kin ya shoot a rifle?"

Alabama smiled. "Now *that* Ah kin do!" he exclaimed with a grin. "Ah kin knock a pine cone off'n a tree from fifty paces, and you kin name de cone!"

He was correct. The Army put all recruits through tests, some of which were for fitness (several whites failed at this point while very few blacks did, since they had to be fit and strong to wrest a living from mean ground) and some of which were for proficiency. When Alabama was given a rifle, he sighted it in on a target, made minute adjustments to the scope on the M-1, and proceeded to score higher than any recruit had ever accomplished at that induction station. Virtually every shot was dead center in the bull's eye, with ten coming from a distance of seventy yards. The major in charge of the camp was immediately informed, and Alabama was assigned to a sniper company consisting of black sharpshooters from all over the country. Without further ceremony, he was given a railroad ticket to Newport News, Virginia, and told to report to the sergeant in charge of troop transport. "And you'd *better* get your black ass to News," the gruff blonde sergeant who handed him the ticket remarked harshly. "Don't even think of skippin' out. If you're so much as a day late, we'll send out a company of men and they'll find you. Ain't missed a deserter yet. When they do track you down, they'll hang you upside down nekkid and use you for target practice, real slow-like. Might take you two-three days to actually die." Alabama assured him that no such mission would be necessary, that he was eager to get to Europe and start picking off Nazis like pine cones.

Alabama was elated when his troop transport ship arrived in England and he and other black soldiers were taken by truck to an American Army-Air Force base that had been hurriedly constructed in a sheep field. The white sergeant to whom he reported took one look at his papers, stared sharply at him, and directed him to a Quonset hut at the back of the base. Alabama toted his duffel bag across the base, watching with eager eyes the marching troops, the aircraft taking off and landing, the hustle and bustle of an army preparing to deploy. When he checked in at the assigned arched metal building, he found a black sergeant who looked at his papers, turned and hollered at a corporal, and told Alabama to go with the soldier. The black soldier, walking beside Alabama, said "'A' rating, huh? Think you kin shoot, boy?"

"Tolerble," Alabama replied easily.

The soldier smiled, revealing huge white teeth. "We goin' see 'bout dat," he said with relish. He led Alabama to a firing range on the outer perimeter of the base. It was buttressed with three stacks of straw bales, one behind the other, so the bullets would be spent in the straw and not fly out into the countryside. The corporal handed Alabama a ten inch by twelve inch target, with concentric circles filling most of it. "Go down an' stick this here target on a bale," he said, pointing to the bales some thirty yards away. "There's nails in the bales. Use 'em."

"Ah know," Alabama replied. "Ah kin see 'em."

The corporal stared at him. "You kin? From heah?"

Alabama nodded. "Second bale, second row from de lef'. They inna clustah."

The corporal stared downrange and then at Alabama. "Whooeee!" he exclaimed. "Dem's some eyes, shootah! Mmm, mmm! Go on, now. Pin yo' target."

Alabama duly complied, mounting his target with a nail in each corner. When he returned to the firing line, the corporal handed him an M-1. "Make yo' adjustments on that papuh there," he said, pointing to another target off to the side of the bales. Alabama nodded, checked to see the safety was off and a shell was chambered, and raised the rifle. He squeezed off three quick shots, lowered the rifle, and peered at the target. Then he reset the safety, made a small adjustment, and fired another test round. After examining that shot, he pronounced his weapon ready.

"Fire away, den," the corporal replied from behind him.

Alabama unlocked the safety, raised the rifle, and methodically placed five bullets in the center of his target. He lowered the rifle, locked the safety, and turned to the corporal. "Five nuf?" he asked.

The corporal stared downrange. "Depends," he replied quietly. "Go an' fetch yo' target."

When Alabama returned with the paper, the corporal gave it a quick glance. He stared hard at Alabama. "*Damn*, thas' good shootin'!" he exclaimed appreciatively. "Ah ain't nevah seen bettah. C'mon." He turned and strode off to the Quonset hut, clutching the paper tightly by its edge. When they arrived, the corporal handed the target to the sergeant without a word. The sergeant glanced at it, and his eyes grew wide. He looked quickly up at the corporal, who nodded wordlessly. The sergeant said "Denton, you're shipping out tonight. Three hours. Get down to the chow hall, use the loo out back, and be back here in two. Got it?"

"Yessah!" Alabama replied with a smile.

The sergeant scowled. "I ain't a 'sir,' you country bonehead! See these stripes? I'm a *real* soldier! You call me 'sir' again and I'll rip your balls off!"

Alabama grinned. "Ah be needin' those when this heah war be done," he replied. "Sergeant."

The sergeant grunted and redirected his attention to papers scattered on his desk. The corporal beckoned to Alabama. "Ah be takin' sharpeyes heah to de chow hall, Sarge. Okay wif you?" The sergeant waved them off without looking up.

Over a meal of typical military issue, i.e. edible and probably nutritious but of inscrutable origin, the corporal explained to Alabama that he was to be assigned to an elite group of snipers. They would operate largely on their own, with orders given as little as once a week in gatherings of those who lived to return. "You be sent to areas where dey lots 'a Germans," the corporal explained. "Yo' job jes' to shoot 'em. Many's you kin. You collect dey dog tags if'n you kin, bring 'em back to prove you doin' some good. You be runnin', you be hidin', you be makin' you own luck. Hide, shoot, kill, run like hell so dey don' shoot you."

"Sound lack fun," Alabama replied with a grin.

The corporal frowned. "Lots be killed," the corporal said plainly. "Day get seen, dey make a mistake, dey get shot in trees and hidey places. If'n you live, you come back to company HQ and get a feed an' a shower. Den you out fo' mo.'"

Alabama shrugged. "Ah small," he replied. "Ah shifty. An' Ah smaht as hell. Ah kin hide. Ah be back."

Now carefully ensconced in his oak tree, Alabama's eyes lit up and his body stiffened as he detected movement on the edge of the woods a quarter of a mile away. Many times such movement would only be a deer or a fox, and the sniper would sigh and settle back down for another wait. But this time Alabama grinned, and his heart began to pulse faster with anticipation. A lone German soldier was walking along the edge of the woods toward him.

Alabama waited, watching closely. If this man was the scout in a platoon, it would be very dangerous to pick him off, because his companions would hear the shot and know there was a sniper in the area. Alabama would have to scamper down the tree after the kill, forget the prized dog tags, and run as fast as possible to escape the infuriated platoon.

The soldier meandered along a thin dirt path toward his waiting assassin. Alabama thought him stupid and lazy, because he could have walked a few steps into the woods and been much safer from the danger of a waiting sniper. *But thas' work, pushin' dem tree branches out de way,* Alabama mused. *An' dese Nazis don' like work. Dey like Jew to do dey work. Bet dey ain't no Jew around today!*

He waited patiently. Step by careless step, the German soldier, who had the audacity to keep his rifle lowered as if he was strolling with an umbrella in a park in Berlin, moved along the path toward him.

He alone, Alabama decided. *An' he dead.* He raised his rifle, rested it on a branch, and sighted down the scope. Two seconds later, the soldier had a clean hole in the middle of his forehead. He fell backwards stiffly and did not move.

Alabama waited, listening intently. Carefully, he climbed down the oak, using his spike attachments and a rope around the trunk of the tree to lower himself in jerky increments. When he was at the bottom of the tree, he slipped off the spikes and paused to listen again.

There was no sound other than an occasional chirping bird.

Alabama crept in a soft zigzag pattern toward the fallen German. When he was within a few yards, he paused and waited. For fifteen minutes, he stayed low, hidden in a patch of bushes, his senses alert. When there was no movement in the nearby woods, he dashed low to the ground over to the soldier, grabbed his boots in both hands, and dragged him quickly into the woods.

Alabama unclasped the soldier's dog tags and stuffed them into his pocket. He rifled through the man's uniform, looking for souvenirs. Rejecting the usual German money, some of which he had scored with several other bodies and now disdained, he came across a small dark blue velvet bag in the upper right breast pocket. He pulled the yellow silk drawstring and peered into the bag.

Four shiny stones met his gaze. He shook them out into his palm. They shone with a flashing brilliance in the middle of his black hand.

Alabama stared at the stones. He held one up to the light. When it caught the rays of the sun and reflected both a stunning blue and mesmerizing yellow ochre, he gasped in wonder. *What kinda rock is dis?* he pondered.

Suddenly remembering the danger around him, he tossed the four stones back into the velvet bag, tightened the drawstring, and stuffed the bag into his pocket. Then he withdrew it, pulled out his trousers and underwear, and stuffed the bag down beside his privates. It felt odd there as he crept away from the body, but he smiled in grim self-satisfaction.

Four years that bag stayed there. It saw many changes of underwear, but seldom did it see the light of day. By the time V-E Day was declared and Alabama joined thousands of jubilant soldiers returning to the United States, he possessed a bronze star for valor, a purple heart for taking a shot in the left forearm which went through the flesh without hitting bone and healed quickly, and a smelly blue velvet bag with a mysterious cargo still secure near his crotch.

On the ship heading from England to New York, Alabama exercised the plan he'd been contemplating for many months. *Got to find me a Jew,* he thought carefully. *Jews be smaht. Jews know thangs normal folks don' be knowin'.* He strolled around the ship, gazing surreptitiously at worn nametags on equally worn uniforms. When he came to a white man with black-rimmed glasses, a crop of curly black hair and the name "Finklestein" leaning on a rail and gazing at the swells below, he sidled up and took a spot a few feet away. The Jewish soldier glanced over, and Alabama gave him a dazzling smile. "How you be?" he exclaimed. "Name's Alabama Denton." He held out his hand to shake.

Corporal Finklestein did not hesitate. He shook the proffered hand and returned the smile. "Nice to meet you, Alabama," he said. "Is that your given name?"

Alabama's smile disappeared. "Given?" he asked. "Whachoo mean?"

Finklestein shrugged. "You know. The name on your birth certificate."

Alabama laughed. "Don' have no birth certificate," he replied lightly. "Down home, da mama jes' have de baby. Doctah hep sometime, sometime not. Dey ain't no certificate." He stared down at the sea and chuckled.

"So, it's just a nickname, then," Finklestein remarked.

Alabama considered, chewing his lip. "No, it ain't zackly," he replied carefully. "Mah real name goofy as hell. Ah hates it, so Ah nevah uses it. Alabama wheah I from. Ah jes' likes it."

Finklestein smiled. "Okay, Alabama Denton, now you have me intrigued! What *is* your real name?"

Alabama resumed his contemplation of the ocean rolling below them. Suddenly he burst into a prolonged giggle and slapped his knee, doing a little jig. Finklestein couldn't help smiling. "What's so funny?" he asked.

Alabama gradually ceased his hilarity and stared at his new friend. "You goan' crap yo' *pants* when you heah!" he replied. "You ready?"

Finklestein nodded.

"Okay," Alabama said mysteriously. "Heah go. My real name Prendergast Adonis Denton." He stared at Finklestein and then burst into loud hilarity again, screeching with laughter. "*Prendergast!* You evah heah such nonsense? *Prendergast!* Sheeit, woman *crazy* to name a boy Prendergast!" He gripped the rail with both hands and rocked back and forth in his howling laughter.

Despite himself, Finklestein began to chuckle, then to laugh, and finally to lose himself in utter abandonment as he watched his wizened black companion hoot and holler and shake with contagious mirth. His eyes teared up, and he began to wheeze and bark uncontrollably. His belly shook, and he bent over and held his sides. It was as if more than four years of stifling heat, unbearable cold, incredible danger, fright, death, stench, destruction, and horror were suddenly dispelled in the cathartic burst of genuine, grateful laughter each man was wholeheartedly experiencing. Other men glanced at them and began to guffaw and hoot out of a need to simply vent pent-up feelings.

It was nearly five minutes before either could speak. Finally, Finklestein straightened up and grabbed the railing again. "Whoo, man, that was brutal!" he exclaimed. "But a *nice* brutal. I needed that! Thanks for a great laugh, Pren...I mean, Alabama."

That set the two of them off for another full minute of hilarity before they were able to breathe normally. When they were again composed, Finklestein asked "How did your family obtain your surname, if I may ask?"

Alabama looked at him strangely, a slight frown on his face. "Surname?"

"Your last name. Denton," Finklestein replied, pointing to Alabama's uniform shirt.

"Oh. Well, Ah don't rightly know. Slave name, Ah reckon."

"Slave name?"

"Uh huh. Lotsa black folk took dey massah name when dey free. Nevah had no last name 'til dat day."

Finklestein nodded, mulling over what he'd heard. "I didn't know any of that," he remarked as if to himself as he stared out to sea. He turned to his companion. "So, Alabama, tell me about yourself," he remarked in an inviting tone.

Alabama regarded him. For a few seconds, he looked down and merely stared at his boots. Then he raised his head. "You really want to know 'bout dis black man?" he asked.

Finklestein nodded. "Really," he replied with genuine interest.

"Ain't zackly pretty."

Finklestein nodded slowly. "I, uh…I don't suppose it would be. But tell me anyway. Please."

Alabama smiled softly and nodded. For the next forty minutes, as the ship rolled and swayed easily below them, Alabama related the life of a black boy growing into a young man in the Deep South in pre-WWII years. He told of the backbreaking work in the soil, the meager return which just barely managed to feed their family of three year after year, the constant threat of lynching, the insults of segregation at every turn, the lack of education beyond the fourth grade he had been able to achieve, and the bleak prospects facing a Negro when he was ready to enter the workplace. "Das' why de Army look so good," he explained. "Ah been lucky. Earnt me some money. Made it back."

Corporal Finklestein, who had listened intently without interrupting, sighed deeply and stared off at the horizon. He shook his head sadly. "I never heard anything remotely like that, Alabama," he remarked softly. "I had *no* idea." He turned and stared at Alabama, a tear leaking from his eye. He raised his glasses, wiped at the tear, and dried his hand on his shirt. "I have a college degree," he said simply. "In accounting. From NYU. It was easy. My father paid for it so I didn't have to have a job. Sailed through in four years. I enlisted because I wanted to serve my country and have a real life away from the pampered existence I'd always known. My family thought I was crazy." He sighed and stared off to sea again, his lips deeply pursed. After a few seconds, he remarked with a firmness beyond his years "I've had a real life now. Lord knows." He turned to Alabama again. "But I'll never experience the difficulties you've faced. What a *horrible* way to treat a human being!"

Over the next few days, as the ship made its way expertly toward New York Harbor, they spent quite a bit of time together. The black/white separation tradition was relaxed on board ship, to the point where several pairs or groups of whites and blacks occasionally mingled easily together. It was as if the war had made Southern Tradition seem largely ridiculous. Both races seemed to be at ease with a lack of societal chains.

At one point, as the coast of the United States became visible and everyone on board gave a prolonged and heartfelt cheer, Alabama took Finklestein by the sleeve and beckoned with his eyes toward a remote part of the bow. He led his puzzled friend to a spot behind some lifeboats, hidden from prying eyes. When they arrived at the secluded hollow, Finklestein asked "What's up, Alabama?"

Alabama sighed. "Ah got to trust you, Jeremy," he replied. "Ah got nobody else. You got to help me."

Finklestein stared at him. He nodded somberly. "You're my friend. Name it."

Alabama reached down into his crotch. Finklestein's eyes grew wide, and Alabama smiled bitterly. "It ain't nuthin' lack dat," he commented wryly. He pulled out the blue velvet bag and held it loosely between thumb and forefinger.

Finklestein stared at the worn bag. "What's that?" he asked in a whisper, glancing over his shoulder.

Alabama loosened the now-worn yellow silk drawstring and opened the bag. He shook out the four stones onto his palm.

"*Damn!*" Finklestein exclaimed, turning quickly to peer back and forth to see if they were being observed. "Where'd you get the diamonds, Alabama?"

Alabama stared long and hard at the stones. "Diamonds," he breathed softly. "Ah *thought* dey might be!"

"May I?" Finklestein said, reaching for the stones. Alabama swiftly closed his hand over them. He stared hard at Finklestein, his face in a defiant scowl.

Finklestein took a step back and held up both his hands, palm toward Alabama. "I'm not going to steal them," he said in a soft voice. "You don't have to allow me to touch them if you don't want. I'm just trying to get some idea of their value."

Alabama stared at him for a few seconds, nodded, and slowly opened his hand. He handed one of the stones to his companion. Finklestein held it up to the light, admiring its gleaming facets. "My, my," he breathed. "These look like very high quality. Where did you get them?"

"In de war," Alabama replied simply. Finklestein handed him the stone and stared at him.

"I din' steal 'em," Alabama said stiffly. "I ain't no thief."

Finklestein nodded. "I believe you. I do. How can I help you?"

Alabama slipped the stones into the bag and stuffed it back down into his underwear. "Ah need to sell 'em," he replied. "Get de money. Goin' buy me some land in Looziana."

Finklestein paused, then nodded. "And you don't know where to turn to sell them without getting taken advantage of."

Alabama nodded. "Black man an easy mark," he replied, a hard edge to his voice.

Finklestein shook his head sadly. "From what you've described these past few days, I believe you're absolutely right," he replied. "Most white men probably *would* try to steal them from you, believing you have no idea of their value. Well, we're going to prevent that. As it turns out, my father, who owns the accounting firm where I worked for a few months after graduation and before enlisting in the Army, knows a lot of people. A *lot* of people! Some of them are diamond merchants. Tell you what: when we get to New York, my family will be there, and I'll introduce you to them. Why don't you stay with us for a few days, a week or two, and I'll ask my father to take you around to several diamond merchants so you can obtain quotes. I'll accompany you so you'll feel comfortable. Will that be satisfactory?"

Alabama didn't know what to make of all the words, but he understood the gist of it: this man was going to help him, and more than likely he could trust him. You never knew with white men, but then some blacks would flash a razor and cut your throat for these stones too, so he'd best go with Jeremy and do what he said. While watching very, very closely, of course. He nodded. "Thank you," he replied simply.

Jeremy Finklestein held out his hand. When Alabama grasped it, Finklestein pulled him in for a hug. "I am so happy to help you," he breathed. Gently, he pushed his friend back and looked him in the eyes. His own eyes began to tear up beneath his lenses. He sighed and turned his head away. "Let's go back," he said, turning to go.

The Finklestein family welcomed their son and his new soldier friend with open arms. Night after night, as Papa Finklestein listened carefully and Jeremy's little brothers gazed with rapt attention, Jeremy and Alabama related tales of the war. They spared their audience the most horrific aspects of the conflict, though Papa Finklestein delighted in descriptions of Nazi deaths and would have stayed up for days to hear more. On the first day of the second week of their stay, Papa Finklestein said to Jeremy and Alabama at breakfast "Today we see what you have, my Southern friend. Several of my acquaintances have indicated considerable interest." He led them on a tour of the diamond district, laying the four brilliant stones before merchant after merchant and bargaining in a rapid singsong that was part Hebrew and part English and well beyond Alabama's comprehension. At the end of an exhausting day, Papa Finklestein treated his young companions to supper at a very fine establishment and remarked in a low voice "I believe Mr. Pearlman will offer you the best price, Alabama. You should do business with this man."

Alabama glanced at Jeremy. He read genuine trust there. "Yassuh," he replied to Finklestein senior, using the term he'd sworn he'd never say to another white man the remainder of his life.

Mr. Finklestein nodded as if in complete understanding. "Tomorrow, then," he replied. They enjoyed their meal and talked of baseball and other matters of great consequence.

The next day, the three of them returned to the diamond district. When the merchants saw them coming, to a man they hollered out "Good day, Finklestein. So good to see you again!" The elder Finklestein nodded politely to each and moved resolutely to the stall held by Mr. Pearlman. "My friend has decided to accept your offer, Mr. Pearlman," he said by way of greeting.

Pearlman nodded formally. "Please be seated," he offered, beckoning to three chairs before his table. "Would you like coffee?"

When the deal was done, and Alabama was handed $12,485 cash, he turned to Jeremy and peeled off $1,000. "Dis fo' you," he said, offering twenty $50 bills.

Jeremy glanced at his father and smiled. He turned to Alabama. "I cannot, my friend," he said softly. "We have a saying. It's in Hebrew, but translated it says 'God watches.' He sees all, Alabama. He sees the blessing you have been to my father's household. May you go in peace."

Alabama stared at him. He looked to Papa Finklestein, who smiled and nodded. "It has been a pleasure to be of service, my son," he said. "I too wish you a safe journey."

CHAPTER 2

The bus ride from New York City to Montgomery, Alabama was a long four days, with all the stops in small towns on the way. Alabama Denton enjoyed every minute of it. He liked looking out the window at the America he had never seen, he liked drifting off to sleep late in the evening, he liked the stops where he could get off the bus, stretch his legs, and buy a Coke and a sandwich. He didn't even mind riding in the back of the bus, because that was where he could have a leisurely conversation every now and then with a fellow black traveler. Besides, it was comfortable back there, with the loose springs giving the ride a lazy bouncy feel. Alabama was glad to be back in the land of the free, at least free from the Nazis. He kept his money securely belted to his waist in a special canvas band that Jeremy Finklestein had purchased for him as a parting gift, putting his hand on it every now and then while he dreamed of land.

When he arrived in Montgomery, he debated walking the two-day journey to Selmon, a distance he could easily accomplish and probably would enjoy even more than the bus ride. But he decided it wasn't fitting for a veteran of the war to walk such a distance, so he visited a hardware store in the Lowertown section and for eight dollars bought a new red Schwinn with fat tires and one gear. He waved at the ladies as he rode an easy pace north. Though he could have pushed himself to make the distance by nightfall, he chose instead to stop at a small combination grocery store and diner in a town populated solely by a few dozen black families. There he invested in a meal of cornbread and honey, pulled pork, and chitlins, flavored by a nip or three of the store owner's homemade whiskey. The bottle came out, courtesy of the proprietor, only after Alabama began to relate his experiences in the war. More than once he was pressed to display his Army ID card and dogtags, eliciting whistles and appreciative comments each time. He was very careful to leave out any mention of his wealth and concentrated hard not to touch the belt under his shirt when anyone in the small crowd that had formed to hear him might be observing.

The proprietor wouldn't hear of Alabama pushing off to spend the night outside. He insisted that his wife prepare a cot with a goose feather pillow and a light blanket so that his guest could sleep in the family's quarters above the store. Alabama gratefully accepted. In the morning, after a fine breakfast, he gave the proprietor a twenty-dollar bill. The man was aghast at such a generous gesture, since a loaf of oven-baked bread could be had in his store for only six cents. Alabama laughed away the man's protests and slapped him on the back. "No, dis fo' yo' famly," he said with a grin. "Least Ah kin do. Buy yo' wife a new dress, and them chirren a few toys. Get yo'sef some new hardware fo' yo' whiskey-makin'." He laughed uproariously at the man's sudden self-conscious grin, wherein he displayed all six remaining teeth. The proprietor wished him Godspeed and waved a hearty goodbye as Alabama climbed onto his bike and pedaled north.

He arrived at the outskirts of Selmon at ten in the morning. The day was hot and beginning to become humid. Alabama paused and peered through rising heat waves at the place he knew so well. *Ain't changed a lick,* he thought. He pedaled slowly through the town, waving at an occasional old friend. Several heads turned and mouths dropped as he rode by, and his name was shouted out more than once. He merely smiled and pushed on, heading for his parents' shack north of town.

He was still a hundred yards down the road when he saw his father sitting on the porch of the ramshackle unpainted wooden two-room home he'd known from birth. Alabama took a deep breath, let it out slowly, and wheeled softly up to the shack. When he was a few feet from the porch, he stepped off, laid the bike on its side, and said "Hey, Pa."

Alabama's father looked at him with rheumy eyes, blinking as if to focus. After a few seconds, he frowned and said "Prendergast? That you, son?"

"Yes, Pa," Alabama replied.

His father stood on stiff knees and appraised his son, looking him up and down several times. Alabama wore tan cotton slacks with the right leg turned up six inches at the ankle to prevent the cloth from catching in the bike chain, and a light green t-shirt. His wiry muscular features were visible on his arms and on his torso when the breeze blew the sweaty t-shirt against his chest. There was a solid look to him. He stood, hands on his waist, smiling softly.

"Mmmm, mmm," the old man opined. "You done put on some weight, son."

Alabama's smile widened. "Reckon Ah done, Pa," he replied. "Army food ain't bad."

Denton senior nodded. "You come back from dat war."

Alabama's smile faded. "Yes, Pa. Ah been in dat war. Fo' yeah, Ah been in dat war. Long tam. Seem lack fo'ty yeah."

The old man sagged down into his chair and nodded. He sighed deeply. "Figured Ah nevah see you again, son. Figured you get yo' ass shot off in dat white man war."

Alabama frowned. "It warn't no white man war, Pa!" he protested. "We's Mericans, all 'a us, fightin' Germans. Some 'a us fought Eye-talyuns, but they warn't much. Hear tell some 'a us fought Japs, way off on de othah side'a de world. Me, I jes' stayed wif de Germans. Put a few in de ground, Pa." He stood an inch taller.

Denton senior nodded. "Reckon you might, at dat," he replied musingly. "You could allus shoot." He peered carefully at his son. "Dey let you eat wif white boys?"

Alabama nodded. "Yes, Pa. We in sep'rate units, but we all men. Dey some rednecks, but mos'ly jes' 'Mericans. Not lack heah, in de South. We all 'Mericans fightin' Germans." Alabama glanced toward the cornfield. "Wheah Mama? She hoein'?"

His father stared at him. A long moment passed.

"Pa?"

"She gone," the old man replied in a soft, phlegmy voice. "She done gone on ta glory."

Alabama took in a sharp breath. He stared at his father, eyes wide. He tried to speak, but no words formed. Finally he croaked "*Mama?* She *gone?*"

Denton senior nodded. "Three yeah ago. She jes' fade away, son. Missin' you too much, Ah reckon. Plus she got some kinda whoopin' thang. Couldn't stop coughin'. Reckon it was the consumption, best a body could tell. She din last long once dat set in."

Alabama sighed deeply. His eyes filled with hot, stinging tears, and he wiped them away fiercely. He stumbled to the steps and sagged down, staring at the packed red dirt at the base of them. For several long minutes he merely sat there, shoulders slumped, seeing only the cheery black face of his mother, with her shiny apple-round cheeks and her sparkling black eyes beneath long, curly lashes. As if from a distance, he saw a boy hugging her around her ample midriff; he saw his mother pull that boy in tight and exclaim "My, ain't you a fine young man!"; he saw her looking up at him one day, hands on wide hips and head tilted, saying "How you get so *tall*, son?"

Alabama cleared his throat and looked up at his father, who sat staring off into the distance. "Ah nevah think she be gone," Alabama said softly. "Men shoot at me ever' day, but Ah nevah think *Mama* be gone."

His father sighed deeply and nodded. "Me neither."

Alabama stood and looked around. The same corn stood tall in the same six acres behind the house. "You bin farmin' good, Pa," he remarked.

The old man nodded. "Keep a man busy," he replied. "Keep yo' mind off thangs. Gettin' hard, though. Mah ol' body don' lack it much dese days. And Ah sho' wish yo' mama was heah to make pone an' tend dem chickens."

Alabama nodded, chewing his lip. He stared at his father. After a moment, he asked "How old you be, Pa?"

The old man looked at him sharply. "None 'a yo' bizness!" he replied indignantly.

Alabama lifted his shirt. He unzipped the money belt and pulled out twenty fifty-dollar bills, counting them carefully. Handing them to his stupefied father, he said "Dis heah a thousand dollah, Pa. You sell dis six acre to a young man wif a fambly. Gim a fair price. Den you go to town, get yo'sef a room. Tell Mr. Roosevelt you be wantin' dat theah Social Security he got. Ax 'round, dey tell you how to get it. Den you take it easy. You hide dis money good, ain't nobody goin' steal it. You live a lotta years in peace, Pa, if'n you rest yo'sef. You been hoein' too long."

The old man stared at the money in his hand. He looked up to his son and down at the wad of bills again, time after time, as if attempting to connect the two. Finally he folded the bills in half with a shaky hand and slipped them into the breast pocket of his denim coveralls. He nodded, a look of respect that Alabama had never seen on him before.

Alabama stared at his father. His face showed no emotion, though he nearly chewed a hole in the inside of his lip. After a long moment, he said "Wayall, Ah be pushin' on, Pa. You be okay."

The old man regarded his son. A tear fell down his cheek, and he nodded. "Take care yo'sef, Prendergast," he said.

Alabama turned on his heel, raised his bike, and pedaled off quickly. He did his best to hide the shaking of his shoulders.

CHAPTER 3

The history of the state of Louisiana begins with Native American tribes who inhabited the land when the first Spanish explorers arrived in the sixteenth century. Many place names in the state, including Atchafalaya, Natchitoches, Tangipahoa, Caddo, and Houma are transliterations of the words used in various Native dialects. At Watson Brake and Poverty Point, thousands of years of Native American occupation can be seen in archeological digs.

The first Europeans to visit the area came in 1528, when the Spanish expedition led by Panfilo de Narvaez located the terminus of the Mississippi River. In 1541, Hernando de Soto's expedition crossed the region and constructed crude maps of it. Concluding that it was basically a swamp-ridden wasteland, the Spanish government generally ignored the area.

In the late seventeenth century, French expeditions, which included government, religious, and commercial groups, established a foothold on the Mississippi River where it enters the Gulf Coast. From that strongpoint, France established a claim to a vast region of North America. It set out to establish a new French colony and commercial enterprise stretching from the Gulf Coast to Canada. The French were not particularly known for their modesty.

Despite the beachhead on the coast, the first French settlement of any importance was Natchitoches, along the Red River in present-day northwest Louisiana. That was established in 1714 by a nobleman by the name of Louis

Juchereau de St. Denis, who had been displaced from his family estate in France over an affair with a very underage female cousin. He proceeded to name the entire region after himself. The name stuck, and Natchitoches became the center of the new colony of Louisiana. St. Denis declared the fledgling town to have two main purposes: to deter Spanish advances into the area from Texas and, ironically, to trade with these same Spaniards. Within a short two decades, the settlement became a flourishing river port and crossroads, giving rise to vast cotton plantations along the river. This pattern was later to be repeated in New Orleans and other towns. St. Denis died in 1752, secure in the knowledge that he had been kinglet of a mighty (if somewhat primitive) empire.

During the eighteenth century, French explorers founded settlements along the banks of the Mississippi and its major tributaries, from Louisiana to as far north as the present-day St. Louis, Missouri and Peoria, Illinois. In 1722, much to St. Denis' disappointment, France declared the new settlement at New Orleans to be the seat of military and civilian authority due to the importance of the vast Mississippi River.

In 1719, two French ships, the *Duc du Marine* and the *Aurore*, arrived in New Orleans with a strange new cargo: human beings stolen from Africa. Eager settlers snapped up the new treasures, paying the slave ship captains a handsome fee for the privilege of free labor and the prospect of good breeders.

The region changed hands twice in the latter half of the eighteenth century. After nearly fifty years of back-and-forth victories and losses in the French and Indian War, followed by claims of large tracts of the central region of what is now the United States by both Britain and France, the treaty of Paris in 1763 ended the war and gave all of North America east of the Mississippi, other than New Orleans, to the British. As compensation for Spain surrendering Florida to the British, the French turned over their claims to New Orleans and the lands west of the Mississippi to Spain.

However, despite the fact that it was the Spanish government that officially ruled Louisiana after 1763, the rate of francophone (French) immigration to the territory increased swiftly. Several thousand French-speaking refugees from the Canadian region of Acadia (now Nova Scotia) made their way to Louisiana after being expelled from their home territory as a result of the British victory in the French and Indian War. These people settled mainly in the southwestern region of Louisiana now called Acadiana. Their descendents came to be known as Cajuns.

After a couple of generations of prodigious Acadian and Spanish immigration to the area, the difference between a Frenchman and a Spaniard became negligible. The term "Creole" was coined to identify such people. Native Americans, Englishmen, Africans, and various natives from the Atlantic and Gulf islands began to mingle and intermarry with Creoles. By the time the newly-named Americans (winners of the American Revolution) took over the territory in the early nineteenth century, the notion of a pure French-Spaniard as a "Creole" was already history. Creoles were considered persons of mixed race with a distinctly Louisianan flavor. Today the term is generally used to refer to a sub-group of people who have colored skin of various hues and a long history but are not "black" per se.

During the years of Spanish rule of Louisiana, from 1763 to the end of the century, both free and enslaved populations increased rapidly. New settlers from France, Spain, and Germany, along with Creoles, purchased large numbers of slaves imported from West Africa and put them to work on their developing plantations. Such was the burgeoning slave trade that soon the majority of people in Louisiana were African slaves.

Napoleon Bonaparte, Emperor of France, acquired Louisiana from the Spanish in 1800. He harbored dreams of establishing a new French empire in the central part of the North American continent, but that dream was dashed when he attempted to take over Haiti and lost many men and armaments. He subsequently sold Louisiana and millions of square miles north of it to the new United States of America in 1810 (the "Louisiana Purchase," for which President James Madison was ridiculed at the time by the Democratic Party).

Louisiana became a state of the union in 1812. Its borders were fixed as they appear today.

With the growth of American settlers in the Louisiana Territory, trade and shipping increased in New Orleans as produce flowed south and imports flowed north along the Mississippi River. The port became crowded with steamboats, flatboats, and sailing ships. Workers speaking languages from many nations mingled freely with Creoles and "pure white" Louisianans. The city became quite wealthy as a result of rich farm production, much of it created by a massive slave population in the area. By 1840, New Orleans had become the third largest city in the union and clearly one of the richest.

After the crushing defeat of the South in the Civil War followed by what white Louisianans considered the intrusive and quite unnecessary Reconstruction, groups such as the White League and the Klu Klux Klan began to dominate freed black citizens. Segregation became the ethos, Jim Crow laws became the established legal system for suppressing blacks, and Southern Tradition kept "order." This situation persisted until the conclusion of World War Two.

CHAPTER 4

Alabama Denton stepped off the steamship he'd boarded in Mobile, Alabama some six days earlier and onto a dock in the Port of New Orleans. Desiring to save what money he could, he'd purchased a ten-pound bag of potatoes, a five-pound bag of apples, and two pounds of beef jerky prior to boarding the ship. This constituted his menu on the journey. In addition, he'd waited until he had secured work as a deck hand on a ship before embarking on the 140-mile journey south from Mobile and then due west to the Port of New Orleans. The sail around the Gulf islands south of the state of Mississippi and up the wide river to New Orleans was exhilarating. The only other times Alabama had ever seen the ocean was his trips to and from Europe, and this was much different. The Gulf was more choppy, filled with interesting sea life, and more alive than the Atlantic had appeared from sixty feet above it. The thought *Ah could do dis fo' a livin'* entered his mind, but the dream of owning land was too strong and he quickly abandoned thoughts of the sea.

Louisiana, Alabama daydreamed as the steamship plowed with its cargo of passengers and cloth goods to New Orleans. *Ah have loved dat word since Ah heard tell of it in school.* He thought back to Miss Wellington, the young, pretty, college-educated black woman who had come to Selmon from Philadelphia to dedicate her life to the education of poor black children in the South. She hadn't lasted in that role for more than a year, having been claimed and swept off her feet by a tall, strong black farmer who had the good fortune of owning twenty-five acres and a motorized tractor. Alabama and seventeen other children had been the beneficiary of Miss Wellington's ministrations that year. She poured all her time and energy into those children, bringing them from a low level of competence in the three R's to considerable improvement. One of the subjects she stressed was geography, insisting that the children should discover the world outside Selmon, Alabama in order to give them a chance for broader horizons as an alternative to a life spent scratching out rows for corn.

That was when Alabama encountered a map of Louisiana.

For reasons he could not identify then or now, the word had a special magic. He borrowed one of the four geography books in the school and took it home each night for a month, diligently returning it the next day. At night, he traced the border of the state with his finger, marveling at how it formed a union with Mississippi on the east, Arkansas on the north, and Texas on the west, with the vast Gulf of Mexico stretching away to the south. He memorized each of the parish names, noting their position relative to one another. The land of Louisiana became a strange fixation to his young mind. He resolved to go there one day, not knowing if it was even possible.

When he stepped off the ship, having first collected his pay in cash from the ship captain, he paused, closed his eyes, and took a deep breath of the city's air. *Ah really heah!* he thought with barely suppressed excitement. Opening his eyes, he spread his arms and embraced the entire city. The money belt tugged at his waist, but he ignored it in his exultation.

Alabama wandered along the Riverwalk with an Army surplus backpack strapped onto his back and a faded quilt carpetbag with a wooden handle alternating between one hand and the other. Though these constituted the entirety of his possessions, he was happy. He was in Louisiana! Moreover, the money belt around his waist confirmed with each step that he was wealthy beyond what most black men would ever earn in a lifetime.

Knowing from his studies of geography that the Garden District was east of the French Quarter, he turned north on Jackson Ave. and walked seven blocks to Magazine Street. When he crossed Magazine and looked to his left, he saw for the first time what neatly-kept, flower-laden yards and gardens could be. Each of the stately homes and mansions in the District was meticulously kept, proudly displaying a panoply of lush, bright, colorful, and exotic foliage. Alabama breathed it in, smiling and marveling at his good fortune in being there just to see and enjoy it.

He turned left onto St. Charles Ave., knowing from his studies that it would take him into the French Quarter. Six blocks later, as he continued to admire the sensuous display of nature surrounding every house in the District, he noticed a white woman standing near her front gate, hands on her hips and a frown on her face. Her home on the corner of St. Charles and Washington featured two large lawn-and-garden botanical creations, each fronting one of the cross streets. He paused before crossing Washington, not wanting to startle or upset the woman. She spotted him and called out "You there! Young man! Come here!"

Alabama sighed. *First day and Ah already in trouble*, he lamented. He stepped across the street and approached the woman. When he was yet ten feet from her, he laid down his carry-all and said "Yes, ma'am? How kin Ah hep you?"

The woman looked him over, appraising him from head to foot. After a few seconds of such scrutiny, she remarked "Well, you're small, but you look strong enough. Come with me." Without ceremony, she wheeled and walked through her open gate into the garden on St. Charles and around the side of the house. Alabama followed more out of curiosity than a sense of duty.

When the woman reached the back of the house, she pointed to a large white wooden structure. Alabama could see that it was a garage, with four large doors and a stone driveway leading to Washington Street. The woman pointed to the right side of the building, where a staircase ascended to a second story. "You'll stay up there," she directed. "There's some furniture. Everything you'll need." She waved her hand as if that settled it. "See Matilda in the kitchen. She'll give you the meal schedule." She turned and took a few steps toward the house. Abruptly she paused and turned back to Alabama. "You *do* have experience, don't you?" she inquired, hands planted on her hips again.

Experience, Alabama mused. *Lessee, Ah kin plow a furrow and plant corn seed. Ah kin dig manure into the soil and tend a veggie garden. Ah kin hoe weeds from dawn to dusk. Ah kin hide for two days in a tree if'n dey's Germans 'round, and they nevah know.*

Ah kin drop a man wif one shot from neah a hundred yahds. Dat de kinda experience you be wantin,' lady? But he simply smiled and answered "Yes, ma'am."

"Good!" she replied. "And I hope you're more reliable than my last gardener! He just *wandered* off last week, pretty as you please! And *look* at my garden!" She swept her hands to encompass the vastness of her magnificent floral panorama.

Alabama did look. He saw a weed here, an untended azalea that needed pruning there, and a piece of paper under a bush that had obviously blown in from the street. He shook his head and made a *tch-tch* sound.

"Exactly!" the woman remarked indignantly. "Well! See Matilda. And I do hope you're not too weary to start today." She peered at him, a frown between her eyes, as if to forestall any thought to the contrary.

"Ah be please to staht today, ma'am," Alabama replied with a smile.

She nodded firmly. "Good. We'll talk later." She turned and strode resolutely to the front door on the wide veranda along St. Charles Street.

Alabama put down his carryall, slipped the backpack off his shoulders, and looked around the garden. Suddenly, without warning, a burst of laughter escaped him. He turned and suppressed it as much as possible so no one in the house would hear him. *Mama do say God love all folk, even black ones,* he mused. *He mus' love me a <u>whole</u> lot!*

CHAPTER 5

After ascending the stairs to the apartment, laying his carryall and backpack on the cot and appraising the small chest of drawers and bedside table that constituted the remainder of the furniture in the small room above the garage, Alabama walked down the stairs and over to the back door of the large house. He ascended the four steps onto the back veranda and knocked tentatively on the back door. "Hello? Matilda?" he asked, hoping he wasn't being too loud.

"Ya'll come in!" a hearty female voice rang out.

Alabama opened the door, noting that it squeaked terribly and making a mental note to oil it. He stepped into a narrow hallway where a rough cotton rug had been laid on the polished wood floor to accommodate muddy shoes. He slipped off his boots and placed them neatly on the rug.

The kitchen was a few steps down the hall and to the right. A small bathroom led off the hallway to the left, opposite the kitchen. Alabama could have found the kitchen blindfolded from the tantalizing aroma of fresh-baked bread that wafted from it. He paused at the door of the kitchen and looked inside.

A tall, ample black woman, perhaps four inches taller than himself and outweighing him by at least a hundred pounds, looked up from the wide wooden chopping block table that occupied the center of the kitchen. She was wearing a loose cotton short-sleeve dress with a white lace collar and a white handkerchief around her massive, shiny curls. She appeared to Alabama to be in her late 20's or early 30's. When she smiled, her teeth were large and white, and her face shone with a special charm from the thin film of sweat upon it. She paused in her kneading of a large batch of dough and appraised him.

"Wayall, wayall, lookee what de cat done drag in!" she exclaimed with a musical laugh. Her voice was strong and deep, yet pleasant to the ear. "Come in! Come in!" She nodded to a wooden chair next to a small table in one corner of the kitchen under a long rack of cabinets and commanded "Sitchersef!"

Alabama duly complied.

The woman continued her kneading, the sinews standing out like ropes in her large forearms. "You de new gahdnah," she remarked. "Missus tell me 'bout you."

Alabama nodded. "S'pose Ah am, at that," he replied with a grin. "Leastwise the lady sho' think so. So Ah reckon Ah mus' be. Name's Alabama Denton."

"Ah'm Matilda," the woman replied. "What kinda name is dat?"

"Wheah Ah from."

She considered it for a few seconds and shrugged. "Wayall, call yo'sef cornpone if'n you like, far's Ah'm concerned," she replied nonchalantly. "Only thang Ah need to know is if'n you hungry!" She smiled hugely. "An' heah is wheah you say 'Yes, Matilda, Ah could eat a horse!', 'cause Ah got plenty!" She laughed merrily.

"Yes, Matilda, Ah sho' am hungry, fo' real," Alabama replied. "An' mighty obliged."

She nodded. "Jes' wait 'til Ah get dis brayud into the oven," she commented. "Den Ah fix you up."

Over a very tasty and generous meal of chopped beef, greens, and corn bread, Alabama responded to Matilda's questions about his background. Despite his normal tendency toward caution, he sensed that he could trust this woman not to run off to "Missus" and spill all that he was telling her. Gradually he began to open up more and more, even telling her about his war experiences. When he was finished relating the tale of his life, which coincided with the last piece of buttered cornbread and the last swallow of cold water, he sat back, licked his lips, and said "You some kinda cook, Matilda. Ah ain't et lack that since...well, since the las' time my mama fed me." He grinned and patted his stomach.

"Don' look lack you et much a'tall anytime," she replied. "You ain't got no extra weight on you."

Alabama shook his head. "Nevah did," he replied. "Burned it off, workin'."

Matilda nodded. "Wayall, you best eat small heah, then," she replied. "Dey ain't much work, tell the truth. Dat last man, name 'a Sylvester, he jes' shifty and lazy. Only work when he had to. Lack to spend his days in dis kitchen. Ah had to shoo him off out into the garden mos' days. Finally he jes' up and leave. Dat was las' week. Missus, she be all agitated de las' few days. Good thing you come along. Ah thought she was gonna blow a gasket!"

"What kinda work she be lookin' fo'?"

"Oh, gahdnin', fo' sho'. They all kinda tools an' such in the garage. You jes' figgah out what to do, mo' or less. Plus maintenance heah and theah, you know. Handyman stuff. She lack to keep a man around fo' dat."

"Wha' she pay?"

Matilda shrugged. "Nevah ax. Room an' board, fo' sho'. Plus, Ah reckon dey's some cash now and then. Best thing is you jes' wait, let her brang it up."

Alabama nodded. "Suits me, leastwise fo' the time bein'. What time you lack for me to come fo' meals?"

Matilda smiled. "Breakfast in de mornin', lunch at noon, suppah in de ev'nin'."

Alabama grinned. "What mo' a man want, 'specially wif *yo'* cookin'?"

Matilda grinned hugely and mock-curtsied in reply.

Alabama cocked his head. "How come she all alone?"

"Who? Mizz Stoughton?"

"Yes."

Matilda sighed. "She warn't always alone. When Ah fust come, ten year ago, Ah's jes' a girl gettin' off de farm up north Looziana way. I ax around, somebody tell me dis lady lookin' for kitchen hep. Ah kin cook, so Ah apply. Mizz Stoughton, she hire me raht away. She a sweet lady. Ver'a kind. Don't nevah beat no Negroes. Her husban', he a good man too. He in de Navy. Ship cap'in, Ah think. He go off to de war, and his ship get sunk. Dat was three yeah ago. She been ver'a quiet since then. Still nice, but a body cain't talk wif her much nowadays. Leastwise, Ah ain't tried to."

Alabama sighed, reflecting on how fortunate he had been to escape some very precarious situations. *In de army, a body always got earth 'neath his feet. No fallin' outa de sky, no sinkin' inta de ocean.* He shook his head sadly. "Po' lady," he commiserated.

"Bes' leave her be," Matilda commented.

Alabama found the work to be simple and easy, as Matilda had mentioned. Immediately after supper he located pruning shears and went through the yard, lopping errant twigs here and there. He cleaned up debris as he went, to the extent that by dusk he had virtually completed the job and the garden was neat and clean. Mrs. Stoughton, the matron of the house, came out onto the front veranda and surveyed his work as he was about to put away his tools and wheelbarrow. "My, that's some very nice gardening," she commented. "And so quickly! Thank you."

Alabama stopped, mouth open. He quickly shut it, hoping he hadn't looked like a fool. *Thank you?* he thought, dumbfounded. *What kinda white woman thank a Negro? Matilda raht about this lady.* "You mos' welcome, Missus," he replied with a genuine smile.

She gazed at him. After a moment, she said "Well."

Alabama nodded. "Night then, Missus."

"Uh…." she replied. "I never asked your name."

Alabama smiled. "And I nevah ax *yo'* name, Mizz Stoughton," he replied courteously. "Found it out from Matilda. My name Alabama Denton."

"Alabama. A very unusual name."

He smiled, his teeth gleaming in the fading light. "Yes'm. Sho' is."

She offered a soft smile. "Well. Very good work, Alabama. I hope your bed is comfortable." She turned and walked back into the house.

CHAPTER 6

For the next three months, basically through the remainder of summer and into the fall, Alabama remained with Mrs. Stoughton, taking his meals with Matilda and working six days a week around the house and yard. By the end of the first week, he had the garden looking meticulous, healthy, and breathtaking in its splendor. Mrs. Stoughton took great delight at sitting in a swing chair on her front porch and chatting with folks who passed by and stopped to admire her garden.

At the end of the first week, toward evening on a Saturday, Alabama was on his knees working with hand clippers around the edge of a garden bed. Mrs. Stoughton approached him with an envelope in her hand. He stood and said "Evenin', Mizz Stoughton."

She nodded and replied "Good evening to you." She gazed around at the garden. "You truly do magnificent work, Alabama," she commented. "My garden has never looked better." She handed him an envelope. "I paid the last man ten cents an hour. He generally put in a forty-hour week, although I suspect half of that was hiding out instead of working. I have watched you carefully. You're out in the garden or making repairs in the house from dawn to dusk, less time for meals. I calculate that that amounts to about ten hours a day, six days a week. You're a very fine worker, Alabama. Therefore I am paying you fifteen cents an hour, and you'll have Sundays off. Will that be satisfactory?"

Alabama did a rapid calculation in his head. *Nine dollah fo' a week's work. Cain't earn that growin' corn. Made more on the ship, and 'bout three times that in the Army, but this be good workin' conditions fo' the time bein'.* He smiled and replied "Das good, Mizz Stoughton. Ah thank ya."

She handed him the envelope and said "I've included an extra dollar in case you wish to attend a Christian church tomorrow. You can put it into the offering plate. There is a very fine Baptist church for you people on the corner of Royal and Barracks, just inside the French Quarter. That's about a mile west of us here." She paused and smiled. "Matilda attends that church. Perhaps you could accompany her."

Alabama smiled. "Ah thank ya, Mizz Stoughton. Ah bin thinkin' 'bout church. Mama took me when Ah's a chil'. Been a while, though. Meantime, Ah done some thangs need confessin'. So tomorrah Ah be takin' me to dis church you tellin' me 'bout."

"Very commendable," Mrs. Stoughton replied. "Good night, then." She turned and walked back to the house.

On Sunday, his day off, Alabama did indeed visit the New Orleans Negro Baptist church with Matilda. She laughed gaily as they strolled the mile to the one-story brick building, promising Alabama that he would enjoy the experience. Once there, they were greeted heartily by the pastor and his wife. Matilda introduced him to several of the congregation, receiving inquiring looks from the women but choosing not to respond. As promised, Alabama did indeed enjoy the worship service. As he'd mentioned, during a prayer time prior to the sermon, he laid out his heart before God. *Lawd, you ain't heard the sound of my voice or the seen the shape 'a my prayers fo' quite a while,* he confessed. *Das my fault. Ah know you is always theah. Ah knows you is watchin' out fo' me. Else how could Ah find dem stones, or dat job on de ship, or Mizz Stoughton? You is way bettah to me than this Negro deserve.* And he listed his sins, omitting none: the one hundred and eighty-seven German soldiers whose lives he took in the war, his less-than-loving attitude toward his father, his failure to be more generous with the money with which God had graced him. When it was all spread before the Lord, he asked for forgiveness. *An' Lawd,* he prayed, *Ah ax you to find me land an' de right woman fo' me. Thank you, Lawd.*

In the afternoon, he strolled through the French Quarter. Its reputation for rowdiness was known to him, courtesy of fellow deckhands on the steamship, and he stopped in at two mixed-race bars for a drink. No one asked him for an I.D. He was content just to sip his beer and watch the lively dancing to spirited music and would have left each bar early if it was up to him. In the second bar, however, a good-looking young woman in a tight-fitting long red satin dress with white ruffles along the collar, hem, and sleeves sidled up with a wide smile. "How you, handsome?" she asked grandly, leaning backward on the bar with both arms and gazing into his eyes.

Alabama smiled back. "Ah jes' fine," he replied. "An' so are you. *Mighty* fine!" He laughed along with her.

The woman leaned back against the bar, emphasizing the curves of her body. "You in the mood for some fun?" she asked.

Alabama sighed. He had been approached once in this same manner by a mulatto girl in a bar in Paris while on R & R over Christmas during the last year of the war. She had asked basically the same question, and he'd given that girl the same answer he presented to the young woman before him now. "Honey," he replied, "no disrespect, fo' sho'. You is cert'ly a handsome woman. But you ain't mah wife. Ah's waitin' 'til she come along. Hope you don't mind."

The woman stopped smiling. She gazed deeply into Alabama's eyes. After a moment, she leaned back and sighed. "Any more lack you wheah you come from?" she asked sadly.

Alabama shook his head. "Ah wouldn't know," he replied. "But Ah be pleased to buy you a drink. Whachoo havin'?"

The woman put her hand on his forearm in a loving gesture. "Thanks, handsome. But Ah got to work. Take care 'a yo'sef." She smiled fleetingly and moved on. Alabama downed his beer and left the bar.

When he felt he'd seen enough of the life of the Quarter, he strolled through the streets, always being careful to avoid groups of white men and to keep his money belt well concealed. Sometimes the narrow streets made it necessary to step aside into a doorway when two or more white men walked toward him. He was careful to keep his gaze upon the ground as they passed by, as he did not know how much alcohol they'd consumed or what was in their heart.

Toward evening, Alabama found what he'd been seeking. On the northern edge of the French Quarter, on the corner of Burgundy and St. Peter Streets, he saw a sign: "Crescent City Real Estate. Commercial, Residential, Land." There was a name, Pasqual duFresne, and a phone number on the sign as well. Alabama took out a piece of paper and a pencil he'd brought, anticipating such a find, and wrote down the information in careful block letters. He folded the paper and put it securely into his pocket.

CHAPTER 7

It was a week and a day before he could contact the real estate office. On the eighth day after his visit to the Quarter, a Monday, he found the garden in near-perfect shape and the list of to-do's in the house totally accomplished. After lunch, he sought out his employer fanning herself in her accustomed swing chair on the front porch. "Mizz Stoughton?" he asked, hat in hand as he approached her.

She looked down at him as he stood on the lawn, five steps below her. "Yes, Alabama?"

Alabama cast his eyes around the garden. "De work all done fo' the time bein', Mizz Stoughton. Out heah and in de house. Leastwise far as Ah know. You got mo' fo' me raht now?"

She gazed at him. "No, I don't believe I do, not at the moment," she replied. "Why? Do you want the afternoon off?"

Alabama shook his head emphatically. "No, ma'am. Not de whole aftahnoon. Jes' two hour. Den Ah be back." He stood with his hands before him, holding his hat and waiting for her answer.

Mrs. Stoughton offered a brief smile. "Why, I suppose that would be all right," she replied. "You seem to have everything in hand. Why don't you take the entire afternoon? We'll count it as work time. You deserve it."

Alabama gazed at her. He sighed and nodded. "Dat mighty generous, Mizz Stoughton. Ah thank you."

She looked at him, a strange expression on her face. "Matilda tells me you were in the war," she commented softly.

Alabama nodded. "Yes'm."

She nodded. "And you made it back."

"Yes'm. Ah was fortunate."

She sighed. A slight shudder passed over her. After a long moment, she said "Some are."

Alabama dropped his gaze to the grass. When he looked up, she was looking off into the distance. He caught her wiping a tear away.

"Mizz Stoughton?" he said.

She turned to look at him.

"Mizz Stoughton, Ah…" He pursed his lips, took in a deep breath, and let it out slowly. "Ah don' know wha' to say. Jes'…jes' Ah'm ver'a sorry, Mizz Stoughton."

She nodded. "So am I, Alabama. So am I." She offered a brave smile. "Thank you for saying that."

"Yes'm."

Still smiling, she waved her hand. "Be back for supper, Alabama," she remarked lightly.

Alabama nodded. "Yes'm. Thank you, Mizz Stoughton." He turned and walked toward the back of the house.

Though there was no shower for Matilda or him, the bathroom they shared off the kitchen had a fairly large sink. As often as necessary, sometimes more than once a day if the work had been especially strenuous or the humidity was high, Alabama locked the bathroom door, stripped down, and cleaned himself with a sponge and soapy water. His platoon sergeant in

Europe had emphasized the need for cleanliness. "You don' wanna be upwind from a German and smellin' lack a field niggah," he said. "Keep the stink off'n yo' body. Don' give 'em no chance to sniff you out and blow yo' black ass outa yo' tree." The habit had stuck with Alabama, and he was careful not to offend with body odor whenever he could help it. Matilda assumed the task of washing his clothes, even though Alabama protested that he could do it himself. "Whas' the diff'rence?" she asked. "Ah do mine, Ah do yo' clothes at de same time. Hang 'em out wif mine. Dat is," and she smiled coquettishly, "if'n you don't mind yo' thangs hangin' wif a lady's underwear."

Alabama grinned. "Might make mah ol' rags look special!"

When he was clean and wore fresh clothing, he walked to the French Quarter and located the real estate office. He stepped up the two concrete steps to the tan brick two-story building, noticing now that there appeared to be a residence on the second floor with an iron railing enclosing a narrow overhanging deck. The foyer of the office was empty. Alabama peered around for a few seconds and then tentatively said "Hello?"

"Be right with you!" a cheery male voice rang out. Alabama could hear him say "I'll call you back. Got a client to see. Adieu!"

Seconds later, a light-skinned man of medium height and slightly Negroid features stepped out of a side office. His hair was light brown and wavy, almost kinky in places, and his eyes were gray. *Creole,* Alabama thought. *Das what dey talkin' 'bout, dis heah man.*

The agent smiled widely. "Hello! I'm Pasqual duFresne. How can I help you?" He strode up in three steps and offered his hand.

Alabama shook the proffered hand and introduced himself.

"Tea? Coffee? Chicory?" duFresne asked. "I make a memorable coffee-chickory beverage with just a hint of chocolate and brandy. Does that sound appealing?"

Alabama stared at him. The thought of such an exotic drink was overwhelming.

"Want to try one?" duFresne asked, eyebrows cocked and an inviting smile on his face.

"Uh…sho'," Alabama replied. "Light on de whiskey, please."

Pasqual duFresne winked and pointed an index finger with raised thumb, as if it were a pistol. "Bingo!" he exclaimed. "No sense getting tipsy before doing business, I always say! A fine choice, my good man. Please! Take a seat. I'll be right back!"

Alabama sat in one of two tan upholstered chairs, gazing around the office. It was decorated with travel posters of Louisiana on beige walls, one featuring a steamboat on the Mississippi, one a bayou scene with huge banyan trees growing out of the water and Spanish lace dripping from their branches, and one a lively depiction of a French Quarter bar. On a central carved wooden coffee table sat a glass vase with fresh flowers. A brown-and-red area rug sat on the polished wood floor below the table. Alabama took it all in, marveling at how such a small room could appear so elegant.

Pasqual duFresne stepped back into the room in a few moments. He balanced two white china cups on matching saucers, being careful not to spill either. Delicately, he set one of the sets down on the coffee table before settling into the other chair with his own cup and saucer. He raised his cup. "Cheers, as the British say!" he exclaimed. "Here's to mutually profitable enterprise!" He took a sip, watching Alabama do the same.

Alabama carefully sipped, checking for temperature. When he was satisfied the drink would not burn his tongue, he took in a larger amount and held it in his mouth for a few seconds. An amazingly delicious sensation set his taste buds into a frenzy. He swallowed reluctantly and put the cup back into the saucer, hesitant to take in too much too soon.

"How do you like it?" duFresne asked with a wide grin.

Alabama sighed. "Don' think Ah evah had somethin' so good," he replied softly.

duFresne laughed. "All my guests say the same thing!" he exclaimed. "It's my own special creation." He sat back in his chair and tented his fingers below his chin. "So!" he inquired. "How can Pasqual duFresne be of service to you today?"

Alabama leaned back into his chair. "Ah'm lookin' fo' land," he replied.

duFresne raised his eyebrows. "Land, my good sir? What sort of land? What do you propose to do with your new estate?"

"Ah intend to farm it," Alabama replied.

duFresne smiled. "Ah!" he exclaimed. "Then you must be seeking substantial acreage."

Alabama shook his head. "They jes' me. Mayhaps twenty acres."

Hiding his disappointment, duFresne smiled professionally and replied "Ah, yes. A small farm, as it were. Yes, of course I can supply that for you. Tell me, do you have a particular area in mind?"

Alabama shook his head. "Nothin' partik'ler. Just good farm land."

duFresne thought for a few seconds. "Do you require that it be in this immediate area?"

Alabama stared at him.

"Uh, are you willing to acquire a plot outside the metropolitan New Orleans area, is what I'm asking."

Alabama shrugged. "Yes, dat would be all raht. Ah ain't choosy. Jes' want a good piece wif water handy."

"Ah, yes," duFresne replied smoothly. "Naturally you must have access to water. But are you aware of the water table in this state?"

Alabama paused. The truth is that he hadn't given that matter any thought. But he remembered from his geography studies that all of Louisiana was fairly flat, and that there was a fair degree of swamp and bayou country in the state. He quickly concluded that the water table must therefore be relatively close to the surface. "Reckon it's fairly high," he replied.

duFresne nodded. "Quite right. High indeed. Almost anywhere you go, you can dig a well and hit good, clean water within twenty to thirty feet. And wells don't dry up in this state. So water shouldn't be a problem for you."

Alabama considered. He pursed his lips and shrugged. "As you say."

duFresne smiled. "Well! As it happens, I have several good parcels for you to consider. Tell you what, uh…" He colored slightly. "I'm so sorry. What did you say your name is?"

"Alabama Denton."

"Yes, yes, of course. Please forgive me. Alabama. Well, I won't forget *that* name again!" He grinned widely. Turning serious, he said "If you will be so kind as to give me a few days, I'll compile a selection of favorable offerings and have it ready for you to peruse. Would that be satisfactory?"

Wha' de hell dis half-crackuh sayin'? Alabama wondered. He merely stared at duFresne. An uncomfortable few seconds elapsed.

duFresne peered at him. "Uh, Alabama? Would you like to, you know, talk about some properties? In a few days?"

Alabama nodded. "Yes. Sorry. Dat would be good. Has to be Sunday, though. Afternoon."

duFresne frowned slightly. "Sunday? Why?"

"Day off," Alabama replied. "Ah got church in de mornin'. Afternoon's good."

duFresne smiled. The gesture did not appear to Alabama to reach the man's eyes, as if his mouth was working independently of the top half of his face. "Day off, you say," duFresne commented carefully. "What, ah…what sort of work do you do, if I may ask?"

"Gahdnah," Alabama replied evenly.

duFresne stared at him. A long moment passed. Alabama took another swallow of the wonderful brew and set down his cup again.

"Uh…" duFresne stuttered. He began to speak and halted. Drawing in a short, sharp breath, he said leaned forward and said "We, uh…you understand that you, ah…that it's necessary to actually *pay* for land, don't you?"

Alabama stared at him. He was tempted to get up and walk out, leaving the drink and this fool of a man sitting in his fancy drawing room. Fortunately, duFresne blurted "Please forgive me if that sounded, well, misguided," he said rapidly. "I just, well, it's unusual for a…"

"Black man to have money," Alabama finished the sentence. "'Specially a gahdnah."

"Exactly," duFresne commented, leaning back. He tented his fingers again, peering at his guest.

"Ah got money," Alabama stated simply.

duFresne sighed explosively. "*Ex*cellent! Excellent!" he exclaimed, opening his hands in a gesture of glee. "Very good, sir. I congratulate you! So, then. We'll meet here on Sunday afternoon, say two o'clock? Three?"

"Two's fine," Alabama replied. He rose.

"Please, please!" duFresne exclaimed. "Finish your drink! I hate to throw out such good liquor!" He grinned widely.

Alabama nodded. He reached down, picked up the cup, and took a long, hearty swallow, draining the cup. When the tantalizing dark brown liquid was fully gone, he sighed, smiled, and said "Ah surely thank you, suh. Dat was mighty good."

"Oh, there'll be more on Sunday!" duFresne exclaimed heartily. He stepped to the door, opened it, and beckoned to the street. "Well, thank you so much for coming in, Alabama. I look forward to presenting you with several excellent choices on Sunday, two o'clock." He offered his hand. Alabama shook it, said "Sunday," and stepped down the stairs into Burgundy Street.

duFresne gently shut the door and stepped quickly into his office. He slid into his office chair and picked up the phone. Rapidly consulting a notebook, he dialed a number and tapped his fingers as he waited. In a few seconds, he said excitedly "Francois? Pasqual! Come over immediately! I have a fish on the line!"

CHAPTER 8

Pointe Coupee Parish, pronounced "Pwanco Pay" with equal accents on the first and last syllables, was regarded in the period following the war as a relatively useless part of Louisiana. It is located in the inner elbow of the rounded 'L' that forms the state, more or less in the middle. The parish is bordered on the east by the mighty Mississippi River and on the north and west by the Atchaflaya River. Various other rivers and major creeks, called 'bayous,' wind through parts of the parish. Only four towns of any size exist in the parish: Morganza in the center; New Roads, the largest, in the east; Fordoche in the southwest, and Livonia in the south. About one-fifth of the parish annually becomes a wetland as the Atchaflaya River floods to the east of its banks and turns low land into a massive marsh. Point Coupee Parish features good farmland in the north and east, but the southwest was considered largely a write-off.

It was in that southwest section, on the eastern edge of the Atchaflaya flood plain, that one Francois Milet, a forty-seven year-old sometimes actor whose main profession was fleecing bar patrons at poker games, owned fifty acres that he had won gambling. The player who placed the title to the land into the pot when he was riding aces over fours, a seemingly unbeatable hand, had inherited the land from his father, who had in turn gotten it from his father, who had taken possession of the land seventy years earlier by scaring off a small Native American tribe who had hunted the land for centuries. Soon after stealing the land from the Indians, the old man had registered fifty acres with surveyed borders with the Louisiana Land Office. No one had done anything with the land since then except to hunt it on occasion because of the tendency for half of it to be underwater four to five months of the year.

Francois was holding four tens at the time, and he grinned hugely as he raked in the pot and became the new owner of the fifty-acre plot.

Francois had held the land for eleven years, hating to pay the dollar and forty-five cents per acre tax each year but reluctant to part with it, when Pasqual duFresne placed an urgent phone call to him. That afternoon, Pasqual explained the visit from the ignorant nigger who claimed to have money, and the two of them cooked up a scheme to offload the acreage to this fish. Pasqual gathered photographs of prime farm land into an album and entitled it "Pointe Coupee Estates." Francois, meanwhile, arranged to have his only suit cleaned and borrowed a cravat and top hat from the theater where he did occasional gigs. He purchased white spats to wear over his good pair of black shoes.

On the following Sunday, when Alabama arrived at the appointed hour, he was greeted by Pasqual duFresne as a long-lost friend. Waiting for him in the elegant drawing room was a gentleman wearing an old-fashioned but still impressive knee-length burgundy coat over dark blue trousers, a ruffled white shirt, and a blue satin vest. A pearl-gray cravat rested neatly at his throat, and clean white spats covered his shiny black shoes. This man was introduced as Monsieur Francois Milet, a French nobleman who was on a long-term vacation in New Orleans, chiefly to check upon property he owned throughout the state of Louisiana.

duFresne, as promised, brought out three cups of the steaming concoction he had served the previous week. "Much obliged," Alabama said with a grateful smile after the first sip. "Bettah than las' week."

duFresne laughed and pulled a chair up next to Alabama's. "Monsieur Milet is a significant landowner in the state," he explained. "He lives in a chateau—that's a castle—on the Rhine, in Alsace-Lorraine, between France and Germany."

"Ah know the area," Alabama replied. Both men looked at him with surprise, Milet with eyebrows theatrically raised.

"Spent some time theah in de wah," Alabama explained. "Good huntin' grounds. Lotsa Germans not payin' much attention to wheah they steppin', an' then they ain't steppin' nowheah."

"My, my, you have an interesting background!" duFresne murmured, impressed despite himself.

"Oui. We thank you for zees," Milet said haughtily. "Ze Americans, zey have saved France."

Alabama shrugged, offering a soft smile.

"I've asked Monsieur Milet to be here," duFresne explained. He nodded to Francois, who replied "Oui. Monsieur duFresne ees my American agent." Using his best French accent and drawing upon his acting skills, he responded in mellifluous phrases with a condescending air as Pasqual explained to him that Mr. Denton had an interest in farmland and Monsieur Milet had been invited this afternoon to explore the subject. After a few moments of this, Francois said "Deesplay to the gentleman ze portfolio on ze Pwanco Pay holding."

duFresne looked at him strangely. "Really? You don't mean Pointe Coupee Estates, do you, monsieur?"

Mitel smiled beneficently. "Oui. I lack zees man. He ees an American fighting soldier, preserving ze honor of France. He ees worthy of zees property. Go! Go! Ze Pwanco Pay portfolio! Immediamente!" He shooed Pasqual off to his office with an imperious gesture.

duFresne returned in a moment with the fancy photo album. "Frankly, I'm surprised that Monsieur Milet is even willing to discuss this holding," he said in a somewhat surprised tone. "It's his finest acquisition in the state. Here, let me show you." For the next thirty minutes, he showcased the photos, reveling about the unique nature of this land and its proximity to natural surroundings. "There's excellent hunting up there: deer, raccoon, fox, geese, duck. Good trapping, too. Lots of muskrats. And their pelts are going for a premium in the East. The ladies love them. This could be an additional source of income for you."

Alabama said nothing, as Pasqual was doing all the talking. He merely nodded, showing considerable interest. When the presentation was complete, Alabama turned to Milet. "Suh, how much you askin' fo' yo' fifty acres?"

Mitel stared out the window for a few seconds as if the answer was inconsequential. He waved his hand with a feminine gesture and replied "I tire of land in Louisiana. Next I will invest in the Bahamas. Monsieur duFresne handles ze transaction. As for moi, I must depart." He stood and held out his hand. Alabama took it, marveling as he had earlier that it was like a dead animal in his palm. "Adieu, duFresne! Adieu, monsieur ze Denton," Milet exclaimed grandly. He bowed, strode elegantly to the door, and stood waiting. duFresne rushed to open it for him and closed it after Milet had descended the steps.

"I just marvel at that man," duFresne said admiringly. "So generous. He seemed to really like you, Alabama. I'll bet he'll be willing to give you the fifty acres for a song."

Alabama looked at him. "What kinda tune Ah gotta sing?"

duFresne smiled. "Oh, I would say in the neighborhood of $200 an acre. For premium farmland, that's almost a giveaway price."

Alabama sat quietly, thinking. He glanced back down at the album and thumbed through the photos. "Ah got to look at it," he said.

duFresne frowned. He sighed. He adjusted his coffee cup. He pursed his lips. "Naturally, under most circumstances…" he began. He shrugged. "Look, Alabama, that land is not going to last long. I know Monsieur Milet. He's…well, he makes up his mind quickly. I have other buyers ready to jump on a premium purchase like this, and probably at twice the price. If I were you…"

"Ah got to look at it," Alabama repeated. He stared into duFresne's eyes.

duFresne leaned back in his chair, sighing. "Very well. I'm just trying to help you. When can you get away to drive to Pwanco Pay?"

Alabama snorted. "Wha' make you think Ah kin drive anywheah?" he asked, a frown on his face.

duFresne looked at him. A look of understanding dawned on his face. "Oh! Forgive me. I don't imagine you own a car."

Alabama nodded.

duFresne slowly moved his head back and forth as if thinking. "Well, I could take you there, I suppose. It would be an all-day trip, there and back. You understand, I have to be compensated for such an expenditure of time and gasoline."

"Compensated?"

"Paid. For the wear and tear on my automobile."

Alabama regarded him. "How much you need to be paid?"

duFresne shrugged. "For a trip like that…? Normally twenty-five dollars per leg. Total of fifty. For you, I'll make it twenty per."

"Total of fo'ty," Alabama remarked with a slight frown. "Fo'ty dollah to take me to see dis heah land."

duFresne smiled gently. "I'm afraid so, Alabama. Economics being what they are. When can you get away?"

"Tomorrah mornin'," Alabama replied. "Six o'clock. All raht wif you?"

duFresne looked horrified. "Six o'clock in the morning? Good heavens! Why so early?"

"Ah wants plenty 'a time to see de land."

duFresne sighed hugely. "Very well, then. Six o'clock tomorrow morning, right here." He stood and smiled. "I look forward to it, Alabama. See you then."

They shook hands, and Alabama departed. When he had been gone a few minutes, duFresne picked up the phone and dialed. After a few seconds, he said "He bit. We're going up there tomorrow morning. I told him $200 an acre, and he didn't seem to flinch. I guess the man does have the money after all. Where do you think a nigger gets that kind of money?" He listened for a moment and laughed. "Probably did. I wouldn't want to be the guy he stole it from. Well, anyhow, he has it, and we're going. I'll call you tomorrow night, unless we get back late. Right. Adieu, then.

CHAPTER 9

duFresne kept up a steady stream of chatter on the four-hour journey to the property in Point Coupee Parish. Much of the trip involved country roads, requiring Alabama to navigate from map reading. He found it simple compared to the task of maneuvering to attain an attack position or escape from angry Germans in the woods and fields of Europe. They made one stop for a bathroom break and a cup of good Cajun coffee midway. duFresne winced when he spotted the 'White Only' sign over the bathroom door. Alabama shook off his companion's pained gesture with a sour grin. "De good Lawd made plenty 'a trees for black folk," he remarked, heading for the woods. duFresne met him back at the car, a sleek black 1940 Plymouth roadster, with two steaming cups of coffee, properly sugared, and a brown paper bag of pork rinds. "Dig in!" he invited, placing the bag between them on the seat. Alabama looked at him questioningly. "Go on. I really mean it," duFresne remarked. Alabama nodded and took a rind from the bag.

The last leg of the journey was north on Parish Road 77 from Fordoche, the nearest town some eighteen miles from the property. As they drove at a cautious speed on the gravel road, they encountered considerable evidence of fresh road construction. duFresne handed Alabama a hand-drawn map that Francois Milet had given him. It specified a dirt road leading west off 77, two miles north of 'a huge oak next to a tumbledown shack.' They located what seemed to be the tree and shack and counted down the distance. About the mile and three-quarter point, they came upon a group of road-building vehicles: dump trucks, a crane with a scooper bucket, and a road-grading plow. All the vehicles were occupied in the task of rebuilding and smoothing the rough country road.

Sure enough, at the appropriate distance a quarter-mile ahead, a weed-encrusted track led off to the left. It looked to have been unused for some time. duFresne carefully navigated the roadster over potholes and around a fallen tree for a mile down the track.

Suddenly he spotted a tall wooden pole with a red stripe and a white stripe at the top. "There it is!" he cried. "The beginning of Pointe Coupee Estates!" He stopped the car and hopped out. Alabama followed, although with far less enthusiasm.

duFresne pointed west. "Isn't it great?" he exclaimed, sweeping his hand out in an all-encompassing gesture.

Alabama stood, hands on hips, and surveyed the property. As far as he could see, tall grass up to his waist stretched along the narrow track to the west. Clumps of trees dotted the land, with one section heavily forested with good deciduous trees. He peered north and south. "Wheah de property line?" he asked, pointing each direction.

"Well, fifty acres is a great deal of land, after all," duFresne replied. "We'll have to walk a bit along the line here to find the corners."

Alabama sighed. "Let's us jes' go 'long dis path a bit," he replied quietly.

They trudged down the track, looking all directions. For once, duFresne was silent. Now and then he glanced furtively at Alabama.

Two hundred yards down the track, they came to the edge of the land. Ahead of them stretched a swamp. Some of it was reed-infested, indicating shallow water, and some contained only water with a few lily pads. The fact that it had no banyan trees for a considerable distance proved that it was seasonal water. A line of similar wooden poles with the red and white stripes were embedded about eighty yards out into the water, having been mounted in the dry season to mark the edge of the lot. Alabama stood, looking to the right and to the left. Several long moments passed. duFresne wisely kept silent. At length, Alabama turned to the real estate agent. "Dis heah water part of the 'estate'?" he asked.

duFresne looked down and scratched at the dirt with one stylish boot. "Some of it," he admitted.

Alabama stared at him.

"How much of it?"

duFresne sighed. He looked up at Alabama. "About, uh, two-thirds," he mumbled.

"Two-thirds."

"Yes," duFresne admitted.

"Dat be, wha', thirty acres? Thirty-five?"

duFresne nodded, again dropping his gaze to the ground.

A long moment passed. Finally Alabama said quietly "Ah oughta cut you up an' feed you to de alligators."

duFresne looked up, eyes wide, and took a quick step back, hands up. "I only discovered it late last evening!" he protested. "It was too late to call off our visit! Please, Alabama! I...you..."

"Jes' shet yo' mouth," Alabama countered. He stood, observing the land and water. *Time to try a bluff,* he calculated. He turned to duFresne. "Besides draggin' me out to this swamp, you an' yo' fancy French frien' think to cheat me on de price. De goin' rate fo' raw land out heah only $55 an acre."

"It's ninety..." duFresne blurted. Realizing his mistake, he stuttered "Ah, that is, your basic bottom land..."

Alabama held up a hand, palm toward duFresne. "Don't," he commanded. "No mo' lies."

duFresne made to speak again, but he shut his mouth and pursed his lips.

"Ah goan' need yo' car for a short time," Alabama said. "Gimme de keys."

duFresne's face took on a shocked expression. "Alabama!" he cried. "You aren't thinking of leaving me…"

Alabama laughed harshly. "Don' worry, Pasqual," he replied mockingly. "Unlike you, Ah an honest man. Ah don' intend to be gone long. You jes' wait heah and think about dis fine 'estate' you done brung me out to see. Gimme de keys."

"Can you drive?" duFresne asked fearfully.

"Toler'ble," Alabama answered, holding out his hand. duFresne gulped, reached into his pocket, and pulled out the ring of keys. "Please be careful!" he implored. "That's a very rough road."

Alabama walked to the car without comment. Having never driven a car, he stared at the dash and tried to remember what he'd seen others do when driving. Finding the ignition keyhole was easy enough, and fortunately duFresne had left the vehicle in neutral. Alabama turned the key and the well-maintained machine sparked into life and purred. Alabama slipped the gear stick into first gear. The car lurched forward and died. "Use the clutch!" duFresne shouted. Alabama looked down at the floorboard, remembering. He put the gearshift lever into neutral again and re-started the car. After pushing in the clutch, he slipped the car into first gear and eased out the clutch. The car lurched again, but this time more smoothly. At the last second, he stepped on the gas. The car shot out into the dirt track, quickly reaching high rpm's. "Easy! Easy!" the fading voice of an anguished duFresne echoed as he rocketed down the path. After a few seconds, he eased off the gas, bringing the car to a safe speed.

Steering carefully, he reached County Road 77 in a matter of minutes. There he put on the brake, pushed in the clutch, and slipped the gearshift back into neutral. The car coasted to a stop at the end of the path. Alabama stepped out and examined the moving maintenance vehicles.

After a moment, he found what he was seeking. He walked up to a large white man holding a clipboard and conversing with another man. When he was ten feet away, the men spotted him and ceased their conversation.

Alabama stood, hands at his sides and head slightly bowed. "'Scuse me, suh?" he asked.

"Whacha want, nigger?" the large man asked irritably.

"Suh, Ah was wonderin'," Alabama replied. "Kin Ah talk wif you fo' a moment?"

"Talk 'bout what?"

"Yo' dirt," Alabama replied.

The large man glanced at his companion and shook his head, his mouth open. He turned back to Alabama. "My *dirt*? What dirt? You crazy, nigger?"

"No suh," Alabama answered quickly. "Ah'm talkin' 'bout de dirt y'all be movin' heah. Ah see dem big trucks. You mus' be takin' de extra dirt somewheres."

The large man paused before replying. "Matter of fact, we are," he answered. "'Bout seven, eight mile down the road. Why you askin'?"

Alabama smiled. "Ah got some land down dat lane deah, suh. 'Bout one mile. Lots closer den yo' goin' now. Ah could take yo' dirt."

The man regarded him carefully. "You want us to dump on your property."

Alabama nodded. "Yes suh. Save you time an' money."

The man turned to his companion. "Let me talk with this heah nigger for a moment, Buck," he said. The other man took the hint and walked off. When he was back in his truck, the man turned to Alabama. "You own land down that track?"

"Yes suh. Some of it's jes' low land. Floods from de rivah. Ah wants to fill it in, keep it dry when de floods come."

The man rubbed his chin, his eyes squinting. "Cost you five dollah a truckload," he replied. "In cash, to me."

Alabama hung his head. "Ah cain't pay no five dollah," he replied sadly.

"Well then, I guess we ain't gonna do bidness," the man replied, turning his attention back to the clipboard.

"Ah was thinkin' a dollah," Alabama said.

The man looked up. He grinned lopsidedly. "You got the money, nigger?"

Alabama nodded. "Yes suh. Y'all dump, count de loads, Ah be back in a week and pay you."

The man laughed. "How do I know I'm ever gonna see you again?" he asked derisively.

Alabama shrugged. "Ah needs the dirt, suh. You need to save de haulin'. Plus you put some cash in yo' pocket wif'out yo' boss knowin.' Ah be back, suh. An' Ah pay yo', Ah promise. Ah an honest man."

The large man looked him up and down. "Something tells me you are," he said. "All right. But the price is two dollars."

Alabama considered. "Kin you smooth it wif dat machine deah?" he asked, pointing to the road grader.

"You want it smoothed too?" the man asked incredulously.

"Ah make it three dollah if'n you do," Alabama replied quickly.

The man laughed. "Somehow I think you done me, nigger! Took me for a ride. You a lot smarter than you look. All right, then. Three dollars a load. I'll keep a careful count."

Alabama pulled up his shirt and felt into his money belt. He pulled out five twenties and handed them to the wide-eyed supervisor. "Heah a down payment," he said. "Thirty-three truckloads, all smoothed out. Ya'll goan' see wood posts wif red and white stripes out in de water. Jes' dump up to dat point. Far's the edges 'a de lot, they be de same wooden poles mark the edge of de property."

The man nodded, took the money, and slipped it into his pocket. He held out his hand. "Name's Wallis Flatley," he said.

Alabama smiled and shook his hand. "Alabama Denton. Much obliged, Mr. Flatley. Ah be seein' you heah next week."

"I'm countin' on it," Flatley replied.

Alabama nodded and walked to the car. After considerable stopping and starting, much to the amusement of the onlooking road workers, he got the car moving down the track toward the anxious realtor. When he arrived, he stepped on the brake, put the gearshift into neutral, and turned off the key.

"Thank God!" duFresne exclaimed. "I was afraid you were going to strip the gears!"

"Yo' car be fine," Alabama remarked gruffly. He walked up to the realtor, stood two yards away, and planted his hands on his hips. "Ah bin thinkin', Pasqual," he said. "Ninety an acre is de goin' rate. You done admitted that. Fo' dis land, Ah be thinkin' sixty. Das fo' de dry land. Sixteen acre. Plus Ah give you ten an acre fo' dat useless swamp deah." He swept out his arm, indicating the marsh and open water. "Thirty-fo' acres. So, sixteen time sixty be, uh, nine hundred sixty dollah. Ten time thirty-fo' be three hundred fo'ty. Togethuh dat be, lessee, thirteen hundred dollah. Dat what Ah goan' give you. Take it or leave it, raht now."

duFresne stared at him. He sighed deeply, seeing his commission dwindle from five thousand to a mere six hundred and fifty dollars. "You *do* have the money, right?" he asked quietly.

Alabama nodded. "Show it to ya now, if'n you want."

duFresne shook his head. "Not necessary. Very well. It's a deal. Let's go back and I'll draw up the papers."

"An' file 'em propah? Wif de state?"

duFresne smiled. He stepped forward and held out his hand. "It's the least I owe you, Alabama. You're a good man. I'm going to do it right, I promise. You'll have the deed tomorrow with the state stamp on it. Then and only then do you pay."

Alabama shook the proffered hand and nodded, a slight smile on his face. They got back in the car and rode back mainly in silence. Alabama raised his hand to the construction supervisor as they turned on Route 77. duFresne looked at him questioningly but said nothing.

CHAPTER 10

Alabama came to Mrs. Stoughton the day after he received title to the property and showed it to her. Her jaw dropped, and she stared at him dumbfounded. "Why, Alabama Denton!" she exclaimed, a hand to her throat. "I had *no* idea! You have *money*? Why on *earth* would you want to be my gardener?"

Alabama chuckled. "No disrespect, Mizz Stoughton, but *you* wanted me to be your gahdnah. Ah was jes' walkin', mindin' mah own bidness."

Mrs. Stoughton stared at him. "Now I recall, you're quite right. I believe I simply summoned you."

He smiled gently. "'Cause all black men are jes' good fo' gardenin', right, ma'am?"

She blushed. "Well, I..."

"Please, Mizz Stoughton," he interrupted. "Ah been privileged to be heah. You a ver'a fine lady. Ah 'preciate de chance to work fo' you."

She stared at him, shaking her head. "Well, I declare!" she exclaimed with a chuckle. "You're an enigma, Alabama Denton. You certainly are!"

Unsure of the meaning of the word but suspecting it was benign, especially coming from her, he shrugged. "Mizz Stoughton, de reason Ah show you dis papuh is 'cause Ah be movin' up theah come de fall. Octobah, Ah reckon. Is dat all raht wif' you?"

She considered. "Well, it will be wonderful to have you on board that long, if you want to be here. As I've said, my garden has never been so spectacular. But you needn't stay if you'd rather go now. I won't stand in your way."

He shook his head. "No, ma'am. Ah ain't leavin'. Ah want to get yo' garden ready fo' winter, and Ah need time to prepare. Ackshly, Ah show you dis papuh to tell you Ah be goin' sometime, an' also to ax yo' advice."

"My advice?

"Yes'm. See, Ah don't own a car. Don't have no drivin' license, even if Ah had a car. Let me ax you, Mizz Stoughton. What can a body do to get up to Pwanco Pay Parish an' back heah now an' again?"

She considered the question. After a moment, she replied "I don't rightly know, Alabama. That's a difficult challenge. Let me ponder it for a time."

Alabama nodded. "Much obliged, Ms. Stoughton."

A few days later, Mrs. Stoughton came out to the garden while Alabama was on his knees, digging weeds. He stood politely and said "Mo'nin', Mizz Stoughton."

"Good morning to you, Alabama," she replied. "I've made some inquiries. It turns out there's a convoy of trucks that leaves from New Orleans Naval Air Station with a load of oil for the Army Air base in Shreveport twice a week. There are usually five or six of them that travel together. They normally take Highway 190 into Pointe Coupee Parish, then Highway 1 up to New Roads and northwest out of the parish to Shreveport. I confirmed all this with the provost at the naval air station. Your property is west of New Roads, isn't it?"

"Yes'm!" Alabama replied eagerly. "An' if'n dey go northwest on 1, dey have to go through Morganza. Dat's on de Mississippi. Dat's on'y about twenty mile from my place."

"So, if you traveled with the convoy, they could let you off at Morganza and you could go the rest of the distance by yourself. But how would you get there?"

Alabama smiled. He pointed to his legs. "Ma'am, dese done got me all ovah Germany and France," he replied with a grin. "Ah reckon dey can get me twenty mile south now an' again."

Mrs. Stoughton laughed merrily. "Well. It's settled, then. I'll let you know when the convoy is leaving, and you can meet them a few blocks from here as they go past. More than likely you can arrange to meet them for the ride back in, where was it? Morganza?"

"Yes, ma'am."

"Right. Talk with them. No doubt they'd be willing to meet you there and bring you back to New Orleans a couple of days after they drop you off. They'll provide you with a special flag to use to signal them."

Alabama's smile disappeared. "Uh, Mizz Stoughton…"

She smiled. "Yes, they know you're black. Times are changing, Alabama. Not all Southerners are slaves to the foolishness of Southern tradition."

He nodded, unable to speak.

Four days later, he met the convoy by prearrangement at seven in the morning and climbed aboard one of the trucks. The driver, Charlie O'Neal, was a Navy specialist from the Boston area. He and Alabama struck up a lively conversation during the four hour trip to Morganza, especially when he inquired whether Alabama had served in the war and then sat back, hugely impressed, with Alabama's story. Specialist O'Neal shook Alabama's hand when he stepped out of the cab, saying "It was great to meet you, Alabama. We'll be coming through three days from now, as we always do. Be sure to look for me, hear?" Alabama thanked him sincerely, meaning every word of it. He waved the convoy off, saluting as each truck rolled by.

Alabama looked around the small town. Like most towns of a few thousand souls, it contained the usual mix of stores and homes. Alabama walked until he encountered another black man. "How do, brother?" he asked in a friendly tone.

"Tol'ble," the man replied. "You ain't from 'round heah."

Alabama shook his head. "Not yet, but Ah fixin' to be. Tell me, who sell seed and the like to black farmin' folk?"

The man considered the question and answered "Ah don' rahtly know, tell ya' de truf. Best Ah kin say is mos' black folk live on the south side 'a town. You could mosey down theah an' ax 'round."

Alabama thanked him and headed toward the sun.

Within a few blocks, the stores ended and the homes began. It was easy to tell that he was in the black section: the houses were all wood, not stone or brick, and many of them were in noticeable need of repair. Black children played in bare yards or on the streets, and black women chatted as they hung out wash on clotheslines.

Alabama asked his question of four more people. Eventually he was given directions to a general store owned and operated by a black family on the edge of town. Walking down the designated street, he located the store without trouble. It was a two-story wooden structure in good repair, with a good-sized fenced-in yard containing a variety of small farm equipment and other related goods. It was obvious that the family lived above the store, judging from the play equipment in one corner of the yard and the wash hung out to dry on a line off an upstairs porch. He walked in and looked around.

The store, like many that served the black community in the South, had a little of everything, since such establishments were often the only places that would serve Negroes. Alabama took it all in: racks of fresh vegetables; stacks of bags of seed for corn, beans, hay, alfalfa, and melons; tools such as shovels and pitchforks; some clothing; even a room with basic furniture. The store truly appeared to live up to the term 'general.' Alabama was pleased to see that its offerings were so varied and well-stocked.

As he was looking at animal-drawn plows, a voice asked "Hep ya?"

Alabama turned. There stood the proprietor, wearing rough brown cotton trousers, an off-white cotton shirt, scuffed boots, and a blue canvas apron with a variety of pockets in which he had placed receipt books, pencils, and a slide rule. He was taller than average, just over six feet, and featured a full head of close nappy hair. He smiled, and Alabama saw purplish gums holding strong white teeth. Alabama judged him to be about thirty to thirty-five years of age.

Alabama nodded. "Bet you can, suh," he replied, holding out his hand. "Ah'm Alabama Denton. Jes' bought me a piece 'a land, fifty acre, 'bout twenty mile south. Off Highway 77, neah de Atchaflaya Basin. Ah be needin' some thangs."

The proprietor shook his hand, introducing himself as Josiah Freeman. He frowned when he released Alabama's hand, saying "Off 77, you say? How far south from 10?"

"Down 'bout four mile, Ah reckon," Alabama replied.

Freeman mulled the information. "77's dirt in dat part, raht?"

Alabama nodded. "Sho' is. Mah place ain't but a little turn-in lane. Ya go back 'bout a mile down dat lane 'til ya come to de swamp. De's some land theah. Plus Ah'm makin' some new land." He smiled mysteriously.

"New land?" Freeman asked. "How you do dat?"

"You jes' fill dirt wheah dey ain't no land," Alabama with a grin.

Freeman stared at him and shrugged. "Wayall, good fo' you," he remarked admiringly. "So. Whachoo got, and whachoo need?"

Alabama laughed and swept a hand down his body. "Dis what Ah got," he replied. "An' some money. Ah kin buy wha' Ah need."

Josiah Freeman nodded. "Wayall, Ah 'preciate you comin' to me, Mr. Denton," he replied. "Ah make you a good deal. We get you fixed up."

Alabama nodded. "Name's Alabama. An Ah 'preciate yo' hep." He looked around the store. "Look lack ya got ever'thang."

Freeman sighed with satisfaction. "God is good to dis ol' storekeeper," he replied. "Bidness been good. Folks need thangs, we bring it in. New farmers startin' up, mos' back fum de war." He looked sharply at Alabama. "You a soldier?"

Alabama nodded. "Army. Europe. Fo' yeah."

Freeman shook his head exaggeratedly. "Um, um, um!" he exclaimed. "Wayall, welcome back, soldier. Now Ah make you a *special* deal!"

Alabama laughed. "Ah ain't lookin' fo' no favors," he replied. "Jes' an honest man."

"Oh, you got dat!" Freeman replied. "Dey ain't but one way, an' das honest." He nodded firmly.

The relative quiet was interrupted by a boy and a girl running into the store from the back door. The boy, who appeared to be about ten, led the way, eyes wide with mock fear, and his younger sister chased after him with an angry look on her face. "Ah get you!" she yelled. "Jeremiah, Ah get you! You jes' wait!"

"Here, here!" Freeman called out, grabbing the boy as he ran past. He was unable to prevent his daughter from landing a solid blow to the boy's chest, but he held her back from further damage as she flailed against his grip. "Arianna! Stop!" he commanded, holding the combatants apart. The boy smirked while the girl simmered. "Wha's goin' on heah?" he demanded.

"Jeremiah, he grab mah hair!" the girl accused, stroking one of her two neck-length pigtails. "Pull it hard!"

"Ah, it warn't so hard," the boy remarked. "You jes' a pansy!"

Arianna didn't bother to reply. With surprising grace and power, she sprung at the startled boy and smacked him square in the nose. "Owww!" Jeremiah yelled, holding his nose in both hands. His eyes grew wide, and he struggled against his father's grip in fury. "*Ah'm goin' kill you!*" he screamed.

Josiah Freeman roughly pulled him to the other side of his body and pinned him against his hip. "Arianna, you go on now!" he commanded. "Ah talk to you later! Go on, now!" He shooed his daughter away. She turned and walked away, her head lifted in pride.

Alabama watched her go, his mouth slightly open. *She de mos' beautiful little thang Ah evah seen*, he thought with amazement.

Arianna paused at the back door and turned. She saw Alabama staring at her and smiled fleetingly. Then she slipped outside.

In the meantime, Josiah Freeman was on one knee so he could be at his son's height and lecture him face to face. "Jeremiah, Ah tol' you don' be pickin' on yo' sistah!" he said softly but firmly, his face not a foot from his son's. "Ah tol' you not to do dat. Din' Ah?"

"Yes, suh. But *Pa*!" the boy protested, holding his aching nose.

"But nuthin'!" Freeman said. "You go on up to yo' room, an' don't be leavin' 'til Ah tell you. Ah talk wif' you later." He rose and pushed the boy gently toward the staircase at the back of the store.

"Aw, Pa!" Jeremiah muttered, but he turned and walked away promptly.

Freeman watched him go. "Chirren!" he muttered.

Alabama laughed. "Ain't had de privilege, person'ly," he replied. "How old yo' daughter?"

"She be only nine," Freeman replied. "But she de boss. Her mama do what Arianna say. Ah reckon soon Ah be doin' wha' she say too!" He shook his head in mock sadness, grinning all the while.

Alabama grinned. "She feisty, den."

Freeman considered. "Not so much feisty. Jes' smaht. An' she know how to do folks. She know all dey buttons." He looked at Alabama. "'Nough'a them kids. Whachoo be needin'?"

Alabama considered. "Wayall, de fust thang Ah'm goin' need is a cabin," he replied. "And den a well. Or maybe t'othah way 'round. Need 'em both 'bout the same time."

Freeman nodded. "An' you goin' need some seed, and a mule an' a plow."

Alabama sighed, grinned ruefully, and nodded in agreement. "An' an axe, an' a saw…all kinda thang, seem like."

The storekeeper cocked his head and grinned. "Wayall, Ah gottem. Whatever you be needin'."

Alabama grinned. "Figured you say dat."

Freeman eyed him for a moment. "No disrespect, suh," he commented tentatively. "You, uh, Ah mean, it take some consider'ble money…"

"Ah got de money," Alabama interrupted, feeling the pressure of the money belt under his shirt. "You jes' be fair wif' yo' pricin' an' Ah don' buy nowhere else."

Freeman nodded, clearly glad to have that out of the way. "You kin count on it. Say, you figurin' ta do all the buildin' yo'sef?"

Alabama shook his head. "Dat would take too long. Ah wants a crop in de ground in de spring. Ain't got time to be diggin' a well and buildin' a cabin all alone. Goin' need some help. You know any fellas be wantin' ta work fo' me fo' a spell?"

Freeman nodded his head enthusiastically. "Sho' do!" he replied. "Couple boys raised on dey daddy's farm, but they ain't room fo' three famblies on dat piece a' land. Ol' man done give de farm to de oldest brother. Othah two still dere, but dey be lookin' fo' work. Dey good boys. 'Bout twenty, Ah b'lieve. Mayhaps nineteen, one of 'em. Anyway, dey be good workers. Pay 'em a decent wage an' dey do good work fo' ya."

Alabama looked around the store for a long moment. "Good," he replied. "Dey some trees on de land kin be used to make planks. Ah goin' need tin fo' de roof, pipes and chain an' brick fo' de well, some rope, seed, dat mule an' plow…" He rubbed his chin. "You make me a list, okay, Mr. Freeman? Put a price on it. Ah be back dis time next week. Dem boys be ready to work?"

The storekeeper smiled and nodded. "You bet!" he replied enthusiastically. "An' Ah do you one bettah. Ah got a ol' truck out de back. Ain't much, but it holds a lotta stuff. We kin take a load down to yo' land along wif' dem two boys, an' y'all kin get to workin' raht away."

"Deal," Alabama replied, holding out his hand. "Ah 'preciate yo' help."

"Mah pleasure," Freeman replied. "You seem a good man, Alabama. Ah'm bettin' you a hard-workin' fella. Goin' be a good farmer. Dat mean a lotta seed an' farm tools you goin' need in days ta come. An' Ah'm yo' man!"

Alabama laughed heartily. "Figured you say dat," he replied, shaking the man's hand.

As arranged, Alabama flagged down the Navy convoy of now-empty oil tankers at the predetermined spot in Morganza two days later and climbed in with Specialist O'Neal. The four-hour ride back to New Orleans was filled with animated conversation about the impending farm, much of it supplied by an excited Alabama as he poured out his dreams to his new friend. O'Neal was a ready companion, urging Alabama on. "Dang, that sounds good!" he opined. "You gonna have a fine farm there, my man. Only one thing'll be missing!" He gave Alabama a sly glance.

"Wha's dat?"

O'Neal hooted a sharp burst of laughter. "A lady!" he replied with a grin. "It's gonna be mighty lonely out there beside that swamp without a good friend for your bed!"

Alabama grinned shyly. "Dat come later," he replied softly. "Cain't be jes' anybody. She got to be the raht woman, got to be special. Ah ain't in no hurry."

O'Neal paused, thinking. He sighed. "You know, Alabama, you got the right idea there. Seems like most guys're just wanting to get a woman into the sack. If they want a *decent* woman, they gotta marry 'em. So too often they just take the first good-looking woman who ain't whorin' and propose. Next thing they know they're married to someone they don't even hardly know. Best to do it your way. Wait. Look around. Be selective. Be careful."

The next week, when O'Neal dropped him off in Morganza, Alabama walked quickly to the general store on the south side of town. Josiah Freeman met him with an enthusiastic handshake and a pat on the back. "How you doin', Alabama?" he asked jovially.

"Ah'm good, mighty good," Alabama replied. "Whachoo got fo' me?"

"Ah got it all loaded in de truck," Freeman replied. "Come on out de back. Ah show you."

As he led the way toward the back door, Alabama suddenly stopped dead, staring. He said "Ah be raht wif' you," and turned to walk down an aisle. There, sitting cross-legged on the floor in a white cotton dress, was the little girl. Her hair was done into two short pigtails with a white ribbon bow in each. She had spread corn meal that had fallen from a sack into a circle approximately eighteen inches in diameter. The sun shone through a window directly onto her palette. With her finger, she was drawing elaborate shapes and designs, humming to herself.

Alabama softly approached the girl. "Hello, Adrianna," he said quietly.

The girl looked up. Her face broke into a joyful smile. "Hello, suh," she replied. "You de new farmer."

Alabama's jaw dropped an inch. He recovered quickly. "How you know dat?" he asked.

"Saw you las' week."

"But…"

"Plus Ah ax mah daddy. When you gone."

Alabama shook his head. "Mah lands!" he exclaimed. "Ain't you de curious one! So whachoo makin', Miss Arianna?"

She looked down at her creation and smiled. "It's a secret," she replied happily, adding a flourish to one side of the drawing.

"Wayall, it sho' is pretty." Alabama stared at her as she continued to play with her design. After a moment, he said "Wayall, Ah got to be goin', Miss Adrianna. Ah hope to see you agin soon."

She looked up, smiling demurely, and Alabama's heart melted. "Ah do too, suh," she replied.

Alabama turned and walked down the aisle toward the back door, his legs strangely wobbly.

When he approached the truck, Josiah Freeman introduced him to Rufus and Lonnie Mason, the two young men whom he'd mentioned. Both appeared strong and fit and fairly tall, about Freeman's height. Rufus was heavier than his younger brother by about twenty pounds. They greeted him cheerfully. Alabama explained what he had in mind. "Pay's two dollah twen'y cent a day," he said. "Das twenty cent an hour. We be workin' 'bout 'leven hour ev'ry day, hour fo' lunch an' rest. End of de day, you do good work, dey an extra twenty cent bonus. We be eatin' an' sleepin' on de land, so you bes' get yo'sef a blanket and some extra clothes. Ah talk wif' Mr. Freeman heah regardin' food fo' de three of us. Some days Ah be wif' you, some days you on yo' own. Reckon you can handle that?"

"Yessah!" Rufus exclaimed. "Sound real good! We be workin' hard fo' you, suh!"

"Name's Alabama," came the reply with a smile. "Okay. You boys be goin' home, get yo' thangs. Meetcha back heah in one hour." The two scrambled off, loping toward a row of houses. Alabama watched them go. "Look lack dey kin work," he observed.

"Oh, yessah," Freeman affirmed. "Dey good young men. Ah know dey daddy well. He ain't evah had no trouble wif' dem boys. He jus' ain't got nuthin' to give 'em."

Alabama and Josiah Freeman walked back into the store, where Freeman led him to a counter in the back. Behind it were several rows of canned goods. They selected two weeks' worth of food for the three of them, adding three dozen eggs, salt pork, beef jerky, coffee, sugar, a side of bacon, and two pounds of dark chocolate. Freeman pointed out a large frying pan, metal pots of varying sizes, and a few tin dishes with cutlery. He suggested that all these be added, along with a pound of powdered soap for dishes and two bars of soap for personal washing. "An' a large canvas tarp," Alabama remark. "We be needin' that fo' a tent."

Freeman smiled. "Ah put a fold-up tent in de truck," he replied. "Nice one. Got it off de Army when dey sellin' extras in N'Ohlins. You cut a few poles and hang de tent ovah 'em, stake it down good, and you got a nice little place. Goin' fit you men nicely fo' a while."

The last items Alabama purchased were a few boxes of matches, some candles, and a box of first aid supplies. When he was satisfied that all that he could think of was included, he asked "How much Ah owe you, Mr. Freeman?"

Freeman nodded. "It come to six hundred dollar, all told," he replied. "Ah know it's a lot…"

Alabama held up a hand. "Ah suspect it all worth mo' den dat," he replied. "Reckon you cut yo' price a bit. You sure it be fair to you?"

Freeman looked at him strangely for a few seconds. At length he shook his head in mild amazement. "Ah declare, Ah don' think Ah eveh met a man lack you," he said. "Ain't nobody Ah know would have a care 'bout de storekeeper. Yessah, to answer yo' quession, it be fair to me." He reached out to shake Alabama's hand.

When Alabama had paid him from his money belt, which caused Freeman's eyes to widen a bit, he asked to see the mule. Freeman led him out to the stables. There he had hitched a strong, young female to a post. She was the color of a wheat field, and her lines were clean. Alabama walked up and gently patted the mule, running his hand along her neck and soothing her with soft sounds. The mule tried to toss her head but was restrained by the reins and halter. Alabama calmed her, continuing to speak softly. When he had her confidence, he gently peeled back her lips and looked at her teeth. "Good," he remarked. "She healthy. A good animal. She got a name?"

Freeman shook his head. "Naw. Her mama's out back. Ah raised this one, long wif' some others, but Ah nevah name 'em. Jes' gets in de way when you go to sell 'em."

Alabama smiled. "Ah goin' name her Precious," he remarked, thinking of a little girl happily drawing secret designs on a wooden floor. He reached in his pocket and handed Freeman a drawing. "Heah a map of de property," he said. "Lack Ah said, 'bout fo' mile south 'a 10 on 77. You see a place wheah de road crew been workin'. Raht 'bout theah be a lane into de woods, toward the swamp. If'n you come upon a tumbledown shack, you done gone too far. Go down dat lane 'bout a mile, an' you be seein' stakes wif red and white. Dey be some new earth spread deah. Das the place. You jes' unload the truck. Tell them boys to start taking down some straight trees an' debark 'em fo' makin' planks. Ah be 'long in a few hour."

"Whachoo goin' do?" Freeman asked. "How come you don' want to ride in de truck?"

Alabama turned to the mule and smoothed her neck. "Ah be leading Precious heah," he replied. "Don' want her followin' no truck and breathin' exhaust. Ah be 'long bye and bye. Lemme take a drink fum yo' well, give my girl heah some water, and Ah be on mah way. You boys'll pass me on de road."

"You goin' ride her? She ain't been rode."

Alabama smiled and shook his head. "Precious ain't fo' ridin'," replied. "She goin' pull a plow soon enough. Fo' now, she get to walk wif out no load."

Freeman nodded. "Look lack you goin' take good care of her," he remarked. "Tell ya what: Ah'll toss in a bag'a oats, no charge."

Alabama smiled. "Much obliged, Josiah," he replied.

An hour later, as Alabama was walking along the left side of Highway 10 on his way south and leading his mule, a white farmer and his wife in an old Ford pick-up truck came at them and passed by. The wife turned alarmingly to her husband. "You passed mighty close to that nigger!" she exclaimed sharply. "You coulda hit him!"

The farmer sneered. "Ah *didn't* hit 'em, did Ah?" he asked. "'Sides, Ah bet he stole that mule. Niggers're shifty, and they're liars. Ah oughta tell the sheriff."

CHAPTER 11

Alabama and the two young men had been working on the land for two days, cutting trees and lining them up for careful sawing into planks, when Wallis Flatley drove down the lane and spotted them. When Flatley stepped out of his truck, Alabama said "Keep goin', boys. Ah be back in a few minutes." He walked to the truck and shook hands with Flatley. The two young men observed and raised their eyebrows to one another.

"Mr. Flatley, suh. How you doin'?" Alabama asked.

"Good. Real good. We finished up the road work in these parts," Flatley replied. He looked out at the level dirt which now extended clear to the poles in the water. "Six hundred and thirty-eight loads," he said. "Dumped and smoothed. At three dollars a load, comes to nineteen hundred and fourteen dollars, less the hundred you paid me."

Alabama smiled and lifted his shirt, exposing the money belt. Carefully, he counted out the money and handed it to Flatley. "Eighteen hundred and fo'teen," he remarked. "Yo' men done a good job."

Flatley nodded. "It worked out good," he replied, gazing at the land. "I'm gonna share this with the boys. They never asked me what was goin' on. Jes' done what I tol' 'em. They deserve a share."

Alabama nodded and grinned. "Ah understan' de principle," he commented. "Thank you, suh."

Flatley regarded him with a soft smile. "You mighta put one over on me, Alabama Denton. If'n you did, then more power to ya. Anyhow, it worked out for both of us. You got your land, and I got some cash and saved some miles on the trucks." He held out his hand. "Take care, Alabama."

Alabama nodded, returning the smile. "Ah will, Mr. Flatley. Thanks fo' workin' wif me on dis."

After three weeks of steady work, the three men had cut sufficient planks to erect a three-room cabin with a wooden floor raised four feet off the ground on twenty-four solid posts, each sunk two yards deep into the soil and anchored with rocks. Alabama explained to the men that he wanted it that way to afford a breeze under the cabin when it was hot and to keep snakes from entering the cabin. Inside the cabin, they laid a base of smooth rocks a yard square in a corner of the kitchen for placement of a wood-burning stove which Alabama planned to buy from Josiah Freeman in the near future. Their final task was to dig a square well, four feet on a side, hauling out the dirt in buckets as they dug. Every two feet, they paused and lined the sides with bricks and mortar. They were elated when they struck water only fourteen feet down. They dug two more feet, hauling out the mud, and tossed sufficient stones down into the mud to line the bottom of the well at that point. "Dat'll keep de water clear," Alabama explained. When they had built a brick four-foot square wall to line the top of the well and mounted the pipe, winch, and rope-drawn bucket from a cupola, they considered their work done. Alabama drew bucket after bucket, pouring out the muddy water, until the first clear water emerged. He shared it in a large scoop. "Ah, de fines' water God evah made!" he exclaimed. The boys heartily agreed.

"Oh, yes, das' good!" Lonnie remarked, smacking his lips. "Ah sho' am tired of boilin' dat ol' swamp water. No matter how much it boil, Ah still think it goin' kill me!"

At dinner that evening, Alabama said "Ah need to return to N'Owlins fo' a week, fellas. Ah cain't leave Precious heah alone, else she be gone by de time Ah come back. You boys wanna stay an' jes' hunt an' fish fo' a week? Ah cain't pay you for de time Ah be gone. If'n you want, you kin jes' go back home, an' we work some mo' when Ah return. When Ah come back, we goin' start clearin' trees and burnin' grass to clear de land fo' farmin'. Whachoo wanna do?"

Rufus looked at Lonnie, who shrugged. He grinned and replied "Reckon we kin use some time jes' kickin' back. See you in a week?"

Alabama smiled. "A week. Thanks."

The next morning, he arose at the first hint of sunlight and walked quickly to Morganza in order to meet the convoy returning from Shreveport.

Matilda welcomed Alabama back with a hug. "My, Ah miss you!" she exclaimed. "Been a bit slow 'round heah. Siddown, let me fix you sumpin' fine to eat!" Mrs. Stoughton also welcomed him as he was working in the garden the next morning, inquiring with genuine interest how his farming venture was working out. "Goin' jes' fine, Mizz Stoughton," he replied, outlining what they had been able to accomplish in three weeks. Mrs. Stoughton was truly impressed. "To go from virtually nothing, not even supplies, to a fully-built home in three weeks? And a well? My word, Alabama, you truly don't allow any grass to grow under your feet, do you?" Alabama smiled shyly and scuffed his boots.

When he returned to the land, the Mason boys had constructed a latrine with a six-foot hole below it about twenty feet behind the cabin. The five-by-six structure had two doors: one for entry, and a smaller one in the back where the pile of dirt excavated from the hole stood. A small shovel was embedded in the soil. Rufus showed Alabama how to open the smaller door and toss in a shovelful or two of dirt when one's business was done. "Reckon it'll last ya 'bout three-fo' yeah," he remarked happily. "Keep de smell down de' whole time. Den you got to dig a new hole and put dis heah shack ovah top of it." He grinned hugely. "When you do, plant yo'sef a tree in dis spot. Be de biggest tree in the county in a few yeah!"

Alabama gazed with appreciation at their handiwork. "How many hours you boys put in heah?" he asked.

Rufus grinned. "Ain't no hours, boss. Dis heah jes' a thang. Kep' us from gettin' bored, ya know? Dey ain't no charge or nuthin'."

Alabama gazed at the two young men. After a moment, he sighed. "Wayall, Ah thank ya," he said simply.

"C'mon!" Lonnie cried. "We done some good fishin' this mo'nin'! Gots to enjoy 'em while they fresh! We wastin' time yappin'!" He walked happily to a campfire, where four filleted fish sat smoking over a bed of coals.

CHAPTER 12

Alabama left the Stoughton home for good the first week of November. He informed Matilda and Mrs. Stoughton of the exact date on the last day of October. Mrs. Stoughton smiled and said "I will surely miss you, Alabama. You've taken such good care of my grounds. But even more than that, you are a wonderful human being. I hope you'll be able to visit now and again."

Alabama sighed and nodded. "Thank you, Mizz Stoughton," he replied quietly. "You been so good to me. At de time Ah needed to have a base, you done give it to me. An' you hep me wif' de Navy transportation. Dat was huge. Ah surely will come back to N'Owlins and see y'all from time to time." On his last day, he shook hands formally with her and gave her the honor of a bow. "Oh, Alabama!" she exclaimed merrily. "It's been quite a while since a man bowed to this lady!"

Matilda was another story. She was quiet the entire week, often simply leaving his food on a plate and absenting herself from the kitchen. That was very unusual behavior for the normally friendly and talkative lady. Alabama mulled it over each time. Finally he decided there was much about women he didn't know and likely never would, and he happily dismissed the problem from his mind.

On his last day, he came to the kitchen carrying his suitcase and carryall bag, looking for Matilda. She was nowhere to be found. Alabama surely did not want to simply leave, after all the kindness she had displayed toward him, so he took the bold step of setting his bags down and going down the hall to her room. He knocked softly on the door. "Matilda?" he asked.

"Whachoo want?!" came the angry reply.

Alabama took a step back, baffled. *Wha' Ah do?* he wondered. Unsure of what to do, he merely waited. After a long moment, the door was opened. Matilda stood there, her eyes puffy from weeping. Alabama stared at her, his mouth slightly open.

"You sick, Matilda?" he asked.

Matilda scowled and slammed her hands onto her hips. "You de dumbest man Ah evah know!" she exclaimed. "Whachoo mean, 'You sick?'"

Alabama stared at her. He shrugged. "Wayall, Ah mean…"

Matilda shook her head hard. "Don't," she commanded. "Jes' don't say nuthin." She continued to glare at him.

Alabama took in a deep breath and let it out slowly. He stared at her, thinking *Do Ah jes' go?*

Matilda opened the door fully and retreated to her dressing table, flopping into the chair and staring at him with her arms crossed across her breast. Unsure of what to do, Alabama simply stood and watched. "Wayall?" she cried. "Come in! Don' jes' stand theah!" He stepped tentatively into the room, turned back and looked at the door, and shut it quietly. He turned to the angry woman again. "Wha' Ah do to make you upset, Matilda?" he asked plaintively. "Ah nevah…"

Matilda swiveled in the chair and stared out the window, her arms still defiantly crossed.

Alabama gazed at her for a long minute. At length, he said "Wayall, Ah come to say goodbye, Matilda. It sho' been nice…"

He stopped in mid-sentence, shocked, as Matilda turned suddenly toward him and blurted "Why you hate me, Alabama? *Why?*" She burst into tears and covered her face in her hands.

Alabama took a step toward her, then hesitated. He replied "*Hate* you? Wha' in de world you talkin' 'bout, woman? Wha' make you think Ah got anything but good feelin's t'ward you?"

Matilda stopped crying abruptly. She took a linen napkin out of a drawer in the dressing table and dried her eyes. "Good feelin's?" she asked. "*How* good?"

Alabama regarded her with a sinking feeling, suddenly regretting having stepped into her room. He breathed deeply and let it out slowly. "You mah frien'," he replied in a quiet voice.

Matilda snorted and looked down at her dressing table. "Frien'!" she remarked bitterly. She looked up at him. "Das' all? Jes' you frien'?"

Alabama began to speak twice and halted. He motioned with his hands as if to make words, but that didn't work either. Finally he pointed to her bed. "Mind if Ah sit?" he asked.

She shrugged. Her facial expression seemed to indicate that it made no difference to her if he lived or died.

Alabama sat on the edge of the bed, as far from Matilda as he could. He stared at her, and she at him. A long moment of silence ensued. Finally he said "Matilda, Ah guess…wayall, Ah don' know much 'bout women, but Ah be thinkin' mayhaps you expectin' mo' from me than Ah was thinkin' of givin.'"

She sighed, her face softening. "Alabama, why don' you take me wif' you?" she pleaded. "Ah kin cook! You know that! An' Ah be a good wife, sho'ly Ah will! We…"

Alabama held up his hand, palm toward her. She stared, mouth sagging, and lapsed into silence. He said "You evah see geese flyin' in dey big 'vees,' Matilda?

She frowned and stared. "Geese?

He nodded. "From Canada. Dey gray, and black, and white…"

She nodded. "Yes, Ah see 'em. Wintertime, mainly. On dey way to Mexico. Why?"

"Man Ah talk to one time say dem geese mate fo' life," Alabama commented. "De male find a lady, an' dey make some kinda pact, and den dey mates fo' life. If'n one die, de othah nevah mate wif' another goose. Evah."

She stared at him. "So?"

"Wayall, Ah always wondah, how come one goose come to love one othah goose and not anothah goose? How come wif' all dem geese, de male find de lady and das' dat? Wha' make dat happen?"

Matilda blinked. She shrugged. "How Ah goin' know a thang lack dat? 'Bout geese? Ah ain't evah had no goose!" she asked in some frustration.

Alabama pursed his lips and shrugged as well. "Chemistry," he remarked. "Bes' Ah kin tell, it jes' chemistry. De male find a lady and go all goosey. She wave her feathah or somethin,' sayin' das' okay wif' her, and das' dat. Jes' chemistry."

Matilda stared at him. After a moment, she nodded. "An' we ain't got chemistry," she replied in a quiet voice.

Alabama shook his head softly. "Ah don' b'lieve we do," he replied as kindly as possible. "Ah wish you de bes', Matilda. You a fine lady and a great frien', and one 'a dese days some man gonna come 'long and see you and go all goosey. Den you wave a feathah, and das' dat. Goin' happen, Matilda. Mayhaps at church. Dey's some fine men theah, not all 'a dem married. You get yo'sef to every social you kin, and see if Ah ain't raht."

Matilda stood, a rueful smile on her face. She held out her hand. "It been good, Alabama. You a fine man yo'sef. Some lady goin' be honored to be yo' wife."

Alabama stepped forward and took her hand. Softly, he pulled her into his chest and wrapped his arms around her. She had to stoop a few inches to fit, but clearly she welcomed the embrace. In a moment, he pulled apart, nodded, smiled, and walked out her door, closing it softly behind him.

CHAPTER 13

Louisiana experiences freezes during the late fall and winter months, when the Maritime polar air mass dips down low and settles over the state. The winter high pressure fronts, combined with the cool air mass, tend to keep ground temperatures low.

The normal periods of frost vary considerably over the state. North Louisiana can experience it from mid-October to the end of March. By contrast, some areas along the Gulf Coast never experience frost.

Pointe Coupee Parish, being in the middle of the state, typically sees frost a few times each winter, from late November to the end of February. Farmers ensure that the ground is tilled prior to Thanksgiving to capture the nitrogen from any snowfall, if there is any, and to be ready for quick seeding in the spring. Their animals are put into the barn during the winter nights and allowed out during the day if the weather is suitable to graze whatever scrub remains. Like all farmers everywhere, the winter months are used for tool repair and refurbishing as well as any home repairs they've been putting off for 'indoor' weather.

Alabama hitched a ride on the oil truck convoy the day he left the Stoughton residence. When he was dropped off in Morganza, he walked to the general store, hoping to see Adrianna. She was in school, however, and wouldn't be home for a few hours. But Josiah Freeman immediately took Alabama's mind off the girl. "Ah got sumpin' you goin' lack," he remarked with a twinkle in his eye. "Ordered it in 'special fo' you. C'mon." He led Alabama out the back door to the yard. There stood a wooden wagon with a bench seat for two and trace bars into which a horse could easily fit. "Ah figure Precious can pull this wagon jes' fine," Josiah commented happily. "An' lookee heah." He bent down to show off the wheels. "It got steel bearin's. Newest thang! You jes' keep 'em greased an' dey nevah squeak. Plus dey smooth. An' it got iron strips 'round de wheels. Keeps 'em from wearin'." He ran his fingers down one iron band, clearly admiring the workmanship. "Ah already tried it out wif' one 'a mah horses," he remarked. "Works jes' as slick as can be!" He smiled as big as if he'd invented the machine.

Alabama stared at it appreciatively. He moved around the wagon slowly, touching various parts and admiring its excellent workmanship. "How much you axin' fo' dis?" he asked Josiah.

Freeman scowled in mock indignation. "Now, who say anythin' 'bout axin'?" he demanded, hands on hips.

Alabama stared at him, eyes wide. "You…you goin' *give* dis heah to me?"

Freeman smiled hugely. "Ah figure if'n you got dis wagon, you be back to buy mah goods a whole lot more often den if'n you gotta walk!" he exclaimed.

Alabama smiled and shook his head. "Wayall, suh, Ah sho' am grateful. An' Ah sho' *will* be back a whole passel 'a time!"

Freeman nodded. "Tell you what. Les' go to yo' place in de truck. Ah bring back dem boys, and you come back wif' Precious. We load up some supplies fo' you tomorrah. Goin' take you too much time to walk back wif' Precious today to go back to yo' farm tonight, so you stay heah. Tomorrah we send you off in de wagon. Sound good?"

Alabama smiled. "Ah reckon dem boys done had dey fill of campin' on dat farm. Les' go get 'em."

Supper that evening at the Freeman table was a rare treat. Not only was Jasmine Freeman's cooking the equal of Matilda's, the family was a delight for a man starved of such company. It was clear that the Freemans demanded respect from their children in the way they addressed their parents by 'Sir' and

'Ma'am.' Moreover, the discussion at the table was of a higher order than Alabama expected. Jeremiah, who was just eleven, had discovered geography in a big way in the sixth grade and was happy to converse with Alabama on his favorite subject. Arianna, in the fourth grade, was full of spirit and charm. It was everything Alabama could do to keep from staring at her.

After a good night's sleep on the couch following a leisurely discussion with the Freemans after the children had gone to bed, Alabama took a sponge bath in the bathroom and packed the wagon with supplies, including several rolls of a new product which Josiah Freeman labeled 'insulation.' "It's a product of de war," he explained. "Dey use it in dey houses to keep de howlin' wind from freezin' up yo' cabin." He demonstrated how to lay out a roll and tack it between the boards. "When you ready, you kin cover it wif' some mo' boards," he explained. "Keep de place lookin' nice. Wif' dis heah insulation, dat wood stove you got goin' keep you toasty."

"What about in de summer?" Alabama asked. "Ain't it goin' be too hot?"

"Ever' place too hot in de summer," Freeman replied. "You jes' open yo' window fo' whatevah breeze dey be. Othawise you jes' put up wif' de heat, sit on de porch, an' watch yo' crops grow."

Alabama nodded. "Ah kin live wif' dat." He looked at Josiah. "De boys an' Ah built a barn for Precious," he remarked. "An' a chicken coop. Now Ah need to buy some crack corn and oyster grit. An' Ah need some hens and a rooster. Who be sellin' chickens? You know?"

Josiah nodded. "Yep. Fambly down off Highway 10. White man, but decent. He sell you chickens." He gave Alabama directions to the farm in question.

It was a month before Alabama returned to Morganza. In the meantime, he wrote to Mrs. Stoughton on paper he'd purchased from Josiah Freeman:

Dear Mrs. Stoughton, I am fine are you fine. I have got a wagon it is a good one now I can haul stuff and not have to walk. I hope Matilda is okay. Tell her hello. I have found the girl I will marry.

Respect, Alabama

By this time, the air was cool during the day and cold at night. A layer of snow had fallen but melted away the next day. Alabama spent his days cutting trees for fence posts, chopping and sawing fallen timber for firewood, digging holes for the fence posts, and fishing for his supper. Every other day, he hitched Precious to the wagon and trotted her down the road for a couple of miles and back to toughen her up for plowing in the spring. There was no end of good, physical work, and Alabama fell asleep exhausted each night. He arose with the dawn. By the time he visited the Freemans again, Josiah was astounded at how much Alabama had been able to accomplish. He playfully squeezed one of Alabama's upper arms. "You gettin' mighty strong, brothah!" he remarked. "Workin' mus' be doin' you good!"

Alabama laughed. "It sho' keep me busy," he replied. "Say, Josiah, Ah need some mo' gloves." He displayed the calluses on his hands. "Wore out my only pair. Dat diggin' kin sho' take a toll."

Josiah nodded. "Ah get 'em fo' you." He smiled conspiratorially. "Brothah, have Ah got sumpin' fo' you!" he remarked, walking with Alabama to a tool display. He pointed out a posthole digger consisting of a large steel screw blade attached firmly to a wooden shaft with a solid wood handle at a right angle to the shaft. "You jam it in de groun' an' walk 'round de hole," he explained. "When you got dirt comin' up to de' top of de blade, you lif' it out. Do dat three, fo' time, you got a post hole. Save you a lot 'a diggin'."

"Gimme dat thang!" Alabama demanded. He snatched it up and grinned. "Wheah you bin all my life, sweet thang?" he asked the tool. Freeman laughed aloud. "Jes' got dem in a few day after you leave," he said. "If'n Ah know you diggin' holes, Ah'da brung it to you."

Alabama shrugged. "Work nevah hurt a man," he replied. "But dis heah sho' goin' save me some time." He pulled the envelope to Mrs. Stoughton out of his back pocket. "Mind mailin' dis fo' me?" he asked.

"Cost you two cent fo' de stamp," Josiah replied teasingly. He waved off Alabama's attempt to pay him.

Two weeks later, Josiah Freeman paid Alabama a visit. Alabama smiled when he saw the truck coming down the lane. His heart leapt when the truck pulled to a stop and Adrianna piled out of the passenger side. "How do, Mr. Alabama?" she exclaimed with a big smile. Alabama grinned happily. He had to blink hard to prevent a tear from sliding down his cheek. "Ah jes' fine, Miss Adrianna," he replied. "Sho' is good to see you. An' yo' daddy," he added as Josiah exited the truck.

Freeman grinned. "Come to see the finest farm in Pointe Coupee Parish!" he exclaimed. "You been cuttin' holes wif' dat fancy hole digger?"

Alabama laughed. "On'y 'bout a hundred a day!" he replied. "C'mon. Ah show you."

He led his friend and the excited, gaily skipping girl around the property, showing them what he'd been able to accomplish and indicating what needed to be done. Josiah surveyed it with a careful eye and nodded. "You done good, Alabama," he remarked. "Fence posts in a nice straight line. Good solid house. Good barn. Chicken coop. Looks lack you got some prime chickens, too. An' dat rooster mighty proud, looks lack. He any good?"

Alabama chuckled. "Das' de *stud*, dat one. De ladies mighty busy wif' him 'round."

"Oh!" Josiah exclaimed. "Almos' forgot. Got a letter heah fo' you." He handed it to Alabama, who glanced at the return address and nodded. He looked at Josiah. "Thank you, suh. Ah forgot to tell you Ah use yo' sto' fo' my address, 'cause Ah don' know mine. Reckon Ah best talk wif' de parish, see if'n dey know it."

Freeman shrugged. "Ah reckon dey do, but dey ain't in no hurry," he commented. "Go ahead an' use my store. Jes means you be delayed a bit in getting' yo' mail."

That afternoon, when his guests had left, Alabama sat under a tree and opened the letter. Mrs. Stoughton had written:

Dear Alabama,

What a pleasure to hear from you. Yes, I am doing well, and I am very happy to hear that you are as well. I did convey your greetings to Matilda. She is now seeing a man from her church. I fear she may not be with me much longer. That will be such a loss. First I lose the finest gardener in the state of Louisiana, and soon I will lose a most excellent cook. Ah, me! I must begin to find replacements, I fear.

How intriguing to hear that you have selected a young lady whom you will marry. That happened quickly, I must say! Have you set a date? Perhaps you and your intended—or by then, your wife—will visit with me in New Orleans. That would be most welcome. Just let me know when you might be coming, and I will have the guest room prepared for you.

In the meantime, I wish you and yours a wonderful Christmas season. May our Lord bless you.

Fondly,

Mrs. Isabel Stoughton

Guest room, Alabama mused. *She would put dis Negro in her guest room. Dey ain't many ladies like Mizz Stoughton, das' fo' sho'!*

By the time the weather had begun to warm and plowing time was right around the corner, Alabama had fenced in the entire fifty acres with split rails, right up to the edge of the swamp. He decided not to fence in the swamp side, thinking that the annual flooding and receding would quickly rot the fence posts. At any rate, it was clear from the dirt that the trucks had dumped where the property line lay.

On the first day Alabama awoke and his blanket felt too warm, he arose, stretched, and walked to the door of the cabin. The sun was just beginning to light up a cloudless sky. "Ahhhh," Alabama exclaimed. "Precious, today you goin' discover de joy of plowin'!" After a breakfast of cornbread he'd baked the previous night along with two boiled eggs, he downed a healthy drink from the well and walked to the barn. By the time the sun was fully risen, he was walking behind the plow as the strong mule pulled it through the earth that was just beginning to show green over the controlled burn that Alabama and the boys had conducted in the fall. Alabama kept his eyes on the horizon as he'd been taught in order to plow a straight row. He talked easily to the mule, who tossed her head and snuffled on occasion as if participating in the conversation.

It required eleven days to plow twenty-eight of the fifty acres, the remainder largely covered by stands of trees which Alabama eventually planned to cut in order to maximize his fields. He allowed the mule and himself to rest on two of those days, as it was very hard work to cut a foot down through solid roots that had never felt the plow and turn it over with the roots exposed to the air. On the twelfth day, Alabama hitched Precious to the wagon and allowed her to walk in a leisurely fashion to Morganza. The trip required five hours, but Alabama didn't begrudge the mule's pace, knowing how hard she'd worked to cut the fields.

When he arrived at the Freeman's general store and was warmly greeted, he told Josiah that he'd like to buy several large bags of bean seeds. "Das' all Ah'm goin' plant dis spring," he explained.

"Twenty-eight acres of nuthin' but beans?" Josiah replied. "Das' goin' be a lot of weedin' and pickin'. You goin' get de boys to hep you?"

Alabama shook his head. "No. When de beans be flowerin', Ah goin' turn 'em under."

Freeman stared at him. "*What?*" he exclaimed. "De whole crop?"

Alabama nodded. "Dat dirt ain't soil yet. Jes' highway dirt and prairie sod. It need some good plant material to make it soil. Man Ah knew tol' me to grow beans and turn 'em under. Brings nitrogen into de soil 'cause 'a wha's called 'nodules' on de roots 'a de beans. Plus, de beans demsef' turn into compost. You lose de crop, but you make good soil. Ah figure Ah kin get two crops dis year, so Ah goin' harvest de second crop 'a beans."

Josiah contemplated what he'd heard. After a moment, he shrugged. "Wayall, Ah nevah hear tell of it, but den all de land 'round heah been farmed fo' longer dan Ah been livin'. You de first farmer Ah know wif' bran' new ground."

Alabama nodded. "So Ah goin' need lots a bean seed," he remarked. "An' in a couple months, Ah be back fo' mo'. You make sure you got it when Ah need it, okay?"

Freeman smiled. "Special fo' you," he replied with a grin. "It be ready."

Alabama looked around. "Yo' chirren heah?" he asked innocently.

Freeman shook his head. "School. Weekends de only time dey heah durin' de day."

Alabama nodded, disappointed but careful not to let it show. He said "You sell calendars, Josiah?"

Freeman nodded. "Ah give you one. Seed fella dropped off a couple." He walked down the aisle with Alabama to the front counter and dug out a calendar from a shelf. Alabama accepted it with thanks and said "Whas' today?" Freeman pointed to the proper square. "Tuesday, second of March," he said. Alabama nodded. When he arrived back at his farm with the seed, he tacked the calendar on the inside wall of the cabin and crossed off the first square in the month of March. The next morning, he crossed off the second square. On the morning of the third day thereafter, he walked out to the barn and hitched Precious to the wagon. "We goin' go see yo' namesake today, beautiful gal," he told her. Precious snuffled against his touch along her neck and snout.

CHAPTER 14

Alabama was in the habit of counting the bills from his money belt every now and then. Included with the money was a sheet of paper where he had recorded every expenditure and calculated a balance remaining. Part of the process was to ensure that the final figure balanced with the amount represented by the bills.

After turning his first crop back into the ground and replanting with new bean seeds, Alabama took stock. *Been a while since any money go into dis belt,* he reflected. *But ain't none of it been wasted. Got my Pa off his land and restin', got my own land an' mule and house and buildin's, got tools, got a wagon, got supplies, food for me an' my animals…Wha' mo' a man want?* The thought of a little girl in a white dress with pigtails and the most endearing smile he had ever imagined flitted through his mind, but he suppressed it immediately. *Give her time, give her time,* his mind commanded, but his heart was impatient.

Knowing it was important to actually harvest and sell the second crop of beans, Alabama spent six days a week from sunup to late afternoon, weather permitting, weeding the crop. He divided the twenty-eight acres into six parcels, each four and a half acres, with the final section adding an acre. These he marked with stakes with numbers carved in them. It required most of a day to work through a section with a carefully-wielded hoe, but at the end of each week he had the satisfaction of seeing his work result in healthy, growing, and weed-free plants. The spring rains came once or twice a week, preventing him from walking into the fields, but for the most part he stayed on schedule.

On Sundays, Alabama arose with the dawn and hitched Precious to the wagon for a trip into Morganza. Because she was not plowing, he set the mule into a steady trot. Whereas it took five hours for Precious to walk the distance, she covered the twenty miles in just under two hours at a trot. As a result, Alabama always arrived in time to share breakfast with the Freemans, an invitation they insisted he keep. He delighted in the opportunity to share conversation with friends, attend worship services at the small Negro Baptist church where they were members, and restock with any supplies he needed. He watched Arianna grow, marveling that she seemed to become more beautiful and charming each week.

In the late summer, Alabama engaged Rufus and Lonnie to help him pick beans. He instructed them to carefully grasp the bean with two hands, right at the junction of the stem with the plant, so as to remove the bean without ripping the plant out of the ground or breaking off the bean and making it useless for sale. "If'n de rain come agin one mo' time, Ah get two harvests fum dese plants," he told the young men. "Ah call you back in three-fo' week fo' de las' pickin'." The hoped-for rain did come, two good soakings as it turned out, and the combination of the two crops netted Alabama a large profit when he sold to a broker in Fordoche. Seeing the new bills go into his money belt was a relief. *Farmin' a hard life,* he reflected. *Sometime de Lawd bring de rain, sometime He don't. Sometime He bring strong wind or hail an' destroy de crop. Sometime you get bugs and have to pick 'em off or spray 'em. It all depend. But it all Ah know, 'sides killin' men, and Ah all done wif dat, thank God. Ah satisfied.*

Alabama used the following winter to clear more land. With Rufus' and Lonnie's help, he cut timber, scraped off the bark, and stored the logs in a wooden rack behind the barn, careful to ensure that they didn't lie on the ground and develop rot. The three men dug, chopped deeply-embedded tree roots, and used Precious to help pull stumps out of the ground. When the spring came and the stumps were burned, Alabama had an extra twelve acres to plow for the new year's crops. "Das' fo'ty acre," he told the men. "Dat be 'nough fo' a while. Got mayhaps six, seven acre left to clear, but dat kin wait. Ah got 'nough land fo' a while."

In the meantime, Alabama kept up his correspondence with Mrs. Stoughton. He was faithful to write each Saturday evening so the letter could be mailed on Sunday. Normally he also received a letter from her on Sunday. He often wondered why she was so faithful to write to him and finally put it in the category of questions he would never see answered. Every now and then, Mrs. Stoughton would teasingly ask about the girl he had picked out for his wife, and Alabama would answer with a comment to the effect that the lady wasn't ready yet. *Cain't tell her Adrianna on'y 'leben*, he mused. *Fo' sho' she think Ah crazy.* He agonized over the question of when to pop the question. *Who Ah ax first, her or her daddy? How old she gotta be? Sixteen? Eighteen?* He was not unaware of the fifteen-year difference in their ages and often checked himself from head to toe without benefit of a mirror to see if he was aging and would be unattractive by the time she was ready for him.

In the late stages of Alabama's second winter on the land, having grown a good crop of beans and corn the previous season, he received a visitor while he was sawing logs into planks for future building. A black sedan with a Pointe Coupee Parish emblem on the side came down the lane and pulled into the yard. Alabama took off his gloves, slipped on his jacket against the cool air, and donned a worn straw hat. He walked out to the car just as a middle-aged white man stepped out holding a clipboard.

"You Alabama Denton?" the man asked.

Alabama nodded. "Das' me. Wha' kin Ah do fo' you?"

The man hesitated, as if the lack of the word 'sir' at the end of Alabama's greeting had been noted. He glanced down at the clipboard. "Parish inspector," he said officiously. "You're listed on the records. Need to take a look at your property."

"How come?" Alabama asked.

The man stared at him, his head tilted back just slightly. "We inspect all the farm property in the parish for tax purposes," he replied stiffly. "Just gettin' to you. Says here you ain't paid taxes since you closed on the property."

Alabama nodded. "Thas' raht. De man in de title office say Ah goin' receive notice of how much and when to pay. Ain't no notice come. You de fust Ah heah from de parish."

The man frowned, sighing irritably. He scanned his papers again. "Well!" he remarked, glaring at Alabama. "The tax is $1.45 per acre per year.

We'll waive the interest and penalties for nonpayment, since no one has seen fit to visit you until now. But for the previous two years plus this year, 'cause you gotta pay in advance, you owe the parish $217.50." He looked expectantly at Alabama.

Alabama nodded. "Ah pay you?" he asked.

The man started slightly, as if surprised at the response. "Well, yes, you can," he replied, "if you have it."

"An' you kin give me a receipt."

The man scowled. "Of course! We always provide a receipt."

Alabama nodded. "Wait heah, please. Ah be raht back."

In a few minutes, Alabama returned with $218 in bills. He handed it to the white man and said "Don't have no coins."

The man stared at the money. "Well, I don't either," he replied peevishly. "We can give you a credit on next year's taxes with the extra half-buck."

"Das' okay," Alabama replied.

The man looked off toward the now-full Atchaflaya Swamp and commented "I was lookin' at your land. Seems you got a peninsula, sorta. Square-like. Sticks out into the water, right up to your property stakes. It's obviously artificial. What's that about?"

Alabama explained how the tract had been described as fifty acres but thirty-four of them were actually flood basin. He described how he had purchased dirt to fill in to the stakes marking the property line, though he didn't mention where it had originated. The tax inspector looked at him. "That's illegal, you know," he remarked stiffly.

Alabama frowned. "Illegal? Why?"

"Cain't adulterate the basin with fill," the man replied.

Alabama stared at him. Though he had a strong feeling he knew what the word meant, he asked "Wha's dis 'adul' whatevah? Whachoo mean?"

The parish inspector frowned. "A-*dul*-ter-ate," he pronounced slowly, as if he was dealing with a mentally deficient person or a child. "Means mess with. You can't change the natural shoreline of the Swamp."

"But it mah land!" Alabama protested. "Ah paid fo' it! Got a deed to show, too. You wanna see it?"

A dark look came over the man's face. "Look, nig…Mr. Denton," he replied sharply. "The law is the law. I don't give a damn about some piece of paper you claim you have. You've stolen some twenty or twenty-five acres from the parish. You have to surrender it. That's all there is to it."

Thihty-fo', you ugly crackuh, Alabama thought angrily. *An' Ah paid fo' dem too, when anothah crackuh tried to rob me.* He replied "Mistah tax man, Ah don' really care who you say you are an' what kinda nonsense you be talkin' 'bout givin' up de land Ah bought and got papah to prove. Now you got yo' tax money. Jes' gimme my receipt and git off my land."

The tax inspector fairly steamed. Clearly he had never suffered the indignity of being addressed in such an impertinent manner by a mere Negro. Quickly he scribbled a receipt, tore it off the pad, and thrust it onto the ground at Alabama's feet. "I'll be back, nigger," he said ominously. "And next time I won't be alone." He stomped off to his vehicle, flopped in, and tore down the lane, careening and throwing up dust.

Alabama picked up the receipt. Though his reading skills weren't more than competent, he could see that the handwriting was poorly crafted. *Deliberate,* he blistered mentally. But it appeared to be official, it listed the amount, the credit owed, the date, the years covered, and an address, so he was satisfied that it was indeed an official receipt. He peered at the address: 353 Highway 77, Pointe Coupee Parish, Louisiana. Below it was a plat and lot number. *So tha's wheah Ah live,* Alabama thought with amusement. He resolved to check the legal address with the title that he kept buried in a metal box at the base of the stairs leading up to his house.

And then it struck him. "Ah in big trouble," he spoke aloud. "Oh, Lawd! *Big* trouble!" *An' Ah din' do nuthin' to bring it on,* he pondered, *but dat don' mean nuthin' when a crackuh got a thang agin' a black man.* He walked unsteadily to the wood stack he'd been sawing and sat down hard, staring out at the swamp. *Wha' Ah goin' do?* he wondered with a slack jaw. *A Negro agin' de man. Agin' de* gubmint! *An' dis crackuh say he goin' come back with mo' white men, an' dey won' be comin' fo' tea an' crumpets. Ah ain't got a hope. Do Ah get a gun? Wha' Ah goin' do?*

After a time, he walked into the house and sat at the desk he'd made by carefully cutting planks and sanding the desktop surface into a smooth platform. He pulled a sheet of writing paper and an envelope off a shelf. With his quill pen, he wrote:

> *Dear Mrs. Stoughton.*
>
> *I in trouble I need your help I will catch the next Navy truck and come see you.*
>
> *Please.*
>
> *Alabama Denton.*

As soon as the ink was dry on the envelope, he addressed it to Mrs. Stoughton and donned suitable clothing for the trip into Morganza. Within minutes, he had Precious hitched to the wagon and was trotting down the lane to mail the letter.

CHAPTER 15

Four days later, Josiah Freeman motored down the long lane and onto Alabama's farm. Alabama heard the truck and stepped out of the barn. "How do!" he greeted his friend.

"Tol'ble," Josiah replied with a grin. He approached Alabama and shook hands. "Got a phone call this mornin'," he said.

Knowing that the Freeman General Store had the only phone in the black community, Alabama had no inkling of what was coming. "A Mrs. Stoughton," Josiah reported. "Said she found mah numbah through a lawyer frien,' usin' mah address. Says she wants you to come down to N'Owlins."

Alabama stared at him. After a few seconds, he chuckled and exclaimed "Wayall, Ah'll be hog-tied!"

"Might at dat, if'n you don' change yo' ways," Josiah replied with a grin. "Now lookee heah. White folk don' call if'n dey ain't a good reason. Whas' goin' on?"

Alabama sighed. "Got some good cool well water, Josiah," he replied. "C'mon. Ah'll buy you a cup." He led the way to the well, where he dropped the bucket and raised it full of water on the winch. When both men had drunk their fill, Alabama hitched his rear onto the wall of the well and invited his friend to do so as well. In short, emotionless sentences, he told of his relationship with Mrs. Stoughton and described the visit of the tax inspector. "Couldn't think of wha' to do," he said. "Figured Mizz Stoughton would know. Das' one smaht lady."

Josiah nodded, shaking his head. "White man always try to take black man's land," he mused. "Don' seem lack dat evah goin' change. Wayall, Mrs. Stoughton say she wanna see you raht away. Best you go on down theah."

Alabama gazed out at his farm, the soil ready for plowing. "Dis heah Sadday," he remarked. "Oil truck don' come 'til Tuesday. Goin' be a long wait."

Josiah regarded his friend, scratching his chin. "Y'know," he commented reflectively. "Been a long time since me and de missus took de chirren to N'Owlins. Dey was jes' small, las' time we went. Might be time to go agin'. Ah'm thinkin' mayhaps tomorrow, after church."

Alabama stared at him. "Yo' ol' truck go dat far?"

Josiah grinned. "Oh, she's mo' dan you think, brothah! Ah keeps her up. Cain't go fast, but she go, fo' sho'. Ah buy mah parts fum dat junkyahd fella down wheah 10 an' 77 come togethuh. You know it?"

Alabama nodded. "Pass by it ever' time Ah come up heah. Don't look too kep up, lack de fella don' care much how it look."

Josiah chuckled. "No, he don'!" he remarked emphatically. "Got junk layin' all ovah. Plus he don' lack black folk, thas' fo' sho'. Got 'im two big ugly dogs mus' be trained to attack black skin. When Ah go theah, which is as little as poss'ble, Ah holler out and he has to chain dem dogs."

Alabama frowned. "Why you go theah a'tall?"

Josiah shrugged. "Ain't no black man wif' auto pahts anywheah 'round heah. Got no choice." He grinned. "Dat man prob'ly don' lack me comin' round either, but he lack mah money! Yessah, he sho' do'! Anyhow, Ah got the pahts Ah need and de truck runnin' good. We get to N'Owlins 'n back no problem." He grinned at Alabama. "Ah phone Mrs. Stoughton 'n tell her you be theah tomorrah night."

Alabama took in a long breath and released it slowly. He could only nod at his friend's generosity.

The next day, he arose early as usual and dressed in his best clothes. He hitched Precious to the wagon and set off for the Freeman household. The family was abuzz with excitement with the news of the coming trip to New Orleans. "We stay tonight," Josiah explained to the children. "You be missin' school tomorrah. Ain't dat a shame?"

Jeremiah giggled, and Adrianna smiled with the sweetness that always made Alabama weak.

"So come on, chirren!" Mrs. Jasmine Freeman commanded. "Finish up, now. We got to get ready fo' church, 'n den we hurry back and get on de road!"

The six-hour trip, punctuated by stops for bathroom breaks at selected black-owned stores along the way, was a memorable experience. Alabama found the children to be well-mannered and quite astute. Alabama enjoyed learning that Adrianna had developed an interest in horticulture, to the point where she could name virtually every kind of tree and bush they passed by. Moreover, she was able to predict when each would flower and how they would appear when bedecked with their spring splendor. "How you learn all dat?" Alabama asked with surprise.

"Read about it," Adrianna replied matter-of-factly, looking out the window.

"She reads everything she kin get holt of," Jasmine remarked. "Jes' about read out all de books at de library."

Josiah Freeman dropped Alabama off at Mrs. Stoughton's home just past six in the evening. "We be back tomorrah, 'long 'bout noon," he commented. "You be ready?"

Alabama nodded. "Ah will. Sho' do thank you, brothah," he said humbly.

"Mah pleasure," Freeman replied with a wave. He rumbled off in the old truck. Adrianna leaned out the window and offered a wave and a sweet, sweet smile. Alabama stood looking after the truck for several minutes after they had gone.

He was interrupted by a cheery "Alabama! Come in, come in!" He turned and looked up at the porch. There stood Mrs. Stoughton, smiling down at him. Alabama smiled and pushed open the gate. *Needs a spot'a oil,* he reflected. *Ah catch it in de mo'nin.'* He paused at the bottom of the stairs, but Mrs. Stoughton repeated "Come in!" She walked a few steps to the wide front door. Alabama hesitated, a questioning look on his face. Mrs. Stoughton, noticing his hesitation, said "Alabama Denton, when you worked for me, you used the back door, as is fitting. Now you are my guest and you will come in the front door." Her friendly but firm tone left no doubt. He walked lightly up the stairs and stood before her. "How nice to see you again, Alabama," she offered, holding out her hand in a ladylike gesture. Alabama glanced at it. Instinctively he took her hand and gave it a light shake. "Thank you, Mizz Stoughton," he replied. She smiled and stood to the side of the door. Alabama took the hint and pushed it open for her. She returned the smile and led the way down the front hall to the living room.

"I've asked Mrs. Jefferson, my new cook, to prepare mint juleps," Mrs. Stoughton remarked as she settled easily onto a plush couch. "Please sit there." She indicated a grand chair opposite her. It had a high back on an elaborately carved and polished wooden frame. The upholstery was off-white with a light green lace pattern. Alabama stared at it. He glanced at Mrs. Stoughton. She raised her eyebrows and nodded. "There," she said.

Alabama laid his carpetbag at his feet and settled softly into the chair. It was firm yet comforting. He sat on the edge, not daring to lean back.

Mrs. Stoughton noticed his hesitation and smiled. "Please, Alabama," she said invitingly. "Do make yourself comfortable." She reached over, picked up a small brass bell from a nearby table, and gave it a quick shake. Within seconds, a thin, middle-aged black woman in a housedress and white ruffled apron entered the living room holding a silver tray on which were two tall glasses of opaque liquid. Alabama stood to his feet. The lady served Mrs. Stoughton, who said "Thank you, Mrs. Jefferson," and turned to Alabama. She smiled fleetingly. "Suh?" she asked, offering the other glass to him.

Alabama looked into her eyes, searching for any trace of mockery or other foolishness. All he saw was a gentle and kindly spirit. He took the glass and thanked the lady. She bowed slightly and returned to the kitchen with the tray.

"So," Mrs. Stoughton said with an inviting smile when Alabama sat down. He held the glass in his lap with both hands so as not to commit the awful and unforgivable sin of spilling even one drop. "Tell me about your farm. I've so enjoyed your letters. Tell me everything."

Alabama gulped, glancing hurriedly around the ornate room before turning his gaze to his hostess. In simple sentences, warming to the subject when her encouraging smiles and nods began to relax him, he described the land, the woods and swamp around it, and what he and the boys had built. He mentioned the upcoming plowing season. "You don't push the plow yourself, do you?" Mrs. Stoughton asked with urgency. "Oh, I have no experience in farming, so please forgive my ignorance. But how do you go about it? It must be a very difficult and strenuous task."

"Only for Precious," Alabama replied with a grin. He described his stout and willing mule. Mrs. Stoughton laughed merrily in response.

When he was finished with his recital, Alabama sat silently. Mrs. Stoughton allowed him a few seconds of quiet. Then she asked "What is the problem, Alabama?"

Alabama sighed. He described the visit from the parish tax inspector, the man's remark about land seizure, and his threat to return with company. "Ain't likely to be pleasant folk, Ah don' 'magine," Alabama remarked.

Mrs. Stoughton frowned and stared at him. She was quiet for a moment. Finally she said tightly "The sickness of racism in this nation has poisoned our national soul." She sighed, shook her head sadly, and lapsed into silence again. After a time, she rose and said "Wait here a moment, please." She walked into an adjoining room. Alabama could hear her on the phone.

When she returned a few moments later, she smiled and said "I've asked Mrs. Jefferson to serve us. Will you join me in the dining room, please?" She led the way to the table. Alabama was so numbed by the idea that he was actually expected to join her at that table that he almost missed the fact that she was standing by her chair, waiting. Blushing, he rushed forward and seated her. "Thank you, sir," she said, smiling up. Alabama gulped. He stumbled to the other end of the table and slipped into his chair.

No sooner had he sat down than Mrs. Jefferson returned with the silver tray, this time with two steaming bowls of soup. "Fish chowder," Mrs. Stoughton remarked as the cook set her bowl before her. "One of Mrs. Jefferson's specialties." She smiled up at her cook, who briefly returned the smile as she set Alabama's bowl before him.

As the cook left the room, Mrs. Stoughton said "I always like to thank the Lord for His blessing. Will you join me?" She bowed her head and offered a brief but sincere prayer. When she had finished, she picked up her napkin, slipped the silver ring from it, and spread it out on her lap. "I believe you'll quite enjoy this," she remarked merrily, taking a sip.

Alabama did indeed enjoy the soup, and the roast pork cutlets with asparagus and new potatoes that followed. Mrs. Stoughton offered him a glass of red wine, which he hesitated to accept until she said "It's one of my favorites. You'll quite enjoy it." She nodded to the hallway. Mrs. Jefferson entered with the bottle and two glasses.

As they reached the end of the meal, Mrs. Stoughton said "I've spoken with my attorney. He'll join us tomorrow morning, and I believe he'll be accompanied by a Negro attorney. You'll want to discuss your case with him. You want to be going midday, don't you?"

Overwhelmed, Alabama could only nod.

"I suspect you two can finish your business by then," she replied.

Alabama did indeed sleep in the guest room that night, at Mrs. Stoughton's insistence. It was all he could do to lay down on the bed. He took some satisfaction in the fact that he had taken a sponge bath in the familiar bathroom opposite the kitchen prior to donning a nightshirt and sitting tentatively on the bed.

Alabama was up with the dawn, as usual. He slipped quietly into his clothes and walked down the hall to the back door. He was inspecting the garden, delighted at its upkeep, when Mrs. Jefferson and a black man about her age came down the stairs beside the garage. "Good morning, sir," Mrs. Jefferson said cheerfully. "This is my husband Tyrone."

"Good day to you, sir," Alabama said, stepping forward to offer his hand.

"Tyrone do the gardenin' and maint'nance," Mrs. Jefferson commented. "Ah believe that was yo' job befo'?"

Alabama grinned and glanced at the house. "Ah don' know what to say," he replied sheepishly. "Mizz Stoughton…"

"She a vera, vera kind lady," Mrs. Jefferson remarked as if to save him the difficulty. While she went into the kitchen to prepare breakfast, Alabama and Tyrone walked in a leisurely fashion around the garden, discussing the horticulture and the job. "It ideal fo' me and de missus," Tyrone mentioned. "Ouah chirren done grown an' gone. We be lookin' for somethin' lack dis, and a frien' tell mah wife 'bout it. She come up to apply and mention me. Mrs. Stoughton ax her to fix a meal, an' dat was dat. We been heah 'bout six month, and far as we concern, we ain't leavin'. Dis a vera, vera, fine place. Mizz Stoughton…"

"Ah know," Alabama interrupted. "Dey don' come no finah."

Breakfast consisted of coffee, an egg sardou dish, and bacon. When it was complete, Mrs. Stoughton folded her napkin and said "Why don't we go in the living room. I'm anxious to hear about your lady."

Alabama blushed. "Ah, uh…she…"

"Oh, you don't have to tell me if you don't want to," Mrs. Stoughton said with a merry laugh. "But women are just *so* curious about that sort of thing, don't you know! Come. Join me in the living room."

When they were seated, Mrs. Jefferson brought out the silver tray with fresh coffee along with silver bowls of cream and sugar. When they had each taken a cup and Mrs. Jefferson had walked back to the kitchen, Mrs. Stoughton raised her eyebrows and said "So?"

Alabama looked down at the large Oriental area rug, pursing his lips. He looked up at her and replied "Mizz Stoughton, you goin' think Ah'm jes' crazy. Ah knows it. But Adrianna…wayall, she on'y twelve. Just had her birfday."

Mrs. Stoughton's jaw dropped a half inch in shock. "*Twelve*! My word! Alabama!" She stared at him with wide eyes.

Alabama sighed. "Truf of it is, ma'am, Ah ain't ax her yet. Goin' give her a few year. Den Ah ax her."

Mrs. Stoughton put a hand to her throat, shaking her head and smiling. "My heavens!" she exclaimed. "I never..." She leaned back in her chair. "How did you...I mean, how do you know she's the one?"

"Oh, she de one," Alabama assured her. He told her about meeting the Freeman family and the impact Adrianna had made on him at first sight. "Ah think 'bout her ever' day," he said. "Ah wondah how she doin' at school, and how her brothah treatin' her, and what she learnin', and...Wayall, she on my mind. She de one, fo' sho'."

Mrs. Stoughton smiled hugely. "Alabama Denton, I knew you were special from the day you first walked into my garden," she commented heartily. "Why would I think you would take the conventional route to marriage?" Suddenly she frowned. "But you're...How old are you, if you don't mind my asking?"

"Ah'm twenty-seben. Dey fifteen year between us."

Mrs. Stoughton considered, pursing her lips. "And that won't present a problem?" she asked.

Alabama shook his head. "Not's far as Ah'm concerned," he replied. "Ah'm hopin' she don' see no problem eithah."

There was the sound of shoes on the front porch and a knock on the door. "Oh, there's Jonathan," Mrs. Stoughton said happily. Mrs. Jefferson walked quickly down the hall and opened the door, admitting two gentlemen dressed in business suits. One, as promised, was a Negro.

Mrs. Stoughton and Alabama stood when the men were shown into the living room. "Oh, Jonathan, how good of you to come!" she exclaimed. She hugged the white man briefly and held out her hand to the Negro. "I'm Mrs. Emily Stoughton," she said politely.

The black man gave a slight bow and shook her hand. "Mantor Livingston," he said in a pleasant voice.

"Very pleased to meet you, Mr. Livingston," Mrs. Stoughton replied. "So good of you to come on such short notice. This is my friend Alabama Denton." They shook hands, and Mrs. Stoughton said "Sit, please, Mr. Livingston. Mr. Shelby and I have business to transact. I believe he told you he has been my family's attorney for, oh, I don't know how many years now." She turned to Shelby, who smiled ruefully.

"Too many, I fear," the white man replied with a chuckle.

Mrs. Stoughton smiled gaily. "Mrs. Jefferson will be along with more coffee, gentlemen," she said. "Mr. Shelby, will you accompany me to the drawing room, sir?"

"Delighted," the man replied, following her out of the room.

Alabama looked at the black attorney. He was dressed comfortably but elegantly, and Alabama thought he looked splendid. The man had a soft and easy smile.

"So, Mr. Denton," Livingston remarked. "I understand you're a family friend."

Alabama paused. He looked down at the rug and back up to the lawyer. "Ah don' know wheah de Lawd fin' people lack Mrs. Stoughton," he commented softly.

Livingston chuckled. "He makes them from very different material," he replied. "She is special, no doubt. I do business now and again with Mr. Shelby, and he had commented on her. She's truly one of a kind. And her husband was a true gentleman also, from what I've heard. I never had the pleasure of meeting the man, but I do hope he's in the kingdom of heaven so I can meet him some day."

Alabama looked at him. "Wheah you from, suh?" he asked.

"Philadelphia. I visited a cousin here after graduating from the Pennsylvania State University School of Law and fell in love with the city.

That was six years ago. I've been in private practice here for almost five years, after passing the bar."

Whatevah dat is, Alabama thought.

"But to your issue, Mr. Denton. I…"

"Call me Alabama, suh."

The man smiled. "And Mantor here. Thank you. Now, what seems to be the problem?"

For fifteen minutes, Alabama outlined the history of his ownership of the land and ended with the visit from the tax inspector. Mantor Livingston listened quietly, interjecting a brief question here and there while taking notes. When Alabama was complete, Livingston said "Do you have the title and other paperwork with you?"

Alabama nodded. He reached into his money belt and withdrew the title and the tax receipt he'd been given by the inspector. Livingston examined the title with close attention. "Well, that seems to be in order," he remarked. "It has the official seal, it identifies the land with a legal description and a street address, and it has the proper signatures. Let's look at…oh, my, how sloppy!"

Alabama nodded as he watched Livingston examine the tax receipt. "Yessah. He seem to be in a hurry to write it."

Suddenly Livingston smiled broadly. He leaned back in the chair and held the tax receipt. "Alabama Denton, you just won your case," he remarked. He looked at Alabama with a twinkle in his eye.

"Ah *did?*" Alabama blurted.

"Yes indeed you did," Livingston replied confidently. "My fee is fifty dollars. If you will be so kind as to pay me, I will take care of the rest. You needn't be in New Orleans any longer. It's just procedural from here."

Alabama stared at him, mouth agape. "Suh…Mr. Mantor…how you know…?"

Livingston smiled. "It's all lawyer talk from here," he assured his client. "Truly. Don't worry about a thing. I'll handle everything. Do you have the fee amount with you?"

Alabama reached into his money belt and counted out the bills. "Ah would pay you fifty time that to keep de land," he remarked gratefully.

Livingston smiled as he accepted the bills. "No need, Alabama. A fair fee is a fair fee. Let me give you a receipt. And I'll be sure to write more legibly than the tax inspector did!"

CHAPTER 16

"Court will come to order!" the bailiff sang out, and everyone stood to their feet. "The Honorable Judge Garrett Hanson presiding."

Judge Hanson swept into the courtroom and climbed the three stairs to his massive oak bench. He took his seat, and the courtroom followed suit.

"Docket number 49-04-134," the bailiff cried out, indicating the 134th case to be decided by the court in this month of April, 1949. "Pointe Coupee Parish vs. Alabama Denton." He too took his seat.

An overweight white attorney arose at the plaintiff's table. He was wearing a rumpled brown suit with a red tie secured so short over a white shirt that it only came to the middle of his chest, with the tail hanging four inches below the wide end. "Charles Whitmore fo' the parish, Your Honor," he said with a broad smile.

An impeccably dressed black attorney stood to his feet at the defendant's table. "Mantor Livingston representing Mr. Denton, Your Honor," he said in a quiet voice.

The judge nodded at both men. "Be seated, gentlemen," he commanded. To those assembled in the court, most of whom were waiting for subsequent cases or were taking notes for a newspaper or a law school assignment, he said "Ladies and gentlemen, this is a Summary Court of the state of Louisiana. Under Summary Court rules, cases are presented by representing attorneys before the judge and are decided without benefit of a jury. Both parties have agreed to present in Summary Court. Gentlemen, let's proceed."

Charles Whitmore stood to his feet. "An open-and-shut case, Your Honor," he remarked confidently. "Defendant has violated Parish Code 161.03 by adulterating the borders of his land holding into property owned by Pointe Coupee Parish, specifically the Atchaflaya Swamp. Defendant is therefore guilty of acquiring said acreage illegally and must now surrender it to the parish. Here's a copy of the law, People's Exhibit One." He handed a paper to the bailiff and sat down heavily.

"With respect, Mr. Whitmore," Judge Hanson remarked as the bailiff approached him with the paper, "we'll allow the defendant's attorney to present his case as well before we determine how 'open and shut' this case truly is."

Whitmore nodded obsequiously. "Yes, of course, Your Honor," he replied sheepishly. "No offense intended."

Judge Hanson nodded as he glanced at the exhibit. "Do you have other documents and/or statements to make?" he asked the attorney for the parish.

"No, your honor," Whitmore replied. "Like I said, a clear violation of the law."

Judge Hanson nodded and glanced at the defendant's table. "Mr. Livingston?"

Mantor Livingston rose to his feet. "Your Honor, my colleague used the term 'open and shut.' I believe he inadvertently described this case quite well, though I don't imagine he'll be pleased with the outcome. The fact is that the parish *has* no case. Allow me to present Defendant's Exhibit One, a copy of the original filing that established the boundaries of the land. The property is described in detail. There is no mistaking its boundaries, and you will please notice, sir, that the western border is indeed in the flood plain of the Atchaflaya. Please notice also that that filing is dated July 11, in the year 1876. That's seventy-three years ago, Your Honor, long before the parish law you have before you which is dated 1916. The title predates the law and is therefore grandfathered." He resumed his seat while the judge peered at the title.

After a moment, Judge Hanson looked up. "The title is quite clear, Mr. Whitmore," he remarked. "And it does indeed predate your parish law."

Whitmore stood quickly. "With respect, Your Honor, that may be true, but the defendant adulterated the land by bringing in truckloads of dirt *after* the passage of the law. He may have owned the land legitimately, but he owned flood plain, not adulterated land. He cannot prevent access by the public to those thirty-four acres that would ordinarily be flooded during the season. By adulterating the land, he has in fact claimed it as private land that is subject to parish trespass laws. That is illegal, sir." He sat down.

Judge Hanson looked to Livingston, who stood. "Your Honor, it is true that my client did improve the land. Mr. Whitmore argues that in doing so, he prevented access to that land by the public. But there is nothing in the title to the property which describes it as water, Your Honor. The word 'land' is used exclusively. Land, be it dirt, soil, or horticulture, is not water. My client owns land, and he is entitled to improve it just like any other landowner."

Judge Hanson sat back and gazed at Whitmore.

Whitmore took the hint and rose to his feet. Clearing his throat noisily and thinking aloud, he said "Well, now, uh…well, you know, that *may* be true, Your Honor, *technically*, I mean, as far as it goes. So, okay. Okay. Defendant can alter the land. Okay. But that's only in the past, Your Honor. The law now applies, and he must allow access to the thirty-four acres by ceding that part over to the parish for future public access."

Mantor Livingston stood to his feet. "I'm afraid that's not possible, Your Honor," he remarked quietly.

"Not possible?" Judge Hanson asked.

Livingston shook his head. "No, Your Honor. You see, as demonstrated by Defendant's Exhibit Two, Pointe Coupee Parish is in debt to my client." He handed the receipt to the bailiff, who took it to the judge. Judge Hanson examined it carefully. "What is this?" he asked.

"As you can see if you peer hard enough, Your Honor, it's a receipt from a tax inspector for Pointe Coupee Parish to my client. The handwriting is difficult to decipher, I grant you, but the document is legitimate nevertheless. The receipt describes the legal plat, gives the date and street address, and identifies the plat as fifty acres of land. Not sixteen acres of land and thirty-four acres of water, but fifty acres of *land*. That clearly establishes the fact that the parish recognizes the continual state of the plat as land, land which belongs to my client. Moreover, by virtue of the amount owed to my client as a credit for next year's taxes, the parish recognizes the on-going status of my client's holding as *land*, and as land which belongs to him and is subject to parish taxes. According to established law, such recognition cannot be revoked, now or in the future, for any reason except non-payment of land taxes. And I assure you, Your Honor," he said while looking at Whitmore, "my client does indeed intend to pay his taxes." He sat down primly.

Judge Whitmore took his time examining the document. After a moment, he looked up at Whitmore. "Mr. Whitmore, your tax inspector has behaved unprofessionally with this receipt. I have never seen such sloppy handwriting on an official document. I will have in my possession within thirty days a plan put together by your client, Pointe Coupee Parish, as to how they will re-train this particular individual and all other persons who deal with the public in terms of courtesy and professionalism. Is that clear?"

Whitmore knew his duty. He stood. "Yes, Your Honor," he replied.

"Your Honor?" Livingston said, standing politely.

"Yes, Mr. Livingston?"

"Your Honor, my client's holding is accessible by land only by way of a lane that leads from Highway 77. The land surrounding the lane and my client's holding is owned by an estate located here in New Orleans. It is conceivable that said estate might move at some time in the future to deny access to my client's holding by closing off the lane, since technically the access lane exists on the estate. Therefore I move to amend the title to allow unfettered access to my client's land through said lane, which is to be maintained in good condition by the estate."

The judge chewed his lip. "Mr. Whitmore, do you have any objections?"

In fact, Whitmore *did* have objections, but only in his own mind. As a fallback strategy in the unlikely event that the parish lost this case, he knew the Parish Administrator was planning to talk with the owners of the estate to indeed close off the lane, perhaps offering them an under-the-table tax incentive to do so. *Looks like this uppity nigger from the north preempted that strategy,* he noted with irritation. He shook his head, sensing the inevitable. "No, Your Honor."

Judge Hanson nodded. "The record will show that it is the order of this court to amend the title according to the motion," he stated. "Furthermore, I find this case unassailable for the defendant and therefore rule in his favor. The land in question is indeed the property of Mr. Alabama Denton and not the parish. Case..." He raised the gavel as if to strike it on its wooden pad.

"Your Honor!" Livingston sang out loudly.

Judge Hanson paused and laid down the gavel. Somewhat annoyed, he said "Yes, Mr. Livingston?"

Mantor Livingston, still on his feet, said "Begging your pardon, Your Honor, but there is one more matter in this case to be considered by the court.

Judge Hanson gazed at him. "And that would be?"

"Sir, on the day this receipt was delivered, this tax inspector threatened to return to my client's estate and bring others. The clear implication was that it would not be a social visit. Given the proclivity of white racists to wreak havoc on the person and property of black persons, as has often been the lamentable history of this state, my client is in fear for his life and property. We request a ruling by this court that said remark is acknowledged for the public record."

Judge Hanson sat back in his chair. When he looked at Whitmore, he was visibly trembling. His breathing was steady and controlled, and his visage was dark. "Mr. Whitmore," he said in a quiet voice.

Whitmore stood. "Yes, Your Honor?"

"Mr. Whitmore, listen carefully to me," Judge Hanson said succinctly.

Whitmore's mouth fell agape. He swallowed hard. "Yes, Your Honor?"

"Mr. Whitmore, you are to deliver a message to your client, Pointe Coupee Parish, and its administrators. Make *certain* they hear both the words and the seriousness of this order. If this court ever hears of the parish committing an act of racial prejudice against Mr. Denton or any other person of color within its borders, under any circumstances, at any time, and in *any* fashion, I will have the parish administrators arrested, marched off to jail, and charged with every law that applies, with the intent of imprisoning said individuals for the maximum time allowed. Is that *perfectly* clear, Mr. Whitmore?"

Whitmore nodded. *I will track down that miserable tax lackey and put my hands around his throat,* Whitmore thought vehemently. *I will squeeze it until his eyes pop out. I will hang him from his privates. I will kill his dog.* "Yes, Your Honor," he replied. "Very clear."

Judge Hanson nodded. He picked up the gavel and banged it down hard. "This court finds in favor of the defendant. Case dismissed."

CHAPTER 17

Upon learning of the verdict and the other legal rulings in the case via a letter from Mantor Livingston, Alabama sat down at his desk and wrote two letters. The first, to Livingston, said

Mr. Livingston, I am very happy. You are a fine man. Can you talk to black children so they will be like you. Someday please come to my land so I can give you eggs, vegtables, corn, and fried chicken. Thank you, Alabama Denton.

The second letter, to Mrs. Stoughton, said

Dear Mrs. Stoughton, thank you for helping me to know Mantor Livingston he was so helpful I have no more worries about my land. Thank you also for your friendship to me it is not expected in fact is it amazing you are a special lady. I don't know how the Lord works but I hope He is very kind to you. Respect, Alabama Denton.

It was with a happy heart that Alabama plowed forty acres that spring. He sang whatever songs he knew as he kept his eyes on the horizon and steered extraordinarily straight furrows. Even Precious seemed to sense her master's happiness and whinnied on occasion while laboring. Perhaps it was merely an objection to Alabama's singing that prompted the mule's outbursts, but Alabama always greeted it with laughter and a fond word for his beloved animal.

At breakfast with the Freemans in the fall of that year, Alabama suggested the family might visit him the following Saturday afternoon to see the mature crops and stay for dinner. "Ah got some pigs Ah been raisin,' he told them. "One 'a them goin' become ham an' bacon dis weekend. Ah cain't eat a whole pig by myself, so you have to be there." Josiah laughed and made eye contact with Jasmine, who smiled and nodded agreement. "Goin' invite Rufus and Lonnie too," Alabama said. "Kin you give 'em a ride?"

"No problem," Josiah replied. "Dem boys used to ridin' in de back of de truck. We have 'em wif' us."

Alabama stopped by the young men's residence and posed the invitation to them. Rufus and Lonnie, who had opted to hire themselves out as itinerant farm workers on a year-round basis rather than move away from the family, were thrilled to accept the invitation.

Alabama noted with both embarrassment and joy at the party that Adrianna had begun to develop a young woman's shape and height. *An' das de way it should be,* he mused, recalling girls of her age who had become young mothers in Georgia. In his heart, he wanted to drop to his knees before her and beg her to be his wife right then and there, but he knew that would be looked upon as highly inappropriate by both the girl and her family. *Jes' wait,* he told his longing heart.

He continued to admonish himself thus every day, as he witnessed the metamorphosis of Adrianna from a lean tomboy to a beautifully curved, almost perfect young woman over the next four years. Breakfast with the Freemans on Sundays was almost agony. In an effort to keep from staring at Adrianna, he made sure to confine his gaze strictly to Josiah and Jasmine, only looking to Jeremiah and Adrianna when they spoke. He loved the seconds when her musical voice filled the air, as he could indulge his desire to drink in every detail of her face and float away in the magic of her mellifluous tones. On occasion he had to snap back to attention when she had finished talking, especially when the comment involved him. He worried that one of the family would pick up on his aching for her.

In the winter of 1953, when Adrianna had just turned sixteen, Alabama drove the wagon into Fordoche to visit a black tailor of whom he had heard. He commissioned the creation of a dark blue velvet suit and two white shirts with cuffs made for cufflinks. The tailor suggested a medium gray tie, elegantly striped with light and dark shades, and another that was satin and shiny and pearl in color. Down the street, at a reputable jeweler the tailor recommended, he purchased a set of pure gold cufflinks and a half-carat diamond ring. The whole package set him back nearly half of what he earned from a summer's harvest, but he did not begrudge a penny of it.

The following Sunday, he arose early and stood naked by the well, sponging his body thoroughly in the cool air. He washed his hair with a special shampoo he had purchased in Fordoche and brushed his teeth carefully with a new toothbrush, disdaining the one he normally used twice a day as inadequate for the occasion. When he was clean and dry, he donned his new suit, adjusted the gray tie in a mirror the way he had been taught by the tailor, and put on new black leather shoes. They felt strange on his feet, not being broken in, but he had elected to keep them pristine for the occasion. As carefully as possible, he hitched Precious to the wagon and set off for Morganza. On his way, as the sun rose on his right, he prayed *Lawd Jesus, dis' the biggest day of mah life. Ah in yo' hands today, Lawd. Please be kind to dis man.*

When he arrived at the Freeman store and residence, by sheer coincidence it was Adrianna who answered his knock. Alabama, expecting Josiah or Jasmine, almost fell over at the sight of her. She was clothed in a white cotton dress with lace down the center and at the sleeves, and her long shiny black hair had been somewhat straightened and hung down her back with a white ribbon tying it together. Her face was without blemish and her teeth shone. "Mo'nin', Mr. Alabama," she said merrily. "How you today? My, don' you look handsome!" She stepped aside to allow him to enter.

Alabama couldn't get his legs to work. Nor could he find his voice. When he had stood in place for several seconds, staring at Adrianna and she at him, she grinned and said "Wayall? You goin' come in and enjoy some'a Mama's cookin'?"

Thankfully, he was able to command his legs, and they walked him past her as she held the door open and smiled. Having reached her full height, she was only three inches shorter than his five foot eight, and in her short heels she was almost eye level with him. There was a marvelous twinkle in her eyes as he passed her. *Do she know?* he asked himself almost in a panic.

All of the family remarked jovially on his finery. Josiah asked him if he was going to preach today. Alabama somehow found the strength to laugh it off, though his stomach was churning. At breakfast, though the meal was the usual magnificent banquet that Jasmine normally prepared for their Sunday mornings together, he could eat very little and merely pushed the food around on his plate. He avoided eye contact with Adrianna whenever possible.

When the meal was over and the two children asked to be excused, Alabama stood to his feet. "Josiah, Ah wondah if'n Ah might be allowed to speak wif' you," he said quietly.

Everyone stopped. There was no precedent for such a formal request in such circumstances. Jasmine recovered quickly and nodded to the two children as she rose and left the room.

When they were alone, Josiah sat, waiting. He took a sip from his coffee mug and gazed at his friend over the rim.

"Josiah Freeman," Alabama said in the way he had rehearsed, "Ah wan' yo' permission to marry yo' daughter." He sat frozen, waiting for the scowl and rejection.

Instead, Josiah smiled. "Ah know," he replied softly.

Alabama stared at him. "You *do*?"

"Yes," Josiah replied. "Ah know it fo' some time. You been careful, Alabama, but you ain't fool Jasmine. She tol' me 'bout two yeah ago what to watch fo' when you 'round. She raht, too. You been lovin' Adrianna fo' many yeah."

Alabama sighed deeply. "Since de day Ah set eyes on her," he breathed.

Josiah nodded. "Jasmine an' me talk 'bout it. You consider'ble older den Adrianna."

Alabama nodded. "Fifteen year. Ah thirty-one. But Ah strong, Josiah. An' Ah healthy."

"Dat you are," Josiah agreed. "You a hard-workin' man, and it show on you." He sat back in his chair. "Jasmine an' Ah think it a good idea. You got land, you get yo' legal trouble off you back, you a good church-goin' man, you keep yo'sef clean in body and mind…" He nodded. "Yessah, you a good catch. We goin' recommend she take you."

Alabama sagged in his chair, letting out a long stream of breath. He closed his eyes and moved his lips as if in prayer. After a moment, Josiah said "Should we bring her in?" Alabama nodded.

Josiah rose and walked to the door. "Jasmine, would you please fetch Adrianna an' de two of you come in?" he asked. He winked at his wife, who returned a quick smile.

In a moment, the two women returned. Both men stood to their feet. Jasmine closed the door behind them. Adrianna stood, clearly mystified. Alabama walked unsteadily to her, pulled the ring from his pocket, and dropped to a knee. "Adrianna Freeman, Ah love you wif' all my heart," he said. "Will you marry me?"

Adrianna stared at him. She shot a glance at her father, and then at her mother. Suddenly she burst into laughter, unable to hold it back. Quickly, she covered her mouth with her hand, but the damage was done. "Adrianna!" her mother exclaimed in shock. Josiah merely stared, his mouth hanging low and his eyes wide.

Adrianna took a step back and held out a restraining hand to Alabama. She removed her other hand from her mouth and said "Mr. Alabama, Ah goin' to New Orleans next year, when Ah graduate. Ah goin' to school. Goin' *be* somebody! Ah ain't goin' be no farmer's wife."

"You *what?!*" Josiah shouted. Quickly lowering his voice, he exclaimed "Whachoo talkin' 'bout, girl? Whas' dis foolishness?"

"It's *true*, Papa!" Adrianna replied excitedly. "Dey tell me in school dat Tulane University open up a new school fo' promisin' black folk. Ah kin qualify wif' my grades. Dey say Ah kin get a scholarship and not have to pay nothin'!" Her eyes lit up with unsuppressed excitement.

"Who say you kin go to New Orleans?" Jasmine demanded. "Wheah you get dese ideas?"

Adrianna slammed her hands on her hips. "Ah *smaht*, Mama!" she replied almost indignantly. "Mah grades be at de top of de class! You cain't keep me heah! De day Ah graduate, Ah goin' to New Orleans. Das' *dat*, Mama!"

The argument raged on for some minutes. Lost in the drama was Alabama, who silently rose to his feet and trudged downstairs to the barn. He hitched Precious to the wagon, interrupting her as she munched on oats, and proceeded slowly down the road to his farm.

CHAPTER 18

The next day, Alabama was sitting on his porch at the noon hour when Josiah Freeman turned down the lane and rumbled onto the farm. When Alabama saw the truck approaching, he arose and walked into the cabin. Josiah rolled to a stop and walked to the front door. He knocked and said "Alabama! Ah know you theah! Ah saw you. Now come on out heah an' say hello."

Silence met his demand.

Josiah knocked again. "Alabama! Ah'm comin' in!" He turned the knob and swung the door open. There sat his friend at the log table used for meals, staring at him. Josiah paused. After a few seconds, he walked softly to the table and pulled out the second chair. Saying nothing, he looked around the cabin. It was in a state of relative disarray, which was highly unusual for the normally tidy owner and occupant. He turned again to Alabama. "You okay, brothah?" he asked quietly.

Alabama said nothing. He merely stared at the wall behind his visitor.

Josiah sighed deeply. He hung his head and stared down at the smooth planks that formed the tabletop. A long moment passed. Finally he raised his head and said "She nevah say nothin' lack dat befo', Alabama. *Nevah*! Not 'til yesterday. Jasmine an' Ah caught by surprise."

Alabama made no reply, nor did he shift his eyes.

Josiah swung around so that he was side on to Alabama and draped his arm over the back of the chair. "Yo' animals gettin' fed?" he asked.

There was no reply.

After nearly a minute, Josiah sighed and said "Wayall, Ah bes' fed 'em."

"Dey been fed," Alabama said in a hollow voice.

Josiah peered at him. Alabama returned the stare, his expression vacant.

Josiah nodded. "An' you? You been fed?"

"Ain't hungry."

"Wayall, Ah am!" Josiah remarked. He rose and walked to the henhouse, where he collected six eggs. He returned to the house and built a fire in the Franklin stove with the round belly for heating and the flat plate on top for cooking. When the fire was steady, he located an iron skillet and placed it on the flat plate. "Wheah you keep yo' salt an' brayud an' buttah an' lard?" he asked, rummaging around the kitchen. As no answer was forthcoming, he located the items himself. A dab of lard went into the frying pan and began to sizzle. Josiah cracked the six eggs into the pan and stirred them up with a fork. He laid four pieces of bread on the flat plate next to the pan and stood monitoring them, humming softly to himself. When the eggs and toast were done, he buttered the toast and served the eggs onto two plates. He placed one in front of Alabama and one opposite him. The last step was to locate two forks and sit down opposite his friend.

"Grace?" Josiah offered. He bowed his head and said "Heavenly Fathah…"

"Don't bothah," Alabama uttered in a guttural voice.

Josiah looked up sharply. "*Wha'* you say?"

"Dey ain't no God," Alabama replied hoarsely. "Leastwise if dey is, He a mean, no-care God. Ah got no use fo' him."

Josiah shook his head angrily. "Well, Ah'm prayin'!" he spat. He proceeded to do just that, thanking the Lord for the food and asking for blessings on his family and for Alabama. When he was through, he dug into the food, chewed it noisily, and pronounced it just right. "Yo' eggs gettin' cold," he admonished.

Alabama pushed the plate of food to the center of the table. "You eat it," he said. "Ah tol' you Ah ain't hungry."

Josiah paused, a forkful of food in the air, and stared at Alabama. He lowered the food to the plate and laid both his forearms on the table beside his plate. For a long moment, he stared at Alabama. "Now lookee here," he began. "You think dis de end of de worl'. You think you goin' jes' sit theah an' die. Leastwise you'd lack to. Ain't dat so?"

For the first time, Alabama truly looked at him. He nodded, his lips pursed. His eyes were moist.

Josiah sighed. "You got reason to be down, brothah, *das'* fo' sho'!" he remarked. He resumed eating, his eyes on his friend. "You had yo'sef a bittah blow. Jes' lack Jasmine an' me, you was surprised by wha' she said. On'y difference is you took it personal."

Alabama nodded.

"She din' mean it personal, Alabama," Josiah said quietly. "It ain't 'bout you a'tall. It jes' ain't her plan to marry a farmer."

Alabama merely stared at him.

Josiah took another bite and chewed it contemplatively. He looked down at his plate and back to Alabama. "Nothah two bites, Ah be done," he commented. "Brayud too. So, you goin' die on me? You goin' jes' sit in dat chair 'til you fall outa it an' lie on de flo' and die? 'Cause if'n dat de case, Ah want yo' eggs fo' dey get cold." He stared hard at Alabama.

Alabama sighed and looked down at the plate. He drew it toward himself and picked up a small forkful. Chewing mechanically, he stared at Josiah.

Josiah leaned back and patted his stomach. "Ah allus lack a good cuppa coffee wif a fine meal," he commented with a broad grin. "Wheah yo'...nevah mind. Ah find it." He rose, located the coffee pot, and searched through a few aluminum canisters until he found a bag of ground coffee. "Be raht back," he said cheerily. When he returned from the well with a pot full of cold water, the plate of food before Alabama was half consumed and one piece of toast was gone. He smiled and nodded. "Coffee comin' up soon!" he sang out.

A quarter-hour later, the two men sat on the porch with fresh cups of sugared coffee. Josiah wisely said nothing. It seemed to him to be nearly an hour until Alabama finally spoke, though he knew it was less because the dregs of his coffee were still lukewarm. "Ah don' know if'n Ah'm goin' stay heah," Alabama said softly.

Josiah nodded, staring out at the ground ripe for planting. "You got fambly?" he asked after a time.

Alabama shook his head.

"Den wheah you go?"

Alabama shrugged. "Don' know. Anywheah. Maybe work on de ships."

"An' dis farm?"

Alabama leaned back in the chair and shut his eyes. He made no reply.

Josiah let it ride. After a few moments, he said "One thang Ah learnt. When a big decision got to be made, nevah act in haste. Turn out wrong *evah* time if'n you do. Wait on it. See what happen. When you jes' got to decide, den decide." He rose and took Alabama's cup out of his inert hand, tossing the dregs into the dirt at the base of the stairs. "Ah be back tomorrah," he said simply. He walked into the kitchen, placed the two cups on the counter, and walked out to his truck.

The next day, again around midday, Josiah climbed down from his truck and walked up to the house. Alabama again sat on the porch, staring out at the land. Josiah wrinkled his nose and said "You might wanna think 'bout washin', brothah." With that greeting, he walked into the house. As he expected, the previous day's dishes remained unwashed. Josiah started a fire in the stove, located a large pot, and took it out to the well. When he had two full buckets of water in the pot, he hauled it back into the house and placed it on the stove. In the next half-hour, he washed every dirty dish in the house and tidied up clothing and other items, so that the house again appeared in the neat fashion that Alabama had always preferred. Only then did he pour two cups of fresh sugared coffee and take them out to the porch. As he handed one to Alabama and sat down in the chair beside him, he said "J'eat yet today?"

Alabama nodded. "Some ol' dried apples."

"An' de animals?"

"Dey fed."

Josiah nodded. He sighed deeply and blew out a long breath. "Nuthin' lack a good cuppa coffee, hey brothah?" he remarked. As he expected, Alabama made no reply. But he did take a sip of coffee and sat back, holding the cup in his hands.

It was some time before Josiah said "Ah talk wif' Rufus an' Lonnie. Dey goin' plant dis yeah, if'n dat all raht wif' you. Ah jes' say you feelin' poorly and want dey help. Dat okay?" He looked at his friend.

Alabama stared at him. After a few seconds, he nodded. "Das' a good idea," he replied softly.

Josiah nodded. "Corn?"

Alabama nodded. For the first time in two days, his eyes took on a bit of a shine. "Corn in de twenty by de swamp," he replied. "Beans in de nex' ten. Okra in five, pumpkin in five."

Josiah smiled to himself, hiding it from Alabama. He rose and said "Ah'll tell 'em. See you tomorrah wif' de boys."

Alabama watched him go.

CHAPTER 19

The next time Alabama needed supplies, he hitched Precious to the wagon and headed south to Fordoche. There he shopped at a general store owned by a white man who allowed blacks to shop in his store, though it was obvious to Alabama that he was tolerated and not welcomed. He bought more than he normally would so as not to have to make the trip more often than necessary. Having put up the mule and the tarp-covered wagon at a blacksmith for the night, he went into two bars frequented by black folks. In neither was he approached in a friendly way other than to give his order to the bartender. He sipped his beer and observed. After a short stay in each facility, he returned to the blacksmith shop and slept in the back of his wagon.

Josiah began to stop by every other day, gradually satisfying himself that Alabama was eating, taking care of himself, and feeding his livestock. For two weeks this continued. Often they would sit on the porch and watch Rufus and Lonnie work at seeding the farm. When Josiah was satisfied that Alabama had achieved a semblance of normality, though he was far from his usual self, he limited his visits to once a week.

It was on one of these visits, some seven weeks after the breakfast disaster and now well into the growing season, that Josiah came down to see the new corn, bean, okra, and pumpkin shoots. "You know, Ah nevah get tired of seein' de Lawd's hand in de spring," he remarked happily. Alabama nodded, offering no comment.

"You ain't been back fo' several weeks now," Josiah commented quietly. "Seben, Ah count. Jasmine miss you at Sunday breakfast. She ax me if her cookin' de reason." He gazed at his friend.

Alabama grunted with sour laughter. "She know bettah," he replied in a low voice.

"Das' wha' Ah done tol' her," Josiah affirmed. "You allus seemed to lack her cookin'." After a few seconds, he added "Folks at church been axin' 'bout you."

Alabama made no reply.

Josiah sighed. "Wayall, Ah tell 'em you okay. Dey prayin' fo' you, brothah." He looked expectantly at Alabama. "Hey?"

Alabama looked at him.

"Seems you be needin' supplies raht soon now."

Alabama shook his head. "Ah fine fo' a while."

Josiah frowned. "Alabama, jes' tell me de day you be comin' up to shop. Ah make sho' Adrianna ain't 'round. Don' hurt mah family dis way."

Alabama shot him a puzzled look. For a few seconds, the thought seemed to confuse him, and his eyes welled up. At length, he shook his head and sighed, staring at the floorboards of the porch. "Ah nevah thought 'bout yo' family," he commented softly. "'Bout you. 'Bout Jasmine. Even 'bout Jeremiah, though he nevah seem to care much 'bout me one way or 'thothah. Mayhaps he do. Ah jes' don' know." He looked at Josiah. "Ah'm grateful fo' yo' help, Josiah," he said plaintively. "You a good, good frien'. But try as Ah might, Ah cain't separate you from yo' daughter. Ah see you, Ah see her. An' dat..." Suddenly he stopped and a look of panic came over his face. He leapt up and ran into the house. Josiah could hear him sobbing wretchedly inside. Slowly, he rose to his feet, descended the stairs, and drove off.

When the seeding was over and whatever needed doing around the farm had been accomplished, Alabama dismissed Rufus and Lonnie, paying them in cash. "Y'all come back in a month," he said. "Be ready to spend a few days out heah. Be needin' y'all fo' weedin'."

Rufus smiled. "We happy to help, Alabama. An' we grateful fo' de work. How you feelin' now?"

Alabama gazed at him. *How much you know?* he wondered. *Wha' folks sayin' 'bout me? Reckon dey laughin' dey ass off.* He replied "Ah 'preciate yo' help, fellas. See you in a month. By de way, tell Josiah Ah be up nex' Saddy." The boys gave him a mock salute and a smile, mounted their bicycles, and set off on the twenty-mile trip to Morganza.

On Saturday, after he had completed his chores, Alabama hitched Precious to the wagon and set off north. He paused when he reached the outskirts of Morganza, thinking. On a whim, he proceeded to Rufus and Lonnie's house and dismounted. "Hello de house!" he hollered, and the boys' mother came out the front door, wiping her hands on her apron. "Why, Alabama Denton!" she exclaimed. "Lawd, we been prayin' fo' you! How you doin'?"

"Jes fine, Missus," he replied quietly. "Thank y'all fo' thinkin' 'a me. Rufus be home?"

"Ah'll fetch him," the woman said. A moment later, Rufus came out the door. "Mr. Alabama. You be needin' us, suh?"

Alabama shook his head. "Not fo' a couple weeks, lack we agreed," he replied. "But Ah need you to do me a favor."

"Whatevah you need, fo' sho'," Rufus replied.

Alabama looked north. "Rufus, kin you go up to Josiah sto' and tell him Ah be comin' in a spell?"

Rufus looked confused. "Cain't you jes'…" A look of understanding came over him and he quickly added "Yessah, Ah go raht away." He hollered into the house that he would be gone for a bit and jumped on his bike.

Alabama waited an hour under a tree, shading Precious and himself from the gathering sun. When he judged the time was right, he shook the reins and moved the mule ahead at a steady walk. When he pulled up in front of the Freeman General Store, Josiah and Jasmine both came out to greet him. Jasmine gave him a big hug, and Josiah shook his hand warmly. They welcomed him into the store, Jasmine leading while Josiah put away the mule. Inside, they had a nice meal prepared, much to Alabama's surprise. "You jes' come upstairs and eat," Jasmine insisted. She looked him over and tch-tched. "You losin' weight, Alabama," she admonished. "Man gotta eat if'n he be workin'. Now you come raht on up and sitchersef' down." She led the way, forestalling any argument.

The meal was indeed the best and most complete Alabama had enjoyed in nearly two months. When it was over, he leaned back in the chair and sighed. "Miss Jasmine, das' the finest meal Ah evah had. Leastwise in a while." He patted his spare belly as Josiah and Jasmine laughed in appreciation.

In the next half hour, as he and Josiah talked farming, Alabama completed his purchases and loaded up the wagon. He said goodbye to Josiah, asked him to be ready to receive him about noon on the Saturday two weeks hence, and set off for his farm. Josiah and Jasmine, standing arm in arm on the porch of the store, watched him go. Jasmine began to weep, and her husband held her close. "You know Ah love mah daughter," she said softly. "She a fine, fine girl. But she 'bout de dumbest woman Ah evah known!"

CHAPTER 20

Adrianna graduated from high school the following June, in 1954. Alabama, having been to New Orleans to visit Mrs. Stoughton and Matilda and her new husband, presented Adrianna with a pearl necklace he had purchased from the jeweler Mrs. Stoughton recommended. Adrianna was delighted with the gift. Alabama was satisfied that her gratitude was more for his gesture than for the necklace itself, though she wore it with delight to show to her friends.

For the next three years, Alabama worked his farm mechanically. In the spring he plowed and sowed, in the summer he weeded and watched, in the fall he harvested and sold, and in the winter he made repairs and passed the time. The sun rose, the sun set, and Alabama watched it happen with little interest.

In all seasons, he fished the Atchaflaya River and Swamp. His preferred catch was a bluegill, as they are a good size for one person at three to five pounds when mature. Occasionally he caught a largemouth bass, some weighing up to twenty pounds. He enjoyed the experience of wrestling such a fish to shore and quite appreciated the taste of this fish. Moreover, with a largemouth there was always plenty to give to the hogs after he removed the spine. About twice a year, he caught and landed a channel catfish. These monsters, some weighing fifty pounds or more, usually snapped his line. When he did haul one in, he smoked and salted the meat, keeping it in an underground storehouse that he had lined with wood planks and steel sheets. The pigs enjoyed the skin and organs.

Josiah and Jasmine Freeman continued to welcome Alabama to their home, providing meals whenever he would consent to dine with them. Once again, he began to buy all his supplies from the Freeman General Store, avoiding Thanksgiving, Christmas, and mid-spring when Adrianna might be home from New Orleans. He politely refused all invitations to share breakfast on Sundays or return to church.

At meals with the Freemans, he always asked about Jeremiah and Adrianna. Jeremiah had become a handyman apprentice in Morganza and was always busy. "He learnin' all kinda thang," Josiah reported proudly. "He kin work wif' wood, he kin plumb, he can run 'lectric wahr, he kin do roof, all kinda thang." The plan was for Jeremiah to set himself up in business as a handyman in a year or two, competing with his present employer for business. "Dey plenty 'a room fo' two, mayhaps even mo', in dis town," Josiah commented. "Morganza's growin'. Lotsa folk need buildin'. Jeremiah get some work on his own, save some, build his own home heah soon. Ever'thang lookin' good fo' dat boy."

"He ain't a boy no mo'," Jasmine interjected. "He be twenty-one in July."

Josiah nodded. "Das' raht. Las' week he tol' me he plannin' to vote dis heah Novembah."

"Vote?" Alabama asked. "Since when a Negro get to vote?"

Josiah shook his head. "Don' ax me," he replied. "Ah ain't nevah voted. Nevah tried. Crackuh allus have his rules 'bout registration an' such. Make a Negro take a test, Ah heah tell. Test got quessions lack 'Wha' de capital of Montana?' and 'What state be the twenty-fifth in de nation?'" He frowned and shook his head. "Who give a pig's ass wha' de capital of Montana? An' why a black man got to answer such a quession jes' to vote lack any othah 'Merican?"

"Bet *crackuh* don't have to take no test!" Alabama remarked sardonically.

"Dat be raht!" Josiah affirmed. "But one day dat goin' change. Young black folk lack Jeremiah, dey restless. Dey say dey ain't goin' put up wif' such foolishness. Dey say dey goin' march togethuh down to de votin' place and *demand* to vote. Jes' demand." He shook his head and sighed. "Ah worry 'bout dat boy. Crackuh ain't goin' jes' give dis country to black folk. Mos' of 'em still think we jumped-up slaves. Dey ain't goin' jes' 'low us to vote, pretty as you please, jes' 'cause we say so." He leaned forward, arms on the table. "Ah bet dey be some crackuhs in sheets at dat votin' place," he said ominously.

Alabama nodded. "Black folk could get hurt."

Jasmine shook her head. "Lawd A'mighty, don' let dat happen!" she moaned. "Lawd, don' let dey be no violence. Hep us, Jesus!"

Josiah said "Ah heard de Supreme Court 'a de entire United States done spoke on dis mattah. Two year back, Ah b'lieve. 1954. Ah hear tell it be call 'Brown vs. Board of Education.' De Supreme Court say de states have to integrate schools."

Alabama stared at him, aghast. "*Have* to? Dey *have* to? Wha' dat mean?"

"'Parently dey say 'separate but equal' ain't good 'nough. Supreme Court say blacks and whites gotta go to de same school. Cain't have no schools jes' fo' whites and some jes' fo' black."

Alabama mulled it over. Jasmine sat quietly. After a moment, Alabama shook his head. "Whooeee!" he exclaimed. "Oh, brothah! Dat goin' be no end 'a trouble! Lack you say, Josiah, crackuh ain't jes' goin' lay down an' die." A look of consternation came over his face. "Wha' 'bout Adrianna school? She in a all-black college, ain't she?"

Josiah nodded. "Part 'a Tulane University," he replied. "All black 'til now. Lawd know wha' it goin' be lack wif dis Supreme Court thang."

"How she doin'?" Alabama asked in a quiet voice.

Josiah shot a look at Jasmine. Neither replied.

"Wha's goin' on?" Alabama demanded.

Josiah sighed. He glanced at Jasmine, who rose and began to clear dishes from the table. When she had left the room, Josiah said "Adrianna, she…" His voice trailed off.

"Wha'? Tell me!"

Josiah looked off to the side, breathing out slowly. "We don' rahtly know," he replied. "She call heah two day ago, an' she cryin'. Jasmine cain't get nothin' out her dat make sense. Somethin' 'bout..." He looked at Alabama and then down at the table. "Well, somethin' 'bout a man," he said in quiet misery.

Alabama leaned back and closed his eyes. A long moment passed, Josiah saying nothing further.

At length, Alabama sat up and rested his forearms on the table. "You goin' down theah?"

Josiah shook his head. "She say don' come. She say she got tests, she gotta finish up. She say she come home in June."

Alabama considered. "Das two month! *Two month!* If'n she in trouble, ain't it raht to go *now*? See to her?"

Josiah nodded. "Das' wha' Jasmine say. She ready to go two day ago, soon's she hang up de phone. But Adrianna say no, stay heah, she be okay." He shook his head and frowned. "Ah don' think so," he lamented.

Alabama sat back again. His mind was churning, and his heart literally ached. *A man*, he thought. *A man. Adrianna been wif' a man.* He stared at the wall ahead, not seeing or hearing anything around him. His attention was captured by Josiah's voice. "...end of de term," Josiah said. "In June. Middle 'a June. Ah don' think Ah kin wait dat long."

Alabama stood up. "Ah got to go."

Josiah stood as well. "Ah hep you load up," he said, moving toward the stairs.

Alabama shook his head. "No supplies dis time," he said quickly. "Ah pick 'em up nex' week. Tell Jasmine thanks fo' de lunch." He virtually ran to the stairs and down to the yard, where he pulled Precious from her hay luncheon and slammed her into the traces on the wagon. Within minutes, he was on his way south toward his farm. Once out of the black section and to the country, he stopped, jumped down, and ran to the ditch. He fell to his knees and puked up every ounce of Jasmine's fine meal and then some.

CHAPTER 21

Eight days later, Josiah pulled into the farm and rolled to a stop. He hailed Alabama from the far edge of his farm, where he was inspecting new corn shoots. Alabama heard him, waved, and walked down the row. When he was close, he said "How do, Josiah?"

Josiah shook his head.

Alabama stopped, a worried look on his face. "It Adrianna," Josiah said simply.

Alabama felt his knees go weak and his head grow light. Disdaining pretense, he leaned over and held his knees in an attempt to get blood into his brain. In a moment, he straightened up and stood, his arms hanging limply by his side. "Wha'?" he asked hoarsely.

"She call agin. Two day ago. Sound bad. We go down dis time an' get her. She back at de house."

Alabama stared at him. "Is she…wha'…?"

Josiah sighed deeply. "Mind if'n Ah get some water?" he asked. Alabama nodded. He followed Josiah to the well. When the bucket had been raised and each man had taken a good drink of the cool, clear water, Josiah leaned on the well and said "She had a 'breakdown,' dey call it. She distracted, talkin' crazy, don' make no sense. She cry all de time. Jasmine get her home in bed and she tendin' to Adrianna." He shook his head. "Don' know wha' to make of it, tell you de truth."

Alabama leaned his backside against the well, his arms crossed on his chest. He stared out at the furrows of corn and beans. "Ah nevah hear tell 'a dis," he admitted. He looked at Josiah. "She sick? Ah mean, she…?" He shook his head in frustration. "Wha' happen to make her dis way?"

Josiah shook his head once quickly. "She don' say. She ain't tell us nothin.' Jasmine, she say give de girl a couple days, she be fine. Me, Ah don' know." He spat on the ground and shook his head in frustrated dismay.

Several minutes passed. Alabama said "Whachoo want me to do?"

Josiah breathed in and out quickly, as if he'd temporarily forgotten how. "Give her a few days, Ah guess, lack Jasmine say. Den Ah see wha' Adrianna say. Ah let you know, okay?" His face, ordinarily solid and peaceful, began to wrinkle. Suddenly he burst into tears. "*Mah baby girl!*" he sobbed. "She look so *pain*ful, lack de hurt deep inside! Ah don' know wha' to *do*!"

Alabama took his friend, who was easily four inches taller, onto his chest and held him as the man cried quiet tears and shook. Many minutes passed. Eventually, Josiah took a deep breath and eased back. He looked at Alabama through red and swollen eyes. "Wayall, Ah let you know," he said.

Alabama nodded. Josiah walked unsteadily to his truck and drove back down the lane.

CHAPTER 22

A full two weeks later, Alabama could stand the suspense no longer. He hitched Precious to the wagon and trotted her to the Freeman General Store. Once there, he mounted the three steps to the front porch and pushed open the door. Josiah looked up from the counter. His face fell. "Alabama!" he exclaimed. "Ah *so* sorry, brothah! Ever' day Ah been meanin' to come see you, but ever' day somethin' come up." He shook his head in remorse.

"How she be?" Alabama demanded.

Josiah smiled. "Much bettah. She walkin' 'round, she eatin' some, she talkin' sense. Took mos' ten day, but she bettah now." He shook his head, his eyes wide. "Whooo!" he exclaimed. "It a *long* ten day, das' fo' sho'!"

Alabama sighed. He looked around the store, seeing nothing but the sweet face of Adrianna. "Kin Ah see her?" he asked eagerly.

Josiah pursed his lips and considered the request. "Ahhhhh don' know..." he replied slowly. "Ah mean, it ain't lack..."

Alabama held up a restraining hand. "Okay, Josiah. Jes' thought Ah ax." He pulled out a list of supplies he needed and proceeded to walk around the store, placing them in a basket. Josiah watched him for a moment. Then he disappeared, walking up the stairs. He returned in a moment. Alabama had placed the items on the counter and was seated on a feed sack, waiting.

"She want to see you," Josiah said. He looked uncertain.

"Up?"

Josiah nodded, motioning with his head toward the stairs.

Alabama rose, walked quickly to the stairs, and proceeded steadily up them.

When he arrived at the top of the stairs, he knocked on the door. "Come in," a tiny voice said. Alabama gently pushed open the door. Adrianna sat in a wicker chair, wearing a white linen dress. The light was perpendicular to her face. Her long, straight hair was braided and hung down her back with a white bow holding it together. *She look lack she sixteen agin'*, Alabama thought with a rush of love.

"Hello, Mr. Alabama," Adrianna said quietly. She smiled faintly.

Alabama entered, closed the door behind him, and stood looking at her. Before he could stop himself, he said "How you, sweetheart?" A flash of remorse poured through him. *Idiot! Wha' give you de right...?*

But Adrianna saved him. "I'm fine, Alabama," she replied. "Fine and getting better."

Alabama nodded, lips pursed. He gestured to a chair near her. "Mind if'n Ah sit down, Adrianna?" he asked.

She smiled and waved toward the chair. "Be my guest, please."

Alabama walked to the chair, pleased but puzzled. There was something about her that was changed. It was not her appearance, which was more than beautiful. It was not her demeanor, which was pleasant and appealing. It was...

"I'm so happy you came by today, Alabama," she said.

Her speech! She so fine in her speech!

He eased himself into the chair and smiled nervously. "They teach you to talk real good down theah in N'Owlins," he remarked.

Adrianna laughed gently. "Oh, that they did!" she affirmed. "From the first day. 'No more field hand speech,' they said. 'If you're going to be in the world of business, you need to speak like ladies and gentlemen.' Every day they drilled us on proper grammar and pronunciation." She mused. "Who knows? Perhaps there's a career in teaching young black children all across America to speak like white people." She chuckled. "But then what would the crackers use as an excuse?" Alabama had to laugh with her.

They sat for a moment, he gazing at every inch of her and she alternately glancing furtively into his eyes and staring at the floor. After a time, he said "Adrianna, you look so beautiful."

She took in and released a quick breath. A tear came to her eye, and she wiped savagely at it. It took her a moment to compose herself, but at length she replied in a very quiet voice "You have no idea how much that comment means to me."

Alabama started. "Sayin' you beautiful? You *are* beautiful! Ever' foo' know dat!"

Adrianna burst into laughter. As she giggled, Alabama smiled. His amusement rapidly changed to consternation when her laughter became jagged and then turned abruptly into sobbing. She buried her head in her hands and wailed. "Oh, God, forgive me!" she cried loudly. "How *could* I! Oh, Lord, *please* don't hate me!"

Alabama was on her in a flash. He knelt at her feet, his back straight, and held her to his chest. She readily melted into his arms, wailing and shaking. Hot, wet tears flooded down her face and dampened his shirt. Neither of them saw or heard Jasmine open the door, look worriedly into the room, and quietly close the door. For some minutes, they stayed that way, rocking, holding, crying, soothing, whispering. Alabama wept bittersweet tears along with his beloved, not truly knowing why yet deeply and viscerally aware that years of pain and numbness was coming out of him along with whatever anguish she was experiencing.

Finally, Adrianna pulled back, sniffled, and took a cotton handkerchief out of her sleeve. While she dabbed at her eyes and cleaned her nose, he sat back in his own chair, wiping at his eyes. They stared at one another tenderly for a moment. *Ah could die happy raht now*, Alabama thought. *She have feelin's fo' me. Ah jes' know it.*

"Alabama," she said raggedly, eyes on the floor. "I…" She paused, tense and shaking. Her eyes found him for a brief second before resuming their lock on the floorboards. "Alabama, you sweet man. You sweet, *sweet* man! I know you love me. But I…" She sighed deeply, her lips trembling. "I'm *flawed*, Alabama!" she cried, tears falling down her cheeks. "I've…well, I've *s-sinned*! I'm not worthy, Alabama. I can never be forgiven. *Never!*" Tears flooded her eyes. Alabama thought he would fall into them if he wasn't careful. Suddenly she leaned forward and rocked violently, sobbing and wailing. "*I killed my baby, Alabama!*" she cried. "I killed him! My *son!* He was *perfect!* His little arms, and his legs…*Oh, my God, I killed my baby!*" She fell onto the floor and curled into a fetal position, wailing and thrashing. Spittle ran from her mouth, and she gasped for breath as she moaned and shuddered.

Alabama rose, bent down, and swooped her up into his arms in one motion. He held her to himself, rocking and soothing her, holding her as close as his own skin. Adrianna put her arms around his neck and bawled with abandon. Alabama kissed her, held her, whispered to her. Strength flooded his legs and arms to the point that she felt like a feather. *Ah was born to hold dis woman,* he said to himself with clear certainty.

When she was settling into mere whimpering some minutes later, he gently placed her back into her chair and knelt beside her. He continued to hold her for many minutes, stroking her cheek, gently rubbing her back, and whispering his love to her. When she was settled, her eyes closed, he carefully released her and allowed her to sleep. Quietly, he rose and approached the door. He straightened his shirt, wiped his eyes, took a deep breath, and opened the door.

Jasmine stood on the landing. Alabama smiled shallowly. "She sleepin'," he said quietly.

Jasmine looked deep into his eyes. For a moment, they simply traded knowing looks. Finally, she said "Ah so happy you come, Alabama. Thank you." He reached out his arms and held her for a few seconds. Then he pulled away gently. "Please tell Adrianna Ah be heah tomorrah, midday," he said. Jasmine nodded.

Alabama walked downstairs, told an open-mouthed Josiah that his daughter would be fine now, collected his goods, and carried them to the wagon. Precious seemed happy to begin the trot to the farm, picking up on her owner's mood.

CHAPTER 23

As he'd promised, Alabama trotted the wagon up to the general store when the sun was high the next day. Josiah saw him coming and came out to meet him. "Alabama!" he cried. "Wha' she tell you?"

Alabama stared at him, frowning. "She okay?"

"She fine, far's Ah know. Slept all afternoon an' all night. Jes' wake up mid-mornin'. Jasmine feed her somethin'. Adrianna restin' now. Wha' she tell you yestiddy?"

Alabama considered. "You bes' ax her," he replied after a pause.

Josiah sighed deeply. "Whooo!" he exclaimed. "Dat some cryin' fit, 'cordin' to Jasmine. She 'bout cried ten pounds off!"

Alabama nodded. "Reckon she be okay to see me? Ah kin wait. Or come back tomorrah. Up to her."

"Ah find out," Josiah replied.

Alabama sat on a bench on the front porch of the general store for a few minutes. When Josiah returned, he stood up expectantly. "She say give her ten-fifteen minutes," Josiah reported. "Den she see you."

Alabama smiled. "Fine wif' me," he replied happily.

A half-hour later, Alabama sat in the same wicker chair he'd occupied the day before, and Adrianna again sat by the window. When he first came in, he had bowed and kissed her hand. She'd blushed and smiled, saying "Please sit down, Alabama."

He merely gazed at her, a smile of satisfaction on his face. He was content to simply drink in her beauty and bask in the glow of her presence. After a moment, Adrianna remarked "It's so good of you to come back, Alabama. I was afraid I'd never see you again."

He looked at her with wide-eyed surprise. "Nevah see me…why, Miss Adrianna, Ah couldn't stay away if'n Ah tried!" He smiled grandly. "An' Ah sho' ain't goin' try!"

She nodded and stared out the window, lips tightly sealed in a thin line. "So now you know," she said quietly. She turned to look him full in the face.

Alabama nodded. "Ah wept las' night, thinkin' of yo' pain," he replied quietly. "Ah figure deah be mo' tears comin,' p'haps fo' many yeahs. But now you got it out. Das' de main thang. On'y thang left is to tell yo' parents. Dey got a raht to know wha' cause yo' pain. Den you kin move on."

"Oh, my," she remarked softly, again staring out the window. "Oh, oh, oh! I just can't imagine…" She turned to him anxiously. "Could you…would *you* tell them? For me?"

Alabama shook his head. "Ah be wif' you if'n you want when you tell 'em," he replied. "But you got to be straight wif' 'em yo'sef. Othahwise dey allus feel cheated, lack you give me sumpin' dat was theirs."

She gazed at the boards and nodded. "Okay. All right. Tonight. But not now!" She looked at him eagerly. "Now is *our* time. You and me." She leaned back in the chair. "You were so kind to me yesterday," she said sadly. "I'm sorry I…"

Alabama waved her off, shaking his head emphatically. "No apology, Adrianna. You needed to get it out. Ah jes' glad Ah kin hep."

She gazed deeply into his eyes. "Can you ever forgive me, Alabama?" she asked. Tears again flooded her eyes and burst down her face. "*Can you please forgive me?*" She buried her face in her hands and wept bitterly, her body shaking.

Alabama gave her a moment to cry. Then he rose, handed her a clean linen handkerchief that she had previously laid on a table beside her, and sat down again. When she had subsided and cleaned her face, he took both her hands in his. "Ah will allus love you, Adrianna," he said quietly. "You couldn't do nothin' that would change that. An' yes, Ah forgive you. Now you bes' ax dat quession of yo' parents." He leaned back, releasing her hands. "An' God too, Ah imagine, though Ah don' know much 'bout Him dese days."

She looked at him strangely. "Aren't you going to church anymore?"

Alabama shook his head. "Not since you lef'."

Adrianna leaned back, regarding him. She sighed and shook her head in remorse. "It must have been very hard for you," she commented in a quiet voice.

Alabama also leaned back. He crossed his legs and gazed around the room before returning to her. "It was...wayall, it was many yeah ago, Adrianna. Empty yeahs."

She frowned. "Alabama, it's only been three years since you proposed to me!"

He shrugged. "No it ain't," he replied. "It been three hundred yeahs."

Adrianna colored and stared down at her lap. She took several deep breaths. At length, she looked up and said "How do I begin?" She laughed bitterly. The sound was not pleasant. "I'm a very different person than that naïve, excitable, know-nothing girl who left Morganza three years ago," she said firmly. "I've been introduced to the world of business. I've learned to speak the English language with proficiency. I've learned to train my mind to acquire knowledge and apply it." She paused. A surprisingly soft look came over her face. "And I've learned what's important."

"Wha's dat?" Alabama asked. "Wha's important?"

Adrianna chuckled knowingly. "Perhaps it's best to say what isn't important," she replied. "I'll tell you what isn't important. Money. Status.

Power. Position. Popularity. Alcohol. Parties. Sex without love." She gazed at him, her mouth prim and steady, inviting his gasp or rebuke.

Instead, Alabama merely nodded. "Ah know dat," he replied. "Somehow, Ah been knowin' dat all my life. Seems Ah heard my own Mama sayin' dem thangs a long tam ago."

Adrianna smiled softly. "Your mother must be a wonderful lady. I'd like to meet her some day."

Alabama shook his head. "You got to die first."

Adrianna gasped, a hand to her mouth. "Oh!" she exclaimed. "I didn't...I'm so sorry, Alabama!"

Alabama shrugged. "She die young, when Ah in de wah," he replied. "Got de whoopin' cough, so mah Pa say."

Adrianna shook her head sadly. "That must have been difficult for you."

"Ah din' know it 'til Ah get back," he said reflectively. "Yes, it was hard news. Lack a punch in de gut. Ah did love dat woman, das' fo' sho'."

"I can see that," Adrianna expressed sympathetically. "Is your father still alive?"

"Far's Ah know. He retired, in Selmon, Alabama."

Adrianna read in his tone the distance between Alabama and his father and said nothing further on the subject.

It seemed an eternity passed while they were absorbed in their own thoughts. Then she spoke. "Alabama?"

He looked at her, his eyebrows raised.

"I'd like to start over," she said quietly.

"Ovah?"

"Yes," she affirmed. "With you and me. I mean, not like when I was a child, but…but as friends. Without history between us. Without hurt."

Alabama smiled. "Ah kin certainly do dat," he replied. Adrianna laughed gaily.

For an hour, they sat and chatted of farming and black culture and the peculiarities of white folk and life in general. Alabama could not recall passing such a pleasant time in his entire life. When she appeared to be tiring, he stood and took her hand again, brushing a kiss against it. "Ah love you, friend," he said with a soft smile.

Adrianna's eyes glistened. She nodded.

"See you tomorrah?" he asked.

"Please do," she replied. "Come for lunch."

Alabama turned and walked to the door. When he opened it, he turned and regarded her in her chair by the window. She looked to him like one of those Renaissance paintings he had seen in picture books. He waved, smiled, and closed the door behind him.

CHAPTER 24

On the last day of summer, when the corn was beginning to dry on the stalk, the beans and okra had been harvested and sold, and the pumpkins were beginning to swell from the late rains, Alabama presented the ring to Adrianna for the second time. This time, having heard from her what she had learned from bitter experience is important, he offered her access to those things in a marriage with him: a loving and faithful husband, children, land to walk and farm, family nearby, a strong church readily accessible for worship and social events, and the peace of knowing that God is in His heaven and all is well with the world. "Ah ain't sophisticated, my love," he admitted. "But Ah's solid as ground. An' Ah want nothin' but a life makin' you happy. Dat would be as close to heaven as Ah'm gonna get is dis worl'."

The wedding was set for the first of November, a Sunday. Alabama wrote to Mrs. Stoughton and practically begged her to come. She readily accepted, asking if she could bring Matilda and her husband Patterson Willingham and their two children. "I will arrange for a small bus from the Naval Air Station," she wrote him. He quickly wrote back and said "If Specialist O'Neal is still stationed there, would you please ask him to drive the bus?" She wrote in the affirmative. Alabama was excited about seeing the young man who had been so kind and to show him that all was now complete, according to his own definition.

Alabama also wrote to Mantor Livingston and invited him. Much to his surprise, Livingston accepted, saying that he and his wife of less than a year would be delighted to attend.

Upon hearing of the guests who would be attending, Josiah immediately set about locating overnight accommodations for Mrs. Stoughton, the Willingham family, the Livingston family, and Specialist O'Neal. One of the families in the church with young children of their own agreed to host the Willinghams overnight. The Livingstons were offered Jeremiah's old bedroom in the Freeman residence for the evening. Mrs. Stoughton and Specialist O'Neal were offered separate rooms in a boarding house on the Mississippi which was operated by a white widow. All parties found the lodging much to their satisfaction and replied with enthusiasm.

The wedding, held an hour after the conclusion of the worship service in the Negro Baptist church in Morganza, was packed. It seemed that every black family in Morganza and surrounds knew the Freemans and wouldn't think of missing such an event. Much to Alabama's surprise, there were about a dozen white faces in the pews as well when he looked out at the crowd from his position beside the preacher. In the reception line, with Josiah standing beside him, he learned that these were business associates of Josiah, mainly suppliers, and Josiah was an important customer due to his access to the entire black community in the area. These people were absent from the reception following the wedding, all having offered a reasonable excuse which was graciously accepted. The only two white faces at the reception were Mrs. Stoughton and Specialist O'Neal, who sat near the head table with Jasmine's sister and her husband and teen-aged daughter.

Alabama was certain he was going to faint as he stood nervously at the front along with Jeremiah Freeman, the best man. *She ain't goin' come*, he told himself. *She done run off. No way she walk down dat aisle. You thirty-seben yeah ol'! You an ol' man! Who you think you foolin'? Adrianna too young an' beautiful fo' de lacks 'a you. You jes' a farmer. Ain't got no education. Talk lack some field Negro. Wha' you think...*And then there she was, holding her father's arm, dressed in a beautiful white gown that a number of seamstresses in the church had been making for a month. Her long hair was done up high, with a white lace hat and short veil trailing down. Her dazzling smile seemed to glow. At that moment, Alabama remembered the first time he had seen her, nearly fourteen years earlier. His heart melted at the sight of her. She filled all his vision as she slowly walked, her eyes only on him, down that long and wonderful aisle.

The reception, held in the church social room, was unique. Because of the large number of people who wanted to attend, Jasmine Freeman, who planned and coordinated the event, issued invitations to two different receptions: one an hour after the wedding, and the other that evening. A two-hour break between the events was scheduled to resupply the kitchen and prepare the second meal. She even went so far as to bake two enormous wedding cakes, layer by layer. "Ah nevah hear tell of such a thang!" Alabama said when informed of the plans. Adrianna simply smiled. "It's a woman thing," she said mysteriously. "You men have just one job: show up. Oh, and dance, of course." She laughed merrily as Alabama shook his head in amazement.

The dancing part did not require urging. Virtually from the first note from the band, a group of church musicians who had practiced together for a month to be able to perform flawlessly, men and women leapt to their feet and writhed with enthusiasm. When Alabama had a chance to visit with Mrs. Stoughton at her table, she laughed with genuine merriment and said she had never seen anything like it. "My husband and I attended several balls at the Naval Club, as was expected of us," she remarked. "They seemed like funerals compared to this. You people really know how to celebrate!" Specialist O'Neal had no trouble becoming part of the festivities. He was snatched up by one young lady very early on in the proceedings and virtually passed around among the female contingent all afternoon and evening. "Don't think I'll ever have a chance to dance with so many fine-lookin' women ever again!" he told Alabama late in the evening. "Wait 'til I tell the other guys what they missed!"

In each reception, when the meal was nearly complete and the speeches were made, Alabama stood and introduced his guests from New Orleans. He asked the folks to make them feel welcome, and much to his delight that was exactly what happened. Later, Mantor told him that Negroes in Philadelphia weren't nearly as friendly and eager to extend hospitality as those in the South, especially in the country. "It seems the further one travels from the grandeur of the big city, the more genuine people become," he remarked to Alabama and Josiah. "Thank you for giving my wife and me a healthy dose of the best side of humanity."

When the last guests had left and the wedding party and volunteer workers were all who remained, Alabama and Adrianna departed in a sedan driven by one of Josiah's suppliers. The man had asked Josiah what was appropriate as a wedding present, and Josiah mentioned transportation to the farm as a possibility. The man jumped at it. "Mind if my wife comes along?" he asked eagerly. "She really loves this kinda stuff." When they approached the car, Alabama found it shiny and spotless. A bottle of champagne in a pewter bucket with ice sat on the back floor, along with two glasses. The driver delighted in opening the bottle with an elaborate gesture, and his wife graciously poured a glass for each of the wedding party. On the way to the farm, the white couple happily engaged the newly wedded couple in conversation about their life experiences. Later, Alabama told Adrianna "It's a strange worl' when some white man try to rob yo' land an' othahs drive you home an' serve you champagne." Adrianna laughed happily. "They aren't all rednecks," she remarked. "New Orleans has many enlightened white people who secretly loathe the segregation system. Maybe it's because of the Creoles. They move in and out of both societies at ease. I'm delighted to find there are some white people out this way who are decent folks too. I never bothered to think about it when I was growing up in this area."

It was nearly dark when Alabama bade a thankful goodbye to the chauffeur couple and led his bride up the stairs into the house. He had previously scrubbed it spotless and laid a white linen tablecloth that he'd purchased in Fordoche on the wooden table. A new area rug with a green and gold theme covered the bare floorboards under the table. Two months earlier, Alabama had painstakingly shellacked the table, chairs, and floor of the house, and the smell was still faintly detectable. To counter it, he cut marigolds from his vegetable garden which he had grown to keep insects away, never dreaming they would fulfill such a magnificent purpose. Adrianna was absolutely delighted with his care and preparations. Alabama, anxious about her reaction, was relieved to see her so happy.

Without hesitation, they disrobed and laid in the bed. "Ah nevah been wif' a woman," Alabama whispered as he nuzzled her neck and softly caressed her stomach. "You goin' have to show me what to do." Adrianna laughed merrily and proceeded to do just that. The lovemaking went on all evening, to the point that when the dawn began to break, Alabama quietly slipped out of bed, covered his sleeping wife, and eased on his work clothing.

He hummed as he spread cracked corn for the chickens and slop for the pigs. When he walked into the barn and his eager mule tossed her head in greeting, he stopped and smiled. "You look 'specially beautiful dis mawnin," he said, stroking her neck. "De good Lawd mus' give animals special understandin' at times lack dese." He gave her an extra helping of oats in celebration. On his way back to the house, he stopped at the henhouse and gathered a dozen fresh eggs.

CHAPTER 25

Josiah and Jasmine Freeman drove into the farmyard three days later at midday. Alabama was loading pumpkins fresh from the field onto the wagon for the trip to Fordoche to meet his broker. He spied the Freeman truck and walked eagerly to meet his parents-in-law. Simultaneously, Adrianna heard the vehicle and came running out of the house to hug her mother and father.

During a farm lunch of stewed chicken and fresh vegetables complemented by clear, cool well water, the four discussed the necessity to add rooms to the house to accommodate the addition of hoped-for children in the next few years. "Look lack Ah goin' keep Rufus and Lonnie busy," Alabama remarked with a smile. "Trees to cut, planks to saw, rooms to build. Should be an interestin' winter." Adrianna chatted on eagerly about how much fun it was—and a surprise at that—to be a farm wife. "Every day I wake up, go outside on the porch, and smell God's beautiful earth," she remarked happily. "And then I collect eggs and go inside to make a huge, wonderful omelet for my husband. And Mama, I'm learning to can vegetables and fruit. What a fun thing to do!"

New rooms did indeed go onto the house, four of which were bedrooms and one a bathroom with an iron clawfoot tub and a toilet connected to a septic tank. In the bathroom, Alabama installed a Franklin stove with a flat plate on top, similar to the one in the kitchen/living room, so buckets of water could be heated for a hot bath. It was still necessary to haul water in buckets for use within the house, but the addition of the bathroom was a blessing.

In the spring, when Alabama was guiding the plow behind Precious and seeds were being planted, Adrianna wondered when her baby would come. Try as they might, at various times and places, the couple had not been able to conceive. Adrianna watched the new shoots come out of the ground and anguished. *Have I cursed my body with my sin?* she pondered. *Has God closed my womb forever in His anger?* Alabama was patient, never missing an opportunity to make her happy. Often they sat on the porch and talked about children, Adrianna with longing sometimes leading to tears, and Alabama with stoic determination. "Ah know de Lawd do what He please," he remarked once. "We pray fo' chirren. An' we eat right, get rest, work to keep strong. Ain't nothin' missin. We jes' have to wait on Him."

"Oh, I know that!" Adrianna muttered irritably, seated beside him on a porch swing and cuddling into his body. "But it's been three years! When is He going to favor us?"

Alabama chuckled. "Don' ax me, sweet thang," he replied. "He ain't used to hearin' from me all that much, 'sept when Ah began to go to church agin' the las' few yeah. Mayhaps mah prayers jes' waitin' in line up theah."

"Well, Lord knows *I* pray up a storm," Adrianna replied, burying her head in his chest. She paused for several minutes and sighed. "It's hard seeing Jeremiah's wife pregnant every year," she remarked wistfully. "He has four children now and more coming, judging from Samatha's shape this last Sunday. When will we be blessed with even *one* child?"

Her lament echoed down the years, in all seasons. By the date of their tenth wedding anniversary, Adrianna was beginning to despair. Her nieces and nephews delighted in coming out to the farm to visit every second or third Saturday, and she enjoyed cooking a feast for her parents and extended family on those days. But her eyes had taken on a vacant look, and her skin no longer held the vibrant luminosity it once had. She was more quiet than usual, going about her tasks listlessly. Alabama was worried about her and took her to a doctor in Morganza for a series of tests. As Adrianna was getting dressed again in the examining room, the doctor came out and beckoned Alabama into his office. "Your wife will be here in a moment, Mr. Denton," he said quietly. "Please have a seat. I'll be right there." When he returned, Adrianna was seated beside her husband. The doctor sat down and said "There may be a problem." He explained that because he was not a specialist in women's health, he would be recommending a doctor in New Orleans who would be able to do a more complete examination and provide an opinion. Adrianna leaned forward. "Is it…my…ah, operation, Doctor? Is that the reason?"

"Your abortion?" the doctor asked.

Adrianna leaned back. Tears flooded her eyes, and she nodded. Alabama took her hand and squeezed it.

"As I said, Mrs. Denton, I'm not a specialist," the doctor replied. "I see some, shall we say, abnormality in your reproductive system. It may be causative, and it may not. That's why I'm sending you to a specialist."

"Wha' 'bout her health? In general?" Alabama asked.

The doctor nodded. "All our tests are normal," he replied assuringly. "Blood pressure is good, heart rate is normal, lungs sound good."

Alabama stared at him. "No disrespect, Doctah, but den how come she don' look so good?"

The doctor cocked his head and frowned. "Well, sir," he replied, "I'm a general physician, Mr. Denton. I examine bodies and determine if anything is amiss. I don't make medical statements about emotions or mental conditions. Frankly, Mrs. Denton," he said to Adrianna, "there's a developing science concerning what the profession is labeling 'depression.' As far as I understand it, depression is a general symptomatic condition with physical manifestations that is generated by an emotional unbalance."

Alabama stared at him. "Wha' dat mean?"

"Mrs. Denton," he replied, looking at both of them and leaning forward onto his elbows, "you may not be physically ill at all, other than what your mind is doing to your body. It's a new field of study. Basically, the science is tending to indicate that you can make yourself sick and you can make yourself well." He paused.

Adrianna glanced at Alabama, who sat chewing his lip.

"Mrs. Denton, is there anything on your mind?" he asked. "Anything that would cause you to be especially sad?"

Adrianna dropped her head and began to weep. Fat tears coursed out of her eyes and fell onto her lap. Alabama put his arm around her and drew her in. "We want a baby," he said simply. "Adrianna feel it 'spesh'ly bad. Been a long tam since we's married. Ten yeah. She also 'fraid dat she mighta...ah, messed herself up wif' dat operation all dem yeah ago."

The doctor nodded and leaned back. "Well!" he remarked. "I suspect that that is indeed the cause of your physical languishment, Mrs. Denton. Your mind is so desperate for a baby that it's affecting your body negatively." He wrote on a pad and handed a piece of paper to Alabama. "This is the name of the specialist in New Orleans. He's a woman's doctor and will be able to tell you if there's any physical reason you can't have children, Mrs. Denton. If he finds you capable physically, it may be necessary to recommend a psychiatrist who can discuss your emotional condition with you." He rose and held out his hand to Alabama. "Thank you, folks. Please see my secretary on your way out to take care of the bill."

Alabama and Adrianna took the hint, stood up, thanked the doctor, and left.

On the way back to the farm, Adrianna was silent. Unlike her previous listlessness, a bright fire burned in her eyes. Alabama looked over at her. "Whachoo thinkin'?" he asked.

"We need a prayer time," she replied quietly.

"But we pray all de tam!" Alabama replied. "You pray, Ah pray, yo' folks pray..."

Adrianna shook her head. "No. We need everyone. *All* of them, in one place!"

Alabama considered it. "Wayall, you outa my area 'a understandin'," he replied. "But you know wha' you doin'. Ah go see de pastor."

Adrianna nodded. "Turn around, Alabama. We have to go see him now."

"Now?"

"*Now*!" Adrianna's eyes were fierce, and the color rose in her face for the first time in months.

Alabama immediately turned to check for traffic over his shoulder, and shouted "Yo, Precious! We goin' back! Get you some oats, girl! C'mon, now!" He turned her expertly to the left and urged her into a trot for the two-mile trip to the church.

The word got out quickly in the church community, and the sanctuary was packed the next Sunday. Neighbors buzzed to neighbors, and an air of excitement pervaded the room. "Brothahs an' sistahs!" the pastor boomed after the heartfelt singing was complete. "Today we goin' seek de Lawd in a *mighty* way! We goin' get on our knees and we goin' pray an' pray an' *pray* 'til de Lawd answer Sistah Adrianna and give her a baby! Dis de day of de Lawd, brothahs and sistahs, an' we goin' call on His mercy lack we *nevah* done befo'!" He proceeded to lead the congregation in a long, heartfelt, almost agonizing prayer, mopping his forehead from time to time with a white handkerchief. "*Yes, Lawd!*" people cried, and shouts of acclamation and urgent pleading rang out on a steady basis. Well into the second hour of prayer, the pastor nodded to the organist, who broke out into a frenzied series of chords before settling into an old hymn with which everyone was familiar. Everyone stood to their feet and sang with gusto, some with eyes closed and tears streaming. When the song, which the organist stretched out an extra five stanzas while the congregation hummed, sang, and moaned along, was complete, the pastor motioned for everyone to sit. "Folks, we goin' pray some mo', an' den we goin' take a break. Y'all who gotta go, feel free. If'n you kin stay an' be part of a sightin' of de Lawd, please stay an' hep us to beseech His holy presence." He launched into another dramatic prayer. People shouted, alternately rose to their feet and sat down, and cried out with loud exhortations for the power of God to descend upon Adrianna. No one left during the half-hour break, though many simply sat with closed eyes while others continued to offer silent prayers.

It was well into the evening when the exhausted pastor waved everyone to their seats. By this time, the air in the sanctuary was rank with the smell of sweat and expelled carbon dioxide. Many people lay spent against one another, looking up with exhausted eyes at their leader. He took a deep breath for one last try. "Lawd Jesus," he began, and the congregation was strangely silent. Every eye was on him. "We done give you praise today lack we nevah knew we could," he intoned imploringly. "We done prayed 'til we ain't got no mo' stren'th. We beseeched yo' mercy, we cried out to yo' kindness, we give it *evrythin'* we got! So Lawd, Lawd, sweet Jesus! Give our sistah Adrianna a baby, Jesus. *Bless* dis po', devout, God-lovin' woman wif' a child, Jesus! She done suffered enuf'!" He paused, panting shallowly. "Now we goin' trust you, Lawd. We goin' trust you." With that, he fell into a dead faint. Ushers rushed up to tend to him, and in a moment they had him seated on the steps beside the pulpit with wet rags to his head.

Josiah Freeman stepped as quickly as his tired body would allow to the front. "Suppah at our place!" he cried. "If'n you kin, stop by yo' house an' bring somethin'! But come by tonight. All 'a ya'll! We got some celebratin' to do, 'cause de Lawd is goin' to work raht *now!*"

Too exhausted to return to the farm that night, Alabama and Adrianna retired to the spare bedroom upstairs and shut the door. With unspoken agreement, they disrobed and made love. Despite their fatigue, it was the most frantic, needful, desperate act of love they had ever consummated. When they were spent, Adrianna lay on her back, Alabama gasping for breath beside her. "He did it!" she exclaimed raggedly. "I can *feel* it! God is making a baby in my womb!" She burst into tears, laid her head on her husband's chest, and hugged him tightly, crying tears of pure joy.

CHAPTER 26

Darrius Josiah Denton was born nine months later, to the day. All during her pregnancy, Adrianna arose in the morning, walked out the door to the well, and knelt with her forehead against it, giving prayers of thanksgiving. "Just as this well is the source of life for the sustenance of our bodies, Jesus," she prayed, "you are the source of life for our souls. And you have created life within me. Thank you, Lord. Thank you." Jasmine came out to the farm three times a week and fussed over her daughter. Occasionally Josiah accompanied her, and then he and Alabama would separate themselves from the women and talk farming. Usually this was done in Alabama's rowboat, anchored in the swamp, as they fished for bass and bluegill. If it was raining, they retired to the barn and sipped corn whiskey until it was time to eat.

The birth was quick. Jasmine and Adrianna had made plans for her to go to Morganza a week ahead of the anticipated date so she could be accessible to a doctor and a midwife at a moment's notice. But the day before she was to be taken in the wagon to her parent's home, she cried out to Alabama as he tended his crops with a hoe. By the time he got to her, running for all he was worth, her water had broken, and she sat on the porch steps holding her swollen belly. "He's coming!" she cried. "My baby is coming!"

"*Wha' do Ah do?*" Alabama shouted.

She lay back against the top step. "Get me into the bed," she panted. "Quick. I can feel him coming!" By the time Alabama had laid her in the bed and gotten her sopping underclothes off, she was crying in pain. Alabama stared in horror as his son's bloody head emerged from the birth canal.

"*Help me*!" Adrianna cried.

"*Push*!" Alabama shouted from the other side of the room, his back and hands solidly against the wall. "Push, Adrianna!"

She did, and Darrius emerged screaming. Adrianna lay her head down, exhausted. "Put him on my breast," she said softly. "Let me see my baby."

Alabama edged forward, his eyes wide as plates. Carefully, he picked up the crying infant and stared at him, shaking his head.

"Alabama! Put him on me!" Adrianna commanded.

Alabama shook his head, as if to break a trance. He carefully placed the baby on his wife's breast and ran to fetch a bucket of water to boil.

An hour later, when he had cut the umbilical cord, bathed the baby and his wife, taken the bedding and afterbirth outside, and changed the sheets, Alabama wrapped the infant in a clean white cloth and lay with him between Adrianna and himself. For some time they stayed that way, Adrianna resting and occasionally sleeping, and Alabama on one elbow staring into the face of his sleeping son. He could not take his eyes off the boy.

CHAPTER 27

Darrius was nine months of age and crawling around the floor when Adrianna came in with a bucket of water. Alabama jumped to his feet, his pleasure in playing giggle-wrestle with his son evaporating at the sight of his wife laboring so. "Hon!" he exclaimed. "Jes' tell me when you need water! Ah fetch it. You shouldn't be doin' that."

Adrianna shrugged it off. "Keeps me fit," she replied nonchalantly. Indeed, she had worked hard in recent months, going for long walks while Alabama tended to the baby, to regain the form and shape she'd enjoyed prior to her pregnancy. Alabama encouraged the exercise, saying with concern "Mayhaps the fresh air will raise your spirits a bit too, hon."

Adrianna had sighed at that statement, replying "I hope so. Lord knows I could use some cheering up. I'll be damned if I know what's the matter with me."

Alabama held her close and smiled. "Ah love you, happy or sad," he whispered in her ear. "You goin' cheer up soon, Ah jes' know it." He drew back, looked her in the eyes and said "All Ah ask is you talk to me, sweetheart. Ah don' read minds, an' Ah cain't hep you none if'n you keep yo' thoughts to yo'sef'."

Adrianna looked into the eyes she loved and nodded. "You're right," she murmured, looking down at the floor. "I don't mean to mope around the place. It's just that...well, I can't explain it. I wake up in the morning, I go out to the well like I did before Darrius was born, and I just can't feel joy." Her expression became perplexed. "Seems like I can't even talk to the Lord anymore. How could that be?" She shook her head in frustration. "I have the finest man in the world as my very own husband, I have a beautiful little son, I have great parents, I have a wonderful church..." She frowned and pursed her lips into a thin line. "I don't know," she sighed. She looked deeply into his eyes again. "Alabama, my love, please be patient with me!" she pleaded. "I don't know what's going on with me. I don't know why I'm sad all the time. I love you, I love Darrius, I love this house and this farm and our life together..." A deep breath exploded from her. "It's so *frustrating!*" she exclaimed. She leaned into his chest. "Just be patient with me. Please," she whispered raggedly.

Alabama caressed her hair with his lips and rocked her comfortingly. "Ah couldn't love you mo', no mattah wha' state you in," he reassured her. "Don' worry. Jes' take yo' walks. Clean out yo' mind. Fresh air do you good. Ah look after de baby."

She sighed and nodded. Abruptly she pulled back and held him at arm's length. "Say!" she remarked forcefully. "I want you to build a lid for that well. Make it heavy enough that Darrius can't move it. He's going to be toddling around pretty soon, and we don't need any accidents."

Alabama nodded. "Ah work on it today," he agreed.

The next day, Adrianna inspected the square wooden lid which Alabama had built to sit on top of the well, extending four inches beyond the brick wall in each direction. Alabama had placed a large stone in the center of the lid. The stone was securely fastened in a rope basket he had woven to hold it, and the basket was attached to a rope looped through a brace made of two large bent nails on one post that held the winding axle for the bucket. Alabama showed Adrianna how to pull on the rope that held the stone and secure it with a twist to a hook on the post. "Jes' give it a tug an' raise it a foot," he instructed. "Das' all you need. Den tip de lid off de well and let de edge rest on de groun'. You kin draw water wif' no problem. When you done, you raise de lid back into place, lower de stone, and she secure. Darrius ain't goin' be able to move dat 'til he a grown boy."

She inspected the set-up, nodding in approval. "I guess it should work," she remarked, giving the rope that held the stone a pull. It moved up easily, despite the thirty-pound weight of the stone. She fumbled the first try at securing the rope to the post, resulting in the stone falling a foot onto the lid, but the lid was thick and strong. The stone merely bounced an inch and settled. On her second try, she lifted the stone and twisted the rope easily. Alabama grinned. "Easy when you get de hang of it," he remarked.

She chuckled. "No pun intended, right?"

He smiled in return. "Hey, das' good!" he remarked. "Nice to see you makin' a joke, sweet thang!"

Josiah and Jasmine delighted in visiting the farm to play with their grandson. Jasmine would have come every day if she could, but she did not drive and was limited to the one or two days a week when Jeremiah was willing to mind the store in their absence. Darrius began to recognize them at three months and giggled happily at their arrival when he was six months old. "Ah love all my gran'chrirren," Josiah admitted, "but dis little fella got somethin' 'bout him. He a special baby, fo' sho'."

"Don't say that when Jeremiah or Samantha is around," Adrianna cautioned.

Josiah laughed. "Ah be careful," he replied, gently bouncing Darrius on his knee.

Darrius took his first steps at thirteen months, and from that moment he refused to crawl any longer. The first couple of weeks of walking were perilous since his balance was imperfect, and his parents made many a dash to keep him from falling onto hard or sharp-edged furniture. Occasionally they missed or were late and Darrius let out a howl of pain when he crashed to the floor. Adrianna was distraught when he fell, but Alabama usually just shrugged. "He got to learn," he cautioned her. "We cain't always be aroun' to catch 'im."

"I know, I know," Adrianna fretted, rushing to catch Darrius again. "But this is the most active and curious boy I've ever known! He's just *every*where!"

When Darrius was sixteen months, Alabama built him a miniature hoe from a single piece of tree branch so the boy could be with his mother in the garden and 'help' her. Adrianna showed the boy how to chop weeds and guided him to recognize the difference between a wanted plant and an invader. "He's very clever," she told Alabama with pride. "I only have to show him once and he knows what's a weed and what isn't." Alabama shrugged and grinned. "Wayall, jes' look at his mama!" he replied. "Is theah any wondah?"

Adrianna's "darkness," as she and Alabama termed it, began to lift around that time. One Sunday when Precious was trotting back home from church and the usual afternoon meal with the Freemans, with Darrius playing with toys in the back of the wagon under Adrianna's watchful eye, she remarked "You know, I really enjoyed the worship service today. I felt close to the Lord again. It's been a long time."

Alabama glanced at her and smiled softly. "Lots 'a folks been prayin' fo' dis day," he replied.

She sighed and nodded. "I know. And I'm grateful. Let's just see if it continues."

Thankfully, her moods did indeed lighten, almost on a daily basis. She began to enjoy standing in the sunshine, eyes closed, allowing the heat to invade every pore of her face, for minutes at a time. Meal preparation was once again a pleasure and not a chore. Little things, like the feel of satin on her skin and the color of a blooming flower, gave her pleasure once again. She began a practice of reading to Darrius for a few minutes each day. Alabama looked on silently. *Dey say You work in mysterious ways,* he prayed when alone. *Sho' look lack das' true.*

Though they began to try for more children after Darrius was six months old, it became apparent that it was not going to happen. "Somehow I knew it," Adrianna admitted. "Darrius is truly a gift from God. I can't see the Lord granting us a second child after what it took to get His attention the first time."

"Should you be sayin' dat?" Alabama asked worriedly.

She shrugged. "Look," she replied. "I believe in God. I trust in Jesus. But I've long since given up trying to figure out why God does what He desires to do."

Alabama considered that statement, rubbing his chin. "Me too," he admitted. "Sometime Ah think God jes' messin' wif us, lack He playin'. Othah tam Ah think He leadin' us to trust Him mo' an' mo', an' He have our bes' interes' at heart. Ah jes' don' know. Reckon we ain't s'posed to know. Jes' trust an' obey, lack de Bible say."

Adrianna nodded, gazing down. When she looked up, she said "You know, I often think about Proverbs 3:5-6—'Trust in the Lord with all your heart, and lean not upon your own understanding. In all your ways, acknowledge Him, and He will make your paths straight.' I hear those words, and I know they're virtually breathed into the Bible by God Himself. But I have no idea what they really mean."

Alabama shook his head. "Nor me. But we jes' wait, Ah s'pose. We wait, we watch Him work, and we say 'Amen, Lawd.'"

Seasons came. Crops were planted, tended, and harvested. Short mid-Louisiana winters were endured and even welcomed for their respite. In the meantime, Darrius grew solid and began to lose the chubby look that many toddlers have. By his fourth birthday, he was following Alabama in the fields with his own little plow that his father had made. The plow had a rope attached that Alabama tied around his own waist as he directed Precious down the furrows. Darrius delighted in hollering "Giddyup, Daddy!" as he skipped along behind a grinning Alabama. The boy helped Adrianna in the garden, collected eggs and plucked feathers from slaughtered chickens dipped in boiling water, shucked corn with his daddy, and talked non-stop. Darrius rarely walked; running was his preferred means of locomotion. "We gotta stop feedin' that chil'," Alabama remarked. "Ah kin hardly keep up wif him no' mo'!"

One day, at noon on a lazy summer day after Darrius had turned four, Alabama was cranking the axle over the well, drawing water and thinking aimlessly, when he heard Darrius holler "Daddy! Lookit me!" Alabama whipped around toward the sound, but he saw nothing. Curious, he let the bucket down into the water and peered around.

"Up here! Up here, Daddy!" Darrius shouted.

Alabama looked up. There on the pitched roof of the house, Darrius waved his arms and shouted in glee. "Lookee here, Daddy! I climbed up here all by myself!"

Alabama took off running toward the house. *"Hol' still, Darrius!"* he shouted. "Don't move! Daddy be raht theah! Hol' still!" He scuttled around toward the back of the house and located the ladder he'd made and left leaning against the side of the house. Scrambling up as quickly as he could, he yelled "Ah'm comin', Darrius. Daddy's comin'!"

When he reached the top of the ladder, Darrius was making his way cautiously along the peak of the wood tiles toward him. Suddenly he lost his balance, swayed precariously, and tumbled down toward his father. Alabama braced himself on the ladder, leaned forward onto the roof, and caught the boy with his left hand just as he was sliding off the edge. With an iron grip, he pulled Darrius into the ladder and hung on tight with his right hand. Darrius gasped, his eyes wide, and grabbed the ladder with his own hands. Together they climbed down the ladder. When they reached the ground, Alabama released his grip on his son and sat down, breathing heavily.

Darrius stood, holding onto the ladder and looking up. He burst into a boy's laughter. "That was *fun*, Daddy!" he shouted. "Let's do it again!" He was just lifting a foot to place it on the ladder when he was grabbed by the back of his trousers and yanked backward a full yard. Alabama sprang to his feet, gripped the boy's shirt front, leaned down, and pulled Darrius' face within six inches of his own. *"Don' you evah do dat agin'!"* Alabama shouted. *"You lack to scare de daylight outa me!"* Spittle sprayed his son's face in his fury.

Darrius burst into tears, screwing up his eyes and doing his best to twist away from his father's steely grip. "I was just having fun!" the boy screamed. "Lemme go! Lemme go!"

Adrianna came running around the corner. *"What's going on?"* she shouted. "Alabama! Let him go! What's going on?"

Alabama released his grip, and Adrianna knelt and held her bawling son to her chest. She looked up at Alabama with an angry expression. "Was that *necessary?*" she inquired acidly.

Alabama leaned against the ladder, his eyes closed. "He mos' fell," he said quietly, his words almost drowned out by the boy's wailing. "Off de roof."

Adrianna gasped. She pushed Darrius away and held him at arm's length. "Darrius!" she demanded. "Did you climb up on the *roof*?"

"I was just having fun!" Darrius cried, bawling anew. Adrianna pulled him in and rolled her eyes, exhaling explosively. "Thank God!" she murmured.

Alabama walked to the barn, muttering to himself.

It was near supper time when he walked back to the house. By this time, he had cooled off and prepared himself to sit his son down and quietly explain the difference between fun and outright foolishness. He stepped inside. Adrianna looked up from peeling potatoes, a question in her eyes. "You okay?" she asked.

Alabama nodded. "It was close," he said quietly.

Adrianna shuddered, closing her eyes and leaning against the sink. "That boy!" she exclaimed. "I swear, he is *always* into something! A body has to watch him every minute!"

Alabama looked around the room. "Wheah is he?"

Adrianna straightened up, a panicked look on her face. "Isn't he…I haven't seen him since…" She dropped the potato and peeler and rushed to the porch. "Darrius!" she yelled. "*Darrius*! Where are you?"

Silence met her demand. After a few seconds, she yelled "Darrius! I'm not fooling! Where are you? *Answer* me!"

When there was no reply, she whipped around, eyes wide, her hand to her mouth. "Alabama!" she shouted. "Where is he? Where is Darrius? I can't find him!"

Alabama walked rapidly to the porch. "Darrius!" he yelled at the top of his voice. "Boy, you bes' come in dis house raht *now*!"

They listened carefully. Only a lonely crow off in the woods returned his shout.

"Oh, Lord!" Adrianna exclaimed. "He's in trouble! I just *know* he is! *Darrius!*" she screamed, tears beginning to form in her eyes. "Darrius! Where are you? Darrius! Answer me!" She bawled, rocking back and forth while gripping the porch rail. "Oh, Darrius, please answer! Darrius!" she screeched.

Alabama leapt from the porch to the ground and ran to the barn. When the boy could not be found there, he shouted "Darrius! *Darrius!*" and set off for the swamp. For a quarter of an hour, he ran up and down the shoreline and then along the border of the woods, hollering for his son. Finally, he staggered back to the house, breathing heavily and covered in sweat. "Ah cain't find him!" he said raggedly.

Adrianna had slumped onto her knees. She merely rocked back and forth, her hands on the rail, and wailed.

Suddenly Alabama froze. The hairs on his arms rose up as if of their own accord. His eyes grew wide as saucers. As if in slow motion, he turned toward the well.

The lid lay canted on its side, against the wall. *Oh, Lawdy, Ah lef' it off!* "DARRIUS !" Alabama yelled. He sprinted toward the well and leaned over.

His son's body floated in the water, fourteen feet below him.

"Darrius! Oh, Gawd, Darrius!" Alabama breathed. He glanced at Adrianna, now standing tensely on the porch. She took one look at the anguished look on her husband's face and collapsed straight downward in a dead faint.

Alabama leaped into the well, lowering himself hand over hand down the rope. When he was at water level, he stepped into the water, straddling his son's body. He swept the inert boy up in his arms. Darrius' head drooped at an impossible angle, and water poured from his mouth. A deep gash on his scalp oozed blood. Alabama pulled the boy's head to his chest, trying to make his spine straight again. He held the boy's rear with his left hand and blew frantically into Darrius' mouth. More water poured out of the boy's slack mouth. Alabama tilted his son perpendicular, allowing the water to drain. "Darrius! Breathe, son!" he exclaimed frantically. "Breathe! C'mon, now, Darrius! Make yo' neck straight agin', son! *Breathe!*"

For nearly an hour, Alabama alternately blew into his son's mouth and massaged his chest. Whenever he didn't hold Darrius' head straight, it flopped onto his chest or back. Alabama screamed when that happened and resumed his mindless blowing and pounding.

At length, spent, exhausted, and staring, Alabama sank to his knees, holding his son's body tightly to his chest. "How could dis be?" he whispered. "How de boy fall…" Gently, he let the boy fall away a foot from his chest so he could look into the boy's face. "*Oh, Gawd, Darrius!*" Alabama wailed. "*You cain't be dead! Darrius! My son!*"

It was another hour before Alabama rose, holding his son's body tightly. With one hand, he tore his shirt off his torso. He set his son's small rear end in the bucket and tied him to the rope with the shirt. When Darrius' head lolled to the side at a sickening angle, Alabama screamed and grabbed it. He pulled off his belt and strapped Darrius' head to the rope. Carefully, sliding with his back against the wall of the well, he strained with his legs to inch his way to the top. Once there, he climbed out, flopped over the edge, and lay on the ground, staring at nothing.

Eventually he rose, turned the winch with both hands, and cranked the body of his only son to the top.

Alabama pulled Darrius' body out of the bucket and lay on the ground by his son for a time. When he arose, ponderously carrying the body to the porch, he found Adrianna still unconscious. He walked hunched over to the barn, mechanically hitched Precious to the wagon, and laid a blanket in the back of it. After leading Precious by the reins to the porch, he lifted his inert wife into the back of the wagon and stretched her out on the blanket. Then he walked into the house, located a bed blanket in the linen closet, and returned to the porch. As carefully as possible, he wrapped Darrius' body in the blanket and laid him beside his mother.

Alabama rolled to a stop in front of the Freeman general store and residence an hour after dark. He knocked listlessly on the door. When there was no answer, he knocked again. He repeated this process, head down, for ten minutes, bloodying his knuckles. Finally Josiah peered through a slit in the door, saw who was there, and flung the door open. Alabama stepped aside as if in a dream. "De well no good no mo'," he said by way of explanation.

Josiah rushed to the wagon.

In minutes, the wails of anguish from Josiah and Jasmine brought out the neighbors. Their own cries summoned the entire black community until almost everyone was gathered at the Freeman General Store and wailing. Alabama plodded to the barn and fell down in a horse stall, his eyes staring at the wall. He saw only the smiling face of his beautiful son.

Josiah found him in that position around midnight when he was putting Precious away for the night. He slipped into the stall and slid down next to Alabama. Wordlessly, he put his hand on Alabama's shoulder and rubbed it affectionately.

Alabama sat up. Spittle ran from one corner of his mouth, and he rubbed it away. "Adrianna okay?" he croaked.

"Dey take her up and put her to bed," Josiah replied hoarsely.

They were silent for several minutes. Eventually, Alabama said "Ah been tryin' to put it togethuh. Bes' Ah kin figure, Darrius climb up on de wall of de well and tried to walk it. Lost his balance, lack on de roof. Fell 'ginst de wall of de well an' break his neck. Den he fall in de water."

Josiah shook his head. Tears leaked down his face. "Don' sound lack he suffered no pain," he offered raggedly.

Alabama nodded. "De on'y blessin'." He stared at the straw in the stall. Listlessly, he flicked a piece from his shirt. "She say anythin'?"

Josiah did not reply.

Alabama turned to look at his father-in-law and friend. "Adrianna. She say anythin'?"

Josiah picked up a piece of straw, examined it, and flicked it away. "We bes' go," he replied, beginning to rise.

Alabama put out a hand to restrain him. "*Did* she?"

Josiah sat back again and shook his head, staring at the wall of the horse stall.

Alabama half-swiveled to stare at him. "Do dat shake of de head mean she din' say nothin' or you ain't goin' say?"

Josiah glanced at him and quickly shifted his gaze to his boots. "Ah ain't sayin,'" he replied quietly.

Alabama stood up. He stared down at Josiah. "She mah wife!" he exclaimed heatedly. "Ah got a *raht* to know! Now wha' she say?"

Josiah shook his head and sighed deeply. "Leave it be, Alabama," he replied in a quiet, raspy voice. "Jes' leave it be."

Alabama shook his head and crossed his arms in front of his chest. "Ah *ain't!* Now wha' she say?"

Josiah remained silent.

"*Dammit, wha' she say?*" Alabama demanded.

Josiah slowly rose to his feet. He looked his friend in the eyes. He replied "Alabama, she ain't in her raht mind. You know that! Now leave it be. You don' want to know."

Alabama stared at his boots for a long moment. When he looked up and desperately croaked "Ah *got* to know," his eyes were wells of sadness.

Josiah nodded. His mouth formed a wrinkled grimace. "She say 'Ah kilt mah first son, and my husband kilt mah second son.'" An explosive sob escaped him. Alabama reached out and held the taller man tightly to his chest, both of them sobbing. It was many minutes later before they returned to the house.

CHAPTER 28

Early the next morning, Josiah walked down to the residence Rufus and Lonnie shared with their parents. He knocked on the door, loudly crying "Rufus! Lonnie! Come out heah, boys!"

Two sleepy young men stumbled out of the house, both in various stages of dress. Like most of the black community in Morganza, they had gotten to bed quite late after many tears and much shared mourning. "Whas' up, Mr. Josiah?" Rufus asked, rubbing his eyes.

"Got a job fo' y'all," Josiah explained. "Want you to go to Alabama farm and take out de well. Take Alabama mule an' wagon wif some brick an' mortar an' tools. Use wha' you can from de well to build a new well after y'all dig a hole. If'n you got to use new brick, use it. Jes' keep a tally. Oh, an' feed de animals. Y'all kin have de eggs. Ah 'spect you be three-fo' days at it. Ah'm payin' dis time."

Rufus looked at Lonnie, who nodded. "Wheah you want de new well, Mr. Josiah?" he asked.

Josiah chewed his lip and shook his head. "Ah don' know. Ah don' care. Bes' on de othah side de house, Ah reckon, if'n dey room. Y'all figure it out."

"Yessah," Rufus replied. "C'mon, bro, les' get us some breakfast. We got a job to do!"

When Josiah returned to the house, he found Alabama sitting on the front porch. "She don' want to see me," he said anxiously.

Josiah stopped, one foot on the bottom stair. He frowned. "Say wha'?"

Alabama shook his head. "Jasmine say jes' wait. Say Adrianna too upset raht now. Plus she sleepin'."

Josiah slipped down and sat on the stair. He picked a stalk of grass from beside the stairs and chewed on it. After a moment, he said "Wayall, c'mon, les' get sumpin' to eat. She still be theah later on."

Alabama shook his head. "Ain't hungry."

Josiah looked sharply at him. "Guess dat raht," he replied. "Lack befo'. But 'ventually you got to eat. Might's well start now." He arose and walked into the house and climbed the stairs to the residence above the store. In a few minutes, he returned to the porch with a large piece of beef jerky and two glasses of water. He handed one glass to Alabama and tore the jerky in half. Alabama listlessly nibbled on his half and sipped some water.

"Jasmine say Adrianna still sleepin'," Josiah remarked. He glanced sideways at Alabama. "Jasmine say she don' seem raht."

Alabama looked at him and frowned. "Wha' kinda not raht?"

Josiah shrugged. "Say she don' look *at* a person. Kinda look *through* 'em."

Alabama considered this news. After a moment, he replied "Mos' likely she got de darkness agin', but dis time she got it really bad."

Josiah nodded. "Ah reckon."

Alabama bit off a piece of jerky and chewed for a long minute, his thoughts in turmoil. "Ah don' know nothin' 'bout funerals," he said in a low voice. He shuddered, fighting for control.

"Already happenin'," Josiah replied soothingly, a hand on Alabama's shoulder. "Pastor takin' care of it."

Alabama shut his eyes and sighed. "When?"

"Tomorrah. Early evenin'."

Alabama stared into the distance. Finishing his water and tucking the remaining jerky into his shirt pocket, he rose and said "Ah goin' look after Precious."

"No need," Josiah replied. "Rufus an' Lonnie lookin' after yo' farm fo' a few day. Dey take de mule an' wagon. Bes' you stay heah fo' a bit. Be wif' yo' wife."

Alabama stared at him. After a moment he nodded. "Ah sleep in de barn."

"No, no!" Josiah replied, rising to his feet. "Adrianna stay wif' Jasmine in de main bedroom. Ah bought one 'a dem fancy new reclinin' chair fo' de family room. Ah sleep in dat. You take de othah bedroom."

Alabama shrugged. "Whatevah you say." He leaned back against the riser, staring at the distant horizon.

It was late in the day when Josiah came out to fetch him. "Jasmine say supper in an hour," he reported. "An' don' say you ain't hungry."

"Okay. Ah won't. But Ah ain't."

"You eatin' anyway," Josiah replied firmly.

"Wha' 'bout Adrianna? How she doin'?" Alabama asked, leaning forward to hear the answer.

Josiah shook his head. "She still sleepin'."

Alabama's mouth dropped. "All *day*? How a body sleep de entire day?" He shook off Josiah's reply. "Ah know, Ah know. Ah see her after supper."

But that did not eventuate. Adrianna continued to sleep. Jasmine woke her just as the sun began to set and insisted that Adrianna take some soup. After half a cup of it, Adrianna said "Thanks, Mama," and settled back to sleep again. Jasmine tucked her in, a rush of tears escaping her and falling on the bedclothes. Adrianna never knew it, so deep was her almost instant slumber.

It was the same in the morning. Jasmine woke Adrianna from a deep sleep and fed her a small bowl of oatmeal with milk and honey. In the early afternoon, she woke her daughter and virtually pulled her out of bed. "C'mon, Adrianna, it's time to get ready," she said, holding the unsteady woman on her feet.

"Ready? For what?" Adrianna asked, her eyes unfocused.

Jasmine stared at her. "Honey, it's been three days," she replied softly.

Adrianna turned to look at her. Once again, Jasmine had the deeply uncomfortable feeling that Adrianna was looking through her into a world far, far away. As understanding dawned on Adrianna, she collapsed in her mother's arms. She was too big for Jasmine to hold, so she allowed her daughter to slip back onto the bed. Adrianna was asleep when her head hit the pillow.

Jasmine literally ran downstairs and explained the situation in frantic tones to Josiah. He immediately left the store, fired up the still-new pick-up truck that he'd traded up to acquire the year before, and drove to fetch the doctor.

The Freeman family physician, a black New-York educated native Louisianan named Demetrius Thibideoux who had helped Jasmine give birth to Adrianna and patched up all the girl's scrapped elbows and knees as she was growing up, came out of the bedroom an hour later and sighed. "She doesn't appear to have anything wrong physically," he reported. "Vital signs are good. That's the good news. But she can't stay awake. I could give her a stimulant so she can attend the funeral, but frankly, I don't recommend it."

"Why?" Josiah asked.

The doctor frowned. "From what you describe she was experiencing over those many months, and from her previous experience with what you've called 'the darkness,' I believe there's a possibility she's suffering from a syndrome the researchers are beginning to call 'depression.' Because she has no physical symptoms of distress or malfunction, I have to think it's a brain

172

issue. They say it could have to do with hormones and other chemicals that affect the part of the brain that controls emotion and energy. No one knows a great deal about it at the moment. There's a strong possibility this tragedy has exacerbated the situation. I'm very hesitant to give her a stimulant that might react adversely with whatever's going on in her body. With what she has to face tonight if she wakes up, it could cause hysteria and perhaps some lasting psychological damage."

"But if you don't do sumpin', she goin' sleep through her own baby's funeral!" Jasmine wailed. She turned to her husband and wept in his shirt.

Dr. Thibideoux nodded and sighed. "I realize that. The whole thing is…" He shook his head and looked at Alabama. "I don't have the words for it," he said sadly.

In the end, they elected to let Adrianna sleep. Josiah and Jasmine quietly explained why Adrianna was missing to whoever asked. Adrianna's absence only added to the deep, deep sorrow of the occasion. Not one person left the funeral or the sunset burial in the church graveyard with dry eyes. The community supper in the church following the burial was somber to the point of being almost silent. It was punctuated now and again with sudden wailing and sympathetic words.

CHAPTER 29

When Adrianna hadn't awakened by dawn the morning after the funeral, Jasmine gently shook her. "Adrianna, baby," she said softly. "Time to wake up. You need some food and water. C'mon, now."

Adrianna slept on. Jasmine shook her more forcefully. "Adrianna! Wake up!" she said loudly, close to her ear. Still there was no sign of consciousness.

"Adrianna!" Jasmine shouted. Josiah leapt from his chair. "Wha'? Whas' goin' on?"

"She don't wake up!" Jasmine wailed. "Ah cain't get her to wake up!"

Josiah sat on the edge of the bed. He slipped his hands under Adrianna's back and lifted her at a forty-five degree angle. Adrianna's head lolled back, and she gagged for air. "Adrianna! It's yo' daddy! Wake up, girl!" he shouted. She did not stir, and he looked worriedly at his wife. "Ah'm goin' fo' Dr. Thibideoux!" he exclaimed, laying the girl down again.

The doctor arrived a half-hour later in Josiah's truck. Once again, he examined Adrianna's pulse and blood pressure while her anxious husband and parents looked on. Gently, he peeled back her eyelids and examined her pupils with a penlight. Then he ran his fingers along her jaw, checking for swelling. When the examination was complete, he put his instruments back into his bag, stood, and said "She's in a coma."

"Whas' dat? Wha' dat mean?" Alabama demanded. He peered in at his wife, who lay on her back with a gentle expression on her face.

"She's below the level of conscious mental activity," the doctor explained. "She can't be awakened except by the insertion of certain chemicals into her bloodstream. Even then, there are prescribed times and means which have to be observed so as not to damage her. I'm not in a position to do that. She has to be taken to New Orleans."

The three exchanged glances, eyes wide. "Oh, Lawd Jesus!" Jasmine exclaimed breathlessly, a hand to her throat.

"I have connections at Mercy Hospital in New Orleans," Dr. Thibideoux commented. "We need to arrange immediate transport so she doesn't suffer from dehydration. I'll go back to my office and phone them to expect her this afternoon. Give me an hour to prepare and I'll be back here to accompany her."

"How we goin' do dis?" Josiah fretted. "Ah cain't jes' lay her in de back of de truck! She get all sunburned!"

"We'll take my sedan," the doctor offered. "We can lay her in the back seat as comfortably as possible. Every now and then we'll have to stop and rearrange her, but it should be okay."

"Ah'm goin' too," Alabama said emphatically.

"An' me!" Jasmine exclaimed.

"Ah take de truck," Josiah offered. "One 'a y'all ride wif' me, de othah wif' Doc. C'mon, Doc. Ah take you back home."

In the late afternoon, after Adrianna had been admitted and was under observation in a ward, the four sat in the hospital cafeteria and sipped coffee. Dr. Thibideoux looked around the large room and smiled crookedly. "I can't tell you how much I appreciate Dr. King," he remarked. "The 'Colored' signs only went down in this hospital in 1972, two years ago. Segregation is *such* nonsense."

"It ain't entirely gone," Alabama remarked.

The doctor nodded. "No, there are still fools and rednecks. But look at us. We're at a table in what used to be the 'Whites' section of this cafeteria and no one is bothering us. Little by little the Declaration of Independence seems to be read and understood down here."

Josiah waved his hand restlessly. "Doc, whas' goin' happen wif' Adrianna? How long she goin' be lack dis?"

Dr. Thibideoux shook his head. "No one knows, Josiah," he replied. "I've read in the literature of coma cases that have taken…" He looked uneasily at them. "Well, years," he added.

"*Yeahs*!" Alabama exploded. "Wha' dat mean, 'yeahs'?"

"It means she could be in a coma for years," the doctor answered patiently. "Or she could come out of it tomorrow. Coma is a condition of the brain in a state between life and death. I've seen two coma cases in my time. One was a complete non-attachment to anything worldly, and eventually the woman died. She was elderly, though, not young and vigorous like Adrianna. In the other case, it was like the young man was an inch under water. He could hear us and respond, but it took almost a minute for his brain to process that someone was talking to him, and then he'd move his hand or change his facial expression in relation to the topic or the emotion of the person talking. For example, whenever anyone mentioned the automobile accident that put him in the coma, he became quite agitated, even weeping. If someone mentioned baseball, his favorite sport, he smiled and moved his hands as if playing the game in a very awkward and slow-motion fashion. And I read of a person who awoke from a coma after nearly a decade. It's all individual. In Adrianna's case, she experienced periods of prolonged depression in the years leading up to this incident, which makes me think she's predisposed to brain chemistry abnormalities. Also, I have no doubt her mind is telling her to sleep in order to escape the trauma of her son's accident. Who knows what all is involved here? All I can tell you is that some very fine doctors are watching her, some great nurses are tending her, she's being fed intravenously and changed often, and nothing more can be done for her."

"Nothin' in dis world," Jasmine remarked, her eyes full of tears. "We kin still pray!"

"That we can," Dr. Thibideoux agreed. He held out his hands to Alabama and Jasmine, who took them and then connected with Josiah. "Why don't we do that right now?"

When they'd each prayed, Jasmine with great difficulty due to her sobbing, Alabama asked "How Ah goin' pay fo' dis?"

Dr. Thibideoux shook his head and smiled. "That's one ray of good news in all this," he replied. "Your wife is a ward of the state as long as she's in here. By the way, there are some papers you have to sign before we leave."

"Papuhs?"

The doctor nodded. "To allow the medical staff to intervene on her behalf when and as necessary."

Alabama looked at Josiah, and then at Jasmine. They both nodded.

Alabama sighed. "Nothin' Ah kin do from Pointe Coupee," he muttered. "Show me dem papuhs."

CHAPTER 30

Four days after Adrianna had been hospitalized, Alabama drove the wagon to the Freeman General Store. He put Precious up in the barn and walked into the store from the rear. Josiah smiled sadly at him. "You doin' all raht, Alabama?" he asked.

"Toler'ble," came the reply. "Ah goin' catch de oil convoy dis' afternoon so Ah kin visit Adrianna. Come back tomarrah. But fust Ah need to talk about a new mule."

Josiah considered. "Precious gettin' old?"

"Das' raht. She still good, but she slow. Couldn't trot fo' long comin' heah. Ah reckon it's tam to put her out to pasture."

"Wayall, Ah got one or two could do de job," Josiah remarked, "but mayhaps you oughta get yo'sef a tractor. Save you some work."

Alabama shook his head. "Ain't tam fo' dat yet. Dis body still good. Ah get a new mule, she can pull de plow. When Ah cain't walk, Ah get me a machine."

Josiah smiled. "Okay, brothah. But de day you come in limpin,' we go lookin' for a good used tractor." He led the way out to the barn.

After a half hour of examination of three good quality mules and some negotiation, Alabama purchased a two-year-old filly which he named "Chestnut" for the color of her coat. "Ah pick her up tomarrah aftanoon," Alabama commented. "This be Precious' las' visit heah. She walk back tomarrah, den jes' graze her days away."

Josiah smiled sardonically. "She been a good mule fo' you. Kinda sad to see her windin' down."

Alabama sighed. "Das' de trouble wif' livin' so long. Ah wish Ah could jes' go to pasture too. Jes' eat, look 'round, an' forget 'bout all das' happened."

Josiah nodded, staring down at his boots. "Know what you mean."

When Alabama hopped out of the oil truck in New Orleans, thanking the driver and promising to be at the same location the next morning for the trip back to Morganza, he walked resolutely the seven blocks to the hospital. He explained his identity to the receptionist and was admitted to the floor where Adrianna lay, still comatose, in a room with another coma patient. As he was the only visitor, the nurse on duty allowed him to pull a chair up to his wife's bed so he could talk softly to her. "Some coma patients can hear what you're saying," the nurse commented optimistically. "We've seen them react now and then. Hopefully your wife can hear also. You'll want to bear that in mind." She nodded to the other patient. "Please do keep your voice down, won't you?"

Alabama nodded and thanked the woman for her kindness. The nurse left the room, closing the door quietly.

Alabama sat so close to the bed that his knees touched the bed frame. For a half hour, he watched Adrianna's chest slowly rise and fall and stared at the tubes and bottles that dripped fluids into and out of her. He wondered how she could maintain any weight on such a diet. *But some live dis way fo' yeahs,* he remembered Dr. Thibideoux saying. *Guess dey know wha' dey doin' heah.* He stared at Adrianna's face. The same gentle expression had settled upon her. *She look peaceful,* he mused. *Hell of a lot less pain den Ah feel, das fo' sho'.* He leaned on the bed with his forearms, depressing the mattress slightly, and sighed deeply. For a long moment, he stared at her face.

"Adrianna," he suddenly blurted, his voice full of pain. *"How could you say dat?"* He began to cry. Fat tears ran down his face and dripped onto the mattress. "How could you *say* dat?!"

He leaned back, snuffling, shaking, and wiping his eyes. "Don' you think Ah *know* what Ah done?" he asked her raggedly. "Don' you think Ah feel lack *hangin'* myself? My *son* gone, Adrianna! Why you have to go an' say Ah kilt him?" The tears returned, and he shut his eyes and sagged in the chair, weeping in wrenching, tearing sobs.

After some minutes, he rose, found a tissue, and cleaned his sinuses. He stood, watching his wife breathe slowly. He leaned down, kissed her softly on the cheek, and whispered "Sleep good, mah love. Ah be back nex' week."

Alabama walked out of the hospital, feeling a hundred years old, and trudged the three miles to the Stoughton home on St. Charles Street. He was both pleased and terrified to see Mrs. Stoughton sitting on the front porch. When she saw him coming a half block away, she rose and waved. "Alabama!" she cried. "Oh, how delightful! Come sit and have some lemonade!" Alabama smiled. Out of the corner of his eye, he caught sight of Mrs. Stoughton's across-the-street neighbor standing on her own porch. The woman had her hands planted firmly on her hips and her nose in the air. Mrs. Stoughton saw him glancing at her and hailed her neighbor. "Oh, hello, Francine!" she shouted artificially loudly, waving in a friendly manner. "How nice to see you! Why don't you come over for tea some afternoon?" The woman merely 'hmmphed' and turned to walk back into her house. Mrs. Stoughton laughed as Alabama approached the front gate. "She lives in the past, just stewing away over there," she commented. "One of these days she might actually read a newspaper and see how the world has changed around her. But do come in! Come in!" She greeted Alabama with a two-hand grip and leaned back to take a good look at him. "You look sad, Alabama," she commented with concern.

Alabama sighed and nodded. His lower lip trembled.

"Oh, my!" Mrs. Stoughton exclaimed. "Something is not right. Come in the house." She opened the door and proceeded through it. Alabama closed it behind him.

"Please, sit down!" Mrs. Stoughton remarked, waving to the overstuffed chair Alabama had found so comfortable before. "Mrs. Jefferson!" she said loudly down the hall. "Would you please bring some lemonade? Alabama Denton is here!"

In a moment, Mrs. Jefferson came into the living room with a silver tray on which sat a large glass pitcher of cold lemonade and two glasses. "How are you, Mr. Denton?" she asked warmly. "So good to see you, sir."

Alabama rose with a smile. "Thank you, Mrs. Jefferson. Nice to see you agin' too. An' you know mah name Alabama. Ah ain't no 'suh.'"

Mrs. Jefferson laughed softly. "Well, enjoy your lemonade, Alabama." She set down the tray and poured two glasses, handing one first to Mrs. Stoughton and the second to Alabama. "I'll be in the kitchen, ma'am," she said to Mrs. Stoughton.

"Thank you, Mrs. Jefferson," Mrs. Stoughton replied. She took a genteel swallow of lemonade and set her glass down on a coaster. "Now," she said firmly. "Tell me what's happened."

In less than a minute, she was in tears. When Alabama had related the whole story, right up to his visit to his wife that afternoon, Mrs. Stoughton was distraught. She rose and fetched a box of tissues. "Oh, how *horrible*, Alabama!" she exclaimed with a hand to her throat. "How absolutely *wretched*! I just wish...Oh, I don't have the words to say. It's just...just..." She closed her eyes and waved the thought away, weeping anew.

Alabama merely sat, staring at the large Chinese rug on the polished wooden floor.

"Poor, poor Adrianna," Mrs. Stoughton remarked softly. "I can't imagine her pain."

"She in no pain at de moment," Alabama remarked. "Das' a blessin', anyway."

Mrs. Stoughton nodded, sighing deeply. She looked at her guest and shook her head. "I am so sorry for you, Alabama. I truly am. I can see in your face that you're in a great *deal* of agony, and no wonder! Life has taken a very difficult turn for you."

Alabama nodded, his lips pursed. "Thank you, Mizz Stoughton. You know, Ah been thinkin' of wha' Adrianna say to me a while back. She tell de Proverb wheah it say 'Trust in de Lawd wif' all yo' heart, an' lean not upon yo' own understandin'.'" He laughed bitterly. "Dat ain't no trouble fo' me, dat not leanin' on my own understandin'. Ah *got* no understandin' 'bout all dis! Ain't got *no* clue what the Lawd up to." He stared at the rug and said "Ah ain't got no choice but to trust Him."

Mrs. Stoughton regarded him. "So you aren't angry at God?"

Alabama leaned back in the chair. He took a sip of lemonade and considered. "Angry? No, ma'am. Ah ain't angry. Ah been readin' in de book of Job. You know how it go. God allow Satan to mess wif' Job 'cause Job so righteous an' God want to show Satan dat Job won't break. Satan take Job's chirren, his animals, his tents, an' make him sick wif' boils. Job *wife* angry wif' God, das' fo' sho'. She say 'Curse God an' die!' But Job don' fall into dat trap. He say 'Naked I come from mah mothah womb, an' naked shall Ah return. De Lawd give, and de Lawd take away. Blessed be de name of de Lawd.' Job faithful. He trust God fo' everythin', and he even trust dat God know wha' He doin' when everythin' gone. Das wheah Ah am, Mizz Stoughton. Ah ain't peaceful, fo' sho'. Ah miss mah wife, Ah'm fearful of dat coma thang she in, an' Ah die ever' day fo' de loss of mah son. Some nights, and even some days, de pain so much it take me to mah knees. Ah got to jes' sit down then an' wait fo' it to pass. But somehow, mus' be by de grace 'a God Himself, Ah *know* God in charge, Ah know He love me, and Ah know He goin' be glorified in all dis. Ah jes' hope He give Adrianna an' me a little peace in all of it." He stopped, seemingly out of words.

Mrs. Stoughton stared at him. More than once she started to speak and stopped herself. Finally, she said "Alabama Denton, you continue to amaze me. I would like to pray with you. Would that be all right?" She rose and held out her hands. Alabama rose too, a look of surprise on his face. "Take my hands, Alabama," she said. "We are two children of God, in His sight at this moment." Alabama gripped her hands, and she began to pray. For some minutes, she praised the Lord for His bounty, for His goodness to her and to Alabama even in the face of adversity, and for His Son. Then she offered heartfelt pleas for Alabama's health and safety, for his prosperity, for Adrianna's health and hoped-for soon return to consciousness, and for the soul of Darrius Denton. When she was through at last, Alabama was quietly weeping. She held out her arms, and he willingly came to her, his emotions spent.

In a moment, when they were both seated again, she said "Please dine with me tonight and stay in the spare bedroom. Won't you?"

Alabama sighed. "Das mighty kind, Mizz Stoughton. Ah greatly 'preciate it."

Mrs. Stoughton smiled. "So!" she exclaimed with as much bravado as she could muster. "Tell me about your farm. I never tire of hearing about it!"

CHAPTER 31

For three years, Alabama flagged down the oil convoy on Wednesday around noon and rode it back to Morganza on Thursdays. Every Wednesday evening he visited Adrianna in the hospital. She never seemed to change: the same soft smile on her face, the same bottles and tubes. Once he arrived when they were changing her, and he caught sight of her naked waist. He was shocked when he saw how thin she was. When the nurse was coming out of the room, he took her aside and worriedly asked her about Adrianna's condition. "She's in a stable state," the nurse replied kindly. "Yes, there's little fat on that frame. The human body tends to reduce itself to minimums when it doesn't receive exercise. But we massage her limbs daily so the muscles won't atrophy. When she awakes, she'll be very weak. She'll need physical therapy to learn to walk again."

Alabama considered. "She goin' lose anythin'?"

The nurse frowned. "Lose? What do you mean?"

Alabama groped for words. "She goin' be the same Adrianna? Smaht? Beautiful?"

The nurse smiled. "She is beautiful, you're very right. As for intelligence, there seldom seems to be a falloff of cognitive abilities after the patient regains consciousness. Somehow the brain maintains its capabilities. I don't believe you need worry."

Alabama sighed, his lips pursed. "Thank you, ma'am," he replied humbly.

Three Wednesday nights a month, after sitting beside Adrianna, stroking her and softly talking to her until visiting hours were over at ten, he found a chair in the visitor's lounge and settled into a semblance of sleep. After breakfast in the hospital cafeteria in the morning, he sat beside Adrianna again until it was time to leave to catch the oil convoy. One Wednesday night a week he visited Mrs. Stoughton, always bringing her a bouquet of fresh flowers he'd purchased in the hospital gift store.

On one occasion at the hospital, Alabama took a break from sitting at his wife's bedside and wandered into the visitor's lounge. There was only one other person there, a well-dressed elderly white man. Alabama hesitated. The man looked up, nodded to Alabama by way of greeting, and resumed contemplating his shoes. Alabama tentatively entered and sat in a chair opposite the man.

After a long silence, the man spoke up. "Your wife, I presume," he said, leaning back in his chair and regarding Alabama.

Alabama nodded. "Yessah."

"Cancer?"

"No, suh. Mah wife in a coma."

The man raised his eyebrows. "Hmmm," he mused. "This is a long-term therapy ward. She must have been in her state for some time. If you don't mind my asking."

Alabama looked at the man, his head cocked. "Yes, das' raht," he replied. "She, uh…" He hesitated. Sighing deeply, he continued, wondering why he was opening up to this stranger. But the pull for human companionship was so strong he couldn't help himself. "She fell into a coma de day our son died. On'y fo', he was. Couldn't keep him corralled. He…well, he had an accident. Mah wife, she found de grief too much, an' she…jes'…" His voice trailed off, and he stared down at the rug.

When he looked up, the man was studying him, a kind expression on his face. "It must be terrible for you," he remarked softly.

Alabama pursed his lips. He nodded, saying "It been a long tam now. Near three yeah."

"Oh, my word!" the man exclaimed. "She's been in a coma *that* long? Good heavens! That's…well, I'm very sorry."

Alabama smiled shallowly. *You sorry. Why? Why dis crackuh sorry fo' a black man?* But he replied "Thank you." Remembering his manners, he asked "Why you heah, suh? If'n you don' mind…"

"My wife has cancer," the man said firmly. "She's dying."

Alabama shook his head, his eyes closed. "Mmm, mmm!" he remarked sadly.

"What is your wife's name?" the man asked.

Alabama stared at him. "Adrianna," he replied cautiously.

"Adrianna. Such a beautiful name. My wife's name is Elaine. Are you a Christian, sir?"

Stunned, Alabama replied "Yes, Ah am."

The man rose. "So am I, for many years. I never needed anything from the Lord before, so I never asked. But I do now. Elaine is my life, and she's dying. Will you pray for her? And I will pray for Adrianna." He looked at Alabama expectantly.

Alabama rose as well. "Yes, Ah will do dat," he replied, unsure of what to do next.

The elderly white man held out his hand. "I'm Marcel Beaujean," he offered.

Marcel Beaujean, Alabama considered. *Ah heah dat name befo'. Wheah?* He took the man's hand. "Alabama Denton."

Beaujean smiled. "Odd how circumstances bring people together, isn't it? Well, I must be going. I'll ask our God to hear your prayers, Alabama."

"An' yo' prayers too, Mr. Beaujean," Alabama replied. "Thank you, suh."

Beaujean chuckled bitterly. "You know, Alabama, I've been very fortunate. I'm a very wealthy man. But right now I would trade *all* of it for Elaine. Do you understand?"

Alabama nodded. "Ah do. Ain't got much, but de Lawd can have all of it fo' Adrianna."

The elderly man nodded. Releasing Alabama's hand, he said "Odd that God would bring us together like this, is it not? Two men in such desperate circumstances. Well, He does what He does. Perhaps we'll meet again, Mr. Alabama Denton. Take care." He turned and walked out the door.

Alabama stared at the door after he had left. After a moment, still puzzled and not sure of what had just taken place, he sank back down into the chair.

As he was returning to his farm in the wagon, watching his new mule pull the vehicle while Precious walked behind, it struck him. *Marcel Beaujean! He de big shippin' man. Saw his name on a warehouse on de docks, an' Ah ax 'bout him all dese many yeah ago. Heah tell he own most of de shippin' dat go on in dese pahts.* "An' he took de tam to speak kindly to an ol' Negro," Alabama said aloud. Chestnut peered back for a second, as if to say "Are you talking to me?"

Alabama kept up the habit of church attendance he and Adrianna had established, more out of respect for and reverent fear of God than any need to socialize. By and large, the members of the congregation tended to leave the subject of his wife alone, being quietly updated on a regular basis that there was no change in her state. On Sundays, he loaded the wagon with whatever supplies he needed and headed back to the farm. Jasmine insisted that he have breakfast with her and Josiah prior to church, and Alabama honored that demand out of duty and friendship. Once or twice a year, another church family would invite him for Sunday supper, or there would be a church picnic on an afternoon after worship services. That was the extent of his socializing. If Josiah didn't drive down to the farm during the week, Alabama seldom spoke with the Freemans or anyone else from Morganza. Seasons came, and seasons went. Alabama plowed, sowed, tended, harvested, and sold, sometimes with help from Rufus—Lonnie having married and moved north—and sometimes by himself.

He had just experienced his 57th birthday, passing it uneventfully by himself, when Josiah slowly drove down the lane and parked the truck on a Friday afternoon.

Alabama came out of the barn when he heard the truck. He stopped, watching. Josiah did not come out of the driver's door but instead sat, looking at Alabama through the windshield. It was nearly five minutes before either man moved. By then, Alabama knew.

Josiah eventually swung the door open tiredly and stepped down. He shut the door shut and stared at Alabama. *He look near a hundred yeah old,* Alabama thought. *But he on'y twelve yeah oldah den me.*

Alabama approached his father-in-law. He saw the dried tracks of tears on the suddenly old face. Wordlessly, he folded his friend into an embrace. Josiah shuddered against his shoulder, and Alabama could feel the tears wetting his shirt. After a moment, he pulled back and looked up into Josiah's face.

"She gone to glory, ain't she," Alabama stated.

Josiah nodded, his eyes red and his face reflecting near exhaustion. "Las' night," he replied. "Jes' slipped away. Dey call me dis mo'nin'."

Alabama released him and leaned against the truck. He stared out at the farm, thinking *Fo' yeah she lie theah, an' den de Lawd take her. Why now?* He shook his head. *Ah mus' be dead,* he decided. *Ah don' feel nothin'. Either Ah dead or some kinda madman. How could Ah feel nothin'?* But the truth, which he had kept in a cage in his mind because it terrified him, was that he never really believed Adrianna would pull through. *Dey don' jes' wake up, mo mattah what kinda mumbo-jumbo dem docs say,* he had reasoned more than once, but he'd quickly banished the thought. Now it faced him and demanded recognition. *It finally happen, an' Ah feel nothin'. What kinda man am Ah?* He turned to Josiah and led him by the arm. "Bes' come in fo' some cool water," he remarked quietly. Josiah allowed himself to be led with no resistance.

Alabama awoke that night and stared out the window at the full moon. As it was his custom to sleep in the nude, when he wandered down the front steps his feet trod upon the grass near the house and his skin felt the cool air. He stared up at the moon. In a moment, it took on the features of Adrianna's face. Alabama began to weep. He sank to his knees, the tears increasing. Within seconds, he was bawling, rocking back and forth on the grass and holding his knees. Precious looked up and whinnied from her place near the fence of the corral, and Chestnut snuffled in confusion.

Alabama thrashed, rocked, moaned, and shook for a solid hour. For many minutes after his spasms, he lay still, staring at the grass. The moon slowly coursed its appointed way across the night sky. After a time, Alabama stood and brushed himself off. He returned to the house and fell into bed. He was asleep instantly. That was the last time he ever cried for his beloved Adrianna.

Unbeknown to Alabama, that very night a baby was born three miles north of his farm, in the ramshackle home of the auto junkyard owner Cletus Pickens. Marjorie Pickens, whom Cletus had married when he was thirty-two and she was fourteen in their small town in the Ozark foothills of Arkansas, had suffered three miscarriages before this baby in the two years they'd been married. All were the result of beatings by Cletus when he was in a drunken state, as he was the literal definition of a mean drunk. The third of these fetuses was nearly six months old when Cletus accused Marjorie of ruining his life in this godawful junkyard in the godforsaken state of Louisiana where only a crazy man would allow himself to be taken by a conniving wife who was desperate to leave her parents—none of which was true—and therefore she needed to be punished. Marjorie was small, barely five feet tall, and Cletus stood six feet and outweighed her by a hundred pounds. She did what she could to cover her abdomen and protect the baby, but eventually the instinct for self-preservation prevailed and she put up her hands to ward off another blow to her face. That was inevitably when Cletus' fist found her stomach with a mighty blow. In all three cases, the result was great physical pain accompanied by vomiting and a copious flow of blood as she lost the baby. In the third case, the emotional damage was even greater, as she looked with horror at the perfectly-formed son she'd been so close to birthing and was now slaughtered.

The next morning, when Cletus was asleep and snoring in their bed as he always did after a night of drunkenness, Marjorie went out to the yard. She bathed her swollen face in cool well water, wincing when the water found fissures and sores. Feeling her face carefully with her fingers, she realized that she'd have another horrible black eye and sore jaw. She wandered into the auto parts area and found an old pitchfork that Cletus had taken in trade for a carburetor, thinking he might one day have horses but never quite getting around to building a barn or purchasing a horse. She carried the pitchfork into the shack and laid it against the wall near the bed where her husband lay slumbering. Then she walked out to the well and drew a full bucket of cold water. She trudged into the shack, leaning far to the left in order to balance the full bucket in her weakened state, and stood near her husband, gathering her strength. When she felt ready, she bent down, lifted the bucket, and poured it all onto the slumbering man.

Cletus awoke, sputtering, and leapt from the bed. He blinked twice and saw his wife standing there, the pitchfork leveled at him and a look of quite unusual determination on her face.

"*What the hell?*" he sputtered. "Woman, you *crazy*? What the hell you doin', you stupid bitch?" He stopped abruptly when she advanced, inch by careful inch, with the pitchfork aimed at his groin. He fell back onto the bed, his eyes suddenly huge. The expression on Marjorie's face was like nothing he had ever seen before. "Hey, be careful!" Cletus exclaimed nervously as she moved closer.

Marjorie stopped a yard short of the bed so he could not reach out and grab the pitchfork. "Cletus Pickens," she said in a quiet, hoarse voice, "if you ever hit me again, you'd better kill me. Otherwise I'm gonna to come at you when you ain't ready and put this thing into your neck. Then I'm gonna cut off your manhood off while you watch."

Cletus smiled, but his eyes were wary. "Marjorie! Honey! Look, I'm sorry, sweetheart! You know I love you, don't you, peach blossom? It was jes' the drink, Marjorie! I would never hurt you by myself, don't you see, sweetheart? C'mon, Marjorie, put that thing down! Ain't no need to panic here! Les' jes'…"

His eyes grew huge as she suddenly thrust the weapon at his face and drew it back again, quick as a snake. "You see, Cletus?" she asked with quiet venom. "You see how easy it is? You'd be wearin' this thang like a necklace 'fore you even knowed it. On'y thang you could do then is watch me go and get the butcher knife. You see, Cletus?"

"I got it! I got it! Now be careful, Marjorie! A body could get *hurt* with that thang!" Cletus exclaimed, scuttling as far back against the wall as he could and holding his hands in front of his face.

Marjorie put the pitchfork by her leg, its tines against the floorboards. "That's the whole idea, moron," she commented bitterly. She stared at him. "I mean it, Cletus. Hit me again and you bes' slit my throat. Otherwise this is yours to take to your grave." She held up the pitchfork and shook it.

Gaining confidence, Cletus sat up in the bed. Though he was still wary, he grinned, displaying his eight remaining teeth. "Hey, Marjorie, I got it, okay?" he exclaimed soothingly. "I ain't gonna touch you again, sweetheart, I mean it. I'm really, really sorry, Marjorie. Really I am, sweet thing. You believe me, don't you, Marjorie?" He stood up and made to advance on her, but she stepped back quickly and held up the pitchfork. Cletus shrank back.

"You ain't sorry," she replied. "You just sober now. Or not so damn drunk as last night. Either way, you better know that I mean what I say." She lowered the pitchfork and stared at him. "Cletus Pickens, it's gonna take me a month, maybe two, to heal up from what you did when you murdered my baby last night. When I'm ready, we gonna have sex one more time. If I don't catch a baby then, we go again. But when I'm pregnant again, that's the last time. You understand?"

"Oh, now baby..." Cletus began, but he stopped dead still when Marjorie raised the pitchfork and held it in a rigid horizontal position toward him. She had dropped one foot back in a position of strength, as if she did indeed mean to thrust the instrument through his midsection. "You *bastard!*" she seethed. "You selfish, mean, bully of a *snake!* Don't you *ever* sweet talk me again! I know who you are, Cletus Pickens. You mighta fooled me these past four years, but you ain't gonna fool me ever again. You jes' do your duty by me when I'm ready and no tomfoolery, you hear?"

Cletus slowly held up a hand in a peace gesture, palm toward her. "I got it, ba…I mean, Marjorie. I got it."

Marjorie stepped back and lowered the pitchfork. Suddenly, in an instant of pure wrath, she plunged it straight down into the floorboards and walked out the front door. The pitchfork swayed back and forth in a tight arc. Cletus stared at it, suddenly unable to move.

CHAPTER 32

Shortly after Alabama's 60th birthday, which he failed to remember and only noticed when he glanced at a calendar page nearly a month after the event, Rufus drove Josiah Freeman's pick-up truck down the lane. Alabama, sitting on the porch and indulging in a corncob pipe break from weeding his garden, saw him coming, waved, and rose when the truck rolled to a stop. He winced when he stood to his feet. *Thas' new,* he thought. *Mus' be dat arthuritis dey talk 'bout.*

Alabama was surprised to see Rufus step out of the truck instead of Josiah. Now in his forties, Rufus had never married, preferring to live with his parents and continue his odd-job lifestyle. His younger siblings had all moved out, some married and some in pursuit of better opportunities. As his older brother owned the farm, Rufus had no hope of inheriting, but he remained loyal to his aging parents. Recently he had taken on the role of caretaker for his elderly mother, as his father was not far from his own sedentary years and found it difficult to help his wife with her balance.

"You steal dat truck?" Alabama said by way of greeting, a friendly grin on his face.

Rufus, ever the genial companion, did not return the smile. Alabama stared at him.

"Josiah, he in a bad way," Rufus stated. He nodded, confirming his own statement. "He dyin', Alabama. Mizz Jasmine she say come raht away."

Alabama nodded. "Lemme put de mules away," he replied. "Gimme a minute."

"Ah hep," Rufus said. He walked with Alabama to the corral. When the mules came to Alabama's call, the men slipped halters over their noses and led them to the barn. Both animals went quietly, knowing there was a good feed coming. Alabama tossed some extra cracked corn to the chickens and tipped a half bucket of crabapples into the pigs' trough. After filling the water trays for all his livestock from the well, he wiped his hands on his trousers and pronounced himself ready to roll.

"Josiah heart no good no mo'," Rufus commented as they rolled and pitched down the lane toward Highway 77. "Jasmine say she find him gaspin' fo' breath. She go fo' de doctor. He come, he put that thang on Josiah chest, say he got to go to de hospital. Das' wheah dey is now."

Alabama nodded. "Man cain't live forevah," he replied softly. "Ah hope we get theah in time to see how he doin'."

"Me too," Rufus replied, gunning the engine.

A half-hour later, they pulled into the parking lot at Morganza Community Hospital and asked for directions to Josiah Freeman's room. The nurse checked the roster and replied "He's in the ICU. The intensive care unit. You won't be allowed to see him. I believe his wife is with him now." She pointed down the hall.

They thanked her and proceeded as quickly as they could to the ward. It consisted of a large circular desk station, with a chest-high counter running all around except for a cutout for a waist-high door, and rooms fanning out in a larger circle around the desk station. Jasmine sat outside one of the rooms. When she saw them coming, she jumped to her feet and walked quickly toward them. She hugged both men, lingering for a few seconds with Alabama.

"He ain't doing too well," she admitted fretfully to Alabama's question. "They done some tests, and den dey took him to the operatin' room. They some new kinda procedure they do now, wheah dey open de arteries with some kinda metal mesh-like thing. Dey leave it in theah permanent. I don't understand it, mysef'. But dey say it may not take with Josiah 'cause de walls of his arteries so thin and damaged. The doctor who did the surgery, he tell me de next twenty-four hours be critical."

"How long ago was dat?" Alabama asked.

Jasmine glanced at her watch. "'Bout fo' hour."

Alabama sighed. "So dey nothin' we can do fo' him now? Kin Ah at least look at him?"

Jasmine shook her head, indicating the closed door. "Dey want him to sleep fo' several hour."

Alabama nodded. "Okay. Les' go git sumpin t'eat. Ah'm buyin'."

"Music to mah ears," Rufus said with a grin. Remembering where he was, he stopped the smile abruptly.

As they were sipping thick beef noodle soup in the hospital cafeteria, Jasmine remarked "Funny thang happen t'othah day in de sto'. Ah'm behind de countah, an' dis white girl come in 'bout noon. She been cryin'. She carryin' a carpetbag all stuffed wif' clothes and whatnot. She ax me wheah de bus stop. Ah say Ma'am, you lookin' to go into Morganza? 'Cause de bus, it don' run but twice a day, once in de mo'nin' and once in de afternoon. You got to wait 'bout fo' hour. She say no, Ah lookin' fo' de long bus, de one go outa state. Ah say das' down on Main, 'bout Fifth Street. She ax how far dat? Ah say 'bout three mile. She look real sad. Ah say whas' de mattah? She say she don' think she kin drag dat ol' bag dat far, and whas' she goin' do? Ah say, wait heah, an' Ah go fetch Josiah. He come, he say he take de lady to de bus station. She ax how much, an' he say no charge.' She look at him funny. Josiah, he say Ah seventy-two year old, don' worry 'bout dis ol' man. De lady, she go to de truck wif' Josiah. When he come back, he say das' de wife 'a de auto junkyard man. She tell Josiah she done had 'nough. She cryin,' say she leave her three-yeah-ol' son 'cause her husband, he won't let de boy go. She say she got to get away, he beat on her and she try to kill him but he wary. She on'y twenny, plenty 'a time lef', staht a new life. But she got to leave de boy so she kin be free of dat man or he kill *her* some day. Already done shot at her once when he drunk. She run an' hide in de swamp. Ain't dat sumptin?"

"Whooeee!" Rufus remarked, shaking his head. "Mmmm, mmm! Das' crackuh fo' ya!"

Alabama stared down at his bowl, breathing deeply. He remarked "Whatevah color, folk lucky 'nough to have a son, dey ought not go off an' leave 'em. It ain't raht."

Jasmine nodded. "You raht, Alabama. But dat junkyard man, he a *devil*! Josiah say he nasty all de time. Josiah go all de way to New Roads to buy pahts now so he don' have to put up wif' de man's bad looks. Das' twenny-five mile one way."

"Cain't 'magine de boy growin' up wif' dat man," Alabama commented. "Goin' be a redneck fool, jes' lack his ol' man."

"Ah reckon," Jasmine replied.

Josiah remained in the ICU for two weeks and was then moved into a ward. Alabama asked Rufus to take him back and forth from the farm to the hospital each day, and Rufus was happy to comply. At the end of his second day in the ward, Josiah was well enough to talk briefly with visitors. Alabama sat in a chair by his bedside, holding his old friend's hand. Josiah breathed raggedly, but there was a smile on his wan face. "Din' get me dat time!" he whispered with glee.

Alabama chuckled. "Nah, you too ornery to die."

Josiah frowned. "Don' feel ornery raht now. Feel weak as a kitten." He looked at his friend. "Sho' glad you heah," he commented softly. "Got sumpin to tell you."

"Ah had to come. You owe me a large bag'a oats for puttin' up wif' yo' bad jokes. Figure Ah bes' come get you outa heah so's you kin pay up. Whachoo got fo' me?"

Josiah shut his eyes. "Ah had a vision," he replied. He turned his head and looked at Alabama. "'Bout *you*, brothah. It warn't no dream, either. It was a *vision*. Ah was lyin' heah, by mysef', when de room seem to get all misty. Ah say 'Oh, no, das de heart goin' bad agin,' but Ah din' have no trouble breathin.' Den Ah see a shape at de end of de bed. Warn't human, weren't nothin' Ah evah seen befo'. All misty lack, jes' lack de room. De shape, it say 'De Lawd heah Alabama prayah. Alabama goin' have a blessin'.' Den it disappear. De mist, too. Jes *poof*! Gone! Ah see clearly, and dey no pain nowheah in me." He smiled at his old friend. "Din' Ah tell you dat God look afta His chirren? Din' Ah?"

Alabama sat back, staring at Josiah. He shook his head. "Dis fo' *real*?" he asked, incredulous.

Josiah nodded. "Sho' as Ah'm talkin' to you, brothah. Ah don' tell no lies when it come to de Lawd. Don' mind lyin' to you any othah time, but not when it come to God." He winked at Alabama. "No, it fo' real," he affirmed. "Angel say it, so it goin' happen. You bes' jes' thank de Lawd and get yo'sef ready."

Alabama frowned. "How Ah do dat?"

Josiah shrugged. "Das when Ah run outa ideas," he replied. "Ain't no prophet. Bes' Ah kin figure, you jes' live lack you livin'. Worship on Sundays, pray all de time. Lack de Apostle Paul say, 'pray without ceasin'.'"

Alabama glanced at the far wall. "Hmmm," he mused. "A blessin'. Dat sho' would be nice." He leaned forward and put his hand on his old friend's forearm. "De very bes' blessin' would be if'n de Lawd take me now so's Ah kin be wif' Adrianna in de kingdom," he said softly. "Next bes'...wayall, Ah jes' have to wait an' see. Don' Ah?"

"Reckon das' true," Josiah said. "Now get yo' skinny butt outa heah so's Ah kin sleep. Ain't easy bein' a messenger 'a God."

Alabama laughed and rose to his feet. "Ah still goin' collect dat bag 'a oats," he replied. "Get some sleep, you ol' cuss."

CHAPTER 33

It was the middle of the summer two years after Josiah was hospitalized. He did indeed pull through, the stent working better than even his doctors had hoped. After a check-up, he reported to Alabama "Doctah say Ah in good shape, 'spec'ly fo' a man seventy-fo'."

"Lack Ah said, you too ornery to die," Alabama replied. "Reckon you put *mah* ol' body in de groun' some day."

"Been thinkin' 'bout dat," Josiah replied. "Mayhaps Ah'll jes' plant a tree ovah yo' body. Peach tree. You make nice fat peaches, Ah reckon."

Josiah retained his driver's license and delighted in spending time at Alabama's farm. "You on'y come fo' de fishin' an' de cornshine," Alabama commented. "Ain't no good fo' real work."

"Don't hafta," Josiah replied, sipping iced tea with Jasmine and him on Alabama's porch after supper one evening, as the sun was making its way down toward the far edge of the Atchaflaya River behind the farm. "Ah a retired man. Retired gemmen don' do no work. Got Jeremiah workin' in de store so's he kin learn de ropes. 'Sides, you don' know nothin' 'bout fishin' yet. Need me to show you how it's done."

Alabama chuckled, knowing that Josiah was fully aware that Alabama pulled his supper out of the river four or five nights a week. "Wayall, leastwise you better company den de livestock," he replied. "But on de othah hand, dey don' tell no bad jokes."

"He gettin' worse, too," Jasmine commented wryly. "Reckon his mind is goin'."

"Ah been noticin' dat for 'bout twenty yeah," Alabama reflected.

"Hmmph!" Josiah replied. "Y'all jes' don' know quality humor. Need me 'round to educate y'all."

A moment of silence ensued as they listened to the bullfrogs beginning to croak. Josiah rose and stretched. "Das mah signal," he commented. "Dem frogs always know when an ol' man needs his nightly rest. C'mon, Jasmine. Les' get our ol' bodies back to Morganza."

Alabama walked them out to the truck. "If'n you come tomarrah, bring me a sack 'a cracked corn, willya?" Alabama asked. "Seems Ah got mo' chickens den Ah know what to do wif. Mayhaps we stew one fo' supper tomarrah."

"Ah bring a nice apple pie," Jasmine offered.

Alabama smiled. "Das' good. You kin come. An' bring him fo' de entertainment value." He clapped his old friend on the shoulder and helped him up into the driver's side. Josiah grinned, waved, and drove off.

Alabama was walking back to his house when a movement toward the river caught his eye. *Deer,* Alabama thought, resolving to get his rifle and come back out to stalk it. Venison was always a welcome addition to his diet. In addition, not too long before he had paid the parish to string electric lines from Highway 77 along his lane and into his house, so he now had many modern conveniences including a freezer. *Catch you, Ah cut you up and save mos' all 'a you,* Alabama broadcast mentally to the deer. *Tan yo' hide an' make a jacket fo' Mizz Stoughton.*

He peered closely. Something was very undeerlike in the movements of the creature he'd spotted. "A boy!" Alabama said aloud with surprise.. *Wha' a boy doin' 'round heah? An' at dis time of day? Mo' lack night, soon enough. Ain't but an hour of daylight lef'.* He crept quietly along a row of waist-high corn toward the river.

When he arrived at the spot where he'd seen the lad, he stopped and looked around carefully. The sun was now almost touching the horizon, and Alabama shielded his eyes. Slowly he turned, left and right, scanning the riverbank. There was no movement. *Musta heard me*, Alabama concluded. When it was almost dark, Alabama walked back toward his house.

The next morning, as Alabama went to the chicken house to feed the birds and collect eggs, he noticed that two tomatoes he'd had his eye on for picking were missing from a vine in his garden. He looked on the ground to see where they'd fallen but found nothing. In the soil near the vine, he found a small oblong indentation. He stood, looking around carefully.

As he and the Freemans were enjoying stewed chicken, fresh garden vegetables, and Jasmine's apple pie, Alabama mentioned the incident. "You know of any new famblies moved in heah'bouts?" he asked.

Josiah thought for a moment and shook his head. "Not down dis way," he said carefully. "A few up in Morganza. Ah ain't seen any settlin' in 'tween you and town." He looked to his wife, who shook her head. Suddenly Jasmine raised her eyebrows. "Might be de boy from de junkyard," she remarked. "He what now. Five? Six? Been two yeah since his mama run off, Ah reckon."

"Five yeah ol' boy creepin' 'round heah neah nighttime?" Alabama asked. "Dat junkyard, it what, three mile up de road?"

"'Bout dat," Josiah agreed.

Alabama considered. "He steal two tomatah off mah vine."

Josiah stared at him. "You know dat?"

"Found a small footprint. Leastwise, Ah think it a footprint."

Josiah considered. "Mayhaps you could set out a bear trap. Put out a choc'lit cake fo' bait."

"Jos*i*ah!" Jasmine exclaimed, taking an awkward swing at her husband. "Das' jes' *terrible*!" Josiah ducked out of the way, laughing.

Alabama chuckled. "Naw. Bear trap cut a boy in half," he mused. "Mayhaps Ah jes' shoot 'em."

Jasmine took in a shocked breath as Josiah and Alabama grinned. "You men worse den varmints!" she spat, glaring at them.

When the Freemans departed near sunset that night, Alabama hid in the corn near the vegetable garden. For nearly two hours, as the sun dipped below the horizon and all light left the sky, he squatted quietly, his senses alert. When there had been no movement by then, he rose and walked into his house to prepare for bed.

For the next four nights, Alabama repeated the ritual, waiting in the corn and eventually going in to bed when it was completely dark. On the fourth night, just as the sun was sinking down into the swamp, Alabama spotted the boy as he crept down the corn row toward the vegetable garden. Alabama watched him go past from his hiding place. *Ain't nothin' but a sprite,* he thought.

The boy peered around the edge of the corn row. Seeing no one about, he dashed to the garden and quickly picked a ripe tomato off a vine. When he turned to grab a handful of ripe green beans, he nearly bumped into Alabama's waist. The boy looked up in horror, his eyes round as plates. He dropped the tomato and made to dash off, but Alabama had him firmly by the shoulder strap on his overalls. The boy thrashed and kicked, screaming "Let me go! Let me go, nigger!"

Alabama held the boy away from himself, dodging the kicks and flying fists. When the boy had spent himself and merely sagged, bawling in terror, Alabama knelt down, turned the boy around, and held him firmly by the waist from behind. "Ah ain't goin' hurt you," he said softly into the boy's ear. "Jes' relax. Jes' relax, now. You be okay. Ah ain't goin' hurt you. Okay?"

The boy abruptly halted his tears, turned his head around, and stared at Alabama. The expression on his dirty, tear-streaked face was one of surprise, barely concealed terror, and wariness.

Alabama smiled, holding the boy at an arm's distance as he continued to grip his waist with strong hands.

"What you want, nigger?" the boy demanded imperiously.

Alabama slowly turned him around so he could see the boy's face. "First, Ah ain't a nigger," he said softly. "Don' evah use dat word 'round me agin'. Ah'm a Negro. A black human bein'. Dey's a big difference." He stared solemnly at the boy.

When the boy did not reply, Alabama said "Second, you kin have all de veggies you want from mah garden. You on'y take 'em 'cause you hungry. If'n you need food, an' it look lack you do, take all de food you want."

The boy's mouth dropped. He stared at Alabama, blinking hard.

Alabama released his grip and leaned back on his haunches. He was now at eye level with the boy and about four feet away. "You free to go if'n you want," he said. "On'y one thang Ah ax of you."

The boy eyed him with suspicion. "What's that?" he asked warily.

Alabama smiled, his large white teeth gleaming in the horizontal light. His face was lit by a soft smile. "Jes' tell me yo' name."

The boy looked into Alabama's eyes. His gaze dropped to the tomato on the ground. "Okay if I eat it?" he asked.

Alabama laughed. "Sho'! You eat whatevah you want from mah garden. Anytime you want. Jes' come up, knock on de do', and say 'How do, Mr. Alabama, Ah comin' to pick some veggies.' Kin you do dat?"

The boy cocked his head. "That's your name? Alabama?"

Alabama chuckled. "Yes. Strange name, ain't it?"

The boy shrugged. "I ain't ever hear it."

"So whas' yo' name?"

"Tony," the boy replied. "Tony Pickens."

Alabama nodded. "How old you be, Tony Pickens?"

The boy stood as tall as he could. "Just turned six," he replied proudly.

Alabama grinned. "Well, you a grown-up boy fo' six, and dat jes'," he replied. "Lissen. Ah got some chicken in the house. How 'bout Ah go in an' brang you out some?"

The boy literally began to salivate. "Chicken?" he replied with wonder.

Alabama rose to his feet and chuckled. "Yessah, chicken! Roast chicken been in de 'frig. Y'all jes' wait heah." He turned and walked directly to the house. In a moment, he returned with two pieces of cold roast chicken on a plate along with a paper napkin and a glass of water. "C'mon up heah," he called to the boy. "Eat yo' chicken on de porch."

The boy didn't need further prompting. In seconds, he was seated on the steps, gobbling the chicken. "Dang! That's real good!" he exclaimed, smiling at Alabama on the porch swing. He gulped down a long drink of water, leaned back, and belched heavily. He grinned at Alabama.

"See you done et de tomato already," Alabama noted with a grin. "Was it good?"

The boy smiled hugely. "*Real* good!" he replied enthusiastically. "Pa, he tries to grow 'em, but they ain't like this. 'Sides, he whups me good if I take one."

Alabama's smile disappeared. He watched the boy devour the chicken, a firm set to his jaw. "You live at de auto yahd?" he asked.

Tony nodded, intent on his meal.

Alabama allowed him time to finish his meal. When the boy was done, he wiped his face with the napkin, took a long drink of water, and smiled up at Alabama. "Thanks a lot, Mr. Alabama!" he exclaimed.

Alabama smiled. "You welcome, Mr. Tony Pickens," he replied softly. He gazed off into the distance. "Ain't you bes' be gettin' home?"

Tony shrugged. "It don't matter," he replied, staring down at his bare feet. He shifted his weight on the stair, adjusting one strap of the denim overalls on a brown bare shoulder.

"Don' matter?" Alabama asked with a frown. "Don' yo' Pa get worried?"

Tony laughed. The sound was guttural, not at all like a child's merriment. "Pa, he drink every night," the boy replied. "Likker. Makes him all dopey-like. He don't know if I'm home or not." He reflected. "'Sides," he added. "It's better if I ain't home."

Alabama frowned. "Why?"

The boy shrugged and flicked a piece of chicken off his fingers. "Pa, he gets mad," he replied nonchalantly.

"Mad."

The boy nodded.

"An' mean?" Alabama asked softly.

The boy nodded.

Alabama sighed. "So you stay outa his way."

The boy shrugged. "Pretty much. Sometimes he catches me."

Alabama stared at him. "Tony," he said, leaning back in the swing chair. "How you lack to stay heah tonight? Out in de barn? Ah make you a nice bed. Got two mules to keep you company. In de mornin', Ah wake you an' take you home in de wagon. Drop you neah yo' house so yo' Pa don't get upset. Would you lack dat?"

The boy stared at him. He glanced at the barn and then down at his feet. A moment passed while he eyed the sinking sun. "Gettin' dark," he replied in a low voice.

Alabama nodded. "Sound lack yo' Pa ain't goin' miss you tonight."

The boy nodded.

"Wayall," Alabama remarked, rising to his feet and stretching, "we bes' get yo' bed ready. C'mon. Ah introduce you to Precious an' Chestnut."

Tony's eyes lit up, and he smiled with boyish enthusiasm.

CHAPTER 34

Tony came early for dinner the next night. When he'd dropped him off that morning, Alabama had promised him roast chicken straight off the grill and a big piece of apple pie. The boy leapt down from the wagon, grinned up at Alabama, and dashed off to the front gate of the auto junkyard. Alabama kept going toward Morganza. He pulled up at the Freeman General Store an hour later. After giving Chestnut a half bucket of water and tying her to a rail in the back, he walked into the store.

Josiah and Jasmine were shocked when he told them the previous night's events. "Ah promised Tony a piece 'a yo' apple pie," he said to Jasmine. "Ain't got none in de fridge 'cause Mr. Retirement heah done et it all. So you have to come wif' a new pie tonight."

"Ah wouldn't miss it fo' de *world*!" Jasmine crowed. "Lawdy, Lawdy! He do His work in mysterious ways!"

"He sho' do," Josiah commented. "Imagine bringin' dat boy to a ol' geezer don' know nothin' 'bout farmin' or fishin'!" Alabama merely shook his head, grinning despite himself.

When Tony came to the farm in the early evening, he hung back for a few minutes at the edge of the cornfield as the three adults sipped Alabama's homemade cornshine on the porch. Alabama spotted him and sang out "Tony! C'mon up, boy! Meet mah ol' frien'!"

Tony slowly advanced toward the house. Even from a distance, it was obvious there was something wrong. When the boy was yet thirty yards off,

Alabama jumped to his feet and walked quickly down to him. Tony hung his head. A large, swollen black eye marred his tanned face, and a bruise was evident on his upper left arm.

"Tony!" Alabama exclaimed, on his knees before the boy and holding him by the arms. "Wha' happen…" He frowned and spat in the dirt to his right. "Yo' Pa," he said bitterly.

Tony nodded.

"Tony," Alabama said in a quiet voice, "Ah would lack to give you a hug. Would dat be all raht wif' you?"

Tony lifted his head and gazed into Alabama's eyes. "You stink," he replied without rancor.

Alabama cocked his head. "Dat yo' opinion? Or did someone tell you dat?"

"My Pa."

Alabama shrugged. "Wayall, Ah goin' give you a chance to find out fo' yo'sef." Gently, he pulled the boy into his chest and held him. After a few seconds, he released Tony and held him at arm's length. "Wayall?" he asked.

Tony looked Alabama up and down, a look of surprise on his face. "Gee, you don't stink!" he said wonderingly.

Alabama chuckled. "If'n Ah been workin' in de sun, den yes, Ah stink, jes' lack you and yo' Pa do," Alabama replied. "We's all human. But Ah keep mahsef' clean. Learned dat in de Army many yeah ago."

Tony nodded, gazing into Alabama's eyes.

Alabama sighed. "Das' a nasty eye," he commented softly.

Tony dropped his gaze to the ground.

"Why he *do* dat?" Alabama asked, anguish in his voice.

Tony shrugged. "Pissed him off."

Alabama sighed sharply. "He told you dat? Used dem words?"

Tony nodded. Alabama shut his eyes and sighed. Rising, he said "Wayall, c'mon, Tony. We put some ice on dat eye, an' den we have some dinner. You hungry?"

Tony smiled, and Alabama felt a stirring in his heart for the first time since Adrianna had died. He put his arm around Tony and drew him in close as he led him to the porch.

Josiah and Jasmine were delighted to meet Tony. Jasmine didn't hesitate to rise and gather the boy into her ample breast. "Mah, oh, mah, jes' look at dat eye!" she exclaimed worriedly. "You come wif' Jasmine, Tony. We goin' get some ice on dat. C'mon, now."

"Not 'til Ah get a chance to shake dis young man's hand, meet him propah," Josiah remarked, rising to his feet and leaning over to shake Tony's hand. "Pleased to meet you, Tony Pickens," he said with a big smile. "We honored to have you as our dinner guest dis evenin'."

Unsure of how to handle all the attention, Tony merely nodded, his mouth pursed in a straight line. He glanced at Alabama, who smiled and beckoned with his head that Tony should go with Jasmine.

While Tony lay on Alabama's bed with an ice-laden towel on his face, with Jasmine in constant cooing attendance, Alabama completed the roast and served the meal of chicken, fried onions, steamed green beans, and lemonade. Tony's appetite was not the least diminished by the beating he'd taken. Now feeling confident around these formerly strange people, he opened up and chatted enthusiastically, answering all their questions about his life and the adventures he had each day. Josiah and Jasmine laughed heartily, egging the boy on and continually replenishing his plate. Alabama observed with a smile, saying nothing.

When it was over, and Tony's plate was nearly as clean as before it had held food, the boy said "Whooo! Don't think I could eat another bite!" He grinned hugely, displaying an abundance of yellow baby teeth. Two had obvious signs of decay.

"Whachoo wanna do 'bout sleepin'?" Alabama asked. "Lack to go home, or do you wanna stay wif' Precious an' Chestnut agin?"

Tony considered. "My Pa, he already drinkin'," he mumbled, eyes on his plate.

Josiah's eyes flared angrily, but the boy didn't see them. He looked at Alabama, who nodded. "Bes' you stay heah tonight," he said quietly. Tony nodded.

Alabama rose to his feet. "C'mon!" he exclaimed. "Ah got some cold iced tea. How 'bout we go on de porch and have a glass?"

"Put some corn sweetnin' in mine," Josiah remarked with a wink to Alabama. He nodded and looked to Jasmine, who smiled and ducked her head coquettishly. "Dat make three," he remarked. "An' one natural. Y'all go out. Ah be 'long sho'tly wif de tea."

When he walked onto the porch, Jasmine had Tony beside her in the swing, her large arm around his shoulders. Tony leaned into her, eager for the embrace. Within minutes, as the adults chatted, he was sound asleep. When it was time for the Freemans to leave, Alabama gently gathered Tony in his arms and carried him out to the barn. Precious whinnied when she saw the boy, nuzzling her gate with delight.

CHAPTER 35

Tony came to stay with Alabama two to three nights a week for the rest of the summer, the exceptions being when Cletus Pickens was relatively sober and would notice that he was gone. Tony spent many an afternoon on the banks of the Bayou Fordoche, which ran directly behind the junkyard, trying for a fish that he could broil for dinner for him and his father. Some nights, when he was unsuccessful fishing, the boy merely boiled eggs from the meager flock his father had bought and subsequently found too uninteresting to feed or tend. The flock's diet consisted mainly of corn which Tony took from the edge of Alabama's farm and long blades of grass which Tony pulled along the riverbank. He delighted in watching a chicken grab a blade with its beak, tilt back its head, and swallow the grass as if it was a snake. Once a spider unwisely scooted across the fenced-in yard of the henhouse and instantly became the target of a four-hen chase. Tony hooted with delight when the winner seized the spider and dispatched it in one gulp.

Tony usually received a cuffing when there was no broiled fish on the table when Cletus was ready to eat. At such times, his father invariably reminded him of how lazy and stupid he was, and how much he resembled that useless, cowardly bitch who had birthed him and then ran off to leave a poor man to tend to him.

By contrast, when Tony was able to spend time with Alabama without his father's awareness, he delighted in gaining knowledge that opened new worlds. At the boy's eager questioning, Alabama explained the seasons of farming and what was necessary to keep a small agricultural concern prospering. Tony fed the pigs; watched a flock of chicks incubate, hatch, and begin to grow; witnessed the literal 'henpecking' ritual of mature chickens who naturally sort themselves into rank order by pecking the neck feathers from weaker birds; helped Alabama to slaughter a hog and prepare the meat into various cuts for freezing; and even began to learn the alphabet as Alabama taught it to him. "See, dis heah lettah is 'A,'" Alabama explained. "De first one in de alphabet. Look lack two pole leanin' together wif' a piece 'tween 'em a boy kin walk on. See?" He mimicked the action with his fingers across the horizontal bar of the letter he'd drawn large in the dirt. "An' dis one a 'B.' Second lettah. Say 'bird.'" Tony complied. "De lettah 'B' be de first lettah in the word 'bird.'" Alabama wrote the rest of the word in the dirt and helped Tony to pronounce each letter. Within weeks of lessons two to three times a week, Tony had the alphabet memorized and developed a habit of spotting an object and spelling it aloud.

That habit landed him in trouble one evening. He placed a bowl of boiled eggs on the rickety wooden table that constituted the eating facility in his father's shack and happily said "Egg. E-G-G." His smile evaporated at the look of rising fury on his father's face.

"Where you learn that?!" Cletus Pickens demanded.

Tony shrank back. "Jes'...jes' kinda picked it up, Pa!" he replied in a low and fearful voice.

Cletus raised his hand to strike his son. "Ain't nobody jes' pick up a thang like that!" Cletus growled. "You been gettin' some learnin'! Where you been when I ain't lookin'?"

Tony held up his hands before his face in a defensive gesture. "Jes' a teacher, Pa!" he cried. "He show me a couple of things. That's all. Really, Pa!"

Cletus moved the hand as if to deliver a blow. "Who? Where is this teacher? Don't you lie to me, boy!" Tony flinched at the move.

"Jes' a farmer, Pa! Jes' a ol' farmer. I see him fishin' now and agin'. We talk, and he show me a couple of letters. That's all, Pa!"

Cletus slowly lowered his hand and stared, eyes narrow and slitted. "Lissen here," he hissed. "If they be any learnin' goin' on in this house, *I* be teachin'! Not some farmer! You hear, boy! *I* be teachin'! *Me*! Your *Pa*!"

Tony had scuttled as far toward the wall as his small bench seat would allow. "Yes, Pa!" he cried. "I hear ya!"

Cletus scowled hard to drive home the message. He gazed disdainfully at the offering on the table. "Couldn't catch no fish, huh?" He looked disgustedly at his son.

"Caught two, Pa, but they was small!" Tony replied in a whimper. "Too small to gut out."

Cletus sneered. "Jeez, you're useless!" he snarled. He picked up an egg, smashed it against the table, and began to pick the pieces of broken shell out of the egg. He looked up at Tony and leaned forward, his face menacing. "Look here, boy," he said in a gravelly voice. "I want some variety in my dinner. Some tomatoes, and some corn, and…well, some potatoes and the like. I'm tired of having to go into town and buy that stuff jes' 'cause you too lazy to get it yerself. From now on, you make sure my dinner is worth eatin. Hear me? 'Cause if you don't, I'm gonna whip the skin right off your little ass! You got that?"

"I hear ya, Pa!" Tony whimpered.

Cletus swept his hand across the table and slammed the egg onto the floor. He rose and stormed out. In a moment, Tony heard his father's patched-together Ford coupe fire up raggedly. He watched through a window as plumes of white smoke poured out of the exhaust pipe each time Cletus gunned the engine. With a powerful burst of oily smoke, the clunker roared out of the yard toward Morganza.

Tony bolted out of the shack, tears pouring from his face, and ran the three miles along the bank of the Atchaflaya River to Alabama's farm. Once there, he fell into Alabama's arms and related what had happened. "How am I gonna get Pa all them fancy food things he wants every night?" Tony wailed. "He'll beat me down to a grease spot, I just know he will!"

Alabama knelt, holding the sobbing boy to his chest. "There, there, Tony," he soothed. "Don't you worry. It goin' be okay, jes' you see. C'mon, now. Dry dem teahs. Thas' bettah." He smiled into Tony's face, no more than a foot from his own. "You look kinda hungry," he remarked. "Ready fo' some bacon an' chitlins? Mayhaps some apple pie Ms. Jasmine lef' ovah?"

Tony's eyes lit up, and the tears stopped abruptly. He nodded, a wrinkled grin on his face.

Alabama leaned closer. "Open yo' mouth," he said gently. Tony complied.

Alabama grinned. "Lost you some teeth!" he remarked. "Two, looks lack."

Tony grinned, a large gap showing in two places. "Sure did!" he exclaimed. He ran his tongue around the gaps proudly.

Alabama nodded. "Now lookee heah, Tony," he explained. "You goin' get some new, strong teeth in dey place. You got to take care of dem new teeth. Keep 'em brushed twice a day. An' don' jes' eat sugah, sugah, sugah all day. Make yo' teeth rotten, jes' lack dem baby ones you got."

Tony nodded soberly, looking up at his friend.

"C'mon!" Alabama exclaimed heartily, putting his arm around Tony's shoulders and walking beside him to the house. "We got some eatin' to do!"

Mutually agreeing that Cletus would probably be drunk again that night and therefore deeming it safe, Alabama prepared a bed in one of the bedrooms he had built for the sons and daughters he'd dreamed of fathering. "You sleep in de house from now on," he commented to Tony. "De barn good fo' a visit, if'n you lack it, but you mo' fambly now. Fambly sleep in de house." Tony looked at him wide-eyed, merely nodding. When the meal had been consumed and the dishes cleaned, and the sun was almost over the horizon, Alabama heated a tub of hot water for a bath for Tony. "You need a good cleanin," he remarked with a smile. "Be sho' to use plenny of soap. Got a bunch of it, so don' hold back." He closed the door behind him and stood outside, listening as Tony oohed and aahed as he slipped slowly into the warm, caressing water.

The next day after breakfast, Alabama told Tony to stay on the farm. "Ah'm goin' talk wif' yo' Pa," he commented.

Tony looked at him with wide, frightened eyes. "Pa, he don't like your kind!" he croaked. "He's mean, Alabama! He'll sic Bear on you!"

Alabama smiled. "Ah won' let dat ol' dawg get me," he replied easily. "Got a hog bone in de freezah. Dawg be mo' int'rested in dat dan an ol' black man!"

Tony stared fearfully. "Be real careful, Alabama!" he said softly. Tears were but a few seconds behind his voice.

"C'mere," Alabama said, scooting back his chair and patting a knee. "C'mere, Tony."

The boy quickly rose and went to Alabama, where he hitched himself up on the offered knee and leaned in to his friend's welcoming chest. Alabama put both arms around the boy in a soft, protective gesture and rocked him gently. "Don' worry 'bout me," he said confidently. "Ah be back soon. You jes' have some fun today. Mayhaps do some weedin' in de garden if'n you feel lack it. Othawise go fishin' or sumpin. Don't take out de boat, though, heah? Das' fo' you and me to do togethah 'til you get a little older. Dey's some good fishin' from de bank. Dig you up some fat 'ol worms in the de garden. Fish be lovin' 'em!" He stroked the boy's head and held him, his eyes closed.

For a long moment, they sat like that, both reluctant to leave. Finally, Alabama released the boy and Tony slid to his feet. He looked across trustingly at Alabama. He smiled, mouth sealed, at a loss for words to express the emotions raging within him.

Alabama nodded and smiled. He rose, patted Tony on the shoulder, and said "See you 'round midday, son."

An hour later, Alabama pulled up at the junkyard fence. He tied Chestnut to a tree in the pitted gravel driveway and approached the fence. Suddenly a fierce, blood-curdling howl came from his left, and a massive canine launched himself at the fence in Alabama's face. Knowing he was a safe distance, Alabama stood his ground, one hand behind his back. The dog yowled, barked, slobbered, and altogether expressed his yearning to make a meal of this visitor.

"You hungry, Bear?" Alabama asked with a grin. He held out the ham bone so the dog could see it. The canine instantly went silent. The only sound was the licking of hungry lips and the 'splat' of spittle as goobers ran off his large lips onto the hard ground.

Alabama tossed the hambone over the fence, a good twenty feet away. Bear lost no time in going after it.

When the dog was safely occupied in consuming the bone, Alabama approached the fence. "Mistah Pickens?" he hollered. "Yo'! Mistah Pickens!"

A bleary-eyed Cletus Pickens stuck his head out the door of the shack a moment later, pulling one strap of his stained overalls onto a shoulder. He was shirtless below the overalls. Staring and blinking, he ran a hand over a scalpful of disheveled hair. "What you want, nigger?" he sneered.

"Want to buy sumpin," Alabama answered.

Pickens stared at him. He took in and expelled a deep breath. "Aw, what the hell," he remarked coarsely. He sat on the steps leading up to the shack and pulled on boots over dirty socks. When that was accomplished, he glanced over at the busily engaged dog and stared at Alabama. "That your doin'?" he asked suspiciously.

Alabama cocked his head and peered through the fence. "Look lack he found him a treat," he replied candidly.

Pickens glanced from Alabama to the dog and back. "Hmmph!" he snorted doubtfully. He arose, stretched, and proceeded to the fence. He stood, hands on hips. "What you lookin' to buy, nigger?" he asked sneeringly.

Alabama stared into Picken's eyes. "Mind openin' de fence?" he asked.

Pickens' mouth opened, and he stared at Alabama as if he was trying to calculate whether he'd just been insulted. He reached out, opened the latch on the fence, and stood aside as Alabama entered.

"Thank you," Alabama said politely as he walked past. Pickens watched him as he walked into the yard.

When Alabama was close to the shack, he turned and stood, his weight balanced. Pickens shuffled up. "What kinda part you lookin' for?" he asked.

Alabama shook his head. "Ain't lookin' fo' no part," he replied evenly.

Pickens stared at him. A dark cloud came over his face. "Then why the hell you wastin' my time!" he demanded.

Alabama shook his head again. "Ain't wastin' yo' time, Mistah Pickens," he replied quietly. "Ah tol' you Ah came to buy. Ah goin' make you a rich man today."

Pickens' eyes narrowed. He stared at Alabama. Suddenly he broke out into a guffaw and cast a disdainful glance out at the yard. "You goin' make me an offer for this place?" he asked with a laugh. "This fine estate? That what you got in mind, nigger?"

Alabama stared into his eyes. "Mistah Pickens, it don' pay fo' you to insult me. Dat ain't goin' make you no money today. Ah ain't a nigger. Dis is 1987, Mistah Pickens. Dat word belong in de las' century. Les' make a deal. Ah don' call you honky, crackuh, paleface, or white brayud, and you don' call me no names neither. Ah a black man, Mr. Pickens, jes' lack you a white man. An' raht now we businessmen."

Picken's jaw dropped. "Why, I swan!" he exclaimed. "Ain't *never* been talked to that way by a nig…" He stopped, mouth pursed, with a scowl on his face. A long moment passed between them. Abruptly, he smiled mockingly. "What can I do for you today, mister black man?" he asked condescendingly.

"Name's Alabama Denton," came the reply, "an' Ah heah to buy yo' son Tony."

This time Pickens' jaw fell an inch. He stared hard at Alabama. Sputtering, he replied "You *what*? You want to *buy Tony*?"

Alabama nodded. "Das' raht. Ah will pay you fo' de boy. Use him fo' farm labor. Feed 'im, take care of 'im. Give 'im some learnin'."

Comprehension dawned slowly on Pickens' face. "*You're* the farmer been messin' with my boy!" he raged. "Why, I oughta…" He raised a hand as if to strike.

Alabama moved in a foot. Now there was but a yard separating them. "You want to make yo' move, Mr. Pickens? See what kinda trouble dat bring you? 'Cause you don' know what you dealin' wif' heah." He stared steadily into the taller man's eyes.

Pickens stared back, looking for a bluff. When he realized that he truly didn't know what he was facing, the coward in him took over and he lowered his hand. "Huh!" he exclaimed with bravado.

Alabama ignored the implied insult. "Ah will give you one hundred dollah for Tony," he said easily. "Ah have a bill of sale heah." He reached into his back pocket and held the paper, though he did not offer it to Pickens. "You agree to give me all rahts to Tony, and you have 'em no mo'. Ah feed 'im, give 'im medical care, keep 'im safe an' healthy. You get de money and you don' have no mo' worry 'bout 'im bein' underfoot no mo'."

Pickens stared at him. "What makes you think a man would sell his son?" he asked incredulously.

Alabama shrugged. "Don' seem lack you pertic'ly care wha' happen to Tony, from wha' Ah kin see," he replied.

A storm of fury crossed Pickens' face, and his body tensed.

Alabama held up a hand. "Don' play no games wif' me, Mistah Pickens," he stated firmly. "We both know you don' give a damn 'bout de boy. He dirty, his teeth rotten—ain't nevah been neah a dentist, fo' sho'— you don' feed 'im, an' Tony but six yeah ol'. Fact is, you make Tony feed you. Dat make 'im a slave in dis state, Mistah Pickens. Dey enuf evidence to bring de law down on you and put yo' sorry ass in jail fo' a long tam. But Ah'm willin' to take dat problem off'n yo' hands. You sell 'im to me, and you be a hundred dollah richer and done wif a boy you nevah wanted in de first place."

Pickens' face began to do a subtle dance as he contemplated the situation. He chewed his lip, ran his tongue around his open mouth, and scratched his nose. In a minute, he said "I couldn't never let him go for less that five hundred. Wouldn't be right."

Alabama smiled bitterly. "Ah brought three hundred dollah," he replied. He reached into his overalls and pulled out a sheaf of bills. "Das de goin' price, 'cause das' wha' Ah got. All you got to do fo' dis money is sign de papuh."

Pickens looked at the money and licked his lips. He laughed, a guttural sound. "What you gonna do with him, mister black man?" he demanded. "Eat him? You jungle bunnies got yer African rit'chels, I been told." The laugh became ugly.

Alabama stared at him, a hard expression on his face. "Ah nevah been neah Africa," he replied. "My fambly fo' Ah don' know how many generations back ain't nevah been to Africa, jes' lack yo' fambly ain't nevah been neah Ireland or wheahevah dey come from. Ah don' know 'bout no rit'chels, Mistah Pickens. Ah a farmer. Das' wha' Ah know. Tony goin' be raised raht, learn to work, learn some schoolin', be treated raht. One thang Ah kin promise you is dat he nevah be beaten no mo'." An expression of suppressed anger set itself on his face.

Pickens saw it, and his gazed dropped to the ground in inadvertent shame. He scuffled a boot on the hard ground. When he looked up, he nodded. "Gimme the paper," he said, holding out his hand.

Alabama gave it to him. Pickens looked up sharply when he saw that the amount of three hundred dollars had already been entered on the 'sales price' line. "Conniving nigger!" he mumbled under his breath. He scrawled his signature and thrust the paper at Alabama.

"Ain't legal 'less you print yo' name below yo' signature," Alabama noted, his hands at his sides.

Disgustedly, Pickens printed his name in large block capitals. "Now gimme the money!" he said gruffly.

"De papuh, please," Alabama replied.

Pickens held out the bill of sale, and Alabama handed over the money. Pickens counted it greedily. By the time he was satisfied it was all there, Alabama was walking out the gate and untying the mule. He stepped up into the wagon and drove off at a leisurely pace, never looking back.

CHAPTER 36

"*Really?*" Tony asked, eyes wide with excitement. "He said I can live here? With you?"

"Das' raht," Alabama replied with a big smile. "He say he want de bes' fo' you, and das' heah."

Tony stared at Alabama, seeking any indication that this dream might not be true. "He ain't mad?" he asked.

Alabama shook his head. "Nope. Not in de slightest. He agree wif' me dat Ah kin teach you mo' 'bout readin', writin,' math, dat sort of thing. An' feed you good. Plus he very busy wif' his business."

Tony cocked his head, mystified. "He din' seem real busy," he replied skeptically. "Only a customer or two a day, far as I seen."

Alabama shrugged. "'Course, you ain't zackly deah much."

Tony smiled. "Guess that's right. I like to fish and walk in the woods. Only thing I like to do in that yard is feed the chickens. Sure don't like to spend time there. That ol' dog scares me half to death!"

"Well," Alabama replied with a smile, tousling the boy's hair, "you don't have to go 'round dat 'ol dawg no mo'. Tell you what: les' have some lunch an' den put out in de rowboat fo' a big fat bass fo' tonight's supper. Sound good?"

Tony's grin lit up his entire face. "Sounds great!" he exclaimed. Suddenly a look of concern came over his face. "What do I call you?" he asked.

Alabama smiled. "Same's de rest 'a mah frien's. Alabama."

Tony smiled and shrugged. "That's easy! What's for lunch?"

For the rest of the summer, they spent the mornings tending to the farm, preparing the crops for harvest. In the fall, while Alabama and Rufus walked the corn rows twisting off the ripened and dried ears and dropping them in homemade carts they pulled behind, Tony did the same in the pumpkin crop. Each brought his picked produce to a central gathering point. Some of the pumpkins were too large for Tony to lift, though he gave it everything and laughed when a big one defeated him. When the crops were picked clean, they loaded as much as they could into the wagon. Alabama and Tony drove each load at a leisurely pace to the broker market in Fordoche, where Alabama had been selling his produce for years. Tony found it very exciting. Alabama watched his enthusiasm with quiet satisfaction.

In the afternoons, Alabama usually napped while Tony explored the woods or fished from the bank. Then they'd spend an hour or two on bookwork, with Alabama patiently laying out the alphabet in simple nouns that related to their life: corn, pig, egg, plow, mule, row, pole, well. When Tony was ready, which happened quickly, Alabama introduced the concept of verbs and explained the various tenses. "Lack dis," he said by way of explanation, "whachoo call it when you look at sumpin?"

Tony cocked his head, unsure. "I look at it?"

Alabama nodded. "An' wha's 'nothah way 'a sayin' it?"

"I see it!" Tony replied eagerly.

Alabama smiled. "Das' raht. An' if'n dis happen yesterday, whachoo call it?"

"I saw it."

"Raht!" Alabama exclaimed happily. "An' tomorrow?"

221

"Tomorrow?"

"Whachoo goin' say 'bout lookin' at sumpin tomorrow?"

Tony cocked his head. "I'll see it?"

"Raht! Good! Now lemme write out wha' you sayin'." He printed the words on a sheet of paper, made sure Tony understood their relevance to time, and moved on to other verbs. When that concept was clear, he moved on to adjectives and adverbs. 'A brown mule,' he wrote, and 'he ran fast.'

By the end of the summer, Tony was required to write ten sentences each day of experiences he'd had that day. Gradually his sentences grew longer, using more words of various types, until the day came in the early fall when Alabama asked him to write a page about the day's adventures. Tony eagerly took the pen and wrote:

Today I got eggs from the chickens. I got six eggs. I fed the pigs. I combed Precious and Chestnut, they liked it. I caught a big fish. We will fry it up for supper. Alabama teaches me good. I can read and write. I love Alabama.

He handed the paper to Alabama with an eager smile. Alabama read it carefully, sounding the words out silently. When he came to the last sentence, he paused, looked off to the cornfield, and sighed. He slid his chair over to Tony and pulled him close, rubbing the boy's back. "Ah love you too, Tony," he said simply. "Way mo' den you evah know." He leaned back and smiled at the boy.

"Today a special day," he said mysteriously.

"Special?" Tony asked, his face eager with anticipation.

Alabama nodded. "Yep. Mighty special. Long 'bout suppertime, we goin' have a surprise."

Tony's eyes lit up. "A surprise? What kinda surprise, Alabama?"

Alabama shook his head. "Cain't tell you. If'n Ah did, it wouldn't be a surprise."

"You can tell me!" Tony replied eagerly. "I won't tell no one!"

Alabama laughed. "De surprise fo' *you*, Tony. If'n you heah what it is, it won' be no surprise. C'mon. Les' go pick a buncha apples so Mizz Jasmine kin come down an' make us a nice pie." He rose and beckoned toward the door.

"Oooo, I can't wait for the surprise!" Tony exclaimed, scampering out the door and running to the barn for a basket.

An hour later, as the sun was beginning to dip toward the horizon, Josiah's pick-up truck came down the lane and pulled up in front of the house. "Heah come de surprise," Alabama said happily to the boy beside him on the porch swing.

Tony looked up at him. "Mr. Josiah and Mizz Jasmine? They been here lots 'a times."

Alabama looked down and smiled. "Yes, but de surprise ain't." He winked at Tony. "Why don' you go see it?"

Tony slid off the swing and ran to the truck as Josiah was just getting out. Josiah reached back into the cab, pulled out a cardboard box, and smiled hugely as he held it out to Tony. "Dis fo' you, Tony," he said. "Present from me and de missus." He set the box on the ground. Tony stopped a few yards short and stared at it. He looked up to Josiah as Alabama and Jasmine watched with eager anticipation.

"Go on, boy! Open de box!" Josiah exclaimed.

Tony took a few tentative steps forward. He knelt down beside the box and glanced up at Alabama. Alabama nodded, and Tony pulled back the four interwoven pieces that constituted the top of the box.

Instantly, a smooth, happy, tail-wagging brown puppy with large floppy ears stood on its hind legs and leaned into Tony's face, giving him an eager licking. Tony's eyes grew huge. "A puppy!" he cried. "Is it for *me*?" He looked to Alabama.

"Sho' is," Alabama replied. "From Mr. Josiah an' Mizz Jasmine. Whachoo gonna call 'im?"

Tony reached into the box and picked up the eager puppy, who continued to coat Tony's face with dog kisses while his little tail waggled up a storm. Tony held the dog close and stared at it. "He sure is a happy puppy!" he exclaimed, laughing as he leaned back to avoid a thorough bath. Suddenly he placed the puppy on the ground and looked up at Alabama. "Hey! That's it! Let's call him Happy!"

Alabama exchanged smiles with the other adults. "Cain't say Ah evah heah of a bettah name," he remarked. "Okay, you play with yo' pup, Tony," he said. "We old folks got some cornshine and catchin' up to do. Ah call you when it time to wash up. Don' take the puppy too far away, heah?"

"I won't!" Tony replied eagerly, running after the pup as the curious dog sniffed around the farm.

CHAPTER 37

On a Thursday morning in the first week of November, Alabama and Rufus piled the last of the pumpkin and corn crops into the wagon. It had been an unusually warm autumn, and the two men and Tony had worked shirtless in the fields for much of it. Alabama's habit was to work Tony for two or possibly three hours in the morning and give him the rest of the day off for studies and just plain fun. "He learnin' the value of hard productive work an' some decent schoolin', plus he get a chance to jes' be a boy," he remarked to Rufus as they drank cool water from the well.

"He a smaht boy," Rufus remarked. "A body kin see it."

Alabama nodded. "He seem to be. Picks up on his schoolin' real quick. An' no draggin' his feet, neithah. He seem to enjoy learnin.'" He smiled ruefully. "Tell you de truth, Rufus, he be passin' up mah ability raht soon. Ah on'y went through de fourth grade. Schoolin' fo' Negroes in Alabama when Ah's comin' up wasn't too fancy."

Rufus watched the boy and grinned. "He sho' do lack dat dawg!"

Alabama laughed, watching Tony and Happy run circles around one another. "Bes' thang a boy kin have is a dawg," he replied. "Good fun, plus it teach 'im 'bout takin' care of a someone who depends on you."

"Goin' teach dat dawg some manners?" Rufus asked. "Sit, lie, wait, dat sort 'a thang?"

Alabama nodded. "In due tam. Reckon we start when he's 'bout six months, in de spring. In de meantam, it bes' jes' to let dem play wif' one another." He glanced at the load in the wagon. "Wayall, Ah thank you, Rufus. As usual, you done a mighty fine job hepin' me out heah. Won't be needin' you 'til plantin', but Ah goin' be sore if'n you don' come an' visit now an' agin' ovah de wintah."

"Ah be heah," Rufus agreed. "Do some fishin', taste some 'a yo' cornshine now an' agin'." He grinned hugely.

"Dat stuff goin' be the end of me," Alabama moaned. "One day Ah make a batch dat drop whoevah take a sip."

"Ah wanna be dat man!" Rufus replied, and the two laughed uproariously.

Alabama looked at the load. "Wayall, time to slip on de jacket and go sell dis load. Tony!" he hollered. "Les' go to town and sell some produce! C'mon, now."

Tony picked up Happy and trotted over to the wagon. He put the pup down and smiled at the men. "Reckon we can pick up a treat for Happy?" he asked eagerly.

Alabama smiled. "Sho', Ah reckon we kin find sumpin' he lack," he replied. "C'mon. Get a drink, den put on yo' shirt and les' get rollin'. Don' forget to put Happy in de barn."

"I won't!" Tony replied eagerly, stooping to give the dog a quick wrestle. Happy quickly engaged his new master by flopping on the ground and mock-biting Tony's hand.

Once in Fordoche, Alabama turned the wagon automatically toward the broker's yard. Within minutes, he was talking with the broker prior to unloading his crop. As they chatted, Tony stood in the wagon and looked around the yard. He always found the piles of various crops fascinating.

A large, overweight farmer stood chatting with another man nearby. When Tony stood in the wagon and caught the man's eye, he asked his companion "Who's that blond kid with the nigger?"

His companion winced and looked around. "You wanna be careful with that word these days," he remarked quietly.

"What word?"

The smaller man looked up at the farmer. "The N-word, man! There's federal hate laws and stuff now. They getcha for sayin' racial-type words."

The farmer sneered. "Huh!" he replied. "Hate crimes! Whadda buncha Democrat horse dung! Say anything Ah damn well please, and the hell with them liberal bleedin' hearts!" He looked at the wagon again. "So. How come that nigger has the white kid with him?"

The other man shrugged. "Beats me. Ah seen 'em down here together a couple 'a times already. Makes you wonder why they always taggin' along 'side one another, don't it?"

The farmer mused, a scowl on his face. "Sho' does," he replied. "Maybe a person oughta check up on it."

The fat farmer lingered until Alabama and Tony had left. Then he sidled up to the broker and asked "Say, who's that black fella with the wagon? With the load 'a pumpkins?"

"Name's Alabama Denton," the broker replied easily. "Good fella. Been bringin' me quality crops for several years now."

The farmer nodded. "He live 'round here?"

"Yep," the broker replied, checking paperwork as he talked. "Has him fifty acres 'bout ten mile north of here, on 77. He invited me up there to see the crops a couple years ago. Runs a tidy farm, that fella. Good worker. Knows his stuff."

"Uh, huh," the farmer replied nonchalantly. "Well, I be seein' ya agin' soon."

The broker looked up and put out his hand. "Thanks, Bubba. Hope to see your next load in the next few days."

The farmer shook hands and left. His next stop was the office of Sheriff in New Roads, the parish seat. The farmer had to make a 42-mile trip one way to get there, but he smiled with grim self-satisfaction the entire way. "Sherf Bill ain't in," the receptionist told him.

"How long will he be?" the farmer asked.

She shrugged. "Don't rightly know. Lemme ask. What's the nature of your business with Sherf Bill?"

"Kidnappin'," the farmer replied ominously.

The receptionist's eyes went wide. "Oh, my," she murmured, picking up a microphone. When she reached the sheriff, she reported that there was a man in the office with urgent business. The radio crackled "Ten minutes" in a gruff voice.

A quarter of an hour later, Sheriff Bill Lamoreaux walked in. He ducked when he passed under the top of the door frame, being six feet, six inches and weighing in somewhere north of three hundred and fifty pounds. His gut was larger even than the farmer's. He looked down at the farmer, who suddenly was on his feet in the presence of The Great Man Himself, the legendary Bill Lamoreaux.

Sheriff Bill was famous for taking down a heroin distribution operation virtually single-handedly when he was a patrolman. He'd received a tip from a black informant and drove directly to the apartment where five black men were packaging the drugs. Without preamble, Patrolman Lamoreaux drew his .45 caliber automatic pistol and shot three of them. Two died at the scene and one in the hospital without regaining consciousness. He lined the other two up against the wall and put the barrel of his gun into the mouth of one of them while the other looked on with trembling. "Lookee here," he said in a quiet voice, all the more to gain their rapt attention. "One 'a them three guys shot at me when I came in. Ya hear? I got the gun he used right here." He reached in his back pocket and pulled out a .38-caliber revolver. While still bracing the man with his pistol as the dealer silently wet his trousers, Lamoreaux fired a shot from the .38 at the wall above the door. "But he was a lousy shot, and he died for it," Lamoreaux commented with a grin. "Right?" The man with the gun in his mouth, his eyes as wide as they could be, nodded carefully. "You?" Lamoreaux asked, pointing the revolver at the other man from a distance of three inches. The man's eyes crossed as he stared down the barrel of the gun. "Yassuh! Yassuh, Mistah Po-lice!" the man stuttered. "He shoot, he die. Das' de way it went down, yessah!" "Very good," Lamoreaux remarked casually. "And if your story changes, you get your equipment sliced off in prison. They'll hold you down and make you watch while they do it. Takes most of a day, way I hear it. We clear?" Both men nodded solemnly. That was the way they testified in court, and Bill Lamoreaux was destined for the head office.

"You the fella with urgent bidness?" Sheriff Lamoreaux asked condescendingly.

The farmer nodded. "Yes sir, Sheriff. Kidnappin'."

Lamoreaux nodded. "My office," he said, indicating a corridor with his cap.

Once in the office, while Lamoreaux flopped heavily into his specially-reinforced chair behind his desk, the man told the sheriff his suspicions about a nig—"I mean a black fella"—who had a blond boy with him at all times. "On'y way he has that kid is he kidnapped 'im," the farmer implored passionately. "It ain't natural otherwise. I jes' know there's somethin' bad goin' on there!"

The sheriff gazed at the farmer and sighed. "That all you got?"

The farmer shrugged uneasily. "Hey, I'm jes' tryin' to do my duty as a citizen!" he replied in a tremulous voice. "The rest is up to you."

Sheriff Lamoreaux nodded. "Well, thanks for comin' in," he noted without enthusiasm. "Give your pertic'lers to the lady out the front, so's we can get in touch with you." He swiveled in his chair and picked up the phone. The farmer took the hint and walked back down the corridor.

Eleven days later, the time lapse revealing the importance Sheriff Lamoreaux assigned to the complaint, a squad car with indicia of the Sheriff of Pointe Coupee Parish on the side rolled down the lane to Alabama's farm. As the crops were in and nothing in the field required his presence, Alabama was in the barn showing Tony how to shoe Chestnut. He was stripped to the waist and shiny from the heat of the furnace where he'd fashioned horseshoes from a strip of iron, banging them on a heavy steel anvil until they were just the right size for the mule. Around his waist was a heavy leather apron to protect his trousers and boot-clad feet from sparks and flying metal pieces. Alabama was just dunking a shoe into a shallow barrel of water to cool it down when a sheriff's deputy walked into the barn. Alabama and Tony stared at him.

The deputy hooked his thumbs in his belt and observed the pair. "You Alabama Denton?" he asked.

Alabama nodded. "Yes, Ah am. Kin Ah hep you?"

The deputy nodded toward Tony. "And who's this?"

Alabama paused. "Dis Tony Pickens," he replied evenly.

The deputy considered, his mouth wrinkled as he watched the two of them for a few seconds. He turned to Tony. "What you doin' here, son?" he asked.

Alabama laid the iron tongs holding the horseshoe on the anvil and stepped forward. "Deah some problem heah, officer?" he asked politely.

The deputy, a full six inches taller than Alabama, rested his right hand on the butt of his gun and replied "That depends." He looked at Tony again. "I asked what you're doin' here."

Alabama turned around and looked at Tony. He nodded gently.

"I…uh…I live here," Tony said fearfully.

The deputy stared at him. He turned his gaze to Alabama, and then to Tony. "You live here."

Tony gulped and nodded.

The deputy nodded knowingly. "I need both of you to step outside," he said, moving back a step to allow them to pass.

Alabama walked back, took Tony by the hand, and led him out of the barn into the sunshine. There he waited as the deputy approached them.

"Now, boy, you tell me *why* you're livin' here," the deputy said to Tony. He stared at the boy, ignoring Alabama.

Tony held Alabama's hand tightly and said nothing.

"He heah 'cause Ah invite 'im to live heah," Alabama said firmly but carefully. "He eat heah, he work heah, he study learnin' heah, he sleep heah. Dat a problem fo' you, officer?" Instinctively, he moved Tony a fraction behind him.

The officer shrugged. "Depends," he replied. "Where'd he come from?"

Alabama paused. "Ah made an arrangement wif' his fathah," he replied.

The deputy stared at him. "An arrangement."

"Das' raht."

"What kind of arrangement?"

"Tony come heah, his fathah don' have to look after him no mo'. He okay wif' dat, 'cause he a busy man. Him an' me agree dat Tony bettah off heah. Das all dey is to it."

The deputy frowned and smiled at the same time. "Somehow I don't think that's quite true," he replied with a hint of sarcasm. "Okay. I need to know who the boy's father is. And I need you to come with me."

Alabama frowned. "Come wif' you? Wheah? Why?"

"I want both of you in the back of the squad while I talk to this boy's father. If he agrees with what you said, I'll bring you back here."

Alabama looked at the ominous squad car. He could feel Tony clinging tighter to his leg and moving further behind him. "Is dat really necessary, Officer?" he asked. "Can't you jes' go talk wif' de man an' come back heah if'n you need to?"

The deputy shook his head. "I want you where I can find you. Don't need neither of you running off."

Alabama held out a hand and indicated the farm. "We live heah, officer. Ain't got nowheah to go. You find us heah, don' worry."

The deputy's eyes hardened. "Get in the car," he commanded in a low voice.

Alabama sighed. "How long we goin' be?"

The officer shrugged. "Depends. Why?"

"'Cause Ah need to button down de farm if'n we be gone long."

The deputy shook his head. "Can't allow that. Now, come on. Get in the car." Again he put his right hand on the butt of his gun. Alabama could feel Tony flinch.

Alabama scowled. "Dis' ain't necessary," he complained. "Least let me get mah shirt on." He nodded with his head toward the interior of the barn. "An' shut de do' fo' mah mule."

The deputy nodded. "First the boy goes in the car. Then you can do what you need to do."

"Alabama, no!" Tony cried, clutching Alabama's leg tightly as he hid behind and peered fearfully at the deputy. "I don't want to go in there alone!"

"Hush," Alabama soothed him quietly, one hand holding his back. He looked up at the deputy. "Officer, show some kindness heah," he implored. "Jes' lemme take de boy to de barn, get mah shirt, put mah mule away, and den we go wif' you."

The deputy pursed his lips. "Okay," he replied. "But I go with you." He nodded toward the barn.

Twenty minutes later, while Alabama and Tony sat in the back of the locked squad car and watched, the deputy stood talking with Cletus Pickens through the fence. Pickens had Bear by his side. Occasionally the dog growled menacingly at the officer and shook slobber off his lips. In a few minutes, the deputy pointed to Pickens' shack and returned to the squad car. He opened the driver's door, slid into the seat, and picked up his microphone. "Unit 6 requesting back-up," he said.

"Six, give your location and situation," the dispatcher replied.

The deputy described the circumstances and gave the location of the junkyard at the corner of Highways 10 and 77. "Roger, back-up enroute," the radio crackled. The deputy hung up the mike and waited.

Alabama held Tony beside him with a protective arm. "Excuse me, officer," he said. The deputy looked at him in the rear view mirror. "Why you needin' back-up? Whas' goin' on?

The deputy's hard expression gave Alabama no joy. "It's illegal to buy children in this state," he replied grimly. "Prolly in the whole country, for that matter. You and Pickens there have committed a felony."

Alabama sat back. A 'whoosh' of air escaped him, and color drained from his face. "Oh, Lawdy!" he moaned under his breath. "Oh, Lawd Jesus!"

Tony swiveled in the seat and looked up at Alabama. "You *bought* me?"

Alabama looked down at Tony and nodded. "Yo' fathah a greedy man," he replied in a shallow voice. "He ain't goin' give you up jes' to be kind."

Tony sat rigidly, staring at the floor and trying to make sense of what he'd heard. In a few seconds, he relaxed and folded up against Alabama's ribs. When Alabama put his arm around the boy, he could feel Tony's quiet sobs. Alabama leaned down and kissed the boy on his head, whispering "It be okay, Tony. Don' worry. We get outa dis mess okay."

When the back-up squad car arrived, the deputy stepped out of the car, briefly explained to the other deputy what was required, and locked Alabama and Tony in his squad car again. The two policemen walked to the fence, where the first deputy hollered "Cletus Pickens! Come out of there! You're under arrest! Now come out quiet, Pickens!"

Pickens appeared on his porch. "Arrest?" he shouted. "What for?"

"Child endangerment," the deputy replied firmly. "Now come out nice and easy, or we're gonna shoot that dog and come in and get you."

"Ah ain't endangered no child!" Pickens shouted. But in the end, he was persuaded to tell his story to a judge rather than to God with a body full of bullet holes. He slipped out and locked the gate while Bear remonstrated behind him.

When they arrived in New Roads, Pickens in handcuffs in the back of the second squad car, Tony was taken by a female deputy. He screamed, calling Alabama's name over and over and thrashing against the grip of the woman. Alabama hung his head, his own hands cuffed behind his back, while Pickens yelled "See what a mess you got us in, nigger? I shoulda shot you on sight! Meddlin' black son of a bitch!"

Once in a cell by himself, Alabama asked for and received a New Orleans phone book. He looked up Mrs. Stoughton's number. With his one allowed phone call, he placed a collect long-distance call to her. Fortunately, Mrs. Stoughton was home and agreed to receive the call when Alabama's name was given as the caller. In short, terse sentences, he explained the situation and asked her to call Mantor Livingston. "Of course I will, Alabama," she assured him. "Right away. Now, if I'm not mistaken, you have a right to wait for him before you talk with the police. I'm quite certain that's the case."

"I won' say nothin'," Alabama replied morosely. "Thank you, Mizz Stoughton."

"Of course! Of course," she replied. "Look, I'll phone my attorney also. Mr. Livingston may wish to confer with him. Don't worry about the expense, Alabama. We'll get through this."

Alabama sighed. "Okay. All right. Mizz Stoughton, would you please call Josiah Freeman at dis number? He need to see to mah farm." He gave her the phone number.

""I'll see to it. Now take heart, Alabama!" Mrs. Stoughton said cheerily. Now in her mid-seventies, she had retained the good health and strength of character that had seen her through the long, dark days and nights after she received news of her beloved husband's death. She hung up the phone and immediately sank to her knees in prayer.

CHAPTER 38

Mantor Livingston drove to New Roads the next day and posted Alabama's bail of $1,000. Cletus Pickens was offered the same bail, but rather than contact a bail bondsman and owe him the interest on the bail bond, he elected to remain in custody. When he heard that news, the arresting deputy dropped by the jail to speak to Pickens. "You just gonna let your place lie?" he asked.

Pickens sneered. "It's locked up, ain't it? Ain't nobody gonna break in an steal nothin' with that mangy dog there."

The deputy rubbed his chin. "Don't the dog need a feed every day? And water?"

Pickens shrugged. "They's a squirrel or rabbit go through the yard now and then," he replied. "And it's gonna rain eventually. He can eat if he can catch a critter. If he's too slow to catch 'em, he can jes' starve." The deputy shook his head and walked off in disgust.

When he walked out into the sunshine with Mantor Livingston by his side, Alabama asked "Where's Tony?"

"He's been taken to an institution for the time being," Livingston replied. "The next step is a foster home. He'll be there until the trial is adjudicated."

Alabama stopped, turned, and looked at him. "Wha' dat mean?"

"Until the trial is over and decided," Livingston replied. "If you're acquitted, we'll apply for custody. If not…" He allowed the sentence to hang.

Alabama stared at him for a moment. "Ah'm up for kidnappin', way Ah heah it," he remarked quietly.

Mantor Livingston nodded. "And human trafficking. That means dealing in slavery. Ironic, isn't it? Both are very serious charges. The penalty if you're found guilty is quite severe. If the prosecutor files for aggravated kidnapping, the penalty in this state if you're found guilty is usually the death sentence. That's especially true for black defendants." He looked gravely at his friend and client.

Alabama searched his eyes, then dropped his gaze to the concrete. "Death," he said slowly, "all for tryin' to keep a kid from bein' beat to a pulp by a mean, selfish bully who don' give a damn 'bout Tony 'cept whether the boy is slavin' proper fo' him."

Livingston nodded. He placed a hand on Alabama's shoulder and looked down at him. "I mention the charges to give you perspective, Alabama," he commented. "But I don't want you to worry. Your motivation was far from aggravated kidnapping, and Lord knows Tony is not your slave. In fact, I hope to convince the jury that your motives were entirely altruistic, and that this is a simple misunderstanding based upon ignorance of the law in your case."

Alabama looked at him. "My Pa once tol' me dat ignorance of de law is no excuse."

Livingston nodded. "Technically, that's correct," he replied evenly. "But we have a strong case nonetheless. For now, let's get you back to the farm so I can ascertain all the facts."

"Ah rather you take me to Josiah Freeman place," Alabama replied. "We kin talk theah. Ah need to talk it all ovah wif' him an' Jasmine."

Livingston nodded. "That's closer, in any case. Yes. Let's be on our way." He handed Alabama his business card. "You probably have my old card," he mentioned. "I've moved offices and added staff since then. Here is my current phone and address. Be sure to use this when you phone me. And call collect. I'll accept all incoming calls from you."

"What 'bout if'n you need to reach me?" Alabama asked. "Ain't got no phone on de farm."

Livingston considered. "I suppose I can phone Mr. Freeman and leave a message?"

Alabama nodded. "Das' de bes' idea," he agreed.

When they arrived at the Freeman General Store, Mantor Livingston allowed Alabama to spend a half-hour with Josiah and Jasmine to explain what had happened. In the meantime, he phoned his office to retrieve messages. Over a lunch which Jasmine quickly threw together for the four of them, Livingston handed Alabama a piece of paper with the name 'Madeline May' and a New Roads phone number. "She told my secretary that she's the social worker handling this case," he noted. "I'll give her a call. Is it all right if I use your phone here, Josiah? There will be a small long-distance charge to New Roads, and of course I will reimburse you."

"Ain't goin' be no reimbursin'," Josiah replied. "We all in dis together. You jes' make yo' calls as you see fit."

Madeline May told Mantor Livingston that she would like to interview Alabama to ascertain the facts of his relationship with Tony, and she inquired as to a convenient time to do so. The attorney informed her that his client would be willing to converse with her but she would have to drive to his farm since he had no phone. A date for the next morning was established. "I won't be there when she talks with you," Livingston remarked to Alabama later. "Bear in mind, she's a state employee and will probably be called as a witness for the prosecution. You must be very careful what you tell her."

Alabama shrugged. "Ah on'y got de truth," he replied.

Livingston nodded. "That's always best. Call me tomorrow afternoon at my office in New Orleans and tell me how it went with you and her."

Alabama nodded. Livingston thanked Jasmine for her hospitality and rose to leave. The other three rose as well. "Thank you fo' takin' dis case an' hep'in' me," Alabama said, shaking Livingston's hand. Livingston smiled. "I don't defend clients I know to be guilty," he replied. "The worst crime you're guilty of is compassion."

"Sho' hope de jury agree," Josiah remarked. Livingston nodded, shook his hand, and walked downstairs to his car.

Alabama remained for supper, after which Josiah returned him to his farm. His first act upon arriving was to liberate Happy from her cage in the barn. The puppy wriggled and cried with unrestrained joy. After he'd allowed the pup to lick his face, Alabama took her to the yard in front of the house. He sat on the porch until dark, rocking back and forth and watching the puppy forage and sniff around. Eventually Happy bounded up the three porch stairs to the swing, and Alabama took her up beside him. Happy turned in a circle three times, gave a satisfied groan, and fell instantly asleep by Alabama's hip.

The next day, Madeline May arrived in a sedan with a logo identifying it as an official Louisiana Department of Social Services vehicle. The sun was near mid-point in the sky when she stepped from the car. Anticipating her visit since soon after breakfast, Alabama, clean-shaven and dressed in pressed slacks, a clean long-sleeved shirt, and brown loafers with matching socks, stepped out of the house and walked to the vehicle.

"You mus' be Ms. May," Alabama said with a smile to the trim, well-dressed black woman. She appeared to be in her late forties or early fifties. He held out his hand, which she took professionally.

"Indeed I am, Mr. Denton," she replied with a courteous smile. She handed him a business card and cast a glance around the farm. Alabama studied the card. "'Fraid Ah don' have a card," he remarked with a grin. "Mine would jes' say "Alabama Denton, farmer. Contact him at de farm.'"

Ms. May nodded, offering a quick smile to acknowledge his humor. "Would you mind taking me on a tour of your property, Mr. Denton?" she asked.

"Ah'd love to," Alabama replied enthusiastically. "If'n you want to see de whole thang, Ah kin hitch up de wagon. Othahwise we kin jes' stroll 'round a bit."

"Walking is fine," Ms. May replied. Alabama noted that she had donned feminine ankle-high boots for the occasion.

For the next hour, Alabama proudly displayed his cropland, extensive vegetable garden, home, and barn. In each case, he explained Tony's responsibilities in contributing to the welfare of the two of them and the animals, noting that the boy had quickly developed a love for the property and a willingness to work hard to do his part. "Ah don' drive 'im," Alabama explained. "Ah give 'im a job, explain wha' need doin', and keep an eye on 'im. If'n it look lack he gettin' tired or de work too hard, Ah step in and give 'im a hand or give 'im tam to jes' play wif' his dawg. He back at it pretty quick, though. Dat boy love to work. He a fine young man in dat way."

Ms. May was especially interested in the home schooling arrangements Alabama had constructed. He showed her the table he and Tony used for reading, writing, spelling, and arithmetic exercises, and he proudly displayed a couple of the boy's one-page essays. Ms. May's mouth opened in surprise, despite her otherwise cool demeanor. "Tony wrote these?" she asked incredulously.

Alabama nodded. "He love words," he replied enthusiastically. He showed her the pile of children's books Josiah and Jasmine had given the boy. "He through wif' dese easy ones," he remarked, holding up the 'Dick and Jane' books. "Now he on to dese." He displayed a book about dinosaurs and another about astronomy. Ms. May looked carefully at Alabama. "He can't actually read these, can he?" she asked skeptically.

Alabama shrugged. "He miss a few words," he replied. "He jes' a boy. But he lack to look up words if'n he don' know 'em. Some words too big fo' him to understand. But he don' mind. Jes' keeps on readin'. He a bit past me now. Ah find it hard to read some 'a dem books."

Ms. May turned the book on dinosaurs over and read the verbiage on the back. "For children nine to fourteen," she read. She looked at Alabama. "Tony is only six."

Alabama nodded. "He is," he agreed. "Seems raht smaht to me. 'Course Ah don' really know. He jes' lack to read." His eyes brightened. "Heah!" he exclaimed, digging out a manila folder. "Dis heah some 'a his 'rithmetic." He handed her the folder. Ms. May examined page after page of exercises, all in a neat hand between the faint blue lines on the paper. "Knows his multiplication tables all de way to ten times ten," Alabama said proudly. "We practice 'em when we workin'."

Ms. May studied the papers carefully. "These last ones are long division," she remarked.

Alabama nodded. "Yes ma'am. Simple stuff. He don' do mo' den three numbahs into three numbahs at dis stage."

"But you've even got him dividing larger numbers into smaller numbers, resulting in decimals!" Ms. May exclaimed. "That's a concept we don't introduce until the fifth grade!"

Alabama shrugged. "He kin do it," he replied. "An' he good at it. Ah 'bout done teachin' 'im."

Ms. May pursed her lips and studied the papers. She looked around the room. "He sleeps in the house, right?"

"Oh, 'a course!" Alabama replied. "C'mon. Ah show you." He took her to Tony's bedroom, where the large bed he and Rufus had made from peeled logs and slats held a medium-firm store-bought mattress he and Tony had picked out in a store in Fordoche. One wall was lined with books and mechanical toys, all neatly arranged. In a small closet, a rack of jeans and shirts was neatly hung. Against another wall was a three-drawer bureau that they'd purchased along with the mattress.

Ms. May took it all in. Abruptly, she wheeled and faced Alabama. "How often does he ask to sleep in your bed?" she asked pointedly.

Alabama looked at her, clearly mystified. "He don' do dat," he replied. "Nevah did. He way too big fo' dat. Ain't a baby no mo'. Nowadays his dawg sleep wif 'im. De bed big enuf, so Ah don' think it a problem. Do you?"

Ms. May studied him for any trace of guile. When she was satisfied that he was telling the truth, she smiled and said "As long as the dog is clean, I see no problem. I presume Tony takes care of the dog?"

Alabama nodded. "Das' one reason Ah got de dawg," he assured her. "Tony feed Happy, keep her water up, and brush her mos' days. If she do a mess in de house, which ain't happen fo' awhile, he clean it up. She a good dawg, and he sho' love her."

Ms. May smiled, studying him. "I believe you," she replied softly. She looked toward the living room. "May we sit down?" she asked.

Alabama smiled. "Actually, Ah was goin' ax you if'n you would lack some lunch," he replied. "Got some nice veggie soup Ah made from the produce from de garden."

Ms. May smiled and shook her head. "I'm afraid that won't be possible," she said. "We generally don't dine with those whom we're investigating. But thank you. However, I would like to sit with you for a moment."

Alabama held out a hand, indicating the hall to the living room. "Please," he said.

When they were seated at the dining table, Ms. May said "It appears from my initial impressions that you and Tony have a good, healthy, perhaps even loving relationship. I'll confirm that when I interview him this afternoon. In addition, if those papers and books are truly his—which I don't doubt they are—he is clearly a gifted child. Whatever happens with him, I will ensure that the Department of Education is fully aware of that so Tony can receive the best education for advanced students the state has to offer."

Alabama stared at her. He dropped his gaze to the table and then looked abstractly around the room, licking his lips. "Ms. May?" he said softly, addressing her after leaning back in his chair. "Tony ver'a special to me. Ah los' a chil' many yeah ago. Boy jes' a bit younger den Tony. My wife, she so distraught dat she nevah recovah. Died a few yeah back. Dese pas' few months, wif' Tony…" He swallowed hard and looked at the table. "Dey been precious," he said quietly. "A real blessin'." He looked up, and there were tears in his eyes. "Ah don' care if'n Ah go to prison, Ms. May," he implored her. "It don' mattah to me. 'Cept dey's Tony. Wha' would happen to de boy? Who goin' love 'im and look after 'im? Who goin' read to him, and hep him wif' his 'rithmetic? How he goin' look after his dawg if'n Ah go away?" He turned his head away in embarrassment and wiped his eyes, rubbing his fingers on his trousers to dry them.

Madeline May sighed. "I can't discuss your court case, Mr. Denton," she replied sympathetically. "My job is to assess Tony's home environment to determine if there is any danger and if it's conducive to happiness and good health. I *will* tell you that I am most impressed. Presuming my interview with Tony confirms all that you've told me and shown me, I will recommend most strongly that the court view your relationship with favor."

Alabama studied her. "Do dat mean he can come home?"

Ms. May shrugged. "That's up to the judge, Mr. Denton. What I will report—again, if Tony confirms all you've said—is that this is a very good environment for him."

Alabama sighed deeply. "Wayall, das' good, Ah guess."

Ms. May nodded and chuckled. "Mr. Denton, had you not shown me the excellent situation you've provided for Tony here, I assure you that there would be no *way* he would return here. Now at least there is a possibility." She rose and held out her hand. "Thank you for a most enlightening tour and discussion, Mr. Denton. I wish you all the best in this situation."

Alabama rose, nodded, and followed her out to her car. He waved as she was turning to drive down the lane. Ms. May nodded with a smile.

CHAPTER 39

The trial date was set for three months hence, in the second week of February. In the meantime, having repaid the bail money to his attorney, Alabama existed alone on his farm. At night he lay awake, sleeping only in fits and starts, with thoughts and dreams of orange jumpsuits and prison beatings running through his tortured mind. During the day he performed necessary repairs to equipment and tended to his animals, all the while with his thoughts on Tony. Despite several requests for information, he was unable to determine where Tony was or how he was being treated. Stewing with frustration, he had to remind himself to eat. By the time the trial began, he had lost seven pounds off his trim and muscular frame.

Mantor Livingston deposed Josiah and Jasmine Freeman as well as Rufus Mason. He also deposed Cletus Pickens, who treated him with open disdain and had to be reminded that failure to testify truthfully in a deposition was a felony on the order of perjury. Pickens did admit his part in the sale of Tony to Alabama, but he couched it as 'bein' forced' by Alabama.

"Forced?" Livingston inquired skeptically. "Would you please expand upon that, Mr. Pickens?"

Pickens looked down at the linoleum-covered table in the jail's interview room, out the barred window, and off to the side. "Mr. Pickens?" Livingston remarked. "Do I need to remind you of the penalty…"

"That nigger said he'd make up some crap about me mistreating my son!" Pickens blurted.

Livingston stared at him for a long moment, and Pickens dropped his gaze to the table. "Are you referring to Mr. Denton?" the attorney inquired.

Pickens nodded.

"For the tape, Mr. Pickens, would you please vocalize your response?"

Pickens looked at him, unsure of the meaning of the word. "Speak up, Mr. Pickens. Don't nod."

"Yes," Pickens admitted.

"Yes, you are referring to Mr. Denton."

"I *said* yes!"

"And you used a racial slur in that reference. Are you aware of the penalty for that transgression, Mr. Pickens?"

"Oh, for Chr…" Pickens mocked a spit on the floor beside him. "Okay, okay, I'm sorry for calling him a nig… a racial slur."

Mantor Livingston paused for a few seconds, staring hard at Pickens until the witness once again dropped his gaze. "The defense team will overlook your insult on this one occasion, Mr. Pickens," he remarked carefully. "But if it occurs again, rest assured it will be reported to the authorities along with a copy of this tape. Do you understand me?"

Pickens looked up. The evil in his eyes was enough to wilt a lesser man. Mantor Livingston merely waited, never blinking. Eventually, Pickens spat "Yeah, I got it."

"So, as to this allegation that my client threatened to invent a fabrication regarding your treatment of your son, will that stand up under testimony in court by your son?"

Pickens stared open-mouthed. "You're gonna make *Tony* testify?" he asked incredulously. "He's only a kid!"

"And a very intelligent child at that," Livingston replied. "With a prodigious memory. I imagine he can remember every blow, every black eye, and every bruise."

Pickens exhaled a long breath and stared at the floor. He uttered a curse under his breath.

"For the purposes of this deposition, I will allow your silence to stand," Livingston commented. "However, we will be calling you as a witness. You might want to think carefully about how you will testify in court and what your words will mean in terms of a possible perjury indictment. This deposition is concluded." He turned off the tape recorder, rose, and walked to the door, where he summoned the guard.

The testimony in the depositions from the Freemans and Rufus was entirely favorable, as Livingston expected. All three, testifying independently, told of Alabama's concern, care, and love for Tony, and how the boy had prospered under Alabama's care. When the prosecutor deposed the three and hinted at sexual abuse of the boy while in Alabama's care, the response was immediate, angry, and vehement denial, along with Josiah telling the attorney to take his perverted mind to a mental hospital and get some help before he hurt somebody. That remark mysteriously disappeared from the tape after the deposition.

The week before the trial, Livingston phoned Alabama by pre-arrangement at the Freeman residence and briefed him on what was likely to happen. "You'll need to be at the courthouse in New Road by 8:30 each morning," he said. "Can you arrange that?"

Alabama put his hand over the phone and conducted a brief chat with Josiah. "All set," he reported to Livingston.

"Do you have a suit and tie?" Livingston asked. "And polished shoes?"

Alabama assured him that he would be dressed appropriately.

"Good. Well, we're ready. Your job is simply to sit beside me, follow the proceedings, and testify to the truth when I call you to the stand. Now, bear in mind that the prosecution will also question you, and they'll do their best to make you look like a pervert and a criminal. Just tell the truth,

Alabama. You have nothing to hide, and the jury will hear and see that. By the way, Cletus Pickens' trial is set for April. Possibly I'll be calling him as a witness. If I do, I expect him to lie, even under threat of perjury. Your testimony must counter his. Also, we'll be calling Tony to testify."

There was a pause. "Please go easy on de boy," Alabama said softly. Livingston assured him that he would be as gentle as possible. "Say," he mentioned, "something else of interest. Do you recall the judge at your trial concerning the land title?"

Alabama paused. "Don't reckon Ah do," he replied. "Seems he was a nice gemmen, but thas' all Ah recall."

"His name is Garrett Hanson. And lo and behold, he's going to be the judge at your trial this time as well!"

Alabama frowned. "But dat was in N'Owlins. Wha' he doin' in New Roads?"

"The trial judges are required to travel once a year and conduct a minimum of one trial in an outlying parish," Livingston replied. "That ensures that they gain exposure to the entire state, because there are some regional differences to take into account now and then, and it gives the outlying parishes some big-city expertise."

Alabama shrugged. "Wayall, das' good, Ah suppose."

Livingston agreed. "I believe it's very good," he replied firmly. "Judge Hanson is a fair and very knowledgeable jurist. I look forward to serving under his authority."

The morning of the first day of trial, Alabama and the Freemans were at the courthouse at eight. Rufus had agreed to live on the farm and tend to the animals until the day he was called to testify, if at all. "If'n dey come fo' me, make sho' dey check de river," Rufus said seriously. "Ah plan to do some serious fishin'."

At precisely nine o'clock, with all parties present in court, the bailiff rose, called out the number of the case, and said "Judge Garrett Hanson presiding. All rise!" Judge Hanson, a few years older than when he'd heard Alabama's land case in summary court, walked into the courtroom and ascended the three steps to his massive oak bench. He glanced at the District Attorney, Ellis Dupre, who was up for election in the fall and had decided to try this case himself for potential political gain. "Are the people ready, Mr. Dupre?" Judge Hanson asked.

"We are, Your Honor," Dupre replied confidently.

Judge Hanson glanced at the defense table. He started with recognition when he saw Alabama and Mantor Livingston. Quickly recovering, he said "And are you ready, Mr. Livingston?"

"We are, Your Honor," Livingston replied.

"Very well," Judge Hanson announced. "Let's get on with jury selection."

Under the laws of the State of Louisiana, the prosecution and the defense were each given ten preemptory challenges, where they could simply declare a potential juror unacceptable with no possible objection from the other side. Out of the pool of seventy-one persons who had been called for jury duty, nine were black. The District Attorney challenged these people, one by one, until only white men and women were left. "This could actually work in our favor," Livingston whispered to Alabama. "It's a point for appeal if things go badly for us. We can claim the D.A. has eliminated all opportunity for a fair trial by challenging all nine blacks but no whites." Alabama looked at him worriedly.

When a jury of ten men and two women had been selected, with two male alternates, Judge Hanson declared the trial under way and asked for opening statements from each attorney. The D.A. painted a picture of a conniving, opportunistic, manipulative black man who had virtually stolen an innocent young boy for the purpose of enslaving and sexually abusing him. Mantor Livingston calmly described the situation as one of rescue and compassion, with none of the heinous motivations the D.A. had portrayed.

When opening statements were concluded, Judge Hanson addressed the jury. "You have five possible outcomes as a result of your deliberations," he said. "It is your solemn duty to come to the right conclusion based upon the evidence you will hear, and *only* that evidence. The five are as follows:

guilty of both of the felonies, that is kidnapping and human trafficking, guilty of one but not guilty of the other, guilty of a misdemeanor misuse of contract law, or outright acquittal of all charges. You have taken an oath to deliberate with the best use of your intelligence and conscience to achieve a fair verdict. Now you'll be escorted to your hotel for the night. None of you are to discuss this case with one another or with any other person unless you're in the jury room. Failure to observe this very strict requirement may result in you being prosecuted with a potential penalty of ten years in prison. We take collusion very seriously, ladies and gentlemen. What we're seeking here and in every other case is a fair and just verdict based solely on the evidence presented in court. Are there any questions?"

There were none. The jury was dismissed and filed out to the waiting van, where they enjoyed a silent five-minute trip to a nearby motel.

The next morning, again precisely at nine, the bailiff called the courtroom to order and Judge Hanson asked the District Attorney to present his case. To warm up the jury, Dupre called the arresting officer to the stand. Whereas Dupre knew there was really not much to be gained from the officer's testimony, he also realized it was good to have the jury see that the police are on your side. When the sheriff's deputy had described the circumstances of the arrest, the D.A. invited Livingston to question him. Livingston declined.

The D.A. then called a clerk of his office, a paralegal, to describe the law under which Alabama had been charged. Livingston objected. "Your Honor, Mr. Dupre can spell out the technical aspects of the law quite competently all by himself. After all, he has a law degree and presumably some experience. This witness is here purely for dramatic effect and is wasting the court's time." Judge Hanson agreed and dismissed the witness. "Kindly seek to reduce the length of this trial, not add to it, Mr. Dupre," he admonished.

Dupre stood to his feet. "Very well then, Your Honor," he announced loudly, "the people call Mr. Alabama Denton."

Livingston leaned over to Alabama. "Be calm. Just like we said. The truth." Alabama sighed and nodded his head. Slowly, he rose and approached the witness stand. He was sworn in with his right hand on a Bible.

Dupre approached the stand with a swagger, smiling to the jury. He leaned with both forearms on the rail of the witness stand, not two feet from Alabama's face. Alabama moved as far back in the seat as he could and Dupre leaned in a few inches further. "Now, Mr. Denton," he said. "*Alabama* Denton." He smiled beneficently. "My, that's an unusual name to give a child!"

Some of the spectators in the court, all black faces being the exception, chuckled at this. Mantor Livingston immediately stood to his feet. "Objection, Your Honor!" he said. "The District Attorney is seeking to shame my client over irrelevant matters. The fact is that this case reads 'People of Louisiana vs. Alabama Denton.' He is entitled to bear that name without comment from the District Attorney."

"Sustained," Judge Hanson remarked, eyeing the D.A. with approbation.

"Mr. Denton, do you waive your Fifth Amendment right not to testify in this matter?" Dupre asked.

Having discussed the matter thoroughly with his attorney and agreeing that there would be little gain in invoking the Fifth, Alabama replied "Ah do."

"So, Alabama Denton," the D.A. continued obsequiously. "You're a farmer."

Livingston was again on his feet. "Your Honor, is there a question in that?"

Judge Hanson sighed. "Mr. Dupre. You know the protocol in court. Address the witness with questions, not statements."

"Certainly, Your Honor!" Dupre agreed innocently. He turned to Alabama. "Are you a farmer?"

Alabama nodded.

"Will you please elucidate your answer for the jury?" Dupre asked.

Alabama frowned. He leaned aside and looked at his attorney. Livingston pantomimed speaking, and Alabama said "Yes, Ah'm a farmer."

"How many acres do you farm?"

"Fo'ty."

"Emmm," Dupre mused, still leaning on the rail. He swiveled to face the jury and smiled knowingly. "Now, I'm not a farmer, Mr. Denton. Never had the privilege. But from what I know, farming is hard work. Farming forty acres must be a real challenge, day in and day out. Wouldn't you agree?"

Alabama nodded. Remembering, he quickly replied "Yes."

"Yes, it's hard work," Dupre repeated.

"I said that," Alabama replied.

"So you did," Dupre remarked. "Now, Mr. Denton, how many farm workers do you employ on a full-time basis?"

Alabama looked at him, a mild frown on his face. "Full-time?"

"That's what I asked," Dupre replied, leaning in a fraction.

Livingston arose. "Your Honor, unless the District Attorney has developed a degree of deafness, there is no reason he has to violate my client's personal space. Would you be so kind as to direct him to display common courtesy to the defendant?"

Dupre immediately backed away, nodding to the judge deferentially. Judge Hanson observed the move and declined to comment.

From a yard away, with his face toward the jury, Dupre said "How many, Mr. Denton? How many full-time workers?"

"Just me," Alabama replied.

Dupre frowned, as if deep in thought. He walked to the jury and placed a hand on the rail. "Just the one. For forty acres. And how many part-time workers do you employ, Mr. Denton?"

Alabama glanced at Livingston, who sat comfortably and did not offer any visual clues.

"One. On occasion Ah ax Rufus Mason to come down an' hep."

Dupre looked at him with surprise. "Just the *one* part-timer? And him only on occasion? My, that must leave a very difficult task for a 62-year-old man!"

Livingston was immediately on his feet. Judge Hanson waved him back down. "Mr. Dupre," he said succinctly. "I will not tell you again. Questions only. The next violation will result in the loss of this witness for further questioning."

Dupre stood tall. "With respect, Your Honor," he replied, "the people are entitled to question the defendant if the Fifth Amendment has been waived."

Judge Hanson gazed at him for a few seconds. "Don't try me," Mr. Dupre," he said ominously.

Dupre sniffed down his nose. He turned to Alabama again. "So, Mr. Denton," he said tersely, leaning in on the rail of the witness stand with both hands and staring hard at Alabama, "isn't it true that you kidnapped the boy, Tony Pickens, so he could be a slave to work on your farm? *Isn't that the truth here?!*"

Alabama shut his eyes and sighed. When he opened them a few seconds later, Dupre was still in his face. "Back up!" he said firmly.

Dupre stood up straight, a surprised look on his face. He turned to the bench in horror. "Your *Honor!*" he protested.

Judge Hanson smiled thinly. "Yes, Mr. Dupre?" he replied, eyebrows raised.

Dupre stared at him, pulled his suit coat down primly, and frowned self-righteously. He turned to Alabama. "I believe I asked you a question, Mr. Denton!" he demanded.

Alabama nodded. "De answer is flat 'No,' Mistah District Attorney. Ah did not kidnap anyone fo' any reason." He sat calmly, hands folded in his lap.

Dupre walked quickly to his table and took a paper which his assistant handed him. "Your Honor, the people introduce People's Exhibit One," he pronounced imperiously. "This is a bill of sale executed by the witness and Mr. Cletus Pickens, the boy's father. It spells out the commodity—that is, the human being known as Tony Pickens—the parties, and the sale price. It even includes a date. No doubt the criminals involved here wanted to be precise! I withdraw the comment," he said quickly when Livingston rose to his feet. He took the paper to the jury box and waved it. "A bill of sale!" he exclaimed. "For a human being! Like an animal, or a sack of oats!" He turned and stared at Alabama. "Or a slave," he said slowly. "A common slave, in this case a white slave." In the hubbub which followed, motivating Judge Hanson to bang his gavel and demand order, Dupre strode to the bailiff's table and dropped the paper on it. "Your witness," he said disdainfully to Livingston.

Mantor Livingston allowed the murmurs to dissipate before rising to his feet. "Mr. Denton," he said quietly. "Did you buy Tony Pickens?"

The courtroom was immediately silent.

Alabama nodded.

"Please, sir…yes or no," Livingston said.

"Yes," Alabama replied.

"You bought him? For how much?"

"Three hundred dollah."

Judge Hanson silenced the instant hubbub with a bang of the gavel.

Livingston rubbed his chin, seemingly in thought. "Three hundred dollars," he remarked. "How much would you have given for the boy if it came to that?"

Alabama stared at him. In a suddenly hoarse voice, he replied "Ah'd'a given every dollah Ah had, plus half mah land, fo' Tony," he replied. Sudden wetness in his eyes made him wipe them with his sleeve.

Mantor Livingston approached the jury and stood off to the side, his hands behind his back. "Really!" he exclaimed. "All your money plus half the land you've fought so hard to obtain, retain, and develop." He glanced at Judge Hanson. "Why so great a price for a little boy, Mr. Denton? A boy you hardly knew at all. Surely a lad of six can't be much of a farm laborer, can he?"

Alabama sighed hugely. "Tony…Ah din' buy him fo' labor. Ah bought him 'cause his fathah was beatin' him an' starvin' him. Tony had to steal vegetables from mah garden jes' to fill his belly. Ah knew two thangs. One, if'n Ah don't step in and get dis boy away from dat man, he goin' beat de boy to death in a drunken rage. Two, Mistah Pickens a greedy man. He don't jes' hand de boy ovah to nobody. Dat three hundred dollah, dat jes' a price. It enuf to satisfy Mistah Pickens, and he sign de papuh. The money ain't important at all. It jes' a number. De on'y thang dat mattered was savin' dat boy's life."

Livingston let the moment ride. After a few seconds, he asked "Alabama, do you put Tony to work on your farm?"

Alabama nodded. "Yes, Ah do. Usually in de mornin' when he got strength. He work two, three hoah. When Ah see he gettin' tired, Ah tell him to stop, go play. He work enuf fo' a boy but no' mo'."

"Why do you want him to work?"

"A boy got to learn dat work is good," Alabama replied earnestly. "Nobody but de inherited rich don't got to work. If'n you got to work, and de Bible say work is good, you bes' work hard and good, so you learn satisfaction from a job well done an' you produce well. Das' wha' Ah teach Tony. Truth is, he love de work. He love to produce an' be part of de farm life. He prosperin', growin' muscles, gettin' tall, breathin' deep of good Looziana air. Workin' good fo' him. But he still a boy, an' Ah ver'a mindful 'a dat. He ain't ovahworked by a long shot."

Livingston nodded, gazing at the jury during Alabama's testimony. "Mr. Denton, did you kidnap Tony?" he asked.

Alabama shook his head. "No, suh. Ah drove mah wagon up to Mistah Pickens' place and did bidness wif' him."

"As indicated by the bill of sale."

Alabama nodded. "Yes, suh."

Livingston smiled. "Now, Mr. Denton," he said gently, "tell the court about your educational efforts with Tony."

"Objection!" Dupre shouted, on his feet. "Irrelevant!"

"I'll allow it," Judge Hanson replied. "Keep it tight, Mr. Livingston."

"Yes, Your Honor," Livingston replied respectfully. He turned to Alabama and nodded.

Alabama smiled. "Tony one smaht boy!" he remarked. "Picks up on learnin' raht quick. Reads up a storm, dat boy, an' he write real good fo' a young'un. He do math real good, he understan' thangs quick. It a real pleashuh to teach him. He jes' lap it up."

"Have you been his sole teacher?"

"Yes. Tony nevah been to school. Ah reckon he need to go, though. He 'bout past all Ah kin teach him now."

"So would you say you've done him good in terms of education?" Livingston asked.

Alabama considered. "Wayall, seein's how he nevah had no learnin' a'tall 'fore he come to live wif' me, Ah guess Ah say yes."

"Do you ever beat him?"

Alabama recoiled with alarm. "*No!*" he almost shouted. Calming himself, he said "A man who beat a boy ain't no mo' den a *coward!*"

"Do you hug him?"

Alabama smiled, dropping his gaze to his lap for a second. "It hard not to," he replied quietly. "Tony a very affectionate young fella. He love to jes' set an' cuddle."

"Do you ever take him into your bed? Or get into his?"

Alabama sighed, frowned, and shook his head. "No. Ah cain't think of no mo' disgustin' thang. Dat boy perfectly safe wif' me, an' he know dat full well."

Livingston frowned. "Alabama, why do you do this for Tony? Feed him, shelter him, give him opportunities to learn and grow his mind, protect him? You even gave him a puppy as a companion! Why do you do all this?"

Alabama looked at him. He looked down into his lap. He looked at the judge. Suddenly he trembled, and it was a few seconds before he could contain himself. He cleared his throat. "Anybody be wif' dat boy fo' a day or so come to love him," he replied hoarsely. He shook his head. "Wha' mo' kin Ah say? Ah do fo' de boy 'cause it give me such deep pleashuh. In a way, he lack de son Ah lost many yeah ago. Ah reckon Ah would do mos' anything fo' dat boy. He goin' be a fine man one day. Mayhaps he look back an' say 'Alabama Denton hep me in a tryin' tam.' Mayhaps de Lawd Jesus be lookin' on, too, Ah don' know. Das' mah reward, Mistah Livingston. Das de reason Ah do fo' de boy."

Livingston smiled. He looked at the jury while he addressed Alabama. "Mr. Denton, in the event the jury finds that you aren't guilty of any crime whatsoever, and in fact you are a wonderfully loving father figure to this very fortunate young man, what are your plans for him?"

Alabama smiled. "He goin' to college, suh. Mayhaps he be a lawyer one day."

Livingston smiled. "No further questions, Your Honor," he said as he walked to his table.

Judge Hanson had to restrain himself from chuckling wryly at Alabama's last comment. "You may step down, Mr. Denton," he said.

Dupre next called a psychologist, Dr. Marianne Matthews. She sat primly in the witness chair after being sworn in. "Dr. Matthews, please explain your educational qualifications for the jury," Dupre instructed.

"I have a bachelor of science, majoring in biology, from Tulane, and a Ph.D. in psychology from the University of Texas."

"And how long have you been practicing?"

"I've been in the field post-doc for twelve years."

Dupre nodded to the jury, inviting them to be impressed. "Dr. Matthews," he asked, "have you dealt with cases of children being deprived of their natural parents?"

"Hundreds."

"And what is your opinion of the merits of depriving children of their natural parents, Dr. Matthews?"

"Oh, there are none!" she replied, a hand to her throat in horror. "At least not to speak of. A child belongs in a home with a mother and a father. That's the norm, and it has stood the test of time while other alternatives have not."

"So, then," Dupre continued, "removing a child from the home of his father when his mother is permanently absent…what is your opinion of such a move, Doctor?"

Dr. Matthews shook her head sadly. "A tragic mistake."

Dupre paused. "And if that child is *sold* out of the home?"

Dr. Matthews exhaled deeply. She shook her head. "Dreadful!" she exclaimed animatedly. "The effects upon the child are most likely to be horrendous! The resulting trauma could be life-long, inhibiting the then-grown person's ability to establish meaningful adult relationships."

Dupre smiled. "Not a good idea under any circumstances, then," he commented.

Dr. Matthews shook her head. "Not at all."

Dupre smiled. "Thank you, Dr. Matthews. Your witness, counselor."

Mantor Livingston stood. "Good morning, Dr. Matthews," he said politely.

She stared at him for a few seconds. "Good morning," she replied noncommittally.

Livingston looked down at his notes. "Dr. Matthews, you testified a moment ago that it is, and I quote, 'not a good idea under any circumstances' to remove a child from the home of his father when the mother is permanently absent. Was that your testimony, Dr. Matthews?"

She nodded. "Yes, it was. And is."

Livingston nodded. "Hmmm. I see," he commented. "So, if said child is required to be the sole provider of food for himself and his father, even though the child is only six years of age, would that change your opinion, Dr. Matthews?"

"Well, I…"

"And if said child is being beaten by his father on a daily basis, would that change your opinion, Dr. Matthews?"

She stared at Livingston.

"And if said child is being emotionally abused on a daily basis, told he is stupid and worthless, how would that affect your expert opinion, Dr. Matthews?" This time he paused, allowing her to respond. When she had said nothing after a few seconds, Livingston said "Perhaps you didn't hear the list of conditions I mentioned, Dr. Matthews. The child is being beaten, starved…"

"I heard them!" she replied tersely.

"And?" Livingston inquired, his eyebrows raised.

Dr. Matthews shrugged. "Well, I just can't *imagine* such a situation!" she exclaimed.

Livingston stared at her. "Dr. Matthews, are you receiving compensation for testifying in this case?"

She regarded him carefully. "Compensation?"

"Are you being paid to testify. You know what compensation is. Is that the case here, Dr. Matthews?"

Dr. Matthews glanced at Dupre. "Well, yes," she replied.

"By whom?"

"Well, by the...by the District Attorney's office," she replied lamely.

Livingston nodded to the jury. "A hired gun, then, are you, Doctor?"

Dupre leapt to his feet. "Objection!" he shouted.

"Sustained," Judge Hanson replied. "Be careful, Mr. Livingston."

"Yes, Your Honor," Livingston replied graciously. He turned again to Dr. Matthews. "Now, Doctor, given the set of circumstances I posed a moment ago, that the child in question is daily being starved, beaten, and emotionally abused by his father, the only other person in the household, what exactly is your professional opinion about the advisability of keeping that child in the household?"

She looked down at her lap. "I suppose he should be removed, under those draconian circumstances," she replied. Looking up, she said "But really, Mr. Livingston, there is scarcely a case in the literature that describes the situation you posed!"

Livingston turned and addressed the jury. "The literature may be a bit sparse on the subject, Doctor, but there is a real life case of it before our very eyes. Soon we will hear from the principal himself, the boy, and he will open your eyes and expand your professional horizon considerably." He walked back to his table.

Judge Hanson said "You are dismissed, Dr. Matthews," to the lady. She left the courtroom in haste.

Dupre rose to his feet. "Your Honor, the state rests. We believe we've proven our case beyond a shadow of a doubt."

Judge Hanson regarded him. "As always, that remains to be seen, Mr. Dupre," he replied. "Let's take a break and reconvene at two o'clock this afternoon. Members of the jury, as always, you are cautioned about discussing any aspect of this case with anyone until you are dismissed to deliberate, and only then in the jury room." He tapped his gavel on the wooden plate and rose. "All rise!" cried the bailiff, and Judge Hanson exited into his chambers.

At precisely two o'clock, the door to Judge Hanson's chambers opened and he walked in. The bailiff called the room to order and the judge took his seat. He looked at Mantor Livingston. "Your case, Mr. Livingston," he invited.

Livingston arose. "Thank you, Your Honor," he replied. "The defense calls Josiah Freeman."

For the next hour, Livingston led Josiah, Jasmine, and the pastor of their church through a recitation of where they had met Alabama, how long they had known him, and what was their opinion of his character. Each was effusive in his or her praise of Alabama. At the end of each testimony, Livingston asked the same question: "In your observation, how has Alabama Denton treated Tony Pickens? Please offer specific examples." In each case, a picture of Alabama's sacrificial love and strong guidance was presented in enthusiastic terms. After he was finished with each witness, he offered them to Dupre for cross-examination. Dupre declined in each case.

Just as the pastor stepped down from the witness box, the back door of the courtroom opened and a matronly white woman entered. Tony, coming along behind her, stopped and stared at the packed room. His entrance caused a bit of a commotion, and Alabama turned to see what was the reason for it. Tony spotted him and yelled "Alabama!" He ran around the woman down the central aisle to the defense table on the right. Alabama had risen when Tony reached him, and the two embraced, eyes closed and smiling hugely.

"How you been?" Alabama asked.

"Good! They feed me pretty good and all. But I sure miss you! How's Happy?"

Alabama laughed self-consciously, aware of all the attention they were receiving. He separated from the boy and said "Happy is good. She growin' lack a weed. An' she sho' miss you, Tony. Ah jes' know it. Now you bes' go wif' dis nice lady and sit and watch. Okay?"

Tony gave him one last squeeze around the waist and walked to a seat with the woman, who smiled at Alabama.

Livingston said "Apologies for the interruption, Your Honor. The defense calls Mrs. Isabel Stoughton." He smiled with relief and gratitude as Mrs. Stoughton rose from her position in the gallery. He'd phoned her only that morning upon remembering her, and she agreed to drop everything and drive to New Roads to testify. Alabama turned and gawked at her, never expecting to see her in the courtroom. She smiled at him as she walked elegantly to the witness stand. Judge Hanson banged the gavel and ordered "Order in the court!" to hush the excited hubbub over her appearance.

After she'd been sworn in, Mantor Livingston smiled and said "Good afternoon, Mrs. Stoughton. How good of you to be here."

Mrs. Stoughton returned the smile. "I wouldn't have missed it, Mr. Livingston," she replied firmly.

He nodded. "Now, Mrs. Stoughton, please tell the jury how you came to know Mr. Denton."

For the next ten minutes, Isabel Stoughton related the story of their relationship, from her original recruitment of Alabama as a gardener to their on-going friendship. She told of the wonderful experience at Alabama's wedding, her delight in his life partner, great joy in the birth of Darrius after ten years of barrenness, and the inexpressible sorrow she felt when hearing of Darrius' death and Adrianna's hospitalization. "I cried for days!" she told Livingston. "Such fine people, and to suffer such tragedy...well, it was too much. I don't know how he survived." She brightened. "But he did, sir! Alabama Denton is a man of character, and a good Christian. He called upon the Lord and made it through that awful, awful time. Now, this is actually the first that I've heard of young Tony, because Alabama has been very, shall we say, 'occupied' with this matter of a trial. But I have *no* doubt, no doubt whatsoever, that that boy will enjoy a wonderful, exiting, and loving life with Mr. Alabama Denton!" She stared almost defiantly at Livingston and glanced at the jury with the same expression.

"Thank you, Mrs. Stoughton," Livingston said quietly. He turned to the judge. "I have no further questions for this witness, Your Honor," he said.

"Your witness, Mr. Dupre," Judge Hanson said.

Ellis Dupre stood to his feet. "Mrs. Stoughton," he said. He took a look at her solid and defiant demeanor. "Never mind," he said, sitting again.

The judge turned to the witness. "Mrs. Stoughton, you are dismissed," he said. "The court thanks you for coming up from New Orleans in this matter before it."

She nodded primly and left the courtroom, smiling at Alabama on her way out. He mouthed 'Thank you', and she winked.

Livingston then called Madeline May, the social worker, and led her through testimony of her visit to the Denton farm and the interview with Alabama. Livingston asked her if she had interviewed Tony. "I did," she replied. "I found him to be a very bright, enthusiastic, and personable young man. As for his relationship with Mr. Denton, I found it to be entirely healthy and productive. Tony expressed great longing to be reunited with Mr. Denton as soon as possible. He also misses his dog very much and is afraid the animal will not know him." She smiled. "I told him the dog will probably take somewhere between half a second and a full second to remember him." Livingston laughed. He asked "So, Ms. May, would you recommend Mr. Denton as a suitable parent for Tony Pickens?"

"We're not permitted to make a recommendation for non-custodial persons until the court rules that such is a possibility," she replied. "However, if a petition for custody was presented in this case, the State of Louisiana would not object."

"Thank you, Ms. May," Livingston said with a smile. "Your witness, Mr. Dupre," he invited.

Ellis Dupre rose to his feet. He walked over to the jury box and briefly glanced into the eyes of each of the ten white men and two white women before leaning his elbow on the rail in a friendly fashion. The symbolism of white D.A. plus all-white jury vs. black female witness was impossible to mistake. "Ms. May," he said heavily.

She waited, not replying.

"Ms. May, how long have you been a social worker?"

"Twenty-seven years."

"And you're now head of the Louisiana State Department of Child Welfare in this region," Dupre stated. She nodded.

Dupre walked over to her and stood a yard away, hands on hips. "Ms. May, in all your professional experience personally and in all the other cases of which you're aware, which must be hundreds, right?"

"Thousands," she replied evenly.

Dupre nodded. "Thousands. So, in all those thousands of cases, how many have involved a Negro trying to play parent to a white child?"

The courtroom broke into excited conversations. Judge Hanson banged the gavel and shouted "Order! There will be order in this court!" When the room was quiet again, he turned to Ms. May. "Please answer the question," he commanded.

Ms. May was silent for a moment. Then she said "I cannot think of a single one. And by the way, Mr. Dupre, your characterization is prejudicial and your terminology is hopelessly outdated. You might consider a course in professional ethics before your language comes to the attention of the Bar Association."

"*Thank* you for the unsolicited advice," Dupre remarked acidly. He waved his hand as he walked to his table. Judge Hanson said "You may step down, Ms. May." She nodded and left primly.

Livingston announced "Your Honor, the final witness for the defense will be Tony Pickens."

All eyes turned toward the boy. The woman accompanying him whispered to him and he rose tentatively. Mantor Livingston walked a few steps down the aisle toward him and beckoned with a kind smile. "This way, Tony," he said. "Come with me." He walked beside the boy to the front and indicated the witness box. "Up there, Tony," he said. Tony glanced at

Alabama, who nodded and offered a smile. Tony walked quickly up the two steps to the seat in the box. He sat and stared around the courtroom.

"How are you today, Tony?" Judge Hanson asked with a smile.

"Uh...good. Sir."

"Call me Your Honor," the judge said. "Everyone else does, for some reason." The people in the courtroom chuckled. "Now I want you to just relax, Tony. We're going to ask you to put your hand on a Bible and promise to tell the truth here today. You *will* tell the truth when you're asked a question, right?"

Tony nodded. "Yes, Your Honor sir."

Judge Hanson grinned. "Just Your Honor, Tony. All right, now. Two men will ask you questions. One is Mr. Livingston, Alabama's attorney." He pointed to Mantor, who nodded. "And Mr. Dupre, at that table over there." Dupre nodded solemnly. Tony glanced at him fearfully, having been briefed that the man's job was to try to put Alabama in jail.

"Can't I just talk to *him*?" Tony asked, pointing to Livingston.

Judge Hanson shook his head. "I'm sorry, no, Tony. That's not how the justice system works. Just relax and tell the truth to whoever asks you a question and you'll be fine. Okay?" He nodded reassuringly. Tony sighed. "Okay, sir. Your Honor."

"Hello, Tony," Livingston said softly as he approached the witness box after Tony had been sworn in. Tony turned to him and smiled. "Hi!" he exclaimed.

"Tony, I'm going to ask you some questions about your life with your father and then with Alabama," Livingston began. "Let's start with your time when you lived at your father's auto parts yard. Here's a hard question, Tony. Be strong, now. Do you remember your mother?"

Tony reflected. "A little bit. She was nice."

"Did she hit you?"

Tony shook his head. "I don't think so. Leastwise I sure don't remember anything like that. She was nice."

"So you've only really known your father, then," Livingston stated gently. "Is that right?"

Tony shrugged. "Yeah, I guess. Far's I can remember."

Livingston nodded. "Tony, this may be difficult for you to say, but you know you're in a time and place where it's important that you tell the truth. Did your father ever hit you?"

Tony nodded grimly. "Lots of times. Most ever' day. Sometimes he just kinda slapped at me, you know? But other times he used his fists and hit hard."

"Where on your body did he hit you?"

"All over," Tony replied. "On the...well, my butt. With a stick. And on my back with that stick, and on my head. And with his fists. All over."

"Did he ever hit you in the face?"

Tony nodded. "Sometimes when he got likkered up he'd come at me real mad. I tried to run, but he's so big. A couple times he kinda knocked me out, like. Leastwise I think that's what happened. I don't really remember."

Livingston closed his eyes and sighed deeply. He opened them and said "What sort of meals did your father prepare for you, Tony?"

Tony looked at him strangely. "Meals?"

"Didn't your father cook for you and him?"

Tony shook his head. "We just sorta scrounged. Most times he wanted me to fix whatever there was. Lotsa times there wasn't much in the cupboards, and then he'd get real mad and use the stick. Sometimes I could see there wasn't much to eat, so I ran and hid."

"How did you eat, then?"

Tony shrugged. "Sometimes I didn't. Most often when there wasn't nothin' in the cupboards, he'd holler for me for a while, but I stayed hid. Then he'd get in his car and drive off."

"What did you do then?"

Tony looked at Alabama and smiled. "I'd walk along the riverbank to Alabama's farm. 'Course, I didn't know his name then, just that there was food growing there. He always had things to eat in his garden, leastwise in the growing season. A couple 'a times in the winter I went into his barn and ate some of the oats for the mules. It was pretty good." He grinned up at Livingston, displaying gaps between good, healthy teeth.

"How did Alabama feel about that?"

"He didn't know at first. But then he caught me. I was real scared. Thought he'd whup on me, like my Pa. But he never hurt me a'tall!" He grinned hugely. "Told me I could eat anything from his garden I wanted."

"Anything?"

Tony nodded. "Yep! Anything. And as much of it as I wanted."

"All right, Tony. Now let's talk about the weeks you lived on Alabama's farm. What did you eat then?"

"Oh, all kindsa stuff!" Tony said enthusiastically. "We always picked what we wanted from the garden when we could, and we had eggs from the chickens, and some fried chicken, and now and then some pork and bacon from a pig we slaughtered, and…lessee, corn from the field, and…Oh! Fish! Lotsa fish! Alabama can really catch fish good! Once he caught this big 'ol catfish. That thing musta been a mile long! He fought it and fought it, and finally he pulled it up on the bank. We cut that sucker up and put a lot of him in the freezer and fed the rest to the pigs. They loved it! Catfish is really tasty."

Livingston chuckled. "So you ate well. Ate your fill. Is that right?"

Tony nodded. "Sure did. I was never hungry with Alabama. Least not for long, and then we'd eat."

Livingston moved to the jury box and stood beside it. "Tony, can you describe your relationship with Alabama?"

Tony stared at him, frowning. "What's that?"

"How do you get along with him?"

Tony grinned hugely. "We get along *great!*" he exclaimed, looking at Alabama. "He's the coolest guy in the world. He knows all kinda stuff, and he teaches me reading and writing and arithmetic, and he shows me how to fish and stuff about farming and all."

"Did Alabama ever hit you?" Livingston asked gently.

Tony frowned. "Of *course* not! He's my friend! He would never do that."

"Not even when you disobeyed him?"

Tony shook his head. "I never disobeyed Alabama. We were having too much fun!"

Livingston smiled and turned to Dupre. "Thank you, Tony. Now this man, Mr. Dupre, is going to ask you a few questions." He sat down at his table.

Dupre stood and walked over to the witness box. "Hi, Tony!" he said enthusiastically.

Tony stared up at him.

"Well!" Dupre exclaimed, still grinning hugely. "I'm just going to ask you a couple of questions, Tony. Nothing to be afraid of. Let's start with this one. What day is today?"

Tony stared at him. He looked up at the judge. He looked to Alabama. "I don't know," he admitted.

"You don't know what day it is. Do you know the date?"

Tony thought about it for a few seconds. "Um, well, it's winter, so…February?"

Dupre looked to the jury with a sarcastic expression. "February. Are you sure, Tony?"

Livingston arose. "Your Honor, I object to this pointless line of questioning."

Judge Hanson looked at Dupre. "Is this going anywhere, counselor?" he asked.

Dupre nodded. "Yes, Your Honor, as I will soon demonstrate."

Judge Hanson nodded grimly. "Make it quick, Mr. Dupre," he replied.

Dupre turned to Tony. "So, it's February. Very good. What number of the month?"

Tony frowned. "Do you mean the date? I said I don't know."

Dupre looked at the jury when he spoke. "So, you don't know the day of the week, you don't know the month, really, you don't know the date on the calendar, and yet you know that your father did these things to you every day and you ate all this great food at the defendant's house every day? How come you remember those things with such precise detail, huh Tony?" He leaned in for an answer.

Tony stared up at the man. "Some things you remember, mister!" he said succinctly. "If you was whacked every day, you'd remember it too. If you was starvin' and then ate good, you'd remember that."

The spectators giggled, and Judge Hanson shut it off with a whack of his gavel.

Dupre stepped back. "So, Tony, which side of his bed do you sleep on?"

"Whose bed?"

"His." Dupre pointed at Alabama.

Tony looked at him strangely. "I have my *own* bed. For me and Happy. I sleep on the side Happy isn't on."

Dupre shook his head in frustration, staring at the jury. Suddenly he whipped around and leaned in to Tony. "He worked you like a *slave*, didn't he, Tony?" he asked loudly. "Didn't he make you chop weeds and plow furrows and…"

Tony leapt to his feet. "I *wanted* to do that stuff!" he screamed into Dupre's face. "You make it sound like Alabama was mean to me! He *wasn't*! He's the nicest person I ever met!"

Dupre walked disgustedly to his table. "No further questions," he muttered.

Judge Hanson looked down at the irate boy. "Thank you, Tony. There won't be any more questions. You can go sit back down now."

Mantor Livingston came and opened the door to the witness box, holding it open for Tony. The boy looked up at him as he walked past. He paused at the defense table, but Alabama whispered "You need to sit down raht quick, Tony." Tony nodded and joined the woman in the middle of the courtroom.

Mantor Livingston said "Your Honor, the defense rests."

"Very well," Judge Hanson remarked. He turned to the jury. "Ladies and gentlemen, you've now heard all the testimony in this case. Tomorrow morning we'll hear closing statements from the two attorneys, and then you'll be excused to deliberate and reach a verdict. For now, we are adjourned. Everyone in their places at nine sharp tomorrow." He banged the gavel, rose, and left as everyone stood to their feet.

CHAPTER 40

At nine the next morning, when Judge Hanson was seated at his bench, he turned to the jury. "Ladies and gentlemen of the jury," he said, "today you'll hear closing statements by each of the defense and the prosecution, in that order. Listen carefully to their summary of the testimony that's been given here. After both sides have presented their arguments, you'll be dismissed to begin your deliberations. You will not be allowed to conclude your deliberations until there is a unanimous verdict or a hung jury, where you are simply unable to reach a unanimous verdict after many, many hours of discussion. The foreman of the jury will keep me in touch on that matter. Now let me review your possible verdicts. Number one: you can find the defendant guilty of both felonies, that is aggravated kidnapping and human trafficking. Number two and three: you can find the defendant guilty of one or the other felony. Number four: you can find the defendant guilty of a misdemeanor, that is a breach of contract law. And number five, you can find the defendant not guilty of all charges." He turned to Mantor Livingston. "Mr. Livingston, you may begin."

Mantor Livingston stood to his feet. "Thank you, Your Honor," he replied. He walked to the central area before the bench, stood tall with his hands behind his back, and looked the jury members in the eyes. "Ladies and gentlemen," he said. "You've heard a great volume of testimony here. What I want you to focus upon is the character of the defendant. When you hone in on his character, you'll have a very good idea of how to decide this case."

"Alabama Denton is a simple man. He's a genuine American hero, by virtue of the Bronze Star and the Purple Heart he was awarded as a result of four grueling years of fighting to protect the honor and safety of this nation. Alabama would never tell you of those medals; he's too modest. But he earned them, ladies and gentlemen. He earned them." He looked briefly into the eyes of each member if the jury.

"Alabama Denton lives an uncluttered life on a neat, tidy farm that he has built from scratch with his hands," Livingston continued. "Thanks to his hard work, that farm has produced well for several decades with only occasional help. Alabama is a God-fearing man who attends church on a regular basis. He is a kind man, by virtue of the testimony of all those who have associated with him—including a rather well-to-do white woman who had no reason to inconvenience herself to come up here from New Orleans at a moment's notice except to lend her testimony to the outstanding character of this man. He is a giving and generous person, by the testimony of the very individual who matters most in this case, the six-year-old boy whose life was in such terrible jeopardy until Alabama made the extraordinary and highly courageous step of intervening to save the boy's life and give him some hope of a future. He didn't have to do that, ladies and gentlemen. He could have just said 'Well, he isn't my son, let him be.' Or he could have said 'He's white, I'm black, there'll be hell to pay if I get involved and I don't need the stress.' But he didn't. He saw the plight of a very vulnerable human being and stepped up to do what he could. As it turns out, what he could do and *did* do is truly remarkable. Tony Pickens absolutely flourished under Alabama Denton's care, love, and teaching. This young man now has an excellent opportunity for a good life, whereas with his biological father, his only future was being beaten or starved to death. We all wish in our heart that we could be so courageous as Alabama Denton has been."

Livingston paused. "Ladies and gentlemen," he said solemnly, "Alabama Denton has committed no crime. Let these two fine people come together again so Tony can continue to prosper. Find the defendant, Alabama Denton, not guilty of all charges. Thank you." He walked to his table and sat down.

"Thank you, suh," Alabama whispered to Livingston. The attorney nodded.

"Mr. Dupre," Judge Hanson said.

Ellis Dupre stood to his feet. This day he had donned a white suit with a white shirt and a bright red tie with matching handkerchief hanging out of his breast pocket. His shiny, well-coiffured blond hair was impeccable. His teeth shone brightly as he addressed the jury.

"Fellow Americans," he said. Livingston rolled his eyes.

"My fellow brothers and sisters," Dupre continued.

"*Racist bastard!*" Livingston muttered under his breath.

"Y'all have seen the picture the defense has tried to paint here," he remarked laconically, walking up and leaning on the jury rail. "The defense attorney, who represents his ethnic group here, has tried…"

Mantor Livingston stood to his feet.

"Sustained!" cried Judge Hanson. "Mr. Dupre! Sidebar! Now!"

The two attorneys walked quickly to the judge's bench and stood side-by-side before Judge Hanson. "Dupre, how *dare* you refer to race!" the judge hissed quietly. "I ought to declare a mistrial right here and now! And believe me, I am sorely tempted! Now you go back to that jury, and you behave yourself! If I see one hint of racism henceforth, I will stop you in midstream and you can try this matter all over again some other day!"

Dupre nodded. No trace of remorse was evident in his demeanor. "Your Honor," he replied.

Judge Hanson stared into his eyes for a few seconds, clearly smoldering. At length, he crisply commanded "Back to your tables!"

Dupre walked confidentially back to the jury box and stood near it, smiling and looking at the members of the jury. "Ladies and gentlemen," he said easily, "We don't care for kidnapping in this grand state. We don't care for human trafficking neither. Fact is, it don't matter who's being kidnapped away from his natural home. It ain't right, and the law says so in black and white." He turned to the judge, smiling easily and waiting for a reaction. Judge Hanson allowed it to pass, though he was clearly not happy.

"Folks, when a clear and simple case of swipin' a kid occurs, no matter how it was done like through payment or whatever, when that kid is used for hard labor, why, we have a case of kidnapping and human trafficking. Your duty is to follow the law. This case ain't complicated. The defendant took that child and made him work as a farm laborer. Now that's the way you have to decide it, 'cause it's the law."

He smiled at the jury. "Y'all're pretty smart," he remarked. "I seen that from the prosecution table. I'm confident you'll do the right thing here. Let's put this, uh, person away so's he don't hurt some other little kid." With that, he turned and walked back to his table. He deliberately avoided making eye contact with Judge Hanson.

The judge looked at the jury. "Bailiff will escort the jury to the jury room," he instructed.

After the jury had trooped out, Alabama leaned in to Livingston and asked "Wha' we do now?"

Livingston shrugged. "You're a free man. Let's get in my car and go down to the black section. I'm sure there's a decent café down there." Alabama rose tentatively behind his attorney and filed out after him.

That afternoon, when all were seated again after the bailiff had notified the judge that the jury had reached a verdict and the two sides were subsequently informed, Mantor Livingston leaned over to Alabama and said quietly "This is very good for us. Juries normally don't reach quick guilty verdicts on felony cases, especially those with a possible death penalty." He smiled and patted Alabama on the forearm. "Relax," he advised.

Ten minutes later, the jury filed into the jury box again. Alabama noted with a tight knot of burning fear in his heart that none of them looked at him. But then none of them looked at the prosecution table either, he realized. "Ah think Ah'm gonna faint," he whispered to Livingston.

"Relax," his attorney advised.

Judge Hanson said "Mr. Foreman, has the jury reached a verdict?"

A portly man arose from his seat in the first row of the right corner of the jury box. "We have, Your Honor," he replied. The bailiff walked to him, retrieved a piece of paper, and walked to hand it to the judge.

"The defendant will rise," the judge commanded. Livingston rose promptly, and Alabama struggled to his feet, his knees weak and trembling.

Judge Hanson opened the paper and read it carefully. It seemed to Alabama that hours went by while the judge studied the paper. Eventually, Judge Hanson leaned back and said "What is your verdict on the first count, aggravated kidnapping?"

"We find the defendant not guilty," the foreman replied.

Alabama let out a deep 'whoosh' of air.

Judge Hanson then said "What is your verdict on the second count, human trafficking?"

The foreman looked at Alabama for the first time. "We find the defendant...guilty," he replied.

A blast of sound erupted from the courtroom as everyone except Alabama Denton and his attorney expressed a loud, agitated opinion on the verdict.

Strangely, Judge Hanson let it go on. Not once in the several minutes it took him to study the paper from the jury did he bang his gavel or even look up. An odd silence suddenly pervaded the court as everyone looked at the judge. In the lull, one or two people whispered to their neighbor, but even that died out to total silence after a few seconds. Only the sound of the two large ceiling fans could be heard as they whupped about in the still air.

Judge Hanson raised his eyes. He turned his head to look at the jury. "No," he said succinctly.

When the first sound among the spectators arose, he picked up his gavel and banged it so hard on the wooden plate that the head flew off and spun toward the defense table, striking the table's legs and spinning to a stop on the courtroom floor. "I SAID *NO!*" he thundered. His eyes shone with a fire that actually caused some in the jury to scoot back further in their chairs.

Rising to his feet and facing the jury with clenched fists, he raged "No, I do *not* accept this verdict! You heard your instructions! You had *every* opportunity to do justice based upon what you heard and *only* what you heard in this courtroom. Instead, aided by the prosecution"—he stared acidly and pointed at Ellis Dupre, who sat with his mouth hanging open—"you brought the most virulent form of racism into this courtroom. You did *not* do as you were instructed, which was to leave all your disgusting racial baggage outside and decide this case on its merits. Instead, you have miscarried justice in the most egregious manner!" He glared with smoldering fury at the jury. "I am vacating this verdict under my authority as presiding judge in this case. Based upon the testimony given and evidence presented in this court, and *only* upon such testimony and evidence, I find the defendant guilty of the misdemeanor of a breach of contract law. Defendant is fined one hundred dollars. Upon payment of his fine, he is a free man. The jury is dismissed with contempt. Case dismissed!" He picked up his broken gavel, tossed it down in disgust, and slapped his hand on the wooden plate. Thereupon he rose and stalked down the stairs and out the door into his chambers in the midst of the babble of incredulous onlookers.

CHAPTER 41

Mantor Livingston paid Alabama's fine to the Clerk of Court on the way out. Josiah exuberantly exclaimed "C'mon, y'all, lunch is on me!" and he led them to the same black-owned café where they'd dined the day before. The café was crowded with well-wishers, all of whom wanted to pat Alabama on the back and crow about the win. When Josiah finally was able to place an order for the four of them, the proprietor said "No way you folks payin' fo' yo' lunch today. Lookit all de bidness you brung in!" She smiled hugely.

Alabama merely sipped his soup and nibbled on his sandwich. "Brothah, you gotta eat, get yo' stren'th back up!" Josiah exclaimed. "Ah know all dis been on yo' mind, but now you gotta get back to wheah you was. C'mon, now."

Alabama looked at Mantor Livingston. "Kin Ah get Tony back now?" he asked plaintively.

Livingston nodded. "I don't see any reason why not," he replied. "Your character has been established by the testimony in the trial and by the Department of Child Welfare. I'm sure they won't put up any objection. I'll file a formal petition for custody. No telling how long that takes to move through the bureaucracy, but I'd bet Tony will be back at the farm in a couple of weeks."

"Hey, das' great news!" Josiah exclaimed. "Praise de Lawd!" Jasmine echoed.

Mantor Livingston said "I'm still processing what happened, but I believe race relations made a giant step today. This could be a very historic case. Judge Hanson made a very courageous call there. He was entirely justified in what he did, but it was a magnificently courageous act nevertheless. The judge has a lot to lose with such a stand. I could be wrong, but I'm quite sure Ellis Dupre won't refile and try you again. His evidence is anecdotal and flimsy, and his jury-stacking strategy won't hold up a second time. Since a felony that has a possible death penalty requires a unanimous guilty vote in this state, even one black person on the jury will virtually doom any chance for a conviction on either charge. And Dupre won't get away with an all-white jury the next time." He paused, seeming to consider. "I'm not vindictive, but I'm going to file an ethics charge against Dupre. The Bar Association needs to hear about his behavior in this matter. I have no doubt they'll censure him, and that will only serve to further the gains made today. It's important that every ounce of good comes out of this, because I believe this case will become a landmark for the end of segregation and Southern Tradition."

"Mmm, *mmm*!" Josiah exclaimed. "Alabama, raht soon you be so famous ord'nary folks ain't goin' get to talk to you!"

Alabama smiled sheepishly. "Long's dem ord'nary folks still servin' breakfast on Sunday mornin', Ah be talkin' to 'em."

Four days later, when Alabama did indeed show up as usual at the Freeman residence at eight in the morning for breakfast prior to Sunday worship services, Josiah met him at the door. "Ah got bad news, brothah," he said morosely. "Mr. Livingston call Friday aftanoon. Ah tried mah bes' to come tell you yestiddy, but thangs kep' gettin' in de way. Anyhow, yo' petition fo' custody of Tony was denied."

Alabama stared at him, eyes wide and jaw low. "*Wha'* you say?"

Josiah nodded, a huge frown on his wrinkled face. "Tony fathah file an objection."

Alabama sat down on the step, his mind reeling. "But...but ain't he...Ah mean, don' he got no raht...?" He stared at Josiah.

Josiah shrugged. "Mr. Livingston, he say call dis numbah," he said, handing Alabama a slip of paper. "He say it don' matter when you call."

Alabama took the paper and trudged up the stairs. He sank down into an easy chair and dialed the number with leaden fingers. "Mantor Livingston," came the crisp reply.

"Alabama Denton heah," Alabama said heavily.

Livingston sighed. "Yes, Alabama, I'm sure you've heard of the setback. Josiah gave you the news, right?"

"Yessah. But Ah don' get it!" Tony fathah sell me de boy! *He* ain't got no use fo' him. How come he standin' in de way?"

"Well, he may have several motivations, but my guess is that it's merely racial prejudice," Livingston replied. "The man is a stone redneck."

Alabama thought over that comment for a few seconds. "You raht 'bout dat," he replied. "But if Tony go back deah, he be killed! Ah jes' know dat man goin' be so mean he beat de boy to death!"

"No doubt. And I'm sure that's the way the Department of Child Services sees it, based on Tony's testimony. No, Tony won't be returning to that environment. He'll stay in foster care."

"Fostah care." Alabama shook his head. "Not wif me. Not wif a man who love him and will raise him and teach him education and show him how to be a man."

Livingston shook his head on the other end of the phone, though Alabama couldn't see it. "Look, I'll do what I can," he remarked. "Though it pains me a great deal, I'll call on the man and see if he'll listen to reason. His trial for participating in human trafficking is coming up in April. He doesn't know it, of course, but your amended judgment of a misdemeanor is a strong precedent for his own trial. If he doesn't have a competent attorney who can figure that out, he may be persuaded to relinquish his parental rights on a promise of my help in his trial. I don't know, but it's worth a try."

Alabama did not reply.

"Alabama? Hello?"

"Ah heah," Alabama replied. "Ah jes' don' know wha' to say."

"Well, take heart, my friend," Livingston replied. "Let me work on it. I'll keep you advised."

That afternoon, Mantor Livingston phoned Judge Garrett Hanson at home. Judge Hanson and his wife were relaxing after a lunch following worship services when he took the call. They chatted for a few moments, and the judge came back out to the porch. "That attorney I told you about, the black fella who represented the defendant in that case in New Roads. Remember my mentioning him?" he said to his wife.

She nodded. "Sounds like a very unusual man. And an excellent lawyer, if I remember you correctly."

Judge Hanson nodded. "That he is," he replied. "I wouldn't see him socially, or any other officer of the court, for that matter, if he wasn't very competent and I felt I could trust him not to abuse the privilege. Anyway, he's coming at three o'clock."

Mrs. Hanson rose. "I'll ask Sally to have some lemonade and scones ready. And some glasses and ice. Shall I have her serve in your study?"

The judge nodded and took his wife's hand, raising it to his lips and giving it a light kiss. "You're still the most beautiful woman in Louisiana, you know," he said softly.

"I know," she replied. "I have to employ bodyguards to beat off the hordes of men who pursue me." She smiled and left to see to the arrangements.

That afternoon, after apologizing for taking the judge's time and thanking him for the audience, Mantor Livingston sat in the judge's study and explained the latest development in Alabama's situation. "I truly believe the best place for that boy is with Mr. Denton," he said confidently.

Judge Hanson nodded. "Off the record, I agree wholeheartedly," he replied. "The trial revealed Mr. Denton's character and potential as a mentor and guardian quite well. And we both know that going back to his father is not an option."

Livingston nodded. "No, sir. Not in this lifetime."

"Right," the judge agreed. "So, the question is, what's to be done?"

"That's why I'm here, sir," Livingston replied. "I'm seeking your advice. As you say, off the record. This isn't an official visit, per se, because my representation for Mr. Denton is over. But he is my friend. He's a fine man, and I'd like very much to see what can be done to rectify this dilemma. I figured if any jurist in the state had any insight, it would be you, sir. Not only because you presided and are therefore familiar with the details of the case, but because I know you to be a man of the highest integrity."

Judge Hanson looked into Livingston's eyes. "Well, I thank you, Mantor. And I return the compliment in terms of your own professional ability. I believe you're headed for a judgeship, if you'd like that. I'll help you all I can in that regard when the time comes. In the meantime, let me see what I can do about this Denton matter." He rose and held out his hand.

Livingston rose immediately and shook hands with the judge. "Thank you so much, sir," he replied. "For the hospitality and the advice. Please convey my appreciation to Mrs. Hanson."

"I'm sure she enjoyed meeting you earlier this afternoon," the judge replied with a smile. "I tell her about all the interesting characters I encounter!"

On Wednesday morning of the following week, Judge Hanson phoned an old friend from his country club. "Marcel, how are you?" he asked.

"Oh, the joints are creaking, and my long game is suffering," Beaujean replied. "But I've learned to be much more disciplined with my putting in order to save strokes."

The judge laughed. "We should all be so disciplined!" he replied lightly. "Perhaps we could get out on the course again soon? Like this afternoon?"

Marcel Beaujean hesitated. "I read some urgency in your timing, Garrett," he remarked.

"No urgency, Marcel. Just expediency. I have no trial duties at the moment and would enjoy a round with you today if it's convenient for you."

"Certainly. I'll adjust my schedule and meet you in the clubhouse. Say, three o'clock?"

"That would be wonderful."

"Good. I'll have my secretary call for a tee time."

"Excellent. Thank you, Marcel. I look forward to seeing you this afternoon. Lord knows I could use some advice on putting!"

Beaujean laughed along with his friend. "See you at three, Garrett." He hung up.

As they were going down the fairway in a golf cart after hitting off the first tee, Beaujean said "What's on your mind, Garrett?"

"It's unusual, Marcel," Hanson replied. "Technically it isn't my problem at all. It concerns a case I adjudicated a couple of weeks ago."

Beaujean turned to look at him, eyebrows raised. "The kidnapping case? Where you threw out the verdict?"

Hanson nodded, grinning ruefully. "I'm still waiting for the barbarians to come after me. And they will, no doubt."

"Well," Beaujean noted, "from what I read in the paper, you did exactly the right thing. That was a hanging jury right out of the Klan days. It took an extraordinary act of courage to set them straight, Garrett. From what I hear, your action was a major step in jurisprudence, not only here but in the entire South."

"Well, we'll wait to see how history judges it," he replied. "My concern right now is the immediate aftermath of the case." For several minutes, continually checking behind them to ensure they were not holding up another group on the first tee, he explained the situation. "So the boy will track through the foster system if something isn't done," he concluded. "Not that that's bad. It just isn't the best for him. Not by a long shot."

"How old is this black fella, Denton?" Beaujean asked.

"In his early sixties. But still quite vigorous. I'm sure a life of physical activity and pure food is a better formula than how the rest of us live. He could go to a hundred, as good as he looks." He reached into his wallet and pulled out a newspaper clipping. "Here. See for yourself how young he looks."

Beaujean took the clipping. Immediately his eyes widened. "I *know* this fella!" he exclaimed. "For certain I've seen him before. Alabama Denton, you say the name is?"

Garrett Hanson nodded. "Yes, that's it."

"Hmmmm," Beaujean muttered. "Where in the world…" He studied the photo a moment longer and handed it back to Hanson. "Well," he commented. "Let me study on the matter. Heh! Looks like I'm away, as usual. Might as well climb out of this comfortable conveyance and have a whack at it."

Marcel Beaujean phoned Judge Hanson two days later. "That fella Alabama Denton, the one you mentioned on Wednesday," he said.

"Denton. Yes?"

"I knew I'd seen him before. I had my staff do some checking. Mr. Denton and I met in a guest lounge in Memorial Hospital when Elaine was sick. Must have been six, seven years ago. I remembered he was there visiting his wife, who'd been in a coma for three years. Imagine that!"

"My word!" Judge Hanson replied. "I had no idea. It came up in the trial that he was a single man; in fact, that was one of the issues the prosecution attempted to use. No mother at home for the boy, that sort of thing. But as for a wife and such a terrible illness…did she survive?"

"No, she didn't," Marcel Beaujean replied. "In fact, I think she died just about the same time Elaine did. Right in the same hospital."

Garrett Hanson considered. "What a coincidence."

"Indeed it is," Beaujean replied. "Well, I just thought I'd touch base with you, Garrett. Thanks for the information on this matter. And thanks for letting me whip you on Wednesday."

"By two strokes! That isn't a whippin'!"

"Yet it's a win," Beaujean replied with a laugh. "At my age, any victory is headlines."

"Well, I'm ready to take you on again, Marcel. Just name the time and place!"

Beaujean chuckled. "Just give me a few days to rest, Garrett," he replied. "Take care of yourself."

"And you, Marcel."

Beaujean leaned back in his chair. His eyes fell, as they did many times a day, on the 9 x 12 glossy photo of his wife Elaine in the silver-and-glass frame on his desk. Taken when she was thirty-four, a year after they'd married with him having just celebrated his fiftieth birthday, it showed the very best of Elaine Beaujean. The three-quarters shot highlighted her high cheekbones, shining teeth, glowing eyes, and wonderful, wonderful smile. Beaujean fell in love for the ten-thousandth time just gazing at the photo. "Elaine," he whispered. "Life was so cruel to you."

He thought back to their wedding day. As owner of a massive shipping operation, he'd had the wherewithal to commission the largest tourist boat on the river for a 150-person reception, sailing down the Mississippi River until dusk and then back, arriving at midnight. It had been a magnificent two-meal and many-drinks affair, replete with all the top politicians, social players, and business contacts the boat could hold. Elaine, who had been a relatively unknown secretary to one of Marcel's vendors, had previously dated a few men, none of whom were appropriate or faithful in the long term. In point of fact, she was a virgin on their wedding night. Marcel had previously endured one marriage which ended in failure after four years when he was a young man and working night and day to establish his fortune in the transportation industry. Marcel and Elaine had a whirlwind courtship and instantly discovered they were perfect for one another.

Both were keen to have children, but Elaine strangely could not conceive. Despite trying everything they could think of and all the advice they received, such as making love on a mountaintop in the Alps, in a submarine under the Atlantic, or under the fifth full moon of the year deep in the bayou, nothing worked. In the fourth year of their marriage, Elaine awoke one morning with severe cramps. She literally hobbled into the hospital, Marcel supporting her and frantic with worry. It turned out his concern was founded: Elaine was discovered to have an advanced case of cervical cancer. She lingered for six months, in and out of the hospital, while Marcel frantically poured thousands of dollars into every type of hoped-for cure he could seek out.

It was for naught. Elaine died in her husband's arms.

I lost my beautiful wife, the love of my life, he mused. *Just as this Alabama Denton fellow did. But he lost a son too, as I recall, in an accident. And now, just when God has favored him with another son, he loses the boy because of a mongrel of a man who ought to be taken into the bayou and shot in the head. I doubt if even the alligators would feed on the evil bastard's body.*

He gazed around his sixteen hundred-square-foot office. It held a three-hole undulating putting course, a huge oval mahogany conference table with twenty ornately carved and wonderfully comfortable chairs, a small kitchen, and behind closed doors, a suite with a bedroom, sitting room, large walk-in closet, and spacious bathroom. He rarely spent time in his twenty-thousand square foot mansion on Charles Street any longer, preferring to simply work until he required sleep and occasionally go to the country club for a round of golf. He had most of his meals catered in, and the remainder he consumed in restaurants while discussing business.

I have more money than I could ever use, he thought. *And no heir.* He thought with disgust of the dozens of charities and foundations and educational institutions that constantly pursued him to fund their operations. *Most of them will be disappointed when my will is read and they discover the bulk of it has gone to the Southern Baptist Convention,* he mused with an inward chuckle.

He glanced at a huge potted Ficus Benjamina tree beside his desk. The twisted tree trunk, consisting of a single trunk and over twenty branches which had been cleverly woven and braided into a large whole, never ceased to fascinate him. *It takes an artist to plant and grow and produce something like this,* he'd often concluded. *Someone whose life is botany.* And his thoughts turned to Alabama Denton.

Marcel Beaujean picked up his phone. "Send my attorney over to see me, please," he said. When he received an acknowledgment, he put the phone down and waited.

Three days later, a shiny black sedan with tinted windows rolled to a stop at the gate of Cletus Pickens' auto junkyard. A new dog, this one a nasty-looking German Shepherd, greeted the well-dressed visitor with snarls. Pickens had come back to the junkyard after finally posting bail through a court-appointed attorney to find a hole dug under one part of the fence. Bear had had enough, apparently. After digging the hole, he'd gone onto the porch of the ramshackle house, pulled down a denim jacket Pickens had left hanging over a chair, torn it to shreds, and laid a pile of excrement on it, perhaps as an expression of his canine opinion.

The man waited while the car continued to run in order to maintain the air-conditioning inside.

Cletus Pickens poked his head out the screen door. "What you want?" he asked roughly.

"Mr. Pickens, I'm an attorney. My client wishes to purchase your property here."

Pickens came out onto the porch, pulling up a strap of his overalls over his naked torso. "*What?*" he asked incredulously.

"My client wishes to purchase your property."

Pickens slipped on a worn pair of tennis shoes and flopped his way to the fence. "Hush!" he commanded the dog, slapping at it. The dog whined and slunk away. Pickens hung onto the fence and stared at his visitor. "Your client wants my estate," he remarked suspiciously.

The attorney snorted, smiled ruefully, and glanced disdainfully at the junkyard. "Your 'estate'? Yes, that is correct. He is prepared to give you twenty thousand dollars for the land, buildings, and contents."

Pickens studied him. "Why does this fella want this place?"

"That is none of your concern, Mr. Pickens," the attorney replied. "Are you interested in the offer?"

Pickens spat in the dirt. "I wouldn't give up this fine establishment for any less than fifty thousand."

The attorney paused. "Very well. I am authorized to go up to that figure. There are conditions attached to the sale."

"Conditions?"

"Yes. You must sign a waiver stating that you will leave the state of Louisiana within twenty-four hours and never return. In addition, you must sign a statement waiving all parental rights to Tony Pickens. If you sign the statements and then violate them at any time, you are liable to civil penalties of up to full return of the principal and interest at six percent per annum, for as many years as accrued after the contract is signed." He smiled. "And Mr. Pickens, you can rest assured that my client is *very*, very good at collecting debts."

Pickens frowned. A panoply of angry and confused emotions played across his face. "Hey, what is this?!" he exclaimed. "Some kinda joke? *I know!* It's a set-up! You jes' wanna see if I'll do it, then you take the money and the paper and run!"

The attorney reached into a portfolio and selected a cashier's check. It was made to 'Bearer.' "Do you see this, Mr. Pickens?" he asked. "This is a check drawn on the account of my client at his bank in New Orleans. As you can see, it is a long-established and highly reputable institution, and my client is held in the highest regard at that bank. Anyone who holds and presents this check will receive the funds. In your case, Mr. Pickens, upon signing the agreement stipulating the conditions I mentioned, you will receive this check. You will no doubt then cash it within hours. Then you will leave the state and never return. You'll be a rich man, Mr. Pickens."

Pickens stared at him. "Come closer and lemme see that check," he demanded.

The attorney complied, confident that Pickens could not reach through the narrow mesh and grab the check. He held it within six inches of the fence.

After two full minutes of studying the check, sounding out each of the words silently, Pickens stared into the eyes of the attorney. "I can cash that?" he asked with an eager expression.

The attorney nodded. "That is precisely what I said. 'Bearer' means whoever is holding the check at the time of cashing it."

Pickens' eyes flitted from the check to the attorney. "What's this all about, really?" he asked in wonder.

"I've stated the conditions of the arrangement, Mr. Pickens," the attorney replied crisply. "My client's motivations are not your concern. Now, I've come a long way from New Orleans and have the same distance to travel back. I would appreciate your signature on these forms." He reached into the portfolio and removed a bill of sale. "Don't worry about an exchange of title for your, uh, 'estate' here," he said. "Our office will handle all the details. You need merely sign on the line with the 'X' to transfer ownership."

Pickens stared at him. "And I get fifty large."

"If you're referring to fifty thousand dollars, that is correct," the attorney replied quietly.

"And I gotta sign this waiver thing about Tony."

The attorney gazed dispassionately at him. "Is that such a loss, Mr. Pickens? For the money you'll receive?"

Pickens pursed his lips and frowned. "There's some monkey business goin' on here!" he growled. "I gotta think this over."

"Certainly," the attorney replied politely. "Take as long as you need. Say...any time in the next ten seconds. Then I get back in that car, drive off, and this offer will never be made again." He looked up and stared with hard eyes at the man.

Pickens gulped. "Gimme the paper!" he demanded.

CHAPTER 42

Mantor Livingston phoned Josiah the next morning. "Josiah! Is Alabama there, by any chance?" he asked excitedly.

"No, he be on his farm, far's Ah know," Josiah replied. "Whas' up?"

"Would you be able to go to his farm and bring him back right away so I can speak with him? It's very urgent!"

Josiah looked around the store. "Reckon Jasmine kin look after thangs fo' an hoah," he replied. "Sho'. Ah do dat."

"Oh, thank you!" Livingston replied. "You have my phone number at the office, right?"

"Yessah, Ah do."

"Okay. Right away, please, Josiah!"

"Ah fetch him. Jes' hang on a bit."

They hung up, and an hour later Alabama was dialing the number. Livingston's secretary put him right through. "Alabama!" Livingston exclaimed. "The greatest news you'll ever hear! Other than the good news of the Bible, I mean. Are you ready?"

"Uh…sho'. Ah guess," Alabama replied, mystified.

"Tony is cleared to come home!" Livingston shouted. "His father signed a waiver of parental rights! You can put in for custody now! And equally important, I have a judge's order allowing Tony to live with you on the farm until the custody arrangement is finalized!"

Alabama lowered the phone and stared at it. "Are you there?" Livingston asked. "Alabama? Speak to me!"

Alabama picked up the phone and put it to his ear. "Mistah Livingston, please tell me dis ain't no joke," he pleaded. "Mah heart couldn't take it. Jes' tell me. Is dis fo' real?"

"It is!" Livingston almost screamed. "It's done, Alabama! Tony will be your son! In all but name, anyway. You'll be his legal guardian. That's like his father, except that you won't be able to adopt him. But in all other ways, and certainly all ways that matter, he will be your son."

"Why cain't Ah adopt him?"

Livingston paused. "You're way outside the allowable limits, agewise," he replied. "There's no sense in even trying to fight it. We'd lose. But who cares? Tony can take your name if he wants. He can call himself Tony Denton all his growing-up years, and then at the age of twenty-one he can make it legal. In all respects, he will be your own son."

Alabama sank into a chair. When Mantor Livingston heard the sound of weeping on the other end, he wisely hung up the phone.

CHAPTER 43

It was seven months later, when Alabama, Rufus, and Tony piled the last of the produce from that year's crops onto the wagon for transport to Fordoche. "Boys," Alabama said, wiping the sweat from his brow, "les' us go up on de porch and talk. Have us some cool lemonade. Ah got sumpin' to say."

"Works fo' me," Rufus grinned. "Dis a hot ol' day!"

"Aw, you're just gettin' old, Rufus!" Tony exclaimed, displaying a boy's bicep and a huge grin. Rufus chased him for a few steps, swinging with his straw hat while Tony giggled and danced out of the way.

They sat with cold glasses of lemonade, Alabama on the porch swing with his arm around Tony and Happy curled up beside his young master with his head on the boy's lap. Rufus sat attentively on a seat nearby.

Alabama said "Fellas, Ah be neah sixty-three yeah of age."

Tony gazed up at him, and Rufus nodded respectfully.

Alabama looked out at the farm. "De Lawd been good to dis sinner," he said with a soft smile. "He give me de money to buy dis' land an' good Jews to hep a black man. A Creole an' a white man try to cheat me on dis' land, but de Lawd provide a way out and even make it bettah. A few yeah later, 'nothah white man try to tell me it ain't mah land, but de Lawd provide a fine man, Mistah Mantor Livingston, to get me outa dat jam. An' de Lawd give me Mizz Stoughton fo' a friend. She de finest white lady Ah evah know.

One day she be in de kingdom of heaven, and we be friends fo'evah." He smiled and nodded. "Yessah, Mizz Stoughton goin' be *big* in heaven! Lawd got a special place fo' dat lady."

He sighed, blinking hard. "Lawd take mah wife an' boy," he said softly. "*Whooo*! Lack to drop me to mah knees and put me down fo' *good*, dat did! Mmmm, *mmh*!" He shook his head, staring off at the fields. In a few seconds, he brightened. "But now dey in glory in the kingdom wif' Jesus! Dey walkin' streets 'a gold, yes dey is! Darrius be a *man* in heaven, not a boy, and Adrianna be healthy an' strong wif'out *no* darkness, bless her beautiful soul! Ain't dat sumpin'?" He grinned hugely. "Y'know, Ah be seein' dem in not too many yeahs. Reckon Ah have a young body again. Run an' jump an' do flips in de air if'n Ah want. Das' what de Bible say." He smiled with quiet satisfaction. "Ain't no bettah place den heaven, das' fo' sho'!" He stared off into the distance, as if seeing what no living man can see.

"White man try to put me in prison fo' life," he continued in a quiet voice after a moment. "Mayhaps hang me at de end of a rope, mmm mmh. But de Lawd provide a righteous white judge to get me outa dat jam. How de Lawd know to bring dat white man to dis heah parish at dat partickler tam?" He shook his head. "On'y de Lawd know His plans. He an awesome God, fo' sho'."

He paused and looked down at Tony with a dazzling smile. "White man try to beat on Tony. Woulda kilt him! An' dat man try to prevent a fine boy from comin' to live wheah he loved and protected. But de Lawd provide some fine man somewheah, Ah nevah did find out who, to get dat evil man to sign Tony ovah an' cleah out fo' good." He sighed deeply, held the boy close to his side, and looked out at the farm for a considerable time. "Ah sho' love you, Tony," he spoke softly. Neither Rufus nor Tony said a word.

"An' lookee heah!" Alabama exclaimed. "Fo' a tam Ah walk away from de Lawd. Lack Jonah, Ah din' wan' nothin' to do wif' Him, 'cause He 'low such pain in mah life. But it His plan! All 'long, it His plan. It *allus* His plan, 'cept sometam we jes' too self-centered and dumb-ass to see Him to do His work. But it allus turn out fo' His glory, an' mos' often fo' our own good. Remember that, fellas. And remember dat even when Ah walk away from de Lawd, He forgive ol' stubborn Alabama Denton! *Nevah* left me. Ain't dat sumpin'? He nevah hold no grudge. *How* kin God love a man lack me? A man dat tell Him 'Ah don' need you!' But de Lawd do love dis man! Yessah, He surely do. Das' a mystery ain't no livin' human bein' goin' figure out. De love a' de Lawd jes' too big fo' a man to understan'. Ain't no gettin' to de depth of it, no suh."

He mused for a moment and then chuckled with quiet delight. "Yessah, de Lawd been good to dis' ol' sinner. Ah jes' keep trustin' Him an' not leanin' on mah own understandin,' an' de Lawd *always* come through. He a mos' awesome God, das' fo' sho'. Don' y'all nevah forget dat."

He paused a moment, then sighed with happiness. "Wayall, boys, Ah come to a decision. Ah wrote a new will, an' Ah goin' file it wif' Mistah Livingston. Heah it is: when Ah cain't work dis land no mo', y'all two goin' work it an' take fo' yo'sef' all but what Ah need to pay de bills. Jes' keep me fed and gimme some shine now 'n then. Rufus, you kin move in heah soon's you ready, take you one of de bedrooms. Yo' folks gone to glory, and you fambly now. If'n Tony be off at college when Ah cain't work no mo', or if'n he graduate an' be workin' in some professional job, Rufus work de farm and take de money, 'cept what Ah need. When Ah gone, Rufus work de farm or sharecrop, dependin' on wha' he wan' to do. Take de money. When Rufus gone, Tony get de land. Keep it or sell it, it don' matter, long's it's a good decision dat heps you. Das' wha' Ah decided."

Tony gazed up at him for a few seconds. His young blue eyes stared into his father's smiling black eyes with total trust. Then Tony dropped his gaze to his lap. He slipped his arms around Alabama's waist and hugged him quietly, his face in Alabama's overalls.

Alabama looked at Rufus. Tears were dropping silently from the man's eyes. He nodded to Alabama and trembled.

"Ah, yes," sighed Alabama. "De Lawd sho' been good to me!"

ABOUT THE AUTHOR

Hale Meserow graduated from the University of Hawaii with a degree in political science and from the University of Oregon (with honors) with a masters in business communication. Between the periods at educational institutions, Hale served in the United States Air Force, leaving after five years with the rank of captain. His service as a navigator in Viet Nam resulted in a Distinguished Flying Cross and an Air Medal.

Having lived in ten American States and four foreign countries, including eight years in Australia, Hale has a deep well of experience from which to form the fabric of his writing. Among the topics which are of most interest to him are racism in all its forms, individual courage in the face of great obstacles, romantic love, parenting, politics, and the themes of the Bible. Most of his novels and biographies involve these areas.

Hale and his wife Sue will celebrate 23 years of marriage in 2011. They have two grown sons, one of whom is married.

As a Christian, Hale delights in relating the message of the gospel of Jesus Christ in tales of real people who believe, live, and die in the faith. As an American patriot, he is a champion of the vision of the Founding Fathers.

The author of eight novels, two novelettes, one biography, and numerous short stories and poems, Hale's current project is a sweeping Michener-style novel of the history of the great state of Minnesota.

RACISM IN AMERICA:
THE PLAGUE THAT ROTS MEN'S SOULS

An enigmatic god was Segregation. He had many proponents—all white—many detractors—mainly black with a few courageous whites—many causes, many effects. He was pervasive. He was ubiquitous. He was powerful, stronger than the law, stronger than the Constitution and the Declaration of Independence, stronger even than Jesus Christ in the hearts and minds of those who genuflected to him. He lay like a volcano under the South and into parts of the North, always there, always in danger of erupting. Sometimes he burst out with a plume of hatred and domination, such as a lynching or a cross burning. Most of the time he was content to show himself with a modest hiss of venomous steam, perhaps in the form of a black woman who was severely chastised, maybe even struck with the back of a hand, if she passed a white man on the sidewalk and failed to dip her eyes and move out of his way.

White children in the South who were old enough to navigate on their own two feet began to know of the god Segregation. No one had to tell them, although Segregation had doctrine that was deeply imbedded and repeated often enough to drive home his power: *the nigger is a jumped-up ape only three centuries out of the jungle; they're not fully human; they'll invade your home and rape your women if'n you don't keep 'em down; never call one "mister"; don't let 'em in the union or they'll take your job; would you want your sister to marry one?* White Southern children knew the dual persona that Segregation demanded. The white mother who taught a Southern daughter love, tenderness, and gentility also taught her the harsh, soul-killing rituals of keeping Negroes in their place. The white mother who handed her infant or toddler son to the family's black mammy, that warm and unquestioning nurse who took the lad to her generous black breast and rocked and cooed and soothed and loved him to boyhood, also taught him that the mammy was not to be loved but was to be regarded with an affection one might display toward a familiar and well-regarded dog. The Southern preacher who sermonized that God is love, that His Son came to give mankind eternal life, that all men have a common Father, also either taught or allowed his congregation to hold to the conviction that every white person is better than any black person, that all blacks have a place that is far inferior to the vistas open to whites and must be kept in that place, that it is biblical if regrettably no longer lawful to own another human being.

White Southern boys, girls, and teens learned it is possible to be a follower of the Lord Jesus Christ and a worshiper of Segregation simultaneously; Southern Tradition eased their consciences. White Southern women learned how to be a gentlewoman with impeccable manners one moment and an arrogant, callous, even cruel creature toward uppity blacks the next with complete peace of mind. White Southern men learned that their highest calling was to protect the sacred honor of white Southern women and the Southern way of life from all threats and detractors. All white Southerners learned that the most detestable, unkempt, and drunken white man was to be allowed in the front door—albeit immediately then to a bath and a shave—while the most brilliant, accomplished, and notable black college president was to come in the back door, if at all.

The high priest Southern Tradition did not need a legal or standing army to keep himself alive and well. He relied upon visual symbols, facial expressions, barriers, and the threat of the sleeping volcano to erupt and take lives. In every Southern town when black faces came home from serving their country, there were signs posted over the doors of railroad and bus stations, toilets, drinking fountains, and theaters: *White...Colored.* There were signs without words: big white church shaded by graceful trees on Elm Street, small unpainted church for coloreds on a bare lane on the edge of town; big, well-kept brick school for white children, small falling-down wooden school for coloreds; big white houses with colonnades and sweeping lawns for whites, tiny gray-wood shacks in a neighborhood of earthen paths for coloreds; extensive, well-laid-out graveyards for whites with elaborate marble headstones and statuary, colored graveyard with mounds of dirt and an occasional home-made wooden cross. There were parts of town in which coloreds were allowed and parts where they were whipped if they dared show. There were wide, welcoming front doors for whites and narrow gates in the back for coloreds. There were places a colored could be, like the back of a bus, and places he could not, like the front. Whites learned to hold their heads high; colored people learned to bend, hat in hand. Southern Tradition did his work well: hour by hour, day by day, whites learned the intricacies of their role and blacks learned the necessities of theirs. Soon the dance was so indwelling in every heart and mind that it became reflexive.

Segregation ruled in the South by captivating every facet of society. Politicians paid tribute to him in order to become elected and stay in office; newspapermen echoed the mantras he required so as to sell advertising and reinforce the status quo; authors reinforced his power and legitimacy in essays and novels. Some of what was spoken in public and written upon a page for public dissemination was revelatory:

"...But we will resist to the bitter end, whatever the consequences, any measure or movement which would...bring about social equality and intermingling and amalgamation of the races in our states."

Alabama Senator Richard Russell, in Congress, 1946

"I would say to the Negro: before demanding to be a white man socially and politically, learn to be a white man morally and intellectually. I would say to the white man: the black is our brother, never adult, but a younger brother, not disciplined but tragic, pitiable, and lovable. Act as his older brother and be patient with his failings."

Author William Percy, 1941

"Only a fool would say the Southern pattern of separation of the races can ever be overthrown, or should be."

'Atlanta Constitution' editorial, 1948

"The black is mentally unfit to be directors in our form of government. You cannot change these natural and God-ordained mental processes. The day our voters list contains a large percentage other than Caucasian stock is the day our constitutional form of government becomes impossible and unworkable."

Tom Linder, Georgia Commissioner of Agriculture
Letter to the 'Atlanta Journal', 1948

"Whenever the Constitution of the United States comes between me and the virtue of the white women of the South, I say to hell with the Constitution!"

Author Cole Blease, 1943

"The notion of political equality is absurd. Political equality of the races would mean social equality, and social equality would lead to intermarriage. That would be the mongrelizing of the American race. I cannot and will not be a party to recognition of the Fourteenth and Fifteenth Amendments (to the Constitution of the United States)."

Mississippi Senator Ellison D. Smith In Congress, 1932

"The way to control the nigger is to whip him when he does not obey. Another is to never pay him more than is actually necessary to buy food and clothing."

Author W.J. Cash, 1942

Northerners disdainfully asked: how can one idea, one perspective, one mindset become so hypnotic that it binds forty million white Southern faces together in lockstep? How can such a wide variety of people, a few rich and most sharecropper poor, a few educated and most averaging a sixth-grade education, a few in the pulpit and the rest paying lip service to the church, be so mesmerized that their minds are incapable of seeing the injustice of Segregation?

"Blindness," answered the most perceptive of the northerners. "There is such a love of their white skin that it blinds their eyes." They were right, but it was deeper than that. The god Segregation had a high priest named Southern Tradition. The followers of Segregation were many and varied, but all agreed with the irresistible demands of his high priest and would stand shoulder to shoulder and dig the butt end of their spears into the ground to repel anyone who would challenge their right to worship their god.

And who was responsible? How did the god Segregation gain life in the first place? How did his high priest Southern Tradition gain dominance? One might well ask how a gang forms, pledges allegiance to one another and the goals which drive them, and creates enforced rituals to keep each one in line. *Everyone* was responsible.

Economics was a player. Though the tradition of human ownership of other humans is as old as civilization, early settlers in the South generally did not own slaves, tending instead to hack out a small holding on a Southern creek to plant vegetables while they raised pigs and chickens to feed their families. Every penny went toward seed and cloth and tools and animal feed. Though the average settler in the South would gladly have taken a slave or two to help him with the backbreaking labor if he could, the thought of affording such a luxury was ludicrous. But then in the seventeenth century, England began to demand cotton to feed its insatiable mills, and it was discovered that land in the Southern colonies was ideal for raising this precious commodity. All that was missing was labor. Realizing that one white man could raise and pick only a small crop of cotton, even with sons and daughters to help, the English began to subsidize the importation of stolen human beings from West Africa for selected Southern cotton farmers. Those who agreed to use slaves to hack out a considerably larger plot of Southern forest, delta, or upland for the purpose of planting and harvesting cotton were given slaves on a pay-back basis, with the discounted purchase price coming from the delivery of cotton to the English mill owners. Similarly, the north began to demand 'Carolina Gold' rice, a labor-dependent commodity which grew well in southern coastal states. Slaves led to productivity, which led to plantations and the industry of breeding Negroes for sale. Politicians and preachers who stormed and railed against the mongrelization of the races looked the other way when light brown faces with Negro features began to show up in the slave quarters. Such faces were not allowed inside the plantation houses and were bought and sold just like other slaves.

The availability of wood in the South was another economic driver. Southern pine is fast-growing, rich in turpentine-producing sap, and easy to log and transport. Hardwood trees grow straight, tall, and fast in the humid Southern climate. Some white southerners with a monetary stake were able to build mills to process felled trees into lumber and turpentine. Soon they employed dozens and then hundreds of white workers and purchased hundreds of unpaid black slaves. The whites worked in one part of the factory or tree farm and the slaves, with white supervisors, in another. Savvy mill owners paid the whites the prevailing low wages, worked them the prevailing long hours, built spare but adequate houses for each group—with wooden floors for the whites and dirt floors for the blacks--built churches for each group, saw to it that a white preacher and a black preacher were permanently on the payroll, and arranged for the construction and continual resupply of a commissary which supplied necessary commodities at a high price. They paid their slaves nothing but food and shelter and the obligatory church to salve their Christian consciences. This was called good business in the South. Whites who worked in these facilities knew they were better than the slaves, and still better than black men after President Lincoln freed the slaves and the War Between the States enforced the detestable new arrangement. To a man, the white workers supported the mill system because there was always that remote chance that they too might become A Rich Man like the mill owner. Besides, they had jobs, full bellies, and the satisfaction of knowing that they were inherently better than niggers.

Religion was a player in creating Segregation and his high priest. Early preachers, some entrenched in small towns or developing cities and some traveling the region as revivalists, soon faced a life-defining choice: is Christianity knowing and following the teachings of Jehovah and His Son Jesus Christ and seeking the touch of the Holy Ghost upon one's heart, all the while fighting the horrible injustice of slavery, or is it merely the singing of hymns, reading the Bible from the pulpit (never in the home), and meandering after the traditions of Catholicism or Protestantism while one ignores the most atrocious sin one could possibly commit, i.e. the ownership, beating, buying and selling, and occasionally killing of other human beings created by God in His image and likeness? Early preachers read the words of the Book of John, where Jesus said He came to lay His life down as a sacrifice for whoever would believe on Him and accept the free gift of grace, and they decided that the acquisition of loyal parishioners was critical and the teachings of Jesus were really only for white people. The Christian church in the South, which with moral courage could have been a beacon of strength and consistency in the bleak period of slavery and post-slavery, had made so grave a compromise with Segregation that it lost all legitimacy and became merely an institution, gently coddled and patiently tolerated by Southern Tradition. The ownership of even one human being put a Southerner's mind, heart, and soul in such bondage to the prevailing god that a weak and lifeless Christian church was powerless to rescue the slaveowner from the pit of hell.

Southern parents were players in the scheme of Segregation. With prideful Southern mannerliness, they taught their children that one must say daily prayers while simultaneously keeping the nigger down. They taught their children that the Jim Crow system, which was the blood-drenched code of law that Southern Tradition used to pay honor to the god Segregation, was wrought by God Almighty and quite acceptable to Him. They taught their children that freedom was a high ideal, and that the word democracy was sacred, all the while practicing slavery and/or segregation from the break of dawn until the onset of sleep at night. Little by little, they shut doors of conscience in young trusting minds until there remained only a small room of conscience in which Segregation ruled and Southern Tradition was unbreakable. Like their parents before them, parents did a thorough job of dishonoring honest curiosity and moral inquiry, of making innocent questions about Southern Tradition sound like treason, of teaching their children an unquenchable need to feel superior to Negroes, and to value power, money, and Segregation far more than the natural human need for decency and love.

Finally, the hypocritical North was a player as well. In the early years of this nation's history, while Southern plantations were being built and Southern fortunes were being made on the backs of slave labor, pious Northerners had to satisfy themselves with warm clothing in long winters and the satisfaction of knowing that at least they hadn't committed the sin of owning slaves. Yet an envy for Southern wealth and decadence seethed in their hearts. When machines were invented, and clever Northerners began to erect factories with mechanical devices that performed great service without the costly encumbrances of food and shelter, the balance shifted. While fortunes were being made up north, the South was beginning to feel the pinch of lowered commodity prices, over-farmed land due to ignorance of soil management principles, and the tension of moral indignation by Northerners regarding the introduction of new states into the union: should they be slave or free? The Southerner, increasingly vexed by his waning standard of income and what he perceived as undue criticism from his Northern brother, declared that the North can have itself and he is withdrawing from the union. The North responded with force. In the end, they fought each other mercilessly, with more than six hundred thousand American sons dying in support of their region's preferred system. The truth is, the War Between the States was an issue of ideology and economics. With the clear exception of abolitionists who knew slavery to be the ultimate destroyer of democracy and the Christian church, the plight of Negroes had very little to do with the conflict. Had the South won, it is quite likely that the North would have accepted the institution of slavery with only a token objection.

So the guilty were named: **everyone**, and white faces all. All had a moneyed stake in the game. No blacks favored slavery, just as no fetus favors abortion.

Southern Tradition did not rely solely on the power of largely unspoken symbols to keep the Negro enslaved. The volcano that lay uneasily beneath Southern soil spewed its lava of death when the high priest deemed it necessary. The demon that Southern Tradition unleashed to keep the Negro in his place was the Klu Klux Klan.

The Klan was founded in the immediate aftermath of the War Between the States by six former Confederate soldiers in Pulaski, Tennessee. The six, four of whom were aspiring attorneys, saw themselves as like-minded compatriots and took their name after *kuklos*, the Greek word for "circle." In the early days, their activities were mere sophomoric pranks, such as riding horses through the countryside while dressed in white sheets and pillowcases with eye holes and hollering "The South will rise again!" But others saw the grim potential of such an organization, especially with the anonymity of a disguise, for keeping the Negro in his place despite Reconstruction. Five former Confederate generals took over the leadership of the Klan and made it a multi-state terrorist organization. In 1872, not seven years after the cessation of the war, General Ulysses S. Grant was moved to describe the true motives of the Klan to the United States Congress:

"By force and terror, to prevent all political action not in accord with the views of the members, to deprive colored citizens of the right to bear arms and of the right of a free ballot, to suppress the schools in which colored children are taught, and to reduce the colored people to a condition closely allied to that of slavery."

To which the average Southerner said "Damn right! Whad'y'all think? You damyankees whupped us in the War, burned our plantations and towns, and set the nigger free as if he was a human being. Arrogant pigs! Well, this here's the way we're gonna get back at you moralist sonsabitches!"

The early Klan did its work through distributing pamphlets, shooting, lynching, pistol-whipping, castrating, and lynching men, almost all of whom were black. A few meddling Jews and Northern rabblerousers met their fate at the hands of white-sheeted gangs as well. After a decade of terror, the establishment of Jim Crow laws made the work of the Klan largely unnecessary. That and the threat of federal law enforcement descending upon them convinced them to go dormant. However, in 1915, the Klan was revived by D.W. Griffith's film, *The Birth of a Nation,* and an oft-repeated quote by the President of Princeton University—none other than Woodrow Wilson, a Democrat who would later ascend to the Presidency of the United States of America—which said *"At last there has sprung forth a renewed great Klu Klux Klan, a veritable empire of the South, to protect the Southern integrity."* This was the true face of the Democratic Party revealed.

The new Klan numbered eight million members by the mid-1920's. Ranging throughout the country, it upgraded its attention from merely blacks to include Catholics, Jews, communists, unionists, atheists, immigrants, agitators, and other disrupters of Southern Tradition. Two months after V-J Day, in August of 1945, the Klan burned a 300-foot cross on the face of Stone Mountain in Georgia. This extravagant display, according to one Klansman who bragged to the editor of the 'Atlanta Journal,' was intended "just to let the niggers know the war is over and the Klan is back in business."

Altogether, more than 5,000 lynchings and other atrocities against black men were credited to the Klan from its origin until the return of black soldiers, sailors, and airmen from World War II. Yet no white man was ever convicted of such a crime. Even when it was obvious from observations of unique boots or some other unmistakable feature exactly who was among the perpetrators, the local chief of police—who was as likely as not to be wearing a white sheet and hood when the victim was hanged—refused to take action. White Southern judges rejected indictments against (fellow) Klansmen. Rich white men in the town nearest the hanging, men who had a great deal to lose by permitting Southern Tradition to be challenged, would visit the editor of the local paper and tell him "Better let this one go, Bubba. Write a piece about the glory of Southern Tradition. Tell the folks how good segregation is for everybody. That'll keep any white traitors from thinking about going to the feds, and it'll tell the niggers ain't nothing gonna change. It's here, nothing can change it, not even Godamighty! No, wait. Leave out that part about God. Just say segregation ain't ever gonna change. And while you're at it, write something about union leaders. Leave the rank and file out of it; they're good white men. But give their leaders a kick in the ass. Say something about the AFL-CIO being nigger-lovers; that'll keep 'em outa the South. And write something about them uppity Harlem niggers, and about the NAACP. Keep saying that the South will handle its own race problem. No, call it a situation. Our race situation. Maybe finish it up with a bit about how folks need to go to church and get right and quit worrying about the Klan. The Klan'll keep things good, never they mind."

The black faces who came back from fighting for their country found that their country wasn't *ever* theirs, not when their great-grandfathers were growing up as slaves and not when their grandfathers were young men and their wives were moaning "Lawd Jesus, when you gonna help us?" after news of another lynching and not when their fathers were bowing to the white man, hat in hand, and not when they themselves were growing into young manhood and making themselves available to go overseas and risk their lives for a country that was never theirs. Now, having survived the atrocities of a war that defied imagination due to the barbarity of the Aryans and the little yellow men they had conquered, those black faces were less likely to do as their fathers and grandfathers and great-grandfathers had done. Words such as *"Yassuh, massah"* their ancestors had reflexively mouthed were replaced by *"Crackuhs! Huh! Don't they think they sumpin'!"* and *"Now I done fought to save yo' white ass, how 'bout 'lowin' me to vote?"*

It was a new day. The volcano under the South seethed and bucked, the lava spewed with whippings and death on occasion, and the god Segregation writhed in mounting fury. Angrily he sent his high priest Southern Tradition on mission after mission to quell mounting insurrection from uppity niggers and interfering damyankees, but the priest's power over the hearts and minds of the South was waning. 1963, Rosa Parks, and Martin Luther King were right around the corner.

Such was the state of the world in Louisiana when Alabama Denton arrived in New Orleans.

www.ingramcontent.com/pod-product-compliance
Lightning Source LLC
Chambersburg PA
CBHW051240260626
47162CB00002B/533